A
CROWN
OF
STAR
AND
ASH

Book Cover by KD Ritchie at Storywrappers Designs
Editing by Noah Sky and Jennifer Murgia
Illustrations by Etheric Designs

ISBN 979-8-9897885-0-7 (Paperback)
ISBN 979-8-9897885-2-1 (eBook)
ISBN 979-8-9897885-1-4 (Hardcover)

First Edition: March 2024
Snowshoe Press

SNOWSHOE
— PRESS —

To those who tried to break us,
We are still here.

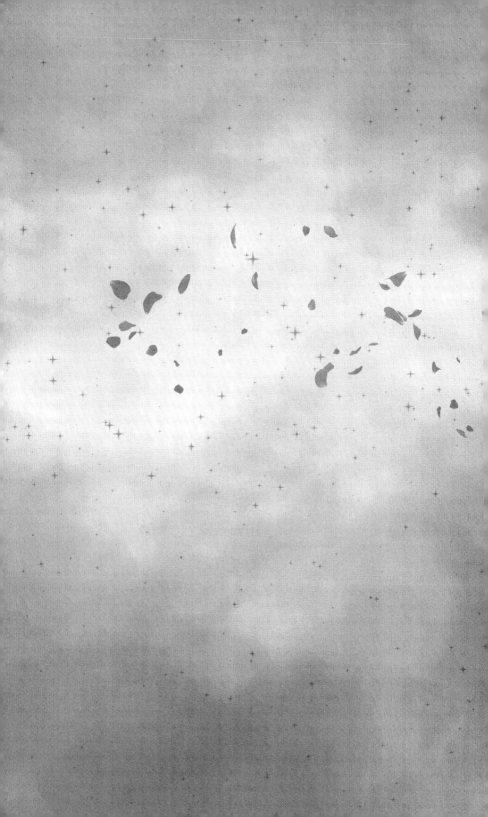

A CROWN OF STAR AND ASH

THE FATE OF ASHES BOOK 1

VICTORIA K. TAYLOR

CHAPTER
1

The sounds of the broken and dying filled the dungeon, and all Deya wanted to do was clap her hands over her ears. No matter how long she had worked as a healer in Stonehall Castle, the sound of death never failed to make her heart clench.

"Shh," she whispered, dabbing a damp cloth against the sweaty, scorched forehead of an older male. "Let the poppy do the work. Hold on. It'll end soon." But she didn't know whether that was his pain or his life.

The male was dressed simply—in a rough spun tunic with worn patches sewn over holes. A farmer, perhaps? Surely not someone dangerous. And yet, his body was covered in severe burns. Magical burns.

The Kingdom of Praiton's castle was quiet and dark. The feeble rays of morning light from the window at the top of the stairs were Deya's only company as she rushed from cell to cell. From dying breath to dying breath.

"Stay still . . ." Deya pushed her arm through the iron bars to reach the male. Her ears started to ring as she pressed against them. The damned material was irritating enough to make any fae's head spin, but she gritted her teeth and focused on the burns covering his body.

Strands of her long, chestnut hair fell out of its thick braid and into her eyes, making her puff it away as she extended her arm as far as it could reach.

The warm feeling of a flame flickered in her core. Her Healing Magic rose through her, filling her veins with the heady sensation of life and light. A glow shimmered beneath her fingers, illuminating the burns riddling the male's arms. Charred skin began to turn from black to red, blisters began to shrink, but still, the burns remained severe.

"*Come on,*" she muttered through clenched teeth.

"Here, let me help," an exasperated voice said from behind her. A tanned hand appeared beside hers, and a second warm glow began to emanate from it. Looking around, Deya saw her only friend in the whole castle, Luc. His face was contorted with a mix of effort and disgust as he pressed his face beside hers against the bars and held his hand above the blistered skin of the patient. Their magic sputtered as it pushed against the scars left by the Ember Magic. Then it faded.

Deya pulled back her hand. It was as she feared. The magic that caused the burns was too strong, even for their combined power.

The door to the dungeon exploded open, making them both jolt in alarm. A group of soldiers stormed down the stairs, carrying two beaten and bloodied prisoners between them. Deya's eyes lingered on them as they were dragged down the steps and thrown into a cell already teeming with bodies. She flinched as flesh hit stone, and the shrieks of pain echoed off the walls.

"More dissenters," Luc said with a sigh. He got to his feet, dusting off his trousers and glancing backwards at the new prisoners. Luc was a lanky male of Ganiean descent—as were all the healers since their magic derived from the Earth Magic in Ganiea—but his skin was darker than hers and most from that region. He rubbed his long, pointed fae ears—longer than even her own—as the screams of the prisoners echoed across the dungeon.

"Not that I don't mind the help, but what are you doing here?" Deya asked. She made to rise from the floor beside the prisoner, but the farmer's hand shot out, seizing her wrist. Deya jumped, resisting the urge to recoil as the charred flesh scraped against her soft skin.

"I didn't mean it . . ." the farmer rasped. "I didn't help the Pillar rebels . . . *Please* . . . I am not one of them . . ."

"Shh," she whispered, her fingers wavering over his burnt hand still clinging to her. The nausea rose through her stomach, and she instantly felt shame. These souls were dying, ailing . . . yet she wanted to throw up at the feel of them touching her. "You know that we are lucky to be Praitonians," Deya whispered to him. "Why would you go against our home?"

The male wheezed as she attempted to extract his fingers from her wrist.

*Why? H*er heart ached as she stood, turning her back on the dying male. All Praiton was trying to do was reclaim the magic of the Mother Goddess. The *true* deity of this land.

"*Please*," the male moaned again. "King Rodric would not want this . . . he *couldn't* want this . . ."

Deya's desire to reach out to him, to comfort him like a good healer should, battled against what she already knew. That these fae were traitors to the Kingdom of Praiton.

Luc watched as the farmer drew a shuddering, gasping breath. The death rattle. With a finite *thump*, his burnt hand fell to the stone floor.

"I'm *here* to save you from yourself, of course. Why are you bothering with these?" Luc asked, his eyes scanning the cells around them. His lip curled. "These are rebellion sympathizers. Praiton dissenters. Possible spies for the bloody rebels of the Pillar Legion. Why waste your magic on trying to save them?"

All the prisoners around them sported a variety of wounds. Being a healer in this realm ensured that there was never an end to the challenges she would be faced with. The farmer's burns from the Ember Magic wielders of Maniel. A male beside him with thick vines wrapped around his neck, courtesy of the Earth Magic users of Ganiea. A woman towards the back of the cell, choking on water, drowning from the inside out after a run-in with the Sea Fae from the Laenimore region. Each injury different; each one more gruesome than the last.

"Because," Deya whispered, tucking the male's hand back to his side. Minus the burns, he almost looked peaceful now. As if he could be sleeping. "They are still souls after all."

Souls that were farmers, seamstresses, cooks. Everyday citizens of the Kingdom of Praiton. Imprisoned for the sin of voicing their disagreement with Praiton's overthrowing of the surrounding kingdoms. But she shoved that thought down. She had to. If there was one thing Deya had learned from helping these traitors, it was that she would *never* be one of them.

"That bleeding heart of yours is going to get you in trouble one day. More than it already has," Luc teased, and although his tone was light, Deya could sense the unease in his words. As if he was worried how her bleeding heart might get *him* in trouble one day, too. "The infirmary just received an influx of injured soldiers," Luc said, grimacing as he took in a female sobbing over her broken arm. "The Pillar Legion decimated Commander Maelor's troops out in Ganiea. If Mother Clarita knew you were down here . . ."

But he didn't have to finish the thought. Deya knew what Mother Clarita would do. As the face of Praiton's one true goddess of the realm, Mother Clarita treated sympathy towards dissenters almost as severely as the rebellion soldiers themselves. *Especially* if that sympathizer was Deya.

"Come on," Luc insisted. "We need to go before she comes looking for you."

Deya cast one last look at the charred body. She knew it was her duty to do what the Mother demanded. Knew it was what was expected of a true Praitonian. Yet why did she feel like a sham of a healer leaving the

4

swells of death below in the dungeon?

The worn stone of the castle was bathed in weak gray light from an obscured sun as they hurried towards the infirmary. A dreary, ever-present fog shrouded the kingdom putting its own weight on her already despondent mood. Even as Deya hurried along the familiar corridors, Luc at her heels, she couldn't help but notice the pall that settled over her home kingdom like a mourner's veil.

The Pillar Legion had been growing in strength lately, causing more uprisings, and with it, more violence and death. Things in Praiton had grown darker since King Rodric had fallen ill. War had erupted under the leadership of the king's steward, Lord Decius.

For years, Praiton had overthrown almost all the surrounding Pillar Kingdoms in the last century. As she and Luc entered the infirmary and looked around at the wounds of the dying soldiers before her, Deya began to get a sense of how angry those kingdoms were.

"Where is everybody?" Deya cried, her head whipping around. Every bed was occupied with wounded soldiers, yet there was not a single other healer to be found. Typical. Mother Clarita had only commanded Luc to fetch *her*.

"They, uh, had to help the High Mother with something else," Luc said, but the way his body shifted, Deya knew he was avoiding the truth. All of the other healers—Luc included—only cared about Mother Clarita's favor. And that was never achieved with hard work.

Steaming with anger, Deya turned away from him just to catch sight of herself in a cracked mirror. Her gray eyes were tired, lined with bags and shadows, pale skin glistening with moisture, concealing the pallor of her complexion.

She let out a sigh that pushed against the exhaustion aching in her chest. Fatigue was already settling in from the amount of magic she had funneled into the prisoners below. Damn Luc for being right. She barely had anything left to give to the soldiers who had fought for them.

"Are you sure you don't want to come with us to the feast tomorrow?"

Luc asked, watching her as she lifted arms to check for pulses, pulled back eyelids, and readied ointments. "I'm sure you'll have fun."

"I'm not sure I'll be exactly welcome, Luc. But thanks," she mumbled, and Luc grimaced, but did not argue.

This was the problem with being friends with one of the most popular healers in the unit, while being the most ostracized one. She and Luc had attended classes together, had struggled through apothecary and herbology before starting in Stonehall Castle. And even when all the other healers had begun to shun her as she continued to upstage them in their everyday work, Luc had stood by her. She was as mystified by his friendship as she was grateful for it.

Her chest ached at the memory of how hopeful she was upon first coming to this castle, of finally making friends for the first time in her life. The wretched loneliness she so often felt within these stone walls scratched at her heart before she shoved it aside.

"But c'mon," Luc remarked, following her around the room. "You have to take a day off every now and then. I'm sure if you just put in an appearance, maybe the Mother will—"

Deya shot him a glare from where she had been studying a soldier's tibia, broken in half like a piece of straw. Because she knew what he was going to say.

Maybe the Mother will stop giving you a hard time.

But she was not Luc. She could not blend into the folds of the other healers anymore, couldn't laugh and charm her way back into their good graces. Not after every time she had to go in and heal someone after them. Not after every life she saved that they could not. Especially when those lives lost were at the hands of the High Mother herself.

"I don't think so, Luc."

"But it smells like an open grave in here," he said, his lip curling slightly as Deya lifted a stained sheet covering another body.

"That's what happens when you receive over a dozen soldiers roasted alive by Manielian rebels," she snapped before she could help herself.

"And really, as healers, the rest of them *should* be in here helping us."

"What good would they do, Dey? Everyone knows you're the strongest healer we have." He gave her a cheeky grin and she felt herself deflating a little, even if her heart sank at his words. "You're even stronger than Mother Clarita. Don't think she doesn't notice."

Flushing, Deya turned to wash her hands in the stone basin by the window. She hated it when someone pointed this out. While the strength of her magic may have been a source of pride at one time, now it was only another log on the fire of the High Mother's personal disdain for her.

"Well, at least give me a hand with this one. This is a bad break." She pointed to the injured soldier's broken body and Luc gave a long-suffering sigh.

"Alright, but this is the only one I'm doing. The smell in here is making me ill."

Deya rolled her eyes before they turned their attention to the soldier. They both raised a palm over the damaged limb. A gentle, warming glow emanated from their outstretched hands. As if some invisible puppet master twitched the strings on his marionette, the soldier's broken bones shifted back into position.

With a groan, Deya dropped her hand. Her stomach hurt as though she had clenched her abdomen for too long. Luc, too, looked winded. If she had not had his help, it would have cost her much more energy. Anger flared in her as she thought of how many more times she would have to do this for the remaining patients. Alone.

"What happened to him, do you reckon?" Luc asked, nodding down at the soldier they had just healed. All of his limbs—once shattered—now lay repaired. Deya's practiced eyes swept over the unconscious form.

Severe compound fractures in the tibia and radius bones. Minor bruising on face and neck. Burst blood vessels around the eyes, as though pressure had increased rapidly.

"Celestial Gravity Magic, I think," Deya replied softly. She felt a small tug at her heart at seeing the soldier's broken body—still beaten and bruised, even after her healing.

Luc scoffed. "The Nodarians are ruthless for a bunch of ruddy stargazers." He paused, before adding, "You reckon they're still holding a grudge for killing their High King and taking over their whole kingdom?"

The flippant, dismissive way Luc said this made a shiver of nausea run through Deya.

The Nodarians had lost much after the siege Praiton had conducted against the Celestial Throne decades before. But High King Castor had put up too much of a fight against Praiton and their mission to restore the Mother Goddess as the one true deity.

The downfall of Nodaria was unfortunate, maybe, but necessary. They all knew that.

"Praiton did what they thought was best," Deya heard herself respond. The canned answer rolled off her tongue with ease despite the twinge of discomfort it gave her. Even then, the discomfort itself made her unconsciously nervous, as though someone, somewhere in the castle could sense that small shred of disloyalty within her.

But Deya did not tell Luc this. She could not. Instead, she kept her mouth shut and gnawed at her lip, biting down on that guilt writhing in her heart. Luc studied her, his dark eyes taking her in. It was as if he could sense the unease his words had elicited.

"What is it?" he asked her, but Deya shook her head.

"It's nothing."

"Rubbish." He followed her as she moved around him towards the next patient, still not looking at him. "Say what you're thinking. I can tell you want to, Dey."

But Deya would not say it. To speak ill of Praiton would be treason. It would be a death sentence. It would mean becoming one of those poor souls in the dungeon. And besides, she had never been allowed to speak freely within these walls.

As if Luc read her mind, he gave her a knowing smirk. "You're much too meek, Deya," he said, his tone light, almost teasing. "One of these days, I swear you'll have to grow a backbone. Even if you have to conjure it with your own magic."

Deya glared at him and opened her mouth to retort, but that's when she heard it. The gentle *thunk, thunk, thunk* coming down the stone hallway. Like a flame from a Fire Wielder's palm, Deya's anxiety shot up, her heart rate quickening.

Strutting as she often did in her velvet flats with the block heel, the High Mother Clarita sauntered into the room with a sweep of shimmering gray fabric. Deya's breathing turned shallow.

"Hello," Clarita crowed. That sickly sweet, pallid smile was plastered across her face, as always.

Clarita was as fake as the gray gemstone in the necklace around her neck—a replica of the one Mav, the Mother Goddess herself, wears. As fake as that simpering, saccharine tone. As though Clarita didn't want the mask to slip, to show her true face.

As if someone were controlling the muscles around her mouth, Deya felt a matching, fake smile pull at her own lips. This was *the* Mother of Praiton, after all. She deserved Deya's respect. With that thought, Deya schooled her features.

"Good afternoon, Mother Clarita," she chirped.

Luc also beamed at the Mother, but it was not forced, like Deya's. "Hello, Mother!"

Mother Clarita's beady eyes swept the Infirmary. Deya watched her take in the broken bodies of soldiers, the deathly moans. Deya wondered if she took in the lack of staff as well but figured it would be too much to expect. The Mother's eyes narrowed.

"So, this is what those pitiful vermin in the dungeon wrought on our kingdom?" the Mother sniffed.

"It was a bloody battle, Mother," Deya supplied, attempting to steady her own thumping heart. Talking to the Mother never came as easily to her as it did to the others. All Deya had ever wanted, all she had ever craved, was the chance to fit in here at Stonehall, to be accepted—like Luc, like the rest of them. To not feel singled out . . . to not feel entirely *other*. Even though she craved it, she did not understand why.

Because when Deya spoke, the Mother did not so much as glance her way.

"I paid a small visit to the traitors," Mother Clarita continued. "And some of them bore traces of Healing Magic. As if someone were trying to . . ." Her eyes flitted to Deya, and the glint of malice that flashed in her irises made Deya hold her breath. "*Help* them," she finished, her voice venomous and sweet.

But Deya was not fooled. She was never fooled when it came to the High Mother of Praiton. Clarita was as mean as the glint in her eye, as deadly as the cat o' nine tails whip she liked to take down to the dungeons to "check on the dissenters."

And while she pretended like she was the Holy Mother, the face of the Mother Goddess, the giver of Life and the balance of the realm, Mother Clarita was none of those things.

"There must be a healer amongst the traitors, Mother," Luc cut in before Deya could even think. "Maybe it was one of them."

Deya's gaze darted to Luc in surprise, but she was forced to look away. The Mother's eyes bore into her, and Deya forced herself to stare back. Why did she get the impression that Clarita did not believe Luc for even a second?

"I see," the Mother breathed. Deya shivered at the poisonous lilt of her voice, a snake flicking its tongue against her skin. Clarita looked away, and Deya wilted with the breath she finally released.

"Are you and the others ready for the feast?" Clarita asked, turning to look back at Luc. "The castle cook has agreed to arrange a special treat for us."

Luc nodded, babbling about how he would go fetch the others. They began heading out of the infirmary, Clarita's gossamer robes shimmering in the weak morning light. As they turned the corner, Luc shot Deya a sympathetic look over his shoulder. All Deya could do was grimace in return.

She was left alone with a room full of dying soldiers with not even a thank you from Clarita. Not like she expected it, anyway. Clarita's praise was saved for her most loyal dogs.

And Deya had never been that.

As she had anticipated, mending the soldiers and their many magical wounds took all night and the remainder of Deya's magic. Every bed was full of wounded soldiers sleeping off their injuries, but every table was covered with the bodies of those she couldn't save—sheets pulled over burned and disfigured faces. Her failures wrapped in neat packages.

Her magic reserves had all but extinguished like the candles flickering around her, casting the empty infirmary into dim shadow. She restocked the shelves with mostly empty bottles as her temples pounded like a mortar and pestle between her ears.

Gods, how long had it been since she had slept a full night? Even when she was spared night duty, she was unable to sleep. Her heartbeat had been out of her control lately. It would quicken of its own accord, even while she lay still in her small bed at night.

She did not understand what caused this anxiety. All she knew was that the panic and fear that kept her awake was the same feeling she got whenever she heard that *thunk, thunk, thunk* noise coming down the stone corridor towards the infirmary.

Deya laid her forehead against the cool stone wall, closing her eyes and sighing. Sometimes she got sick of all the stone in this castle. But she supposed a castle named *Stonehall* should be predominantly stone.

With one last sweep of the infirmary, Deya decided it was time to go to bed. Covered in blood and ointments, she figured she had done all she could. Still, the dozens of bodies wrapped in white sheets taunted her as she blew out the last candle.

The trek through the infirmary and down the spiral stairs of the ward seemed to go on forever. Deya's body ached, the exhaustion bone deep as the stone passages elongated endlessly before her. Echoes of her footsteps bounced off the dreary walls of the castle, the moon high in the sky, casting slivers of silver light in her path as she walked. There was no sound in all of the castle, nor a flicker of movement. As Deya began to wonder if she was the last person awake in the whole castle, she noticed the glimmer of light down the corridor.

Deya's spine stiffened, the hair on the back of her neck standing on end. She knew whose office that was, had been called into it several times in the last month alone for "counseling" on her "poor" attitude in the infirmary.

Mother Clarita's office.

Holding her breath, Deya willed for her heart to calm, even as fear gripped her insides. Clarita was never in the office this late. What could she possibly be doing at this hour?

Leaning forward without thinking, Deya could hear gentle murmuring voices. And then, an all too familiar, horrible cackle. But who was Clarita with? The low male voice was too far for her to recognize as it rumbled through the room, the words muffled by the distance.

Familiar panic and fear flared in Deya's chest again, but she couldn't help it. Something was amiss, something . . . sinister. Her feet began to move. Inching carefully, quietly down the hall, Clarita's voice came into earshot.

"I can make the potion as potent as you want, sir." To hear Clarita use any kind of honorific made Deya's breath catch in her throat. *Sir.* There was only one person who Clarita would address so formally.

The deep, rumbling voice of Lord Decius reverberated in the quiet, stone hall. "We will need a steadier supply of the Nighthold potion, Mother. I believe he is beginning to acquire a certain . . . tolerance."

"The King has been receiving the best quality potions for many years now, my lord," Clarita snapped. "Perhaps you should lessen your dosage for more *efficacy.*"

"I was not questioning your ability, Clarita," Decius said, his voice an unfamiliar, low rasp. "After all these years, I know you are very capable."

Years? Clarita had been supplying the Nighthold potion to Decius for *years*? Why would Lord Decius require something like that? She had only heard rumors about this brew, that it was used only for secretive, nefarious purposes.

Deya backed away from the office door, tripping over her own feet in her haste. She couldn't be caught there. Every fiber in her being was telling her to *go*, to *run*.

But as she stumbled, the room spinning, her heart hammering in her ears, she crashed into a solid form behind her. Bouncing backwards, Deya whirled around.

Luc stood there; his eyes wide. She hadn't heard him approach, had been too busy eavesdropping . . . It only took one glance at his face to know that he had heard everything that was said. And he knew that *she* had heard everything, too.

Deya opened her mouth, a gasp of air coming out instead of words before Luc jerked his head back and forth. He made a slashing movement underneath his neck, then pointed behind her. His movements were furious, urgent, but she knew what he meant. *Go.*

She did just that. Hurrying from the corridor, her heart pounded a fierce rhythm in her temples as Luc followed swiftly behind her.

Could she trust Luc to keep quiet about what she had heard? He had covered for her many times—including today. She *should* be okay . . . shouldn't she?

As she flew through the halls with Luc close behind, her mind kept spinning the conversation over and over again. The Nighthold potion was a Praiton invention. Made with small, diluted amounts of nightshade, the potion could cause everything from paralysis and hallucinations in small doses, to death with a full dose.

What would the king who—according to reliable Maesters and Healers around her—was invalid and incoherent most days, need with a Nighthold potion?

Deya froze so abruptly she almost tripped where she stood. There, standing in the moonlit corridor of Stonehall Castle, the realization hit her with the force of a bolt of lightning.

Luc crashed into her, jolting her out of her reverie.

"We cannot stop here, Deya!" Luc hissed. "We must get back to the residency wing, quickly!"

But Deya did not move. She turned to look at Luc, her mind spinning, her heart hammering, hard in her chest. It came to her, as clear as day. As vividly as a monster moving from the shadows.

The Nighthold wasn't for the King of Praiton. It was for Lord Decius to *give to* the King of Praiton.

Everything in the realm of Krigor changed when Rodric fell mysteriously ill almost a century ago. Since his right-hand steward, Lord Decius, took over, it had become a very different kingdom indeed. Not a kingdom at all . . . rather, an empire.

It all made sense. The king's gradual and then sudden collapse in health, his symptoms . . . Could it be . . . ?

"Luc . . . why is the Mother making a Nighthold potion for the steward?"

Luc's brown eyes blinked, before he shook his head furiously, waving her off. "So what? The Mother probably makes lots of things for the king and the steward—"

"*Nighthold,* Luc!" She wanted to shake him. How did he not see it? Did she really have to connect the dots for him? "Why would Lord Decius ask for the Nighthold potion? Do you not remember what it is used for?"

Luc's eyes continued their chaotic, panicked dance back and forth along the empty corridor. "*I don't know.* Some poison, perhaps?" he spat in an undertone.

"Worse. It disables the mind and body. It can completely addle and incapacitate someone. Why would the steward need that for the *king?*"

Luc opened his mouth again, as though he was about to dispute what Deya knew she had placed so clearly in front of him. That's when she lost her patience.

"Do you think Decius is *poisoning* the king?"

Luc took a step back from her, eyes wide. The fear on his face was vivid. "Deya . . . you can't say something like that. Do you realize . . ."

"Is it crazy, though, Luc?" she breathed. The treasonous words coming from her mouth felt heavy, bitter. They made her heart race, her blood boil. She wasn't supposed to be saying these words, to be thinking them. She knew that. And yet . . .

The walls began to feel small around her, as though they were closing in, as though they were listening. She always felt like those damned walls were listening. Was it her imagination or were the shadows in the corridor almost moving? "Am I crazy to believe—"

"Yes," Luc snapped so forcefully that it was Deya's turn to take a step back. "Now speak no more of this nonsense." And he flew from the corridor, leaving Deya standing on the moonlit battlements, still reeling.

She could barely see two feet in front of her as she stumbled back to the barracks', too shocked by her own realization.

She did not sleep that night. The same panic and fear had overtaken her, but this time worse. This time, it was strengthened by the worry that Lord Decius was poisoning the King of Praiton.

CHAPTER
2

Deya dreaded the return to the infirmary. She was terrified of seeing Luc . . . of seeing Mother Clarita. She was bursting at the seams with fear and worry. This giant, explosive secret rested heavily on her shoulders. But it *wasn't* a secret. There was no proof that what Mother Clarita had said to Decius revealed any sort of elaborate, devious plot.

And, after having a full, sleepless night to dwell on it, it felt ludicrous now. Luc was right. Who was to say that Lord Decius didn't require the potion for the torture of enemies on behalf of the king? Who was to say there wasn't a reasonable—if not *slightly* evil—justification for monthly Nighthold potions to be delivered to the High Lord?

While Deya tried to convince herself of this, it did not sit right in her gut. She *knew*—like she had felt in the corridor last night—that something was *wrong*. If she were being honest with herself, she'd admit that something had been wrong for a long time.

King Rodric had never been a conqueror. He had always been about uniting the realm of Krigor, about peace and unity.

What had changed? And who stood to benefit from it?

Of course, the one who benefitted from it was the one who now conducted business under King Rodric's name: Lord Decius.

She knew little about Decius. Had never so much as spoken a word to him before. All she knew was that he hailed from Maniel and was very, very old. She had seen him from afar before, and he had always looked exceptionally ancient. Fae aged slowly once they hit full maturity. Hair did not begin to gray, nor wrinkles begin to form until several hundred years of life.

So how old did Decius have to be to look like *that?*

She had heard of his three younger brothers. All had been born in Praiton, all had suspicious pasts, according to the gossip mill in the castle. And yet, Decius had placed them into high power positions as generals, ruling three of the five conquered Pillar Kingdoms. They had led the sieges in Laenimore and Nodaria. Were responsible for countless deaths. Now, they not only sat on the Harvest Throne, but the Sea and Celestial Thrones, as well.

Deya had barely crossed the threshold of the infirmary the next day when she realized something was amiss. Perhaps it was from the three years she had been in this toxic place. Whatever the reason, Deya's body seemed to know almost instantaneously when she was in danger. She had felt this way before, the last time Mother Clarita had pulled her into her office.

Restless, on edge, paranoid . . . scared.

What truly tipped her off was the fact that several of the healers that were scheduled to be there that day were actually *there*. Ramona, Bertram, Cledwyn, and Elis. But Luc was nowhere to be seen.

When Deya walked into the infirmary, all of them looked up from their workstations, and then averted their eyes. Deya's heart rate began to quicken, her lungs becoming tight as she tried to draw breath. She tried the tactic she had developed over the years here—to breathe in, hold her breath for a count of five, then release. And repeat. This method usually worked to ease her anxiety, but today, it did nothing. As surely as her gut had known that there was something suspicious about the Nighthold potion, it knew now that something was coming.

Deya moved to her workstation. Gods, her fingers were shaking. She began to prep potions for the day, replenishing her stock of poppy and disinfectants. Her hands moved numbly, but her mind was racing at the speed of a Bayard mare. It was as though every nerve ending in her body was reaching out into space, attempting to sense something, to see it coming . . .

A shadow fell over her. Looking up, she saw Clarita's favorite healer, Ramona standing there. She looked nervous, her eyes darting around.

"Deya," she said. Even her voice sounded unsure . . . almost as if she were *afraid* of her.

And while Ramona had been the most put-out by Deya's healing magic outshining her own—constantly glaring at her, whispering about her behind her back, even spreading rumors of her being late to work, or botching a treatment on an ill royal governor—she had *never* looked at her like that before.

"Hello, Ramona." She also did not want to look at her, afraid of how she may react if she looked into the female's eyes. Ramona's fear was palpable from where she stood, rocking beside Deya's workstation.

"The Mother wishes to see you."

Deya lowered the mortar and pestle she had been using to grind asphodel into ash.

"What is this about?"

Ramona shrugged. "I wasn't told much."

Deya stood, but she couldn't stop the shaking. It had now spread from her hands to her whole body. Her breathing and heart rate had become almost uncontrollable. Why hadn't she thought to shove a sprig of lavender under her tongue before she had started working for the day?

She headed down the corridor. The eyes of the other healers followed her, burning into the back of her rough-spun healer's dress. Their whispers followed her through the infirmary and down that familiar corridor. The one which had haunted her dreams last night.

Deya faltered, but she wasn't allowed a second to question why she was being brought to the Mother's office before the door was thrown open.

There, behind the desk, perched like a frog on a wooden lily pad, sat Mother Clarita. A malicious smile stretched across her doughy face, and she looked positively delighted. For a second, Deya wondered if it was good news, if she had done something, for once, that earned her some sort of recognition from the Mother—other than her passive-aggressive, barely concealed contempt.

But then, she saw who was in the chair before her. Looking stricken and nervous, staring at the ground at his feet, was Luc.

"Hello, Deya," the Mother purred and, as a shiver rolled up Deya's spine, she knew that this was *not* going to be good.

"Good morning, Mother," Deya replied.

Clarita gestured to the remaining empty chair in front of her desk. "Sit."

Deya sat, feeling like a dog obeying a command. But she couldn't stop her eyes straying towards Luc, her heart pounding so hard it began to blur her vision. His brown eyes were wide . . . fearful.

"Now, this is never an easy conversation to have," Clarita began. However, she looked gleeful, that sickly, self-satisfied smile still present.

"What is this about?" Deya asked, her eyes darting between Clarita and her petrified friend still staring at the floor.

Was it her imagination or did Clarita's smile grow even more sinister?

"It has come to my attention that some rather distasteful rumors have been circulating."

All the blood in Deya's veins ran cold. Deep down, Deya had known what this would be about. Luc sitting beside her, white as a ghost, still not looking at her, was enough to spark all the nerve endings in her body. Fear's ruthless chill began to creep up from her toes, spreading like frostbite through her.

"Mother—" Deya began, but Clarita raised her voice, cutting right through Deya's protests.

"Do you realize, Deya, that to speak of such things . . . to *spy on* and *accuse* your superiors is nothing short of treason?"

Deya slowly looked at Luc, but he remained still. A slight wobble began in his lower lip, but still, he did not speak. Every fiber of her being was alight with fear now, as if it knew what was to come.

"I did not accuse anyone!" Deya cried. She could feel Luc next to her trembling, his eyes beginning to fill with silent tears. "Mother, please, I did no such thing! I am loyal to the kingdom, to you and Lord Decius and I apologize if it sounded—"

"It *sounded*, Deya, like treason." Clarita's beady brown eyes glinted, sparkling with mirth. "Do you understand, Deya, that to question *me* is to question the Mother herself? Do you realize, sweet girl, I cannot let you cast doubt on me or this kingdom? To *anyone*."

Deya was shaking but she willed herself to still. Clarita wanted a reaction, an outburst. She wanted to feast on Deya's despair like a fat tick. Deya was not going to give it to her.

"I did not spy," she replied, her tone stiff, but calm. She would not give. Would not yield. Would not admit to anything.

"Oh?" And it was at that moment she realized there was no getting out of what was to come. "Well, Deya, since you do not show any remorse for your egregious actions, I suppose I shall take you to somewhere that may . . . help you reflect." The door behind them opened, and two guards stood, waiting.

At that moment, Luc's head shot up, and Deya could see the shimmer of his eyes. His face was pale, his eyes wide. "Mother, please! There has to be—"

But the look Clarita shot him silenced him in an instant.

Deya whirled around, taking in the soldiers, half rising from her seat. Her frantic eyes found Luc—her friend and confidant. Funny, caring, *weak, cowardly* Luc, who had sunk back into his chair, his face white. "I'm sorry, Dey," he whispered, in a voice so soft she could barely hear. "I had no choice. I'm sorry—"

"Luc—" she began, desperate now, but Mother Clarita spoke over her.

"The infirmary here at Stonehall no longer requires your services, Deya. Thank you for your hard work. I will see you soon, I'm sure."

And then, she was seized by the elbows by the guards in the doorway. Her yelp of shock was torn from her as they twisted her hands behind her back, holding her wrists together as they dragged her from the room.

"Luc!" Deya screamed. It was desperate, pathetic. Deya knew Luc would do nothing to save her. But he was her only hope at this point. *"Luc, please!"*

As the guards dragged her around the bend of the stairs, she caught sight of Luc's face. Shock, grief, and pain creased her friend's features. But still, he said nothing.

CHAPTER
3

In the dungeons of Stonehall Castle, prisoners were not kept alive long. Those sentenced to death were hanged publicly in the city square of Praiton's capital. The not-so-lucky ones were transported to one of the camps in the prison territory of Aunecia on the opposite side of the realm. The fact that Deya did not know which fate she would have filled her with dread.

Deya's hands were clasped in chains, and she was tossed into her own small cell with a straw bed and a bucket.

The fear and panic that had built in her heart in Clarita's office had only grown as she strained against the shackles, rattling them hopelessly around her wrists, the metal making her ears ring.

She knew what it was. Had seen the effects of this substance often in her time healing those in the dungeon. Faerivaine.

A plant grown and cultivated exclusively in Praiton. Only the alchemists in the castle knew how to produce the terrifying substance that suppressed all magic. Iron itself was already poisonous to fae but to mix it with faerivaine—which Praiton did during the forging of the iron shackles for the prisoners—and there was no escaping. No hope.

"No," Deya whispered, pulling on the chains. "No, no, no . . ." But her voice was eaten up by the darkness around her. By the sounds of the surrounding traitors moaning in agony, breathing their last breaths.

At that moment, the weight of her situation hit her with the strength of a sword blow. Her breathing staggered as she slumped against the stone wall of her cell.

She had betrayed the crown. Betrayed herself. And now she would be nothing more to Praiton than a traitor.

Still breathing hard, Deya slid down the grimy stone walls. *Stone, stone, stone.* That was all she would see for the rest of her life.

Shifting around, her eyes attempted to adjust to the lack of light. How long would she be here? Days? Weeks? This was the customary tactic Praiton used on their prisoners. They would starve them until they were sentenced. How long would that be for her?

Hours passed as the panic took hold, her heart still thundering—the only noise in the dark dungeon. She could see the familiar slant of light at the top of the stairs darken and lighten as the time dragged by. All the while, she found herself reliving every moment she had been chastised, the moments when things had begun to go downhill for her in the infirmary. When was it evident Clarita had started to dislike her? Would this have gone differently if she were one of Clarita's favorites, too?

But Deya knew the answer. In the end, *Deya* was the one that had questioned the crown. That had questioned her *kingdom*. It *was*, without a doubt, all her fault. The one thing she couldn't shake, no matter how hard she blinked within the darkness, was the fact that *Luc* had betrayed her.

The memory of the tears in his eyes, how he had mouthed an apology to her, along with the words that still rattled her. *I had no choice.* What had Clarita threatened him with?

Luc had always been content in his circle of healers, had been comfortable being at the center of it all. Had Clarita threatened his place

23

in the infirmary? What had been more important to Luc than protecting someone he called a friend?

At one time, all the healers in the ward had been her friends. They had attended festivals together, feasts, stayed up at night, laughing. When Deya had found herself missing her mother, she had come to think of them as her family.

But things changed as Deya continued to outshine them in healing duties. They began to cloister together more, often leaving her out. If it wasn't for Luc still attempting to include her, she would've been cut out altogether. The thought sent a pang through her heart.

Luc had been her only friend. Her friend had done this to her. Her *friend* . . .

She squeezed her eyes shut. Squeezed so hard she saw lights pop behind her eyelids. A tear slipped down her face before her breathing steadied. And then she fell into a fitful sleep.

The flowers were in full bloom. Lilies and jasmine, lavender, and dandelions—fragrant and heady—framed the window of Deya's childhood cottage. Sunlight streamed through the glass. The world was warm and bright, and Deya looked upon death for the first time.

"Quickly, get him on the table," Deya's mother panted. Deya was no taller than her mother's waist, which was adorned in an apron, muddied from a day of plucking herbs.

The effort to hold the unconscious male's legs aloft was beginning to make Deya sweat, but she did not complain. One look at her mother's determined face silenced all her discomfort. Athena Krey never complained about her job.

Seizing the male's feet, Deya shuffled around her mother, helping to hoist him up onto the kitchen table.

"Deya, the salts." Athena pointed towards the kitchen cabinet, too focused on the Healing Magic she was funneling into the male to say more.

Deya hurried to the cupboard, the familiar potions and vials standing in a line—tiny soldiers ready to do battle again. The salts were in a small vial towards the front, used and replenished often. Swiping them in her small fist, Deya hustled back to her mother, who was sweating with the effort of keeping the male alive.

"Hold them under his nose," her mother commanded, lifting his head aloft. His breathing was growing more and more shallow, even as Deya waved the small bottle under his nose. But instead of reinvigorating him, as it should, the male seemed to fade faster.

"We're losing him," Athena whispered. Her voice was strained, and Deya's eyes widened as she took in the male's pallor, the foam at his lips. Poisoned. Most likely from eating a toxic berry. It happened a lot in this area. People were flocking to Praiton in droves from the fallen kingdoms. Poverty was rampant, food was scarce, and those unfamiliar with the lands and wildlife often fell victim to the same ill fate.

The male drew a rasping breath and then stilled. Deya had never seen life leave something before, as if a large hand had snuffed out a candle's flame.

"Hurry, Deya!" Athena cried, the glow from her hands intensifying. "Help me!"

Deya had only helped her mother heal a handful of times. Athena had rarely been so desperate. Deya's magic was still in its explosive and temperamental stage—vacillating between too weak and too strong. Athena restricted Deya's practice to animals—birds with broken wings, horses with injured hooves. But to actually practice on a dying faerie . . .

Deya threw her hands over the male's limp form, mirroring her mother's actions. The familiar warmth of her Healing Magic crashed over her—a tidal wave of comfort and heat, which she drove into the male on the table. Athena's hands were trembling beside Deya's, her resolve weakening. With a gasp, her mother collapsed back against the cottage wall, too spent to continue.

But Deya did not stop.

"Deya—" Athena began, but Deya shook her head. The hot seed of magic in her core was surging out of her—a powerful wave of pure light, and it was all she could do to keep funneling it into the body in front of her.

Deya's breathing became labored. Her small hands shook, her stomach clenched, and with a cry, she pushed the remaining magic out of her core. Like a dam bursting, *it exploded from her and right into the male . . . who rocketed from the table with a rasping breath. Alive.*

Deya's laugh of triumph burst from her, just as her magic had a second ago. She turned to look at her mother, expecting to see Athena's proud smile, to receive her glowing praise. Except Athena was not smiling. Instead, she was gazing at Deya with something on her face that Deya could not describe, and yet would never forget. Was it awe? It couldn't be fear, *could it?*

Deya opened her eyes.

Gone were the sunlight and warmth from her childhood cottage. Instead, nothing but the bleak stone of the dungeon filled her vision.

Still reeling from the memory of the first life she had saved, Deya reached up and felt tears still fresh on her face.

Athena had raised Deya alone in a small village on the outskirts of Wexbridge. To this day, Deya knew nothing of her father since her mother rarely spoke of him, only that he was from Ganiea.

Even at home in the village, she had few friends. Her mother often shielded her from others her own age. An image of her mother gripping her wrist in a viselike hold, steering her away from a gathering of other children flashed through her mind. Athena whispering, *"Your trust in Praiton is what will keep you safe, Deya. That is all you need to know."*

Athena, like many loyal Praitonians, was wary of others in the outlier villages. No one knew who was a rebel sympathizer or even a rebel themselves. Deya knew it was only to keep her safe, but she never quite managed to chase away the feeling of loneliness that followed her well into adulthood.

When she rose up through the ranks and was hired at Stonehall Castle, her mother was overwhelmed with pride, but saddened. Her mother had been Deya's only real friend, and now she would have to leave her. Gods, she missed her mother.

Deya closed her eyes. A tear streaked through the grime on her face and fell to the stone floor. It had all been an illusion. A stupid, naïve illusion. And now she would die in this cell, her name and reputation soiled, and her so-called friends wouldn't even care. And no one would even tell her poor mother.

It was in that small moment of pain and sorrow which she had allowed for herself, that the door to the dungeon opened.

Thunk, thunk, thunk.

The familiar sound made Deya flinch. She hastened to wipe her eyes. Clarita would not catch her weeping. She would enjoy it too much. A sweeping of gossamer gray fabric brushed against the bars of her cell and Deya looked up.

"Hello again, Deya." Mother Clarita beamed beatifically down at her. It was at that moment Deya realized that, while she had never admitted it to herself, she hated Clarita with every bone in her body. Even now, caged, and hopeless, she wanted nothing more than to rip the female's head from her abnormally squat body.

"What do you want?" Deya replied, not bothering with politeness any longer. She had decided that moment in Clarita's office that she would never kowtow to her again.

Clarita's eyes flashed. She was not used to being referred to in such a disrespectful manner. It gave Deya the tiniest bit of pleasure.

"I was hoping we could have a little chat, Deya." Clarita didn't bother to bend down to speak to her. Instead, she loomed over Deya like a nightmare from the shadows. "Did you tell anyone else of what you overheard about the potion I make for Lord Decius?"

Deya hesitated. This was not the question she was expecting. It was almost as if Clarita was . . . *admitting* Deya had been right to suspect something nefarious. But who would she tell? Besides Luc, that is. And she saw how well that turned out for her. Still, Deya knew that it was best for her to deny everything. She would not put it past Clarita to accept her confession as permission to put her to death.

"I do not know what potion you speak of, Mother," she rasped.

Clarita smiled. "So, that is the game you are choosing to play," she breathed. It was as if she had been hoping for this. Like she had been baiting Deya.

"There is no game, Mother."

"Well . . ." From the sleeve of her gray robes, Clarita withdrew an object. Her favorite cat o' nine tails whip. At the end of each strand dangled a large iron hook.

Deya shrank against the stone, ashamed of the naked fear taking over her body. She was sick of cowering beneath this evil bitch, and yet she was helpless. Wholly at Clarita's mercy—just like she always had been.

"It appears there is more than one spy within this castle," the High Mother breathed. Her eyes were glittering with bloodlust, her smile stretching into a cruel leer. "And if you think I am going to rest until I have smoked all you wretched traitors out, you are sorely mistaken, Deya."

The chill of fear gripped Deya by the throat as Clarita came closer to the bars, the silver hooks on the end of the whip glinting in the dim light.

"I am going to give you one more chance to tell me who they are." She was stroking the ends of the whip as an owner would their loving pet.

"Clarita—" Deya began, holding out a hand, still trying to scramble further away from the High Priestess.

"*Mother* Clarita!" she roared so suddenly that Deya flinched. "How dare you continue to disrespect me, girl." Clarita's face was contorting, the mask falling. "*I* am the High Mother of this kingdom, and you *will* treat me with respect." Clarita's fingers twitched like a spider and Deya's cell was creaking open.

"Mother, please . . ." But the words died on Deya's tongue. She was tired of pleading with this female. Tired of apologizing for every asinine thing she had been pulled into her office for. She had shut her mouth, let them walk all over her, trample her, and now she was tired. Tired and done.

Clarita seized Deya by the hair, dragging her as easily as if she were made of parchment. Deya gasped in pain as she was thrown, face down, onto the stone ground.

Stone, stone, stone.

Deya's face smashed against it, and she choked on her blood and the bitterness of the thought.

"I will ask you again," Clarita said, her voice almost manic with excitement. "Who are the other spies?"

"I do not know what spies—"

But before she could finish the sentence, there was a crack of the whip, her scream of pain, and Mother Clarita's chilling cackle.

Deya lost track of how many times she had been whipped by Clarita. Bound by the faerivaine shackles, she was unable to heal herself. So, there she lay, her back smarting in pain, blood staining her tattered dress.

The days began to blur together marked only by visits from Mother Clarita and her whip.

It was always the same conversation. Clarita would ask her what she knew, Deya would deny it, and she would be whipped until she lost consciousness.

There was so much blood on the floor now that it was no longer an ugly, boring gray. Instead, it was stained a dark, shimmering red. Even the straw of Deya's "bed" was stained with her own blood. Every time Clarita finished, she would heal Deya slightly. Just enough to keep her alive, to keep her wounds from becoming infected. Just enough to keep her ripe for more.

She was Clarita's plaything. The gleam of glee in her eye every time she brought the whip down confirmed she didn't just dislike Deya, she *loathed* her. Wanted her to suffer. Wanted to revel in her agony.

Nobody deigned to come see her in her prison, though she knew Clarita must have informed the others. Deya could practically hear her crowing about it, the others laughing along. The thought of Luc laughing about her dying in a cell made bile rise in her throat. How had she been so wrong about him? About all of them?

Thunk, thunk, thunk.

Deya did not have the strength to lift her head at the sound, though her body reacted to it. A twitch of fear, a tremor of terror. But something was different about Clarita's footsteps this time, and it took Deya a second to realize it was because she was not alone. The blue-gray gown swished into view again, and Deya saw that the Mother was flanked on either side by armed guards.

Deya blinked, dragging her poor, broken body into a sitting position.

"Well, Deya," Clarita said, the sound of the hooks dragging across the floor. The world spun as she weakly raised her head to look up at the evil face of the High Mother. She was grinning down at her, the gray gemstone around her neck winking in the dull light like the flash of a blade. "It seems that our time together has run out."

"What do you mean?" Deya could barely speak, could hardly see through the pain and the blood. The image of Mother Clarita above her swam in and out of her vision.

"Lord Decius has decided your fate. He has agreed to sentence you to one hundred years at Ironbalt Prison Camp. Perhaps, during that time, you'll decide where your loyalties lie."

Deya stared up at her. She didn't have the strength left to be shocked, horrified, or upset. The pain from the whip had now spread throughout her whole being. She felt nothing but numb now.

Ironbalt was the biggest prison camp in Aunecia. They sent murderers there. Rebels. Thieves. People who had done horrible, horrific things.

And then there would be Deya. Imprisoned for questioning the Kingdom of Praiton.

But Deya did not say anything. She kept her face blank, a mask of her own. Clarita's smile faltered, but then her face set, and she snapped her fingers. The guards seized Deya under the arms and every muscle in her body screamed in pain, but she bit down on her lip to keep from crying out.

She would not let Clarita see. She had to hold it down. She would not let that lecherous tick soak up even one more drop of her misery. She had given her enough as it was.

As the soldiers carried her out of her blasted little cell, Deya looked Clarita right in the pallid, squat face. Clarita's smile stretched wide—a frog looking to ensnare a fat, juicy fly.

"You are about to find out how we treat traitors in this kingdom," she murmured to Deya, the end of the whip flicking against Deya's ankles. "It's a pity that I won't be able to see it."

And then, before Deya could even draw breath to retort, she was dragged up the stairs, inevitably, to her death.

CHAPTER
4

A sleeping potion was the one small mercy bestowed upon her by the soldiers tasked with her transport. She realized the soldiers who were responsible for chaining her to the wooden boards of the floor of the prison boat were some she had healed and cared for over the years.

It probably wasn't routine to drug the prisoners for the majority of the weeklong trek towards Aunecia. Deya suspected they preferred the prisoners to suffer through the journey. She didn't see the soldiers give anyone else a potion, and she was barely out of Stonehall's harbors before she felt her eyelids begin to droop. There was barely time to even take one last glimpse of the castle . . . the castle she had called home. The castle which used to represent so much to her and her mother. Oh Gods, her mother . . .

And with that, Deya fell unconscious.

For how long the journey should've taken, it passed in a sleepy haze. The soldiers were diligent with her doses of sleeping potion. She even caught one of the soldiers apologizing to her in a soft whisper as he poured another dose down her throat. She remembered trying to smile at him, but she was already falling asleep again. It was confirmation that the soldiers were trying to spare her suffering, regardless of what Mother Clarita had demanded. She relished the idea that the long, lonely shifts of caring for these soldiers that Clarita had intended to be punishment had, most likely, saved her life.

Without the sleeping potions, Deya didn't think she would have survived the journey from Praiton to Aunecia.

It seemed like it was all one long, horrible nightmare. But when she opened her eyes again, it was to a different, unfamiliar soldier rattling her chains.

"Up," he commanded.

Still groggy, Deya attempted to obey and pull herself into a sitting position only to feel her body scream in protest. After days of not standing or moving, she found that her muscles had atrophied.

The soldier snarled with impatience when her legs failed to hold her, and yanked her up by the chains, hard. Deya yelled, her body jerked upwards, high enough for her eyes to land on the soldier dragging her from the ship. These were not the same soldiers who had cared for her through the journey. Her unsteady gaze found the insignia on their bronze breast plates. A steel peg pierced through the Praiton star. The badge of the Ironbalt Guard.

Deya's chains were yanked forward, her feet still struggling to find the ground. The panic was beginning to build within her—a dam threatening to break. It had been a barrage of endless pain and misery in the dungeons, and then . . . nothing. Nothing but a cold, empty numbness in her chest while bloody pain melted into despair. But now, the fear was coming alive, a feral monster tearing at her heart.

She was at Ironbalt Prison. Not to heal. Not as a servant to her kingdom. But to serve a sentence—for *treason*.

"Move your feet!" the guard shouted. Another yank on the chain. Another aching bite of faerivaine against her wrists.

Deya choked on a sob which was lost in the bark of orders being shouted. Squeezing her eyes shut, Deya forced one foot in front of the other across the rocky ground.

Aunecia was cold and frigid. The sea breeze felt more like an arctic blast, even with the sun high in the sky. Squinting, she attempted to shield her eyes with her still chained hands.

"Keep it moving!" a soldier yelled, and pulled on the chain again, jerking her hands back to her side.

It had been so long since she had seen sunlight. So long since she had felt a breeze upon her face. She didn't know how many days had passed while she was locked in the dungeons of Stonehall, but it felt as if it could have been years.

For a moment, she wanted to revel in the feel of the outdoors, soak in the wind—no matter how frigid—but the yelling of soldiers and the tugging of her chains forced her back into the moment. Forced her to remember where she was.

Soldiers pulled Deya and the small gaggle of other prisoners onto a dock. Worn and weather beaten, the wooden beams were rickety and looked as though a good storm surge would wipe it out. She was chained to five other prisoners, all looking equally as dazed and confused as she was.

"Move!" a soldier shouted, and Deya and the chained prisoners began to shuffle in tandem, dragged along by the soldiers like dogs on a leash.

Deya tried to absorb her surroundings, to make sense of them. She had never been out of Praiton before, had little experience with anywhere but the large Free Kingdom in which she had been born. She knew Aunecia was northeast of Praiton, yet she was shocked to see what the landscape before her offered.

The shore was not white sand and warm breezes, like that of the seas in Praiton. Rocky and coarse, the coast was a collection of sharp, jagged rocks, and the sea looked angry and cold.

She figured the frigid breeze must come from the not-so-distant fjords of the Frost Kingdom which bordered Aunecia. According to every text Deya had read, Bridah was surrounded by menacing and immense mountains of ice.

Even from where she stood on that rocky beach, she could see long, jagged crystalline spears, high and sharp, reaching towards the sky, glinting in the faint sunlight. A deadly wall of pure ice.

It was the only reason Praiton had tried and failed so many times to seize it. Surviving the journey through the fjords and glaciers surrounding it was nearly impossible if you were not a Frost Magic wielder. Now that Bridah was the sole unconquered Pillar Kingdom, it was rare to see any Frost Wielder outside of their home.

As Deya was dragged further and further inland, her panic began to set in. It didn't take her long to feel frozen to the bone. Her healer's dress was tattered, the back shredded and exposed from Mother Clarita's whippings. She was shivering violently by the time the guards loaded them into a rough wooden cart pulled by two Bayard mares.

Teeth rattling, Deya glanced around at her fellow prisoners. One across from her—a fair-haired young male caught her eye. He gave her what she thought might have been an attempt at a grim smile, but his own teeth were chattering. None of them were dressed for these conditions.

It didn't take long for the high, iron walls to loom into view over the barren, rocky landscape. A sharp pain pierced her temples and everyone in the prison carriage winced collectively. The throbbing did not fade, even as they passed through the gates and towards the large stone structure inside.

So, this is what it would be like living in Ironbalt . . . the constant pounding pain from so much iron that she couldn't see straight.

The cart trundled to a stop and Deya waited with bated breath as the soldiers went around to collect them. They were thrust in front of a large, gray structure, which resembled an immense boulder. Deya had read about Ironbalt Prison in the Royal Archives. This was the only reason why she knew that the prison itself wasn't only made of stone, but rather an immense amount of unmined iron ore. The unending pain in her temples made sense then.

The captives were shunted into the prison. Each prisoner was put in front of a guard who took their measurements, hair color, eye color in an almost ritualistic fashion before Deya was separated from the rest of the group and pushed towards a formidable female guard. She was stripped and hosed down, before being given new clothes—a simple long sleeved wool tunic, and brown, rough spun pants. While they weren't made for harsh conditions, they were still thicker and warmer than the fetid healer's dress that Deya was not sad to see thrown into the incinerator.

Now dressed and cleaner than she had been in weeks, she was led through the jail. The inside of the prison resembled a hollowed-out rock. Cells lined the curved walls, the inside lit by flickering candles. The faces she could make out inside their cells all looked empty, lost . . . dead. Was that what she would be? How long would it take for her soul to die, just like theirs had?

She was thrust into a cell towards the end of the curved wall. Inside, there was a bucket, a straw mattress, and a pitcher of water. Deya ran to the water and downed it shamelessly, liquid spilling out the corners of her mouth. She could taste the trace amounts of faerivaine in it, but she was so thirsty she resisted the urge to gag. Gasping, her thirst temporarily sated, she looked around the cell. Was the rest of her life going to be this?

With shaking legs, she sank onto the straw mattress, looking through the bars at her surroundings. Her cell curved along the far wall, allowing her to see into the neighboring room next to hers. It shocked her to see the fair-haired male that had smiled at her in the back of the carriage lying on his own straw mattress.

Exhausted and weak, he had the distinct look of someone who had lost a lot of weight in a very short time. Deya briefly wondered if she looked the same. She had not seen her own reflection since her last day in the infirmary, but she could feel each sharp corner of her body—ribs protruding, hip bones jutting where they once weren't. Even her wrists looked like small twigs within their too big shackles. This, perhaps, was her only saving grace. Her wrists were so thin that the shackles were not digging their faerivaine into her skin.

The male next to her cell, however, looked like the iron surrounding them had drained him. He hadn't noticed Deya—though their mattresses faced each other along the curve of the rock wall. Only iron bars separated them. His eyes were closed, as though he were trying to rest. He must have been finding it difficult to ignore the throbbing ache from all the iron because his face was screwed up in pain.

Deya settled back against her straw mattress. She had slept for a week straight, and yet managed to not feel rested at all.

Struggling to block out the dull pounding of her temples, she closed her eyes and breathed like she would when she tried to heal someone. Her magic rose up. The warm, soothing power flowing up her body— and then stopping, as though someone had dropped a lid on it. It felt as though she had been punched in the gut. Choking on the feeling of nausea that rolled through her, Deya gasped, clutching her stomach. It was evident that magic was more than an impossibility with the faerivaine on her.

And with that, Deya closed her eyes again.

She was awoken sometime later to the sound of her cell door slamming open.

"Up," a guard commanded.

Deya blinked in a daze, lifting her head, and wincing at the sore muscles in her neck. She had fallen asleep awkwardly, leaning up against the wall on her straw mattress. There was no time to rally herself before her cuffs were yanked hard, thrusting her out of her cell.

Guards walked the line, stringing the prisoners together with their chains, pulling them to attention. The bite of the faerivaine and iron against her skin made her gasp in pain before she looked up and realized the fair-haired male was chained in front of her. He had turned at the sound of her cry, and she was struck by how hollow and tired his eyes were. But he still tried to give her the same, weak smile that he had in the prison carriage yesterday.

"Some alarm clock, eh?" he whispered to her.

Stunned by his attempt at a joke, Deya could only gape at him until there was another rough yank on their chains and they began to walk. She had no idea where they were taking them, but she knew it couldn't be pleasant. In all of her readings about Ironbalt, they never said much about what it was the prisoners were made to do.

She got her answer soon enough, however. Outside Ironbalt's main walls—still within its heavy iron gates—lay miles of mines. There had to be at least a hundred of them, all guarded, all filled with people as emaciated as the prisoners chained beside her, carrying pickaxes.

Deya walked in a numb trance as their group was led to a cave on the outskirts of the others. At the mouth of the cavern stood a line of guards, all there to supervise the handing out of pickaxes. Deya received hers wordlessly, the wooden handle unnaturally heavy in her hands—or was she exceptionally weak now? The reason as to why there were so many guards around made sense suddenly. The sharp end of the pickaxe, the heaviness of its stone mallet . . . this was the one weapon she would ever be able to touch in this place.

"Mine the ore," the guard commanded. And that was all. The only direction they received.

Their chains were split. Deya, the fair-haired male, and a few others were separated from the other half, their wrist shackles removed, only to be replaced by ones around their ankles.

Deya stood for a moment, clutching her pickaxe, not a clue in the world how to go about mining for iron ore. The other prisoners shuffled away, their chains clanging and dragging across the dirt floor. One particularly brutal looking Manielian stumbled by, muttering under his breath, wild eyes darting back and forth. His shoulder collided with her so hard that she was nearly thrown to the ground.

A hand reached out and seized her by the elbow, stopping her just short from hitting the dirt floor. The same fair-haired male pulled her to her feet, shooting a venomous glare at the Manielian prisoner, who stumbled away still muttering nonsensical curses under his breath.

"Come on, there's a wall this way," he said to her, mustering a bit more than a grimace this time.

Deya's mouth opened, wanting to thank him, but she found no words came out. As if her voice had been stolen. And even if she knew that everything was working physically within her, the empty brokenness seemed to flow throughout her body, through every working muscle and organ. Everything felt broken now.

She followed him across the mine towards an open expanse of black wall. The mines twisted in long cavernous halls, as though prisoners had been working on it for centuries. Deya wouldn't be surprised if they had.

"What a concept for a prison," the male next to her grumbled. He swung his axe, grimacing as it connected with the wall. "Almost ingenious. Get us to mine for the bloody stuff that makes us want to vomit so they don't have to."

"Never thought of it like that," she mumbled, the sound of her own voice surprising her. With a grunt, she took a swing at the wall, but was so weak that the tip of the axe bounced off the stone, not even making a mark.

"Ah, so she does speak." He glanced over at her. "I was beginning to wonder if you were mute."

"No, not mute." She swung the axe again, this time chipping a bit of stone. "Though, if I was, I probably wouldn't be here right now."

For the first time, a genuine smile spread across his face. "That is something we have in common."

She paused before the next swing and felt her own mouth twitch. There was something about him that made her want to smile along with him.

"I'm Oswallt, by the way . . . or Os, whichever you'd prefer," he said, turning back to his wall.

"Deya," she said softly.

"Deya? Interesting name. Are you from Praiton or somewhere else?"

"Praiton," she said. Her breathing was beginning to grow labored from the swings of her axe. "Deya is short for Deyanira."

"Ah, so with that name, you must hail from Ganiea." For someone who looked so frail, he was surprisingly steady in his swings. "So am I . . . at least, distantly. I've lived in Praiton most of my life."

Deya paused to catch her breath. Gods, she had to do this *all* day?

"This is the first time I've been outside of Praiton," she said, panting. Bracing her hands on her knees, she tried to get her spinning head to still. "Let's just say, I'm not enjoying it thus far."

Oswallt laughed. "I think, my dear, that is the point."

They continued mining throughout the day, sometimes talking, sometimes even laughing, but mostly they gritted their teeth and worked. And it was very, very hard work. Deya had not done work like this her whole life. Even as a child, her tasks then were picking herbs for her mother, grinding up ingredients. She had never held a tool in her life, never so much as swung an axe for wood.

Each indent they made in the stone wall, each slab of ore revealed made Deya's head ache so badly that even her teeth hurt. Hours passed. Eventually she and Oswallt were forced to stay quiet purely to keep going.

When the guards called them back, took their pickaxes, and rechained them, Deya could barely stand upright. Her arms shook and her shoulders burned with every movement. And, for the first time in weeks, she was desperately, desperately hungry.

She had never been so happy to see her cell. Collapsing onto her straw bed, she heard Oswallt do the same in the cell over. Covered in rock and soot, her hands and entire body were almost black, dust from the mines still in her lungs. Her hand scrambled to find the pitcher of water and sipped at it gingerly. She gagged at the burn of the faerivaine but kept drinking.

"Whoever thought of lacing our only water with this shit should be executed," Oswallt wheezed. He, too, was sipping at his pitcher, the same look of revulsion on his face.

Deya was too tired to laugh, but she almost did. "What was it that you said earlier? Ingenious?"

Oswallt groaned. "Ingenious? I meant *evil.* Pure, *evil.*"

They lay in silence for a bit. Their side of the prison was right before a hall leading towards the warden's office. Deya had seen him—a large, imposing male in bronze armor—stride towards it this morning. For the most part, they were almost entirely on their own there. Another small blessing.

"I don't know how I'm going to keep doing this," Deya breathed, more to herself than Oswallt. She heard him shift the straw mattress closer to her on the other side of the rock wall. She did the same. Soon they were leaning against the walls, facing each other within the rounded edges of their separate cells. Mirror images of each other—tired, soot-ridden, and malnourished.

"You can't die on me yet," he said, but his eyes were closed, and Deya saw him wince in pain. "Who will get me through those lovely mining mornings?"

Deya's head lolled from the effort of holding it upright. She was tired . . . so, so tired.

Footsteps rounded the corner, and a guard came by, shoving a tray into both of their cells. Deya leapt on it, not registering the stale piece of bread and cold gruel that was spooned onto it. She shoveled it into her mouth, not even processing its taste—or lack thereof. She could hear Oswallt doing the same beside her. They did not speak as they licked their trays clean. Not one drop of gruel remained, and still Deya's stomach ached.

"Well, that was wholly unsatisfying," Oswallt mumbled.

Deya mustered a small chuckle. "I think, my dear, that is the point."

Oswallt laughed also, and he pointed a blackened finger at her teasingly. "You are learning already."

She smiled at him—the feeling foreign but nice. Comforting. It was similar to the feeling her Healing Magic would give her.

"So, Deyanira, tell me." He shifted on his straw mattress and lay down. She mirrored him. They were head-to-head with only the iron bars separating them. "How did a nice, sweet thing like you wind up in here?"

Deya hesitated. How much should she tell him? Already, the feeling of shame for even shedding doubt on Praiton was beginning to wane, but it still sat within her gut—a sharp thorn in her side. But with each crack of Clarita's whip, she had felt her loyalty shake. Just enough for the anger she had pushed down to bubble beneath the surface.

"Let's just say I got on the bad side of the High Mother Clarita."

"Clarita Killoran?" Os almost sat up to give her a flabbergasted look but found he was too sore and had to settle back onto his straw bed with a wince. "That cow is still wreaking terror then?"

That had Deya almost exploding in an unlady-like snort. "More than just wreaking terror."

"I wondered," he said softly. "I saw them bring you into the dungeons. I heard her whipping you. I'm sorry she . . ." He trailed off.

For the first time since she had left Stonehall, she ran a finger along her lower spine. Jagged, deep scars, torn and healed by Clarita. Forever etched into her skin.

"There's nothing to be sorry about, Os," she whispered. "There was nothing you could do."

"You were one of her healers, right?"

"Yes."

"That explains the guards giving you sleeping potions the whole trip." He chuckled lightly. "I was quite jealous, actually. The journey here almost killed me. Awful seasickness."

Deya smiled. "I would've shared it if I'd known." She saw Os smirk out of the corner of her eye. "And what about you, Oswallt? What horrible, dastardly thing did you do to land yourself in here?"

Os hesitated. It was the smallest of pauses, the faintest moment of uncertainty before it was gone. It was so fleeting Deya almost wondered if she had imagined it.

"Well," Os said, stretching on his straw mat. "I was the king's bard."

This got Deya's attention. "A *bard?*" she cried, unable to hide her surprise.

"A very *talented* bard, thank you," Os replied. She let out a bark of laughter, and he feigned insult. "But yes, I was the throne's personal bard. And your dear *friend*, Clarita Killoran was a frequent attender of the feasts I performed at. One day, she took mighty offense to one of my rhymes . . . How did it go?" He paused, but then sang, "*The fair Holy Mother loves us all, for she did not even care, that the lovely Clarita Killoran is as ugly as a Ganiean ram.*"

Deya let out of a bark of a laugh so hard that her ribs groaned in protest, but she couldn't stop. She could imagine Clarita's face—how it must have turned red, then purple with fury. The humiliation she must have faced from that song. Deya wished with all her heart that she could've been there to witness it.

"You can't be serious! You were in prison because of Clarita, too?"

"My dear, half of Stonehall's dungeon is filled because of her Evil Holiness," Os scoffed, and that earned another peal of laughter from Deya. "For someone so vain, the High Mother has a rather fragile sense of self. You insult that and you may as well write your own ticket to the stockade."

"Then why chance it? Why sing it?"

"Because that imperious bitch swished around the halls like she owned it." Os shrugged. "She talked down to everyone beneath her; always looked down her big nose at me. I wanted to put her in her place." Oswallt picked at a spot of soot on his prison rags. He didn't meet her gaze, and once again, Deya wondered if there was something he wasn't saying. "But perhaps I did it a little *too* well," he finished, smirking.

"I'll say. Especially if it earned you a trip to Ironbalt. How in the Mother did she justify that?"

Os snorted derisively. "She didn't have to. She has that evil git, Lord Decius, wrapped around her stubby little finger. All she has to do is command something, and it's hers. Merely insulting her is considered treasonous."

Deya's chest warmed with molten anger. Os did not know how true this was and she was impressed by his ability to see right through Clarita, even from a distance.

"They shouldn't be allowed to treat people like this . . . especially loyal Priatonians like you and me." she whispered, more to herself than to Os.

Os's hollow laugh echoed amongst the sheet rock around them. "*Loyal*," he scoffed. The word sounded bitter. "Sadly, there is no way to make that stop. Not without toppling the whole regime."

Deya felt a small twinge of fear, a knee-jerk reaction to anything remotely treasonous about Praiton. It took her a second to remember where she was, and that treason hardly mattered anymore.

"Why would I want to topple the whole regime?" she asked him. The small bit of information that she knew —that one seed of doubt— scratched at the back of her mind, but she didn't mention it. She couldn't.

Os, however, turned to face her, his expression bemused. "Praiton has been overtaken by greed and corruption. Surely you have noticed?"

Deya did not answer. Her fingers twisted anxiously in her lap, unsure of how to reply. *Scared* to. As if an invisible hand was forcing her, she shook her head in an attempt to deny what her gut knew was true.

Os did not miss this, though. Scooting closer, he peered at her through the bars, his concern deepening the crease in his brow.

"You served Praiton your whole life," he said, reaching out to touch the bars, as if to comfort her. "And look where that got you."

A sharp pain pierced her heart, an ache that made her throat burn at his words. Because Os was right. Her whole *life* she had devoted her heart and soul to caring for and healing her kingdom. And this was how they repaid her. No trial, no chance to even defend herself. Only a thousand lashes, a hundred scats, and a life sentence in prison.

"Praiton is no longer the kingdom it once was, Deya," Oswallt continued, his voice gentle, but firm. "It might be time for you to realize that."

Deya didn't say anything. The molten anger mixed with sadness was still churning in her chest. Anger that the words Os spoke were both true and horribly unfair. And sadness for the realization that the thing she had devoted her life to was not what she thought it was at all.

They spoke no more after that, and after mere minutes of silence, they both fell asleep.

CHAPTER
5

Life in Ironbalt Prison was a blur of pain and suffering. No matter how many hours and days Deya swung the axe, it never got easier. She hoped she would build her strength over time, but the Ironbalt guards didn't feed them enough for that to happen.

Instead, she and Oswallt guzzled down the meager scraps of food they were given each night after a day of hard mining and then they would lay, side by side, separated by the stone wall, too tired to talk.

Some days were harder than others. Some days, Deya fought against collapse, sometimes even dropping her axe, and falling into the stone walls. When this happened, Os would hurry to her before the guards noticed, pick up her axe, and place it back in her hand. He'd keep her upright until she could gather herself, still swinging his axe relentlessly so as not to draw attention.

No matter the difficulty of the day, Deya knew she would not have lasted one second in that place without Oswallt. She thanked the Mother every night for placing his cell next to hers, as they fell asleep, head-to-head every night.

As a bard, Oswallt knew lots of stories. He had traveled across Krigor throughout his life, learning stories, songs, and traditions from each region. Deya had been shocked to discover he had been to all the Pillar Kingdoms before.

"Well, except for Bridah," he amended one night when they stayed up talking. "The damn ice fjords make it nearly impossible, and I've never been able to find a Frost Wielder to escort me. You can imagine that they're not particularly fond of Praitonians as a whole."

"What were the other kingdoms like?" she asked breathlessly. They were facing each other that night, attempting to slowly eat the small chunk of bread they were given. To make it last, they would talk and eat, one bite at a time. "Which was your favorite?"

"Nodaria," he said without hesitation. "The Celestial Kingdom was the most beautiful place I had ever seen, especially when High King Castor ruled." The battle that had killed High King Castor had taken place nearly fifty years ago. Nodaria had been the last kingdom to fall to Praiton.

"Castor was one of the most powerful High Kings—save maybe for High King Ulf in Bridah. But he not only continuously held the top floor of the palace, Atlas Keep, above the clouds to help with their astronomers' stargazing, but he also kept it permanently at the twilight hours. When he died, they said the top floor came tumbling to the ground."

Deya had not heard much of Nodaria. When High King Castor had been killed and his entire family murdered with him, the Nodarians' hatred for the Praitonians became so strong that they rarely intermingled anymore.

"I didn't know anyone could do that."

Os nodded, taking another bite of his bread. "That is the power of the High Kings. The Royal Bloodlines are said to link directly to the goddesses each region worships."

Deya had known of the five other goddesses of Krigor. The Mother Goddess was said to be the mother of the five, each having their own set of magic that was now wielded respectively in each region where that goddess had come from. Deya knew little of them but had always kept a figurine of the Harvest Goddess from Ganiea, Arista, on her mantle while growing up.

"Praiton outlawed the worship of all other goddesses but the Mother," Deya replied, automatically. It had been hammered into her since the beginning of Praiton's conquests. It had been imperative that she remembered this while working at the castle in order to ensure she never mentioned another Goddess but the Mother Herself.

Os, however, scoffed and waved a hand, brushing away this bit of Praitonian propaganda. "The Five Goddesses are still as important to this realm as they were *before* that blithering geezer, Decius banned them." He shook the small piece of bread he had left at her like a teacher lecturing an apprentice. "Tell me, Deya, how much do you know of the goddesses?"

She blushed a little at her ignorance before muttering, "Just that they are the daughters of the Mother Goddess, Mav."

Os, bless him, didn't judge her. Instead, he nodded and said, "Correct. Mav was the Creator. Her set of scales that she carries represents her devotion to Balance. That's why it's said that she created the human race, to balance against the fae. She is the goddess of life itself."

Deya had never seen a human before. They were said to live on a continent many miles from Krigor. Safe, she assumed, from tyrants like Decius who would no doubt love to enslave a weaker race.

Os continued, "Mav's purpose of balance created her five daughters. The Harvest Goddess, Arista; the Sea Goddess, Eula; the Ember Goddess, Calida; the Celestial Goddess, Astrea; and the Frost Goddess, Flykra. They were created in pairs, to balance the other—except for Arista, that is. Arista was to represent the Earth, the grounding of the realm as a whole. And so, the worship of these Goddesses gave each region their power."

Deya blinked, aghast. "The *worship* itself was the source of the region's power?"

Os nodded, his expression darkening. "Yes, or so our legends tell us. Some believe that the worship of a certain goddess will strengthen that particular power and region. While it hasn't really been proven, those fanatical enough still push those ideals."

Deya processed this. She had never lived in a world where Praiton didn't control most of the realm. Her magic had always been the same level to her. True, it sometimes felt weaker now and then, but otherwise steady. Was this because of Praiton's ban on the Earth Goddess, Arista?

Over the past few weeks with Os, he had been opening her eyes to what Praiton had been doing to the realm. How they had plundered, killed, and destroyed whole empires. Dismantled magic systems, killed the High Kings of Ganiea and Nodaria. And no one within Praiton had so much as batted an eye. Had it all been to make Praiton more powerful? And was it really Lord Decius behind it?

And while it still pained her to realize it—to even *think* it—it was getting harder and harder for her to deny. The words Os spoke during their first night at Ironbalt came to mind.

Ingenious? I meant evil. Pure evil.

To overthrow the balance of the realm on the deluded idea that banning the goddesses to weaken the regions would strengthen Praiton. Would strengthen *Decius*.

Deya was too young to remember what Praiton was like before the goddesses were outlawed. Throughout her life, Deya had always believed Praiton to be doing good in the realm. She was told that the Mother Goddess was the only true deity, that the others were merely sacrilege, and to be discredited. She was ashamed to admit that she had believed it.

And as she sat and listened to Os tell stories of the other kingdoms, of how the goddesses were not sacrilege, but real, *powerful* beings that represented more than just magic to their kingdoms, that shame grew.

"Os," Deya said. Os looked up, the last piece of bread between his fingers. "I wasn't entirely honest about why I am here." She said it so softly, so quietly that only Os could hear. Her heart had begun to beat faster as her hands stilled and he peered at her. "I didn't just get on Clarita's bad side. I overheard her . . . overheard her talking about making a potion for Lord Decius for the king. A potion of diluted nightshade."

Oswallt's eyes widened. Unlike Luc, it had taken him only a split second to understand.

"You don't mean . . ."

Deya nodded, the familiar shaking starting in her hands again. She put her bread down into her lap and wrung her fingers together. "I think so. Someone who I thought to be my friend told her what I had overheard . . . what I had guessed. She and Lord Decius sentenced me to one hundred years here. For treason."

Os swore. Deya didn't know what she expected, telling him this. She wasn't sure if he would react like Luc. Would he dismiss her? Betray her? Would it be any different?

Her hands still trembled where they sat, entwined in her lap. Os, who was lost in thought, digesting what she had told him, noticed this. He scooted as close as he could to the bars, reached out and took her hands in his. It was the first physical contact she had had in months now. Before she knew it, her lips were trembling. Ducking her head, she couldn't stop the tears from coming. So, she let them.

Os held her hand as she cried, not moving, not speaking. He let her cry for everything she had lost and everything that was still to come.

⚜

It was difficult to believe that hard labor would grow to be mundane and boring. But, eventually, it did. While wielding the pickaxe did not get easier, and the constant throbbing of her temples from all the iron did not lessen, Deya found that she was adapting to her lot in life at Ironbalt. Granted, much of this was due to Oswallt.

His support and friendship were more precious to her than anything. She began to look forward to the end of their labor—not just because she was tired, but because it meant she could spend the rest of the night listening to Oswallt's stories about his journeys across the Pillar Kingdoms.

He told her of his run-in with a leshy in Ganiea when he attempted to visit the magical and ancient Mother Oak in the Verdigris Marsh. How he said he almost wet himself running from it. He sang her a song about the Sea Fae he had fallen in love with when he briefly lived in Laenimore, and about legends he had heard of other realms traveling through Maniel.

They laughed together most nights, and every night, Deya prayed to the Mother and thanked her for Oswallt. She knew she would have died without him, would have been wishing for a swift end to her suffering by now if it weren't for him.

But instead, they would laugh in their cells at night, Deya telling him stories of Clarita, Oswallt cackling with glee when she would mimic an impression of the Mother that she had never dared use with Luc. And if the guards noticed they were becoming friends and seeking solace in the other, they did not act. Another small blessing.

"So, this potion," Os said one day as they cracked their axes together in tandem. "I only know a little bit about it."

Deya grunted as her axe contacted with stone. They had not spoken much about what she had told him that night. She had wondered if Os had wanted to forget about it.

"I don't know if here is a good place to discuss that," she said through gritted teeth. It was only halfway through the day, and Deya wondered if she had the strength to swing that damn axe one more time. Somehow, she kept going.

"I know, I know," Os said, brushing her off. "My knowledge of herbs and potions may be a little shaky but . . ." He trailed off and Deya paused a moment to catch her breath.

"Yes, Os," she hissed. "The Nighthold potion addles and weakens. It is basically designed to incapacitate someone while still keeping them alive. Now, doesn't that sound familiar to you?"

Os's brow wrinkled. He had been in the castle, just as she had. No doubt he had heard the rumors, too. How the King was bedridden and incoherent, and no one knew why.

"But if this is true, then how in the Mother has this gone on for so long? What about the Second Lord, Malyk? Surely he wouldn't have stood—" But then he stopped short. The sound of chains being dragged against stone echoed down the cavern in which they stood. Then, a brutish figure loomed into view.

She had seen this male before. His red hair and manic, darting eyes triggered something in her distant memory. It wasn't until he shuffled closer that she could hear the muttered ramblings falling from his lips like stones, and she remembered. It was the Manielian who had barreled into her on her first day in Ironbalt. And, judging by the deep mess of scars across his tanned face, he was as mean as he appeared.

"Too much noise," he growled. His voice was like the gravel beneath their feet, coarse and harsh. "Too much noise . . . too much light . . . too much, too much . . ."

Os's grip on his pickaxe tightened. "I . . . I'm sorry." He began to inch away from the male, his eyes tracking the movement. Deya's spine was rigid as she, too, took in the twitch of muscle, the empty, manic dullness in his eyes. The male was a rolling flame, an unpredictable flicker where one spark could set off a wild blaze.

"Must shut it up . . ." the male continued. "Must make the noise *shut up*. Kill it, I will. Shut it up now . . ."

"Now, that's not very neighborly," Os replied in his usual flippant manner. Deya winced. Sometimes she wondered if Os was brave or just reckless. "But, no worries, friend. We'll keep it down."

Although Os had tried to placate him, it was as though the Manielian was reluctant to leave well enough alone. He edged closer, chain and pickaxe both dragging along the floor.

"All this fecking iron," the male snarled, moving ever closer to her and Os. His hands were gnarled claws around his pickaxe, and Deya wondered how long he had been in here. "My head won't stop pounding . . . and now there's too . . . much . . . noise."

Os took a step back, taking Deya with him. Her feet stumbled over each other as Os scrambled backwards.

"We already said we'd shut up, alright?" Os said carefully, holding a warning hand out between them and the male. "We don't want any trouble."

But the male ignored him. Deya recognized the signs of mania . . . maybe even madness—the male's eye twitched and his brow was furrowed, as though trying to see through a loud noise or bright light. The iron had to have been getting to him, aggravating him.

He staggered closer, lifting his pickaxe and slinging it over his shoulder. Deya seized Oswallt's tunic and gripped it tightly, almost dragging him back with her.

"We'll call the guards!" Os cried, holding up his own pickaxe in front of him as he and Deya shuffled backwards, chains clanging. "Get back! I'm warning you!"

The male's eye twitched as he lumbered forward. "Shut it up," he rasped. "Make it stop . . . *now!*" And then, he swung.

Deya screamed as Oswallt reacted quicker than she expected. He shoved her aside as the male swung the axe. And in that split second, when he could've dodged, he had instead chosen to push Deya out of the way. The pickaxe connected with his shoulder, causing him to yell in anguish.

"*Os!*" Deya yelled. Frantically, she scrambled to her feet and attempted to run towards the male, but her chains slowed her down immensely. By the time she reached them, he had already swung at Os again, knocking his pickaxe flying. Deya launched herself at the male, wrapping herself around his neck, attempting to grab hold of his axe to stop him. He flicked her off as if she were nothing more than a fly and swung again.

Os attempted to roll out of the way, but it was too late. The axe slammed into his chest, and he screamed a loud, horrible howl of pain . . . and then, he was still.

"*Oswallt!*" Deya was shrieking, but the world had gone quiet. She scrambled across the dirt floor towards her fallen friend. There was so much blood . . . staining the stone floor, splattered across the slate wall . . . a flash of memory pierced through her mind of her own cell in Stonehall's dungeons.

Shoving it from her mind, Deya threw herself over her friend, not even paying attention to his assailant who—seemingly satisfied by the bloodshed—had begun to stagger off back towards the mines.

"Os!" Deya shook him, but he did not respond. Her hands were soaked with his blood and the panic momentarily blinded her from acting. How long had it been since she had held someone's life in her hands?

Focus, a small, clear voice in her mind insisted. *Focus. Breathe.*

Deya closed her eyes and took in a long, steadying breath. And just like that, she switched modes.

Throwing herself down on the ground, Deya ripped off her shoes. She was skinny now—too skinny—the shackles were hanging as loosely on her ankles as they had on her wrists. Pointing her toes, she bent, squeezed, and *pushed* with all her might, gasping in pain as the manacles twisted her foot into an unnatural position. One more push of pain and her foot was free. Shocked and shaking, she tore off her other shoe next. *Squeeze, push, pull . . .* With a yell of pain, she ripped her remaining foot free of the shackles.

Immediately, the throbbing in her temples lessened, as if someone had just turned off a high, piercing noise. Not even giving herself a second to revel in this newfound relief, Deya turned to her friend.

Two deep wounds. One to the shoulder, one to the chest. The healer in her began to work. She was weak—made even more so by drinking nothing but water laced with faerivaine and surrounded by iron—but she had to try to save him.

She closed her eyes, hands extended above Oswallt. At first, nothing but a painful, empty ache filled her stomach. Frustration welled in her as the bloodstain on Oswallt's shirt grew darker and darker, but still, her magic fought back.

Please, Deya begged. Out of sheer habit, she prayed to the

Mother Goddess, prayed to the only deity she had ever known. *Please let me save my friend.*

Suddenly, the familiar warmth began to emanate from her core. It surged up her body, wrapping itself around her veins like a hot drink, and then her hands began to glow. Gasping in relief, Deya narrowed her gaze and focused. Channeling as much as she could bear, she drove it down, down, past the weak remnants of faerivaine, and straight into her dying friend.

The sounds of guards filled the caverns around her, but Deya forced herself to ignore it. She had to save him . . . had to save Oswallt . . . couldn't let him die . . .

And then, his eyes snapped open. He let out a horrible, rasping breath and Deya collapsed against the stone floor, spent but relieved, tears running down her face.

Os panted on the floor, still covered in his own blood. Dazed, his eyes fell on Deya, and he gave a weak, humorless smile.

"What are you crying about, love? I'm alright . . ."

Deya's sob burst loose, and she threw her arms around her friend, not even registering the blood pooling around them and soaking her . . . not registering what she had done.

Os sat up with much effort, still looking around confusedly, as though he couldn't remember what had just happened. He looked down at himself—the bloody holes in his tunic—and then, his eyes gradually moved to Deya. They roved from her bloody hands and clothes, and then to her unbound feet, and finally, to her shackles, laying discarded on the floor.

"Deya," he breathed, his eyes wide, horrified. "What have . . . what have you done?"

"I had to," she whispered. The magic had greatly exhausted her, and she felt weak, dizzy. "You were dying . . . Os, you were *dying.*"

The sounds of guards running grew nearer. Os's eyes were wide as he scrambled to his knees. He seized her shackles and began attempting to shove her feet back inside them.

"Deya, do you not understand what you just did?" he hissed, straining under the effort of attempting to contort her foot back into her chains. But it was no use. Her shackles, no matter how hard he tried, would not fit back over her heel. "They will *kill you* for using magic!"

"You were going to die!" Deya cried, furious tears still lining her eyes. "I would not let you die, Oswallt! Not when I could save you—"

"Deya . . ." Oswallt seized her roughly by the shoulders, shaking her. "Listen to me . . . Gods, you silly, sweet, stupid girl . . . Don't you *ever* try to save my life again! Especially when it could get you killed—"

"Don't be—" Ridiculous, was what she wanted to say, but she never got the chance. Guards from all angles began to descend upon them. Os tried to hide the shackles beneath himself, but it didn't make a difference. Hands grabbed her, pulling her up, jerking her away from Oswallt and the pool of blood.

Deya was only vaguely aware of her own sobbing, her instinctual thrashing against the guards who had picked her up like she was nothing. New shackles were slapped on her wrists and ankles, binding her together like a trussed pig.

She was dragged away from Os—to where, she had no clue. She could barely see her surroundings through her tears and panic.

They will kill you for using magic! Os had yelled at her. Were they going to kill her? Was that where she was going right now?

Somewhere between the mines and the main prison, Deya fell silent. She stopped fighting the guards, stopped feeling anything at all.

They are going to kill you, said the little voice in her head. It was the same, clear, calm voice that had spoken to her in the mines. *You have broken the biggest rule in this place. They are going to kill you for saving your friend.*

Deya found that she did not care if they killed her. She would save Oswallt over and over again. If it weren't for Oswallt, she would've been dead by now anyway. Whatever happened to her, Deya didn't think she would ever regret saving her friend's life.

She was brought through the main jail, right past their cells, and down the corridor that held the warden's office. She wondered if that was where she was going, but instead, they kept moving until they reached a small, dank corridor. The stone here was uneven and wet, as though it were so deep inside the rock that the moisture still clung to it. Along the rock wall were small doors—all made of solid iron.

The guard holding her right arm yanked one of these doors open. Deya barely had a moment to register a tiny, cold, wet hole before she was thrown into it. Her face crashed against the rock wall, and her cry was drowned out by the sound of the door slamming behind her. Around her, she could hear other doors on either side opening and slamming shut as well. She wondered if Os was near—if this was where they brought him, too.

She spat her own blood onto the floor and cried, "Os?" But no reply. Frantically, she began to pound her fists against the wall, testing to see how thick and deep the stone ran. The wall was solid—impenetrable.

Collapsing back against the stone, she breathed rapidly. The hole she was in was barely big enough for her to extend her legs halfway. It was tall enough for her to crouch, but not much else.

Solitary confinement. That was where she had to be. This is where they were going to keep her until they were ready to punish her. Until they were ready to kill her.

The panic rose up her throat again and she collapsed to the floor, panting and desperate. She wanted out of that horrible hole, wanted to find Oswallt, to make sure he was okay. Breathing hard, tears still streaking her face and painfully weakened by her use of magic and the reintroduction of her faerivaine shackles, Deya passed out cold.

CHAPTER
6

Days seemed to pass inside that small, dank hole. No sound penetrated the thick stone walls, not a sliver of light to give her a clue as to how long she sat there. Her mind spun out of control inside a useless body that was too fatigued with hunger and fear to tame it. All she could do was sit and think.

Her mind bounced images of Clarita, of Luc . . . and then, of King Rodric and Lord Decius. Her heart was torn. The part of her that had been raised believing she belonged to the strongest kingdom in all of Krigor. To the best army, to the best castle . . . The part of her that believed being a part of Praiton was something to be proud of.

This part of her was now at war with the anger. The hurt and betrayal she felt for a kingdom that had not only lied about the havoc it was wreaking on the world but had also turned its violent and oppressive zeal on her.

Deya leaned her head against the rough stone wall and watched a droplet of moisture plop onto the floor in front of her. *Plop, plop, plop.*

The puddle grew as the hours passed; her eyes glazed over.

Plop, plop, plop.

She felt on the verge of breaking many times in that hole, when, finally, the door to her cage was wrenched open again.

Without a single word, the guard leaned in and seized Deya by the hair and pulled her out of her cell. Deya shrieked with pain and surprise, unable to keep it inside or hide it.

The guard didn't so much as look at her as he held her steady, and she was able to look around, blinking in the light. There was a line of other prisoners who appeared as though they were also pulled from their own tiny holes. There was no sign of Oswallt, though she did see the Manielian who had tried to kill him. Her blood boiled at the sight of him.

Chained together in a line, the prisoners began to walk, led by a guard up at the front. Deya didn't look at anyone else, her gaze zeroed in on the tangle of auburn hair in front of her—all she could see was the monster who had hurt her friend. Deya focused on that prisoner all the way out of the prison house, through the courtyard, and into a carriage similar to the one she had arrived in.

It was only when she was loaded into the carriage with the others that she looked up. And there was Oswallt.

"*Os!*" she cried, unable to contain her relief at seeing her friend there. He looked unharmed, though tired, which was nothing too unusual. The guard yanked on Deya's chain, an indication that she was to keep her mouth shut. Sliding into the seat across from him, she leaned forward to seize her friend's hands.

"Are you okay? What happened to you?"

It was only then she noticed how nervous Os looked. Scared.

"They took me back to my cell," he whispered. He cast a sidelong glance at the Manielian who was the last to load into the carriage. The male did not look at them. "Where did they put you?"

"Solitary," she replied, also in a whisper. "Gods, I'm so relieved you're okay."

"Don't count your blessings yet," Os said, sounding uneasy.

"Why?"

"Deya, do you not realize where we are? Where we're going?"

Feeling like she was lifting her head out of water, Deya blinked and looked around. The small prison carriage held six hostages. Besides her, Os, and the brute, there was also a blue-skinned male with pointed, webbed ears, no doubt a Sea Fae, a Manielian female, and a male with white hair, who looked like he could maybe be from Bridah. But as the carriage kicked off, she realized she hadn't even given a second thought to where they could be taking them.

"Where *are* we going?" Deya whispered.

Os's face was white, his eyes scanning the passengers around them. "The whipping post," he hissed. "I heard the guards speaking of it this morning. This is where they punish, Deya. Where they do *more* than just punish."

Deya's blood ran cold. The scars on her back seemed to tingle as the memory of the hooked whips flashed through her mind. She could still remember what it felt like . . . the sting of metal, the blinding pain, and blur of blood.

"But . . . why are *you* here? You did nothing wrong!"

"Don't you think I wondered that, too?" Os's head was moving on a swivel, trying to see outside the enclosed carriage to where they were being taken. "Why didn't they put me in solitary too, then?"

"I don't know," Deya breathed, but she still had a chill fear in her heart. She knew that Os's panic was well founded, knew that the little voice in her head that spoke to her yesterday was probably right.

They were going to die today.

Within a few minutes, the carriage came to a halt. In that second, it felt as if they were all holding their breath before the door was ripped open. A guard stood there, staring down at all of them with a look of pure disgust.

"You three," he said, pointing to Deya, Os, and the Manielian brute.

"You first."

So, they were dealing with them by case, then. This was a small comfort to her. She would rather they round them all up, whip them together, and be done with it.

Deya, Oswallt, and the Manielian trailed out of the carriage, still being yanked along by the guard.

The whipping posts were stationed in a large, empty expanse of rocky ground. The harsh, cold wind whipped Deya in the face, making her squint against the dust. Judging by the distance from the Ironbalt prison hold, it was more than a mile away. The grounds behind the iron walls were immense—the prison itself only being a fraction of it. Here, though, the only thing for miles around them appeared to be a shallow pit where three lone posts stood sentry.

Deya's whole body felt paralyzed. She had known fear. Had been whipped over and over again until she felt like she would die. But there was something different about this. Something cruel, ceremonial, almost routine.

A large male stood by the posts, holding a large bronze sword. It tapped against his foot while he assessed them, his dark, bottomless eyes looking at them like a hunter appraising which animal to slaughter next. The heavy bronze armor he wore looked old, as if dirt and blood had been cleaned off it many times. She had only seen shadows of this male—seen the other soldiers fall into line and salute when he had walked past: the warden of Ironbalt Prison.

"So," the warden drawled as the prisoners came to a halt in front of him, at the edge of the pit. "These are our troublemakers."

All three of them remained silent. Deya wondered what had possessed the Manielian brute that day, because now, he seemed as docile as a swallow's hatchling. Meek and diffident, he kept his eyes downcast from the warden. Those cold, black eyes flashed in his direction.

"You," he said. "You started it, right?" The male did not answer, and the warden hissed in distaste, before reeling back and kicking the male right in the chest. With a cry, he tumbled to the ground, shock and fear riddling his features.

"Just for that, you're first," the warden snarled.

Deya and Os stood, rooted to the spot, watching in horror as they took the male, unchaining him briefly from their ranks.

Seizing him, the guards hoisted him up, binding his hands to the peak of the post with more iron shackles. The male was shaking, his face white. The mania Deya had seen in his eyes that day was gone, replaced only with blind fear. She felt a twinge of something that might have been pity, until she remembered it was his fault they were all there in the first place.

The warden descended into the pit, pulling a lethal looking whip from his belt. Like Clarita's, it had long metal hooks dangling from the end of its many tails, but unlike hers, this one looked deadly. The tails were longer, like they were meant to be swung with more force and from a farther distance. Deya winced preemptively, knowing how those hooks would smart, hitting her on the already scarred back.

The warden looked to his soldiers first, before nodding. Then he began.

Each crack of the whip had Deya flinching in fear. With each one, her heartbeat quickened, her chest tightening. Faster and faster the whip went, and harder and harder the warden's blows came.

The male was screaming so loudly that Deya understood why the whipping posts were so far from the prison. After maybe the hundredth blow, the male's screams were starting to sound less and less foreign and more like mirror images of her own, echoing off the walls of the Stonehall dungeon. And then, it stopped.

The male sagged against the post. His tunic was in bloody ribbons, and he was no longer conscious. Blood pooled beneath his boots and Deya could feel bile rising up her throat. Next to her, Oswallt was the color of blank parchment.

The warden began to clean the whip, shaking it free of blood. It splattered across the rocky expanse of ground in front of him. Deya's eyes followed the blood splatter, and her vision went black. In that moment, she was back in Stonehall's dungeons. Clarita's cackle filled her ears, as she struggled to breathe, struggled to see anything besides the splatters of her own blood.

"Deya," Os breathed beside her.

Deya turned to face her friend and she saw the same naked fear she felt reflected on his face. "I just wanted to say . . ." He gulped as the warden began to walk, heading towards the edge of the pit, back to them. "That it has been a privilege getting to know you in this festering hell hole."

"Oswallt, stop . . . don't—" Deya's voice trembled, but Os shook his head, his words quickening as the warden came nearer.

"Deya, *listen to me*, this is important," he hissed, his voice desperate now. His eyes pleaded with her as he reached for her hands. "Praiton is not what you thought, not what you have been told. They are doing more than just poisoning the king. I *heard them*. They are looking for something. Something powerful and dark—"

Deya's heartbeat sped up in her chest, her mind racing.

"Os, what—?" But he shook his head, silencing her question as the warden came nearer, his eyes darting up and back frantically.

"If you survive this, promise me," he whispered. "Promise me you will warn them. Praiton cannot get what they seek . . . Promise me that you'll tell them. Promise you will fight this. For the both of us."

Deya stared at her friend, tears now running down her cheeks. But her mind was racing, unable to comprehend this sudden and cryptic warning. She did not know what he was talking about, what horrible thing that Praiton could be seeking—and *who* was she supposed to warn? But, as the warden approached, she feared that she had run out of time to ask.

"Os, what—"

"Now . . ." The warden had climbed up from the pit and stood before them again, ending all chances Deya had to ask Os any more. The dull bronze armor flashed in the sun, now splattered with blood. The warden's eyes then fell on her, and it was like being stared down by a basilisk. Deya felt like shrinking away, looking down, but she didn't. Remembering how he had struck the male who had looked away from him, Deya forced herself to stare back.

To her utmost surprise, the warden chuckled. "They warned me about you," he said, shaking the butt of the whip at her. "Yes, the High Mother told me all about you. You have spirit, girl. Courage." Deya froze at the mention of the High Mother, the remaining blood she had no doubt draining from her cheeks. "But this is why she gave me explicit instructions when it comes to you. For when you step out of line." He reached out a gloved hand and his finger dragged across her cheek. A violent shudder rolled down her spine. She instantly felt sick. "She mentioned how much you *agonized* over watching others suffer."

And then, just as he had struck down the other male, he swung his sword at the chain binding Deya to Oswallt. It cleaved apart and, while they were still staring, dumbstruck at what he had done, the warden sneered. "So how will it feel to watch your friend suffer for you?"

Then he reached out a massive hand and pushed Oswallt into the pit.

Deya's scream mixed with Oswallt's as he tumbled down the rocky ravine. Deya ran after him, no longer bound to anyone, and the warden, grinning cruelly, followed them down.

She reached Os just as the warden did. Seizing Os by the back of the tunic, he began to drag him towards the post on the far right, away from the still unconscious male.

"*Os!*" Deya screamed, but before she could run after him, two guards grabbed her arms.

"Now pay attention, Deyanira," the warden sang, taking Os's hands and chaining them to the top of the post. "He will take your punishment. You should be thankful. It is customary that death be the penalty for using magic within Ironbalt."

"*No!*" Deya shrieked. She fought against her captors, but it was no use. Every fiber of her body was screaming, desperate to get to Os, who looked petrified, quaking where he stood. "Give me the penalty! Leave him out of it! He did nothing!"

"Oh, don't you worry your pretty little head about it," the warden crooned. "I'll give you a beating, too, if you insist. But the Mother wanted to ensure we took *extra* special care of you."

Deya fought and fought, but it was no use. She was weak . . . *so fucking weak*. Even without the iron attached to her hands and ankles, she would have been unable to fight back. The helpless, hopeless, *agonizing* pain overwhelmed her as she screamed her friend's name to the high Heavens.

The warden did not reach for the whip this time. He reached for a club.

The first blow took Deya's breath away, as if he had struck her instead. Then her screams mixed with Oswallt's. Blow after blow until Deya was hoarse. She pounded her feet against the guards' boots, flailed her arms, chains rattling. Prayed and prayed to all five of the goddesses that Os had taught her about, prayed and screamed and cried to the Mother Herself. Begged and pleaded . . .

Someone . . . someone please . . .

Oswallt's face was bloody. The warden struck him in the gut, then the side. He gasped in pain with each hit before the warden swung at his jaw. Deya screamed harder, hearing the crack, knowing he had broken it.

"*Stop it!*" Deya screamed, her throat feeling bloody now. "*Stop it!* He did nothing! *STOP!*"

But Os's bloody head turned to face her. She was so close to him that she had felt each blow to his body in the Earth around her . . . Had been so close to him yet could not save him.

Os's broken jaw moved. "It's alright, Deya," he rasped, the words jumbled and clumsy. Deya stared at him. How he had even managed to speak, how he was still conscious after every blow he had taken, she did not know. But then he spoke again. "*It's okay.*"

The warden wound back, and the final blow made contact with his head. Deya screamed, but it was too late. Oswallt fell, limp, the chains still holding him up, half his head partially caved in, a shadow of the grim smile he had tried to give her still on his broken face.

Deya could not stop screaming . . . could only feel pure, unbridled pain.

Still shrieking and crying, the guards began to drag her closer, pulling her chains free and holding her by the hands and feet, carrying her like a roast pig on a spit towards the middle post.

And, in that brief moment, where she was free of the faerivaine shackles, as she neared the post, she saw Oswallt's bloodied corpse looming closer.

And then the Hell within her broke loose.

A feeling surged from her core—the same place her Healing Magic would begin—but it was different. It was not warm or comforting. Instead, it was unfettered pain. It was agony. It was the purest, rawest form of grief. And it exploded out of her, uncontrolled, unbound.

A ripple of energy, a wave of light and sound mingled with that of her agonized scream. The guards dropped her, and from her spot on the ground, she couldn't see anything as the rock around her rippled. There were other screams—screams that were not hers—and then, silence.

When Deya looked up, there was nothing. Nothing but ashes floating in the breeze.

Her vision began to swim. Large black spots began to appear. She hit the ground, and, with the last bit of her strength, she looked up. She wanted to see Oswallt . . . wanted to see her one and only friend one more time. But there was nothing hanging from the posts anymore. Only a cloud of gray ash and dust. Then she saw nothing at all.

CHAPTER
7

The carriage shook with the force of an explosion. Caelum had to grab at the rough, wooden bench with the tips of his fingers as shockwave after shockwave threatened to blow the prison carriage right over.

"What the—" the Sea Fae beside him cried.

The Manielian female was braced against the wall of the carriage, eyes wide, fearful. The other three remaining prisoners had been dragged out, carried to the whipping posts. Caelum had sat, awaiting his turn to be beaten. It wasn't like it would be the first time. The center whipping post might as well have been engraved with his name by now.

The two that sat in the carriage with him—though no names had ever been exchanged—had also taken several trips to the whipping post with him in the last fifty years that Caelum had been at Ironbalt Prison. He knew they were part of the Pillar Legion, some of the few who often picked useless fights with Praitonian sympathizers. Caelum chose to stay out of it.

The sounds of screaming had not stopped for almost ten minutes now. They could hear the female prisoner they had taken sobbing and crying, shouting her friend's name. The noise had made him cringe, the horrible sound of pain and death all too familiar to him.

But then, the first explosion had torn the world apart. And then there had been more screams—but not the female's.

The cart jolted once, twice, and then went still.

The three strangers in the carriage all looked at each other. There were no more screams. Even the air was all too still.

"Do you think . . ." the Manielian female began, but Caelum did not stop to hear her out. He stood, the chain binding them together clattering loudly as he moved. Using both his feet—which was the only way he could move them without upending the whole group—he kicked the door of the carriage open.

Together, the three poked their heads out.

The carriage had been parked the customary dozen or so yards away from the whipping posts. The warden liked to take groups in threes and string them up on the posts, one by one.

When Caelum looked outside the carriage, however, it was to find nothing. No guards, no warden, no bodies chained to the posts. The only thing that remained in the pit below them was the dark-haired female, lying in a heap in front of where the posts stood . . . and ashes. Nothing but ashes.

Caelum could make out bits of clothes, scraps of bronze metal—he realized, with a pang, that it was all that was left of the warden.

"Holy Mother," the Sea Fae beside him breathed.

Caelum dropped out of the carriage, too shocked to digest the scene before him. Clumps of ash littered the pit, blowing in the wind. And that's when he saw them: swords. He didn't stop to think. He took off, running and shuffling in his chains.

The others let out a cry of surprise. He had forgotten he was still chained to the other two, but he didn't care.

He lunged for the fallen swords, pulling them out of the ash piles. Unsure how the swords had survived when their masters hadn't, Caelum turned to look at his companions.

"Well, are you two just going to stand there?" he asked, before holding the sword above his head and striking the iron shackles.

The other two seemed to catch on, and they both rushed for the remaining weapons on the ground.

He didn't know how long it would take for more guards to come looking for them, but Caelum wasn't going to wait to find out. Prying the shackles open was slow, arduous work, but soon he was able to slip his foot loose. Around him, the other two mimicked his actions, and before long, all three of them were free.

"Round up the weapons," he instructed the other two.

They stared at him curiously but did not argue. They spread out, combing the ash-covered ground, looking for any other surviving weapons. Caelum picked up the remaining shackles and chains and threw them into the carriage.

The cart had been pulled by two Bayard mares, who still stood— far enough away from whatever mysterious blast had given them a rare, golden opportunity.

The other two rushed back, carrying several swords and knives. They dumped them in the carriage and jumped back in as Caelum swung his long, lithe body into the driver's seat.

"What about the girl?" the Sea Fae asked. Caelum paused. His first instinct was to leave the girl behind. He had no idea what that horrible, seismic blast had been, but he had no doubt where it had come from.

"She's a risk," Caelum grunted, seizing the reins of the mares.

"We can't just leave her!" the Manielian female cried. Her red hair was ratted into a nest on the top of her head. It looked like it hadn't seen a wash in many years, much less a comb.

"Do you want to continue to rot in this fetid place?" Caelum snarled, snapping the reins of the horses. "We have a slim chance to get out of here and you want to squander it on a girl who just incinerated half the guard and the warden? Let them come for her, not us."

The female pursed her lips. She seemed the type who liked to argue—an irritating obstacle at this crucial juncture. But she said nothing.

Taking this as a concession, Caelum snapped the reins harder. He would not let the Manielian ruin this. He could taste the freedom, something he had not felt in decades. The horses kicked into a canter, skirting the edge of the pit, beginning to head towards the towering iron gates. Towards freedom.

Caelum was so set on those gates that he almost missed the heated curse behind him. Then, the Manielian female tumbled from the cart and was sprinting towards the pit and the unconscious female within it.

"*Val!*" the Sea Fae cried, running towards the back of the cart, attempting to keep his companion in sight. He whirled around to Caelum. "Stop the cart!"

"I am not stopping this fucking cart!" he yelled. Almost to spite the Sea Fae, he urged the horses faster.

With a curse, the Sea Fae leapt through the window into the driver's seat beside Caelum. Seizing the reins, he jerked upwards, hard. The mares whined, digging their hooves in, and grinding to a stop. Caelum let out a snarl, and almost reached out to hit the male, when a small flash of fire came from the pit.

The Manielian female burst out of the hole, the dark-haired girl slung over her shoulder, a weak stream of sputtering flames propelling her forward. She launched herself, her face screwed up in concentration, her mouth muttering curses as her fire careened out of control, before crashing back into the carriage.

"*Go!*" she cried, but she was smiling, grinning so broadly Caelum almost paused to revel in it. He wondered how long she had gone without using her magic, how good it must have felt.

In his second's hesitation, the Sea Fae beside him grabbed the reins and cracked them forcefully.

The mares took off in a gallop, and for a second—just a second—Caelum found himself rejoicing in the feel of the wind on his face. He had not been free of those faerivaine shackles—hadn't been free of that awful, pounding feeling in his head for fifty years. Was he about to feel that again?

Then the first arrow flew. It struck the ground so near to the mares that they reared in fright.

"Fuck," Caelum breathed.

Five more arrows whistled through the air, landing around the carriage, causing the mares to spook.

"Archers!" the Sea Fae next to him yelled.

"I got it!" the female in the carriage—Val—appeared next to him. Then, she was boosting herself from the driver's bench onto the roof of the carriage.

Two swords in hand, she steadied herself precariously on the roof. Caelum watched her take a deep breath and fire erupted up the base of her swords. But there was something wrong. The fire sputtered, just like it had when she had used it earlier, as if she were having a hard time producing it. It dawned on Caelum then that, although the shackles may have been off, there was still faerivaine in her system . . . in all their systems. Finally, weak surging flames encased the silver blades, flashing as she spun them expertly around her body, her teeth grinding with the effort to keep her magic going.

The next arrow veered towards the carriage. Val twirled her swords, slicing it in half. Caelum was glad the Sea Fae had taken control of the reins because he found himself distracted, in awe in spite of himself. The female's swordsmanship was masterful, a product of obvious training.

The arrows kept falling, and any that were destined to hit the carriage were sliced in half by the female's fire blades.

The iron gates loomed nearer.

"You know," the Sea Fae next to him yelled over the wind, "as swimmingly as this escape mission is going, have you given much thought to how in the Mother's name we are getting through that blasted gate?"

The answer to his question was no, he had not a single fucking clue how they were going to make it through those gates, but he was interrupted by the female from the top of the carriage, yelling, "Guys . . . we may have a bit of a problem!"

Turning, Caelum saw what she meant. More than a dozen horses were thundering on their heels. And each of their riders were holding a bow and arrow.

"We're about to get lit up in a major way!" Val yelled to them.

The Sea Fae breathed out his own curse, but Caelum ignored him. Stepping up onto the driver's bench, he pulled himself onto the roof of the carriage next to the female. She looked over at him in surprise. The carriage was moving at such a fast pace that it took Caelum a second to find his balance. Hands outstretched as though he were walking a tight rope, he made his way across the roof before coming to stand beside the red-haired female.

"I don't know what you plan on doing—" she began, but she was cut off by the sound of over a dozen arrows being loosed at once.

Caelum took a deep, steadying breath. He had stopped drinking the water in Ironbalt years ago, only sipping it when absolutely necessary. Fae could survive without water for long periods of time. He knew his magic was more important, even locked away with shackles. But it had been a long time—too long. He had barely been out of his childhood when he had last been unchained. His magic had been weak then, undeveloped. What was he now?

Slowly, he raised his arms. It was a familiar motion, one he had performed millions of times as a child, often with his brother correcting his form, coaching him through it. An image of his brother lying in a pool of his own blood burst into his mind. As the agonizing pain of the memory rushed over him, a surge of uncontrolled power, so strong it almost knocked him off balance, exploded out of him. And then the arrows froze in midair.

The female next to him let out an audible gasp. The arrows trembled where Caelum's magic held them aloft. They were not frozen, merely hovering, their gravity momentarily suspended. The Celestial Magic churned within him, and he felt like he had taken a breath for the first time in half a century. As the cart raced forward, they cleared from underneath the arrow's trajectory. With a grunt, Caelum released them, and they fell to the ground, burying themselves harmlessly in the rocky dirt.

"*Go!*" Caelum roared at the Sea Fae. He snapped the reins harder and the iron gates barreled into view. Caelum glanced over at the female beside him. "Hold on," he told her.

She stared at him for a split second, like she didn't know what she was seeing, before throwing herself down onto the roof of the carriage and bracing herself. Caelum planted his feet again, drew in a breath, and raised his arms once more. Without warning, the carriage—mares and all—rose into the air. The screams and cries of his companions barely reached him over the roaring wind.

Moving objects with his Gravity Magic in any direction other than a simple up or down was something he had never mastered—even when he had trained as a child. But with the speed of the carriage, the trajectory took them up, up, up until they were over the iron walls. Caelum resisted the urge to yell—the strength it was taking him to lift something this heavy, this big . . . he had never imagined he would've been able to do this much.

The carriage's wheels and the mare's hooves cleared the gate. The headache that had become a constant part of Caelum's existence lessened and then cleared. The relief gave him enough strength to carefully ease the carriage down.

The wheels hit the forest floor, the mares' hooves righting themselves. And then, they were off. And Caelum collapsed onto the roof, completely spent, but a disbelieving laugh exploding out of him for the first time in a long, long time.

He was free.

Deya woke to a loud, hard crash. The surface she was laying on smashed to the ground, almost throwing her into the ceiling. Tumbling and rolling, Deya came to just to find herself in the same prison carriage she had been in earlier. Except, this time, it was moving at a substantial speed. Another large crash as the carriage bucked, caused her face to smack against the wooden bench. Swearing, she spit out a mouthful of blood and slumped onto the floor of the carriage.

She felt numb, spent, like all her magic had come out at once. Briefly, she wondered if everything that happened had been a dream. In flashes, it came back to her: guards holding her back, the warden beating Oswallt, his skull caved in, and then . . . pain. Waves and waves of agony emanating from her. And then . . . ashes.

Deya closed her eyes. She could feel the tears coming again, but her body felt so broken, so empty. There was nothing left in her, no more tears or magic. Had that wave of power come from her? A shiver rolled up her body at the memory of how that power felt coursing through her veins. She had reduced the guards, the warden, the Manielian . . . her friend . . . all to cinders. But how?

She felt diseased, poisoned. A bomb about to go off. What had caused that horrible power? Where had it come from?

And, more importantly, where was she going in this carriage now? And with whom?

A female's face appeared in the window leading to the driver's seat, causing Deya to jolt back in shock. She had a mess of bright red hair—an obvious sign of a Manielian—and skin that looked to be a natural, golden brown. She was bright and beautiful—even beneath all the dirt and soot.

"You're awake!" she cried, and her smile was so big, so pretty that it hurt Deya to her very core. She couldn't explain why it hurt so badly—like a stab to the heart. Maybe because she felt so broken and devastated that the fact someone could still smile so genuinely further broke her inside.

"Wh-what's going on?" Deya stuttered. She recognized this female as one of the other passengers that had been waiting in the carriage earlier. But how . . .

"We escaped," she said. Deya could tell she could barely contain her joy at the news. "Thanks to you."

Deya sat, dumbstruck, as the female pulled herself through the window to sit beside her.

The female's smile faltered, and she bent to peer down at her anxiously. "Are you okay? I . . ." she hesitated before whispering, "I'm sorry about your friend."

Deya nodded, still numb inside. She wasn't able to bring herself to say anything more.

"What happened out there?" the female asked softly. There was something about this girl. Something warm and friendly that Deya hadn't expected to find here at Ironbalt. Though, she supposed, after meeting someone like Oswallt there, anything was possible.

"Honestly, I don't know," Deya whispered. Her voice was hoarse, her throat scratchy. The sounds of her own screams still reverberated in her ears. "I . . . I've never seen that magic before. Much less used it." Deya's voice trembled, and she began to shake violently.

When the female didn't say anything, Deya looked up at her. It was all sinking in, hitting her in a tidal wave of painful memories.

"Why did you save me?" Deya whispered. She could still taste the ashes in the air, could still smell the smoke. She had gotten from the pit to this carriage somehow. Judging by the way the Manielian female was looking at her, Deya knew it had to be because of her.

The female's amber eyes glinted with something that looked almost like concern. "I heard you in the carriage . . . with your friend," she said with a small grimace. "It felt wrong leaving you there after that. I had to go back for you, even if it was just to check if you were still alive."

She hesitated for the briefest moment, before reaching out and taking Deya's hand.

Deya jumped, shocked. Then the wave of sadness fell over her as she remembered the night in her cell, as Os had reached out and taken her hand, just like this. And then that feeling began again—right in her core where her Healing Magic once belonged. With a yelp of fear, Deya threw herself towards the back of the carriage—as far from the female as she could get—curling into herself, her fingers tearing at her hair, pulling at her clothes as though trying to rip the darkness from her chest.

Stop, stop, stop. Deya pleaded for the horrible, agonizing power to stay down. All she could think about was Os and the Manielian, their bodies reduced to ash . . . and in quarters this close, she knew she would kill this poor female. This female who had showed nothing but kindness to her.

She breathed as slowly and deeply as she could. *Breathe in, hold five seconds, then release.* The exercises she had performed while surviving the hostile environment of the infirmary helped to push down on that horrible feeling. And then, a hand was on her shoulder. It was soothing and almost unnaturally warm. Comforting.

"Shh," the female was beside her, holding her steady. "It's alright. You're safe now."

The warm hand on her shoulder seemed to ease the dark beast in her chest. The power began to calm, and then it was still. She opened her eyes. Amber orbs peered back at her.

"Okay?"

Deya nodded and the female smiled. "I'm Val, by the way."

I'm Oswallt, by the way. The memory came back to her, and she felt a slight jolt in her heart. But just like the power, she pushed it down.

"Deya."

Val beamed at her. "Nice to meet you, Deya. And let me just say, that regardless of the circumstances, thank you for getting us out of that rotten hellhole." She held her hand out to her, and Deya took it. Val helped her up and they both sat down on the bench facing each other.

The carriage trundled along underneath them, and Deya cast a curious look towards the window where the driver's seat was.

"Where are we going? Who else is with us?" she asked quietly.

Val followed her gaze towards the driver's seat and shrugged. "My friend, Rayner, and another male. I don't know him very well, only seen him around now and then."

Deya remembered both. The Laenimorian Sea Fae and the white-haired male whom she had thought was from Bridah.

"How did we get through the gates?" Deya asked, noticing how quiet it was in her head. The absence of the constant throbbing was glaringly obvious and an enormous relief.

"The other male used his Celestial Magic," Val said. "Levitated us right over the gates. It was impressive, honestly. My magic is still being throttled by all the faerivaine they made us drink, yet his seemed to be just fine. Nodarians are usually powerful—especially ones that can use Gravity Magic. But, if I were to be honest, I didn't expect him to be a Nodarian. He doesn't look it."

Deya couldn't help but agree. Nodarians notoriously had dark hair and purple eyes. She had assumed the male was from Bridah because of his white hair—usually a signature feature of the Frost Throne region.

"No, he doesn't," she murmured in agreement.

The carriage began to slow down underneath them. Val looked up. "I think we're stopping," she said, surprised.

Then, the door was ripped open, and a sword was thrust into Deya's face. She screamed and leapt back, landing on Val's lap.

The white-haired male stood there; sword pointed right between her eyes.

"What is *wrong* with you?" Val yelled at him, grabbing Deya's arm and pulling her closer, away from the male who was glaring at Deya with a look of undisguised contempt.

"Who are you?" the male demanded. The tip of the sword reached towards Deya's nose and she almost whimpered. She would have if she didn't have Val behind her, snarling in her ear like an angry wolfhound.

"Leave her alone!" Val insisted, but Deya faced the male. His eyes were a dazzling violet with a hint of blue. Besides his Celestial Magic, it was the only other indication that he was a Nodarian.

"My name is Deya," she replied, her voice quivering as she stared down the sharp point of the sword.

The male's expression did not change, but Deya saw his sword arm tremble just slightly, as if he were too tired to hold it up. His violet eyes bore into hers, as sharp and ruthless as the blade still in her face. "What did you do to those soldiers and the warden?" he pressed her, thrusting the sword closer.

Deya's chin lifted, her lip trembled, but still she forced herself to remain calm. She couldn't risk becoming frightened again and incinerating everyone around her.

"I don't know."

His eyes narrowed. "What kind of magic was that?"

"*I don't know,*" she repeated, this time more forcefully. The effort made her weak, her chest still feeling like it was caving in. Her desire to get away from these people was overwhelming. To run, to be alone, to understand what in the Mother's name had happened to her today, what had happened to her *in general* for the last few months.

But instead, she forced herself to stare into the hostile purple irises and tried to appear strong.

The male did not speak. He glowered down at Deya, eyes flashing violently, searching her as if trying to find a sign she was lying.

"Are you satisfied now?" Val demanded. She reached up and valiantly shoved the sword out of Deya's face. "She's petrified, and you're terrorizing her just like those fucking animals at the prison did."

From around the carriage, the Sea Fae appeared, looking winded and bemused. "What's going on?" he asked. He was looking at the white-haired male warily, as if he wasn't sure what he would do next.

The male whirled on the Sea Fae and gestured towards Deya again

78

with his sword. "She is a risk. I told you both not to take her with us. She will either get us caught or kill us all."

Deya flinched and Val stiffened beside her, yet she said nothing this time. Had she sensed it? Deya's power overwhelming her again a minute ago? Had she felt that she was as close to being destroyed as the warden and his guards had?

"Then leave me," Deya snapped. She stood—legs shaking—and stepped out of the carriage, right in front of the male.

He was tall, much taller than she was, and she had to crane her neck to look up into those violet eyes. Tattoos crawled up his neck and arms— thin, straight lines of dark figures she guessed were letters and words written in an ancient language. With a strong jaw and a straight nose, his cheek bones were high and prominent. Dark eyebrows stood out of place around all the white hair, accenting the brightness of his eyes. It made Deya take a quick breath, her face flushing as she took all of him in.

"I will stay here and fend for myself. I won't trouble you."

The male sneered, but Val cut in before he could retort. "Absolutely not," she insisted. "You wouldn't last a second out here. It's wild country. If the bears don't get you the monsters will."

Deya tried not to let her fear show at the mention of *monsters*. She had heard about the monsters that lurked in wild country. Her interactions were greatly limited, what with never leaving Praiton before.

She stared the male down, trying to infuse as much defiance as she could muster behind her own glare. The male did not falter.

"It doesn't matter," she sniffed. "Let my death be on *his* hands then."

One eyebrow rose slightly, almost as if he were taken aback. "I can live with that," he growled.

Val scoffed. "No one will die," she snapped. "Deya will not hurt us. And as for *you*," she said, turning a finger on the male. "*You* leave her alone or *you* can go. What even is your name, anyway?"

"Don't worry about my name."

Val drew herself up to her full height, her red hair virtually crackling like the heat of a flame. *"What is your name?"* she hissed, each syllable elongated.

Deya knew she shouldn't be relieved the male had turned his ire from her to Val, but she couldn't help it.

"What my name is does not matter," he spat.

Val looked murderous, but the Sea Fae cut in. "Look," he said, calmly. "We all know what wild country means. We are being hunted by the monsters of this region, and most likely Ironbalt, as well. We all stand a better chance of surviving and making it out of this if we work together."

The white-haired male said nothing. He stood and glowered. Deya began to wonder if his face was permanently stuck that way.

The Sea Fae seemed to take his silence as a reluctant agreement. He turned to Deya and smiled at her gently. "I'm Rayner," he said. "It's nice to meet you, Deya."

She felt her mouth move into something that—she hoped—resembled a smile but wasn't sure if she knew how to do that anymore. "Nice to meet you, too," she murmured.

They all turned then to look at the white-haired male who appeared as if he were about to detonate with displeasure. After a couple seconds of them all staring expectantly at him, he let out an aggravated huff.

"Caelum."

"There," Val purred, smiling sweetly. "Was that so hard?"

The glare he threw at Val could have levelled a troll, but it only made her laugh. "We should probably find shelter," she said. "It's not smart being out in the open like this." She looked at Caelum, almost as if for his approval.

After a moment, he gave a grudging nod. "We'll keep moving."

"Where do we plan on going?" Deya asked hesitantly. She knew from the maps she had seen that Aunecia was on the far east coast of Krigor. They were surrounded by water on most sides and the only kingdom close by was Bridah. The likelihood of them surviving a journey to Bridah was slim to none.

"I was thinking that we try to make it across the channel," Val said, looking between Rayner and Caelum. "Towards Elbania. The rebel forces are hidden there. They'd take us in."

Deya glanced sharply at her. "Rebel forces?" she echoed. A tremor of fear rippled through her, almost without reason. "Is that why you were all in Ironbalt?"

Val and Rayner both nodded, but Caelum didn't respond. Val noticed this, too.

"If you were not a rebel, how did a Nodarian find himself imprisoned?" Val inquired curiously. "Especially with your caliber of magic."

Caelum grunted. "It's none of your business."

"This again?" Val moaned, rolling her eyes. "If we are to be companions, it is only customary to get to know you. If you were a raging, violent killer locked up for heinous crimes, I think we'd have a right to know."

Rayner nodded in agreement, but Deya stayed quiet, watching. Caelum's violet eyes rolled back in aggravation. "I was in Atlas Keep the day Praiton raided it. I was captured and imprisoned. There is no more you need to know."

Deya couldn't hide her surprise and—in spite of herself—awe. It appeared Val and Rayner were of the same mind. Caelum had been in the Nodarian capital the day High King Castor had died? And he had *lived* . . .

"You were *there*?" Val breathed.

"You were actually *in* Atlas Keep during the Battle for Atlas?" Rayner asked, stunned. "How on earth did you survive—"

"It's not important," Caelum cut in. He sheathed the sword back into the scabbard and Deya realized with a jolt that the swords were from the guards who had restrained her back at the pit. "Elbania is not far once we reach the channel."

But when he turned to go back towards the front of the carriage, he stumbled. Shooting out a hand, he seized the edge of the carriage before he could fall over. Rayner had leapt forward, as if to catch him, purely out of instinct, but Caelum jerked his arm back, out of his reach.

"You overexerted yourself back at the gates," Rayner said. "Using that much magic is a lot for anyone—"

The glare Caelum shot him silenced the Sea Fae instantly. The white-haired Nodarian was weak, his legs shaking. From what Val had told her, he had lifted all of them over the walls with almost little effort. Or so it had seemed. It was evident now that it had cost him much more than it had appeared.

"We have to start making our way eastward. And quickly," he said, before staggering back towards the driver's bench.

Deya's surprise at Caelum's quick acquiescence to going to join the rebels was nothing compared to Val and Rayner's. They stared at him, dumbstruck, as he turned to head back to the driver's side.

"But—" Deya spoke before she even realized what she was doing. The three strangers around her paused and glanced back at her. The Nodarian's stare was colder than the wind gusting from the Bridanian fjords behind them. "I'm not sure if it's a good idea for me to go to the Pillar Legion."

"Why?" Caelum's words slapped her like venom in the face.

Deya flushed, the words sticking in her throat. Her heart began to pump in her ears, but she knew she had to tell them—knew that she could be in a dangerous situation. She was surrounded by rebels. And she was a Praitonian.

"Because," Deya said, her voice wavering, "I'm from Praiton."

The proclamation seemed to hang in the air like a bad smell. Val's brow crinkled, but her confusion was nothing compared to the anger she could feel radiating from Caelum.

"What did you do to have Praiton imprison one of their own?" Val asked.

Deya bristled and shook her head. She couldn't bring herself to tell them, to confess what her crime had been. To tell these rebels she was imprisoned for treason might give them the wrong idea about her. She was not *one of them*, after all.

"They will not hurt you, Deya," Rayner said finally. "Anyone displaced by Praiton is a friend to us."

His words, far from making her feel better, made her heart squeeze painfully in her chest. That was what she was, she realized. Displaced. Exiled and outcast from her home, from the dream her mother had for her. From the kingdom she had given her heart and soul to. But the thought of finding a place, of being somewhere *safe* where she wasn't tormented, hunted, or beaten . . . Perhaps Elbania was not the worst place to be.

Without thinking, Deya found herself nodding. And just like that, she agreed to go to the Pillar Legion. She found that she no longer cared what happened to her next.

CHAPTER
8

They traveled for several more hours with Deya and Val in the back of the carriage, Caelum and Rayner in the driver's seat. Deya did not envy Rayner. Caelum hadn't stopped snapping and snarling from what they could hear from the small window separating them.

Val sniffed. "He sounds like a rabid animal," she mumbled.

Deya tried to smile at her but found her mouth was stiff and uncooperative. The guilt of not being able to respond to the female in the way she wanted frustrated her. Val was funny, confident, and dynamic. She was everything Deya would have loved in a friend back home. But as they trundled along, Deya found she couldn't shake the realization that this female was a soldier of the rebellion. A few weeks ago, being around a rebel soldier would've made her all kinds of uncomfortable. But now, after everything, she felt nothing but numb to it all.

Val was fiddling with one of the knives she had taken off the soldiers, small licks of flame spiraling up and down the blade. "It makes you wonder though," she said quietly. "What his story really is. Nodarians are the biggest part of the rebel forces. For him to have been captured and held since the Battle for Atlas . . ."

Deya couldn't imagine. Oswallt had told her a little of what happened in the Battle for Atlas, how King Castor had perished horrifically.

"They killed most of those they found in the Keep," Val said softly. "If they were full grown, that is. He must have been a child still if they kept him alive."

Deya felt a twinge of pity for Caelum. If he had spent the majority of his life imprisoned, she then understood his demeanor a little better. He bit and snapped like a caged animal because he *had* been a caged animal. She had only spent a few months at Ironbalt. It wasn't even a fraction of her sentence. To think that Caelum had spent *fifty* years there . . .

"He must be a half-breed," Val mused. "With that hair, he can't be *pure* Nodarian."

Deya had seen many half-breeds in her day. Living in Praiton, where fae from all five kingdoms intermingled, she had seen a fair amount of crossed genetics. While the offspring was likely to get a mix of physical features, the magic itself was always ever one or the other. No one was able to inherit two different types of magic.

"Were you there for the Battle for Atlas?" Deya asked.

Val shook her head. "I wasn't in the Legion at the time. But it was a surprise attack, so no supporting rebel forces were able to reach them in time. But I remember it vividly. Castor's death was the reason I left Maniel. It was the reason most of my unit left Maniel." Val's face darkened.

"Your unit?" Deya asked.

Val cracked a small smile. "I captained a small elite unit of Manielian females. We were called the Fireflies." Even through the smile on her pretty face, Deya could see the glimmer of worry there, of fear. She found herself wondering what may have become of the Fireflies while their captain had been imprisoned.

"So just how big is the Pillar Legion?" Deya asked. "Praiton makes it sound like it was nothing more than a scrappy band of resisters."

Val let out a derisive snort. "I'm not surprised that's their take on things. The Pillar Legion is much more than that. There are hundreds of us, all across Krigor. The headquarters are in Elbania, but there are small outposts all across the realm." Her lithe fingers spun the tiny dagger around and around, the flames licking the steel making it resemble a fiery Catherine Wheel.

"I didn't realize there were so many," Deya said in a small voice. Hundreds of people hurt by Praiton's rule. Hundreds of people wanting blood.

Val nodded grimly. "Stopping Praiton is our main goal, but even with the hundreds of soldiers we have, we're sorely outnumbered compared to their military. So, we limit our confrontations as best we can. Between our network of spies and allies, we try to stop supplies from moving to Praiton, stop invasions when we catch wind of it, anything we can do to slow down Praiton's overtaking."

Deya's body rolled with an inadvertent shiver. She had seen firsthand how big Praiton's military was, and even though the Pillar Legion was bigger than she had anticipated, hearing it put that way reminded her of someone attempting to use a small bucket of water to put out a forest fire.

"I am surprised to meet a Manielian rebel," Deya admitted, fiddling with the frayed end of her sleeve. It still had traces of soot on it that made her stomach roil. "Most sided with Praiton, quite happily from what I heard."

"You heard right," Val said bitterly. "I came from a noble family in Maniel who was more than happy to plunder and kill on Praiton's behalf. I was the only one who apparently did not agree with the ruthless overthrowing of other kingdoms. Naturally, my family did not take kindly to it." Val's eyes burned like tiny flames. There was a sadness to her voice that made Deya's heart hurt for her. Through her sympathy for Val, her own bitter guilt burned dully in her gut.

"So, I was chucked out. Fled Maniel and joined the rebels. My unit was a small group from Maniel who disagreed with the regime. There aren't a lot of us, but we do exist."

"What about Rayner?" Deya asked. "Was he part of your unit?"

"No." Val's finger caressed the tip of the knife in her hand absentmindedly. "Rayner was part of an elite unit of skilled archers, but we had fought together before. The Laenimorians have lost much, too. There are many Sea Fae in our ranks."

Deya looked away and fell silent. Val's amber eyes watched her closely. Wearily.

"May I ask you something, Deya?"

Deya looked up. "Yes?"

"What did Praiton tell you the war was about?" she asked. "How did they justify it to you?"

Deya's mouth parted, the question taking her aback. "I . . . They had always told us that it was to preserve the worship of the Mother Goddess and our way of life," Deya admitted, the shame making it difficult to meet Val's gaze. "They told us that the other kingdoms did not worship like we did. That it was a threat to the balance of the realm."

Val nodded, seeming to digest this, but her eyes mimicked the flames she toyed with on her blade. For the first time, Deya saw anger in her.

She knew she wasn't technically responsible for Praiton, but all this time she had served in the castle. She had healed their wounded soldiers, provided them herbs and potions for their battles . . . aided and abetted their overthrowing of kingdoms and the killing of innocent people. And she had believed it always to be for the good of the realm.

"I'm sorry," Deya said softly.

Val looked up at her. "Why are you sorry?"

"I'm from Praiton," she whispered, shame weighing her down. "But I was ignorant. Blind. I didn't know—didn't realize the extent of the horrors my kingdom had wrought on you all."

Val studied her, not saying anything, but her expression softened. Her golden fingers, worn with callouses and faint scars, still traced the edge of the blade in delicate circles.

"You are not your kingdom, Deya," she said. "We have a few Praitonians who have joined us, as well. While some of them may have direct links—family and friends in other ruined kingdoms—they joined our fight. It's not too late."

"Fight?" Deya gave a defeated laugh. "I haven't fought a day in my life. I couldn't do anything. I couldn't defend myself . . . I couldn't save my friend . . ." She fell silent. Tears welled behind her eyes and her heart ached and ached.

The distraction of the last few hours—of escaping Ironbalt with this unusual group—had kept the pain of losing Os at bay. But, in the quiet hours in the back of the carriage with Val, it was becoming hard to suppress. Sadness slammed against the wall she had built around it, beating angry fists on the door, demanding to be let in.

"I was a healer," Deya whispered. "I saved lives. It was the only power I ever had. How did my healing power become so . . ."

Her hands started shaking. Val watched her, her amber eyes filled with sympathy. She reached out and took Deya's hand again and let her cry, let her grieve. She was angry with herself for crying. Angry that Val was there, holding her hand, comforting her when she did not deserve it. She had let Os do the same, and now the consequences of her own weakness rested heavily on her shoulders. But most of all, she was angry at herself for serving a kingdom that had done nothing but lie to her.

Os's last words floated into her mind like a cold wind.

Praiton is not what you thought, not what you have been told.

They made camp for the night in a small cave that Rayner found. They soon realized that the horses were a bit of a risk. Monsters were prone to eat anything they could find, and losing the mares would be detrimental. So, they tied their bridles to the inside of the cave, leaving no room for the rest of them. Instead, they established shifts to keep watch.

Rayner handed Deya a sword, which she took apprehensively. She had never held one before, wouldn't even know what to do with it if the moment arose. She felt Caelum's eyes on her as she lifted the sword as if it were a foreign object. The silver blade winked at her in the night, an intimidating glint which made her shove the sword behind her, out of view. Caelum snorted and Deya glared at him.

"I'll take the first watch," Caelum declared.

Shocker, Deya thought spitefully.

Rayner and Deya gathered kindling and wood for the fire, which Val lit with a flick of her fingers. Caelum proceeded to sit and brood a little way from the fire, facing the clearing, sword in hand.

Deya watched him through the veil of the flame. The light cast shadows across his sharp features, turning his purple eyes a dark violet. It was obvious he wasn't happy about traveling in a group but was too smart to not recognize it was essential for survival.

"Don't mind him," Rayner said in her ear. He sat down beside her next to the fire, an armful of thick branches beside him. Like the rest of them, he was thin and tired. His blue-tinted skin appeared sunken, his cheekbones pronounced, and Deya wondered if he was dehydrated.

The kingdom of Laenimore was home to the Sea Throne. She knew this kingdom was built upon a settlement of nymphs—purely water-breathing creatures with high intelligence but minimal magic. Over time, the fae and the nymphs intermingled, giving birth to most of the population of Laenimore.

Sea Fae had a much more amphibious nature than their ancestors, but still preferred to be close to the water. To this day, pure fae from the royal line were almost extinct in Laenimore, and many still held disdain and prejudice towards the nymphs who resided below their shores.

"His bark is worse than his bite," Rayner said.

Deya gave him a small, wan smile. "I'm sorry we stuck you with him."

He laughed. "It wasn't all bad, I promise."

They sat before the fire, resting in the peaceful crackling of the flames. It had been so long since they had enjoyed pure silence and peace—undeterred by faerivaine and iron. For a while, they just sat and appreciated it; Val laying on her back, eyes closed, Caelum, leaning against his lonely tree. Deya was admiring the flames, and Rayner busied himself by splitting thick pieces of wood in half with a heavy rock and a small knife. It was only then that Deya realized what Rayner was doing with the collection of branches: he was making a bow.

"I feel naked without one," he said when he noticed her watching. "You may think it odd . . . a Sea Fae as an archer."

"No," Deya said, shaking her head. Watching Rayner build a bow purely from bits of tree and plant was fascinating, hypnotizing in a way. Praiton always had the best weapon makers in all the realm at their disposal. She had never even thought someone could make such a rudimentary weapon from nothing.

"Shooting arrows underwater is definitely uncommon," he said, smiling wryly as he carved chunks out of the tip. "But in Laenimore, I was the only master archer in the region. I taught everyone, from the late King Tritan to his daughter, the current Queen Arnora. When Laenimore fell, I became part of an elite set of archers in the rebellion." He scraped the flat rock along the wooden back of the bow, carving it down to a smooth finish. "I was never much for fighting with swords."

After a while, the fire began to dim and Deya found herself volunteering to go collect more firewood.

"Be sure to hurry," Val advised. "Go while there's still daylight."

Deya nodded, the sword clunking against her hip, feeling like someone had attached a foreign limb to her. Yet, all the while, she felt Caelum's eyes on her back as she headed into the forest, watching her.

Weaving between the trees, Deya soaked in the sounds of the forest around her. Bugs chirruped, frogs croaked . . . and all the while, she braced for any ominous rustling that may indicate monsters were lurking. As she walked, her thoughts began to wander dangerously to things she had tried not to think about. Os's face swam in her mind. The frantic look in his eyes as he had begged her, warned her: *Praiton is not what you thought, not what you have been told . . . They are looking for something. Something powerful and dark . . . Promise me you will warn them.*

A lump rose in Deya's throat, remembering the last words her friend had ever said to her. It had not been a normal goodbye. It had been more than that. It had been *a warning*. Now, Deya was filled with more than just grief. Confusion overwhelmed her, questions circling her mind that she had never gotten to ask her friend . . . That she never would.

What was Praiton seeking? Something dark and powerful? And *who* was she supposed to warn? Who was supposed to stop Praiton from finding what they were looking for?

The obvious answer was the Pillar Legion, but Deya dismissed this. Os had not been a rebel. He had been a *bard*. A kind, funny bard who had been imprisoned for singing an offensive song. He wouldn't have lied to her . . . would he?

Deya staggered through the forest, her mind in overdrive. Finding a good brush filled with kindling, she knelt on the ground and began to gather brambles in her arms. The quiet of the forest soothed her consternation. With her knees against the Earth, and her hands within the brambles, she found herself breathing in deeply, her mind quieting.

Her Healing Magic came from the Earth. Because of Os, she now knew that the Harvest Goddess she had liked as a child, Arista, was the source of her power. She had noticed, even when she was in Praiton, that her magic always felt strongest when she was in nature.

She looked around the clearing. There was no one and nothing to harm. If she just . . .

Noticing a wilted wildflower in front of her, Deya held out her hand and closed her eyes. She attempted to find that source of warmth and comfort that had once been within her, tried to draw it up through her core. But she felt nothing. It was as if she still bore the faerivaine shackles, except this time, she couldn't even find it within herself to retrieve it.

Brow furrowed, she breathed in deeply again and pushed harder. She was searching through her veins, clenching her muscles, trying to find it . . . but it was like looking for a piece of straw in a dark room.

Anger surged up inside of her. Anger and grief. With a curse, Deya slammed her fist on the ground. Gods, every feeling she had today was laced—no, *soaked*—in grief and confusion. Losing Os, being cast out and thrust into the wilderness with a group of rebel strangers, the thought of her friend turning to ash replaying in her mind over, and over again. And with that thought, a familiar rush of pain and fury came surging like a violent wave from her core . . . from the same place she had been attempting to extract her Healing Magic only seconds before.

Deya gasped and attempted to shove it back down, but it was too late. Like a hole in a dam, it crashed out of her. A shockwave rippled from her, knocking her flat on the grass, which was now black and brittle, the wildflower in front of her reduced to nothing more than cinders.

Deya's body shook as her breaths came in quick, shallow gasps. Tears of absolute, naked panic were flowing down her cheeks as she stared at the ashes surrounding her. She took in the crater which had expanded several feet around her at all sides and a sob burst out of her.

She had known, deep down. Had dreaded this confirmation. Her Healing Magic was gone and, in its place . . .

Shaking violently, the desire to curl into herself, to sob uncontrollably was taking over. Her body crumbled into a ball, the destructive magic inside her churning, as though it was readying to explode again.

A hand seized her shoulder. Deya yelped and leapt back.

"*Easy,*" a familiar voice hissed in her ear. Hands grabbed her more tightly, holding her in place. Wildly, Deya panted and flailed. Her body instinctually reacted. Panic. Fear.

But Caelum held fast. "Fight it, girl. *Fight it.*"

Fight it? Could she fight this? This pain was so visceral, so unending. She didn't think she could ever escape this feeling. Squeezing her eyes shut, she shook her head fiercely, but Caelum's fingers held tight to her shoulders.

"Picture it like a strong wave." His voice was in her ear, grounding her, an anchor in the black current. "Like a wave you are trying to shut a door on. Push back on it."

She could see that horrible, disastrous power surging forward like a tsunami of death and pain. Letting out a weak cry, Deya felt herself push back, picturing the door he had described slamming shut. She pushed and pushed until, with a gasp, she opened her eyes.

Violet eyes stared back at her. With a start, she realized she had fallen backwards during her fight with her power and—most surprising of all—Caelum had caught her. She was cradled in his arms, still shaking uncontrollably.

"I . . ." she stuttered, staring up at him.

In an uncharacteristically gentle way, Caelum lowered her to the ground, still helping to keep her upright. His gaze roved the crater she had created. Every blade of grass had been drained of its essence. Some blades had disintegrated already, turning into ash in the air. Caelum stood, assessing the radius of the blast while Deya sat and watched him warily.

"You cannot control it," he said. It was a statement. Like he was realizing the gravity of the situation.

"No." Deya's voice trembled, and so did the rest of her—still shell-shocked and shaken.

Caelum shot her a piercing look. "When did this magic start?"

"At the whipping post," Deya whispered, looking down. Her fingers reached for a blade of incinerated grass, and it crumbled beneath her fingertips. "Right after they killed Oswallt."

Caelum didn't reply. He approached the wildflower that Deya had focused her power on. It was black and burned.

"What were you trying to do to the flower?"

"I was trying to heal it," she admitted quietly. "It was dying. I was trying to bring it back to life."

He looked over at her, surprised. "You were a healer?"

Deya nodded.

His brow furrowed and he began to walk the length of the blast radius, occasionally bending to pick at a piece of grass or plant. All turned to ashes beneath his touch. They floated into the wind, caressing

Deya's face, making her cough.

"I've never seen this before," Caelum muttered. It sounded as though he were speaking more to himself than to her. "If I had to wager a guess," he muttered. "I'd say your magic has reversed itself."

Deya blinked. "*Reversed* itself?"

Nodding, still deep in thought, he said, "It appears that the pain and trauma you suffered at the whipping post mutated it. Turned it."

She listened to this theory, contemplated it. Deya had also never heard of something like this. But the thought . . . the thought that her Healing Magic was gone . . . Replaced by *this*.

Deya stared down at her hands. She half expected them to look like the flower—blackened and dead looking.

"I've lost my Healing Magic?" she breathed.

Caelum looked down at her. There was a glimmer of something in his eyes that, for once, was not contempt or anger. Was it pity?

"I don't know," he said. "But we will both die out here if we linger. We need to get back."

She nodded and picked up the fallen brambles and branches she had gathered before following Caelum back to camp.

Deya tossed and turned that night, too scared to fall asleep. What if she had a nightmare about the day's events? She couldn't risk losing control of her emotions and potentially reducing her companions to ash in her sleep.

Eventually, she gave up and offered to relieve Val of her watch early so she could rest. Deya didn't know what she would do if she came face to face with a monster. It was ironic, she thought, that she now possessed this immense, destructive power, yet she couldn't use it without the risk of killing everyone around her.

She is a risk, Caelum had spat at them.

I am a risk, Deya thought bitterly. *He should have left me when I asked him to. I could kill all of them and not even realize it.*

She thought of Oswallt. Of his body. How there was nothing of him left for her to even attempt to bury. In a way she was relieved since there was no way she would've been able to get Os's body out of there. The thought of having to leave him behind in that place filled her with an inexplicable sadness. No, this was better.

She closed her eyes, clutching her sword against the tree she was leaning on. *I'm sorry, Os. I'm sorry I couldn't save you.* Tears came before she knew it, but she still kept a firm hold on that door Caelum had given her. Pushed down on the waves. But the sadness in her was too strong, too heavy. And as she cried, her fingers dug into the bark of the tree and left small, tiny black holes in their wake. Deya ripped her hands from the trunk with a terrified gasp and closed her eyes.

Push, push, push.

She breathed in deeply, focused. It was as she was doing this that she felt something cold and heavy slide around her neck.

The magic instinctively burst loose from where she had held it down . . . and slammed into an invisible wall within her. Shaking, she looked down and saw a thin iron chain that appeared to have been taken from the Ironbalt shackles now resting around her neck. Looking up, startled, it was to find Caelum staring down at her.

"This should keep it controlled," he said stiffly. "So you can rest."

Deya reached up and grabbed at the chain necklace. The links were small and light—less iron than what they had loaded on them in the prison. It only caused a slight tingle in Deya's temples. Nothing she couldn't handle. It was a small price to pay for keeping this horrible power locked inside.

"Thank you," she stuttered, unable to contain her surprise. Caelum nodded brusquely and headed back towards camp. Deya stared curiously after him, wondering if perhaps Rayner was right, and Caelum's bark was worse than his bite.

CHAPTER
9

They packed up the camp and moved on early the next morning. The minute the sun appeared above the trees, Caelum was back to snapping out orders and getting the mares ready.

Val yawned; her red hair even wilder than it was yesterday. Leaves and twigs stuck to its strands, making her look like some kind of woodland nymph.

"Gods, does he ever give it a rest?" she groaned as Caelum barked at Rayner to stamp out the fire and get moving.

Deya fingered the faerivaine necklace and said nothing.

Caelum claimed that they were only a few days' travel from the port that could take them to Elbania. Latchside Landing was a small, forgotten trade port Caelum reckoned would be their best bet to get to sea.

"We need to keep going," he said from the driver's side an hour into their morning trek. Gone was any softness he might have let her see the night before. He was, once again, straight-backed and no nonsense.

Val gave a groan from the backseat next to Deya. "All I want is a hot meal and a *bath*," she moaned. "Do you realize how long I've been in that place?"

Rayner let out a tiny, almost inaudible sigh of longing. "It *would* be nice to find some water."

Caelum's jaw tightened. "You do realize we are fugitives, don't you? We can't exactly just stroll into a bath house and order a hot meal."

Val moaned again, and even Deya couldn't help the small noise of yearning that escaped her. It had been weeks since she had been clean—the last time being when they had hosed her down when she had arrived in Ironbalt. And that hadn't exactly been a pleasant experience.

"Come *on*, Caelum," Val cajoled, leaning through the window to poke at him lightly. "It should take them at least a *few days* to alert the surrounding areas that we've escaped, right? What harm would there be to stop for a while? We're all still covered in soot from the mines. Don't you want to wash all that pretty white hair of yours?"

Caelum's teeth ground together. It looked like he was trying his hardest not to hit something. "How about," he snarled, "when we get to Latchside Landing, I'll pitch you all into the harbor and leave you there to drown?"

Val growled in protest, but Rayner shrugged good-naturedly. "I can't drown, so I wish you the best of luck with that."

The bickering that persisted washed over Deya like white noise as she processed the three people around her. It had been too long since she had felt this free, and yet a niggling pit of anxiety was still wound tightly in her gut. While she might have been free from Ironbalt, she was still surrounded by rebels, people who hated Praiton. Their reassurances aside, she couldn't quite trust that their hate wouldn't turn on her at some point.

But as Val reached through the window to swat at Caelum, who hissed like an angry cat, causing Val to shoot a devious look back at her, Deya found herself hoping that Val and Rayner didn't actually hate her. Caelum on the other hand . . .

They all left Caelum alone and allowed him his quiet brooding time while they continued through wild country—although Val didn't stop moaning about wanting a bath. As the sun began to wane, Caelum veered off course from the rough path and plunged in between the trees.

"Where—" Deya began curiously, leaning through the window to peer out over their shoulders.

Caelum didn't say anything, but Rayner sat next to him, a pleased smile on his face. The mares weaved into and out of trees, branches and brambles scraping along the wooden walls of the carriage. The path began to get bumpier than usual, and Val was beginning to complain about motion sickness, when the trees cleared, and then they heard running water.

"No way . . ." Val breathed.

In the center of the clearing was a small creek. Its clear water churned across rocks and boulders, the burbling and surging of it filling the wooded area. Val whooped and Rayner began to laugh, barely able to contain his joy. Both of them ran from the wagon and sprinted towards the creek, not even bothering to lose their clothes first before splashing in.

Deya clambered out of the wagon as the sounds of Val and Rayner's splashing and laughter filled the air. A shadow moved beside her, and her body instantly responded to the presence.

"That was very nice of you," she said quietly to Caelum's sulking figure.

He grunted in aggravation. "The Sea Fae made me."

"*Deya!*" Val shouted from the creek. She had discarded her clothes by now and was bobbing unashamedly amongst the rocks. "Get in here! It feels heavenly!"

Deya waved at Val, feeling her face twitch. She wanted to smile, yet the muscles couldn't seem to move anymore, as if they were permanently frozen. She glanced at Caelum. "Coming?" she asked.

He said nothing, his face not betraying any sort of emotion—though she could have sworn she saw a tic working in his jaw.

"Leave the grump behind!" Val cried. She was splashing about like a baby nymph, the grin on her face spread from ear to ear.

Giving Caelum one last glance, Deya hesitantly made her way to the creek and splashed in next to the Manielian female. Cool water rushed over her, an instant shock to the system, but she sighed with relief as it eased her aching muscles, wading further in where Val stood, waving her over. Rayner had submerged himself and was sitting at the bottom of the creek, his eyes closed as if he were settling in for a good nap.

Once Deya waded in up to her neck, she shrank down behind a boulder, for modesty's sake. Pulling off her clothes, she laid them out in the sun to dry. Val, however, was floating along freely and without shame.

"Gods, this feels *amazing*," she sighed, giggling. "I don't think we'll ever be able to get Rayner out of here." Deya couldn't help but agree. The Sea Fae looked perfectly at peace beneath the surface.

Out of the corner of her eye, she saw Caelum rise off the rock on which he had been pouting. When he pulled off his shirt, Deya was surprised to see the number of markings across his skin. Aside from the dark tattoos—words and scripture in an ancient Nodarian language, no doubt—there were also scars. Lots and lots of scars. His arms, chest, and back were covered in a mixture of deep, white lines and raised, jagged pink skin—a startling contrast from the otherwise dark marks across his body. Deya found her stare immobilized, watching each scar and line ripple as he grudgingly waded into the water.

"Well, look who decided to join us," Val jeered. She had ripped a piece of lavender off of the riverside and was rubbing it across her body.

Caelum glared at her, but then quickly looked away when he realized that the burbling water did nothing to conceal her.

"Cover yourself," he snapped, before turning his back on them and dunking himself beneath the water.

Val rolled her eyes and floated towards Deya. "He's really no fun at all, is he," she said.

Deya leaned back against the rock she was hiding behind and closed her eyes, for once, content. "Maybe he's afraid to look in case you take offense and roast him alive," Deya said, stifling a yawn.

Unfortunately, they weren't able to spend all night in the creek. It was still wild country, after all. So, when the males had gotten out and dressed, they politely turned their backs so Deya and Val could step out and put back on the prison rags they had been able to clean in the creek.

When they set up camp for the night, Deya no longer felt uncomfortable and grimy. She now smelled of something delightfully like sea, salt, and lavender—thanks to the heaps of the stuff she and Val had plucked from the banks of the creek and rubbed all over themselves.

"Wish we had some pepper flakes for this," Val grumbled, rotating the wild rabbit Rayner had caught over their small fire. "Wild rabbit tastes better when it's not so bland."

Rayner chuckled and Deya smiled in spite of herself. All day, she had felt abnormally . . . normal. Val had a way of prodding her out of her moods, especially when her brain threatened to deviate back to thoughts of Oswallt and Ironbalt. The female's infectious personality often had Deya forgetting about her sadness and apprehension that now constantly lay dormant in the pit of her stomach. It sat there, always, like a thorn buried in her side, awaiting a slight movement in order to pierce her with sudden pain.

"Salt is an easy compound," Rayner said. "Or an herb perhaps?"

Deya smiled, thinking about the kitchens in Stonehall, how the smell of roasting meats and fresh bread used to greet her on the walk to the infirmary every morning. "Back home, the kitchens used to make the best wild rabbit," Deya said wistfully. "The soldiers brought a spice back from their missions overseas . . . illiper, I think it was called. I've never tasted anything quite like it—"

A loud snap caused Deya to stop mid-sentence. All three of their heads whipped around to look at the angry figure standing above them. Caelum had snapped a branch in half, his eyes glowing with a barely concealed rage as he looked at her. They hadn't even heard him approach. But the murderous hatred in his eyes made all the air leave Deya's lungs.

"Because illiper is a Nodarian spice," he growled. His voice was so quiet, a hiss with the same lethal edge as a blade sliding from its sheath.

Deya's mouth opened, then snapped shut, the realization of what her words meant hitting her. But before she could even open her mouth to apologize for her thoughtlessness, Caelum threw the branch into the fire—sending sparks flying—and whirled around, storming away, into the trees.

The silence he left in his wake was deafening.

They ate their dinner quietly after that, before Deya, still feeling guilty and sick over her own indiscretion, closed her eyes, and attempted to get some sleep.

Thunk, thunk, thunk.

A slat of light appeared at the foot of the stairs leading towards Deya's cell. She ached all over, blood pouring endlessly from the still open wounds on her back. That horrible sound loomed ever nearer, and she tried as hard as she could to drag her bleeding body towards the back of her cell. The toadlike, pallid face of Clarita Killoran loomed out of the darkness and that smile was as sinister as it always was.

"Hello, Deya," she purred. The cat tail whip was clutched in her hands, the tails like snakes, hissing at her.

Deya tried to respond, to tell the horrible female to leave her alone, but it was as if her voice had been stolen from her. As if she couldn't breathe. Clarita only smiled wider in her silence.

"You were always an easy one. So obedient," she said. "But you must tell me. Where is the weapon? Where have you hidden it?"

She pulled her arm back, raising the whip. Deya curled into a ball, braced for the whips and iron hooks to lick her skin again and again.

"I don't know!" The words still would not come, and Deya started to sob as she screamed the words inside. "I don't know what it is you're looking for—"

But when Clarita brought down the whip with a crack and a flick, it didn't hit her. Instead, a cry of pain sounded out beside her. Frantic, Deya turned to see Oswallt, face down on the stone floor, his expression screwed up in pain.

"It's okay," Os hissed as the whip cracked down on him again.

Deya fought against her chains. This can't happen, not again. She'd stop it this time, she'd save him. But the chains seemed to shrink into the floor, pulling her wrists closer to the ground until all she could do was shriek and kick while Oswallt was lashed again and again with Clarita's whip.

"It's okay," Oswallt rasped. His jaw hung awkwardly, and he was covered in so much blood she could barely make out his face. She felt for her own wounds on her back but was shocked and horrified to find that they had clotted and scarred—no longer dripping blood. Instead, all the blood was flowing out of her friend on the floor next to her.

"Just warn them, Deya," he breathed again. "Warn them . . . it's okay."

Clarita's whip cracked again . . . right for his head.

"NO!"

Deya's shout rent the air, making the mares beside her bray and snort with alarm. Bolting upright, her breath coming in short desperate gasps, she looked around. Val and Rayner both still lay on their bed of leaves, neither of them stirring. She supposed that after Gods knew how long in Ironbalt they both had learned to sleep through anything.

A sharp *crack* sounded next to her, and she flinched violently. But it was only the fire, crackling away beside her, its embers illuminating the small crevice of the cave they had found hidden by the creek.

Deya panted, her hands running down her body, as if they were searching for blood and open wounds from Clarita's whip. She could still hear Oswallt's screams ringing in her ears, and when she touched her face, she found her cheeks wet with silent tears.

That's when she noticed a pair of violet eyes watching her from several feet away. Caelum had chosen a large boulder as his perch tonight. He still held the brass sword he had taken from the soldiers at the pit. It lay across his lap, glinting as menacingly as his eyes in the firelight. Their gazes locked, and for a second, they stared at each other.

Wordlessly, Deya stood, and crept away from the sleeping forms of her companions and made her way towards the rock the white-haired Nodarian brooded on.

"I'm sorry," she whispered, coming to stand beside him. She wasn't sure what she was apologizing for. Whether it was her thoughtlessly talking about Praiton and the resources they had stolen from his home, or for the nightmare which had disturbed the peace, she didn't know. He looked away from her, his eyes now sweeping the forest and the creek beyond, searching for signs of movement.

"Why are you apologizing," he replied stiffly. "Your nightmares mean little to me."

Deya's mouth sagged open. His cold indifference was one thing, but the hatred and fury burning in his violet eyes welded her in place.

"I wasn't asking for my nightmares to matter to you," she muttered sheepishly.

Caelum gave a disgusted snort. "I can assure you I will never care about a Praitonian female who has served that bastard Lord Decius for all of her pathetic life," he spat.

"I never served Lord Decius," Deya stuttered. She hated how her voice trembled, how she struggled to find the words to defend herself—just like in her dream. "I served in the infirmary. I cared for any who came my way. I did not discriminate—"

"That's rich," Caelum sneered. "A Praitonian not discriminating. Your kind never does, do they? They only discriminate when you choose to not join them in their mission to destroy every last kingdom to ever exist outside its stone walls."

She flinched, his words stinging her like a slap to the face. While Caelum had never been warm to her, he had been at least decent, if not kind. She was so grateful for the faerivaine necklace but hadn't figured out how to express it to him. Especially when he still looked at her with barely concealed disgust. But it was as if her one mistake had reminded him exactly who she was, and more importantly, where she came from.

"I had no idea the extent of the war," Deya snapped, surprising even herself with how viciously she proclaimed this. "Praiton was never forthcoming about their misdoings."

"Please." Caelum sneered down at her, contempt curling his lip. "You probably believed every lie they ever told you. I heard the Praitonians in the prison," he said. "You all believed that your precious kingdom was destroying our homes *for the greater good.*"

He advanced towards her, and her heart skipped a beat. Stumbling, Deya tried to back away from him, but then he was in her face. The smell of him—like a cool forest after a fresh snow—filled her nose as the violet eyes simmered in the dark.

"Do you know what they do to fae who look like me in Ironbalt?"

"I-I—" Deya stuttered, but Caelum was already reaching to the hem of his tunic and ripping it upwards. The black of the tattoos were marred and mangled by the scars Deya had seen at the creek. But now she was face to face with them, so close she could reach out and touch them if she wanted.

The devastation was obvious. Raised lines, vicious and angry, twisted around Caelum's body like rivers on a map. They littered his chest and his arms, snaking up his shoulders towards his back, breaking up the black letters, a mix of pink welts and thin white lines.

"When you look like me, Praitonians think you're hiding secrets on how to get into Bridah," Caelum said through gritted teeth. "They didn't believe me when I told them I'd never stepped foot in the Frost Kingdom. They did, however, enjoy carving pieces out of me in the meantime, trying to get me to talk. Chunk by chunk, and yet it never satisfied them."

Deya's stomach gave an uncomfortable squeeze. Her cheeks burned as she stared at the male's hard chest, the tattoos and scars beginning to blur in her vision as she took them all in.

"Say what you want, but I know better," he snarled, yanking his shirt back down, hatred burning in those purple eyes. "I saw you hesitate about joining the rebels. You know as well as I that you are not on our side in this war."

His words burned through her, a searing white flame of guilt and anger scorching her insides. Her face flushed with rage and shame.

"That isn't true—"

"We both know it is." He recoiled from her, as if disgusted by her presence. "You do not know what it is like to have *everything* taken from you by that fucking empire!" His voice cracked just slightly at the words, and Deya saw a glimmer of pain so virulent that it stopped her in her tracks. "So, *no*," Caelum panted. "You do not matter to me because you will *never understand.*"

Deya was shaking with rage, indignation flared through her body. Her hands curled into fists, his words echoing in her head.

You don't know what it is like to have everything taken from you . . .

But she was too furious to wonder what Caelum could have lost to Praiton. Before she could stop herself, she was advancing back into his space, her face and chest hot with anger.

"Actually, I do," she hissed, fury surging in every syllable. "Did you never stop to think to yourself why I was imprisoned? Why I was targeted specifically by the warden? I was not a rebel nor a criminal. Did you ever bother to even think in that arrogant, cold head of yours why a Praitonian healer was treated this way?"

Panting, eyes shimmering with involuntary tears, which angered her even more, Deya swayed with the effort to remain standing in front of him. Because it wasn't Caelum she was shouting at, it was the universe, the world. She had done everything right, all her life. Had worked hard in the infirmary, saved countless lives, smiled at the dead and the dying, served cruel, cowardly, heartless people.

She had served and sacrificed, and she was rewarded with *this*. This part of her—the broken, angry, aching pain in her chest—was now a permanent scar. Not like the ones that now mangled her once perfect back, but an invisible, perpetual wound that would plague her for the rest of her immortal life.

Oswallt's face as he died for her. Clarita Killoran haunting her from her seat of undeserved power. The betrayal of finding out the kingdom she loved had been destroying the realm. And she had helped them do it.

It was all too much, all too unfair.

"I am not denying you your pain," Deya continued in a furious whisper. "And I am sorry for what you all have likely suffered at the hands of Praiton, but I have suffered too. And I continue to suffer now."

And with that, she stormed off, too angry to look at him, staring at her with that deadened expression on his face. As though nothing she said or could ever say would change how he looked at her.

Steaming with rage, she barreled through the forest, surprised at her own outburst. Exploding in rage was not her style. She typically chose to let things go, to roll off her back—let people walk all over her. What was it Luc had said to her?

You'll have to grow a backbone. Even if you have to conjure it with your own magic.

The memory made her almost blind with anger as she beat past bushes and brambles, picturing Caelum's face in the branches she savagely knocked back. Deya had wanted to get as far away from him as she could, but soon realized she had nowhere to go. It was nightfall in wild country, and there was a very good reason as to why Caelum was sitting up, keeping watch. She kept going though, her pride pushing her through the trees. Monsters be damned.

But this thought was dashed from her head by the first snap of an errant branch, causing her to yelp in alarm. Okay, maybe she misjudged letting her pride thrust her right into wild country in the middle of the night. Still, she pressed on until she reached the creek. Here, there was nothing but boulders and cliffs over the water, perfect for her to sit and stew over the infuriating Nodarian.

Plunking down onto one that appeared to be dry enough, she stared down at the creek rushing below her dangling boots. Moonlight danced on the surface of the running water, and her nails dug into the gravel underneath her in an uncharacteristic fury. But inside, her heart was heavy and aching. Caelum's cruelty and viciousness didn't shock her, but it did hurt her for a reason she couldn't fathom.

For her whole life, she had believed a lie, helped a corrupt kingdom plunder and kill. And what was more, she had inadvertently helped Praiton ruin the lives of the people who had saved her from Ironbalt.

All of this filled her with a cloud of fury and confusion, but the thing that consumed her like a noxious poison was the fact she had helped a kingdom that killed her friend to punish her. So why did she still hesitate to join the rebels?

Praiton had always looked down on the Pillar Legion. Known as a misfit group of amateurs, they were hardly considered a threat to the military machine of Praiton. However, in her few short years at the castle infirmary, she had seen a lot of damage done by the rebels.

For a moment, she sat and stared, transfixed at the moon, relishing in its silver lighted beauty . . . until a shadow rippled into view. Deya froze, her spine stiffening as a large black beast emerged from the trees.

Bent and shriveled, like someone failed in an attempt to turn a dog into a man, the creature had black skin with tufts of dark fur stretched tight over elongated bones. It had the head of some strange mutation— part man, part ghoul, but all nightmare. It padded towards her on all fours, front legs sporting long, sharp, silver claws, each looking like an extended finger.

Fear held Deya in place, digging into her like those long, needlelike claws would. It prowled out of the shadows, its red eyes seeking, searching. They landed on her, and its flat nose holes flared, as though it smelled her. It let out a low, deep snarl.

Move! The small voice in Deya's head screamed at her. But her limbs felt leaden and numb, too terrified by the thing stalking towards her.

The beast let out a low growl, and as if the sound had awoken all the muscles in her body, Deya turned tail and ran. With a roar, the beast took off after her.

Deya hadn't run in weeks—maybe months—and yet, her feet carried her as fast as they could, darting between trees and branches that grabbed and scraped at her face and skin. She tore under brambles, the creature hot on her heels, its panting and growling so close she could almost feel its breath on her face.

She had no idea where she was going, only that she was running as far and as fast as she could, attempting to lose that nightmarish beast. *Maybe*, she thought, *if I can make it to the other side of the water . . . maybe it can't swim . . .*

But as she chanced a glance behind her, a glint of a silver blade flashed through the trees. The head of the monster went spinning off into the darkness and the grisly body dropped in a heap. Deya gasped, her feet skidding to a halt as she attempted to see who wielded the blade, when she barreled into something hard and heavy.

Deya was about to let out a scream when a hand clamped around her mouth. Falling backward, Deya's heart skipped a beat as harsh laughter echoed in her ears. The scent of smoke and dirt filled her nose as the male's grimy palms pressed into her mouth and nose.

"I got her!" the male yelled, his voice almost perforating her eardrums. "I got the traitor!"

CHAPTER
10

Deya's breath was coming out in short, desperate gasps against the man's hand, her fingers scrabbling against his grip, attempting to pry him off her face. But she had not missed what he had called her. *The traitor?*

Thundering footsteps sounded through the clearing, and then a group of soldiers burst through the trees, swords gleaming, armor sparkling under the moonlight. Deya then noticed there was something different about these soldiers. Something . . . familiar. With a pang, she recognized the green and white crest on their breastplates.

They were Praiton soldiers.

"Bind her up!" Deya identified the captain of the group, who was regarding her like a large hog he had bagged for dinner. "Quickly, before she attempts to use her dark magic!"

Her hands were jerked behind her back, ropes tightening around her wrists along with the clinking of chain. Faerivaine shackles. Deya fought and struggled against the soldier holding her, desperate to free her hand, to grab at the sword dangling uselessly from her hip.

"Stop moving!" the male barked, and a fist connected with the side of her head. She crashed to the ground, vision blurring, the faces of the soldiers around her turning white and fuzzy.

"Let me go!" Deya's voice found her, but it shook as she spat blood from her teeth.

The captain of the group leered, bending to stare her right in the eye. She did not recognize this male. He was pale and scruffy, and the insignia on his badge told her that he was not a mainland Praiton soldier. Which meant that they were sent from Praiton's Aunecia unit to find them. Or, more specifically, to find *her*.

"We'll let you go, traitor," the captain breathed, his eyes glinting with excitement in the light from the torch held over her head. "After we bring you back to the High Lord."

Deya's blood ran cold.

Instinctively, she began to squirm more underneath the soldier's grasp, bound hands clawing against the hilt of the sword sitting uselessly against her waist, her fingernails succeeding in prying it out half an inch.

Just a little closer, Deya thought. *Just a little . . . closer.*

But it was no use. The sword's brass hilt lay out of reach of her trussed hands.

The soldier holding Deya grabbed her hair, jerking her up, making her scream in pain.

"What does Decius want with me?" Deya cried. Her mind was racing. How was she to get out of this? She was surrounded by at least half a dozen Praiton soldiers, her hands bound. At that moment, her whole body was screaming for the Nodarian male to feel she was in trouble, to come find her. All she could think of doing in the meantime was to buy herself time, to keep the soldiers talking.

The captain appraised her with a cold, almost apprehensive stare. "You know full well what you did, demon girl."

Deya shifted back and forth on her feet, her heart pounding an uncomfortable rhythm against her ribcage. "Escaping from Ironbalt is punishable by death," she said, willing her voice to stop shaking. "Yet you want to take me back to Praiton. Why?" As she spoke, she wiggled her thin wrists in circles inside their bindings. The faerivaine shackles were loosely strung around the rope, a safeguard to keep her magic at bay.

"Don't play stupid with us," the captain sneered, drawing his sword from his scabbard.

Deya flinched backwards, her eyes alighting on the sword. For some reason, up until he had drawn his blade, she hadn't thought they would actually hurt her. These were the soldiers she had spent years caring for, who had kept her alive on the journey to Ironbalt . . . had taken pity on her. And yet, *this* male looked like he would enjoy nothing more than cutting her to ribbons, his beady eyes glittering with bloodlust.

"You incinerated the warden, and a half dozen guards," the captain murmured, the tip of his sword nearing her face. "Lord Decius finds this dark magic concerning. You have a fat bounty on your head, demon girl. And *we* will be the ones that collect it."

The males surrounding her let out chuckles of appreciation, menacing murmurs that made her heart beat even faster. She twisted and strained more against her bindings. Then, she felt her wrist slip free of one loop.

Moving without thinking, she seized her sword and brought it swinging through the air blindly. There was a scream of pain, a shower of blood, and she took off sprinting through the forest.

Panting, her legs screaming, she lowered her head and ran as fast as her weak muscles could carry her. But, in her haste to get away, her feet stumbled, tripping over rocks and brambles on the ground.

The soldiers were shouting. The sound of thundering footsteps filled the forest as Deya struggled to her feet before a shadow fell over her. There was a slash of silver and she fell to the ground again with a scream of pain and an arc of blood.

"Do not kill her!" The captain's voice rang out from the clearing. "Lord Decius wants her *alive*! Do not kill her, dammit!"

But his words were lost on the hulking brute that she had not noticed lurking on the outskirts of the group. He advanced towards her, sword slick with her blood, a fiendish grin on his face. Deya scrambled backwards. The pain from the wound made her vision fuzzy, her fingers scrabbling over the deep gash on her back.

"Please," Deya whispered, her hand outstretched. But the Praiton soldier didn't stop.

He raised his sword above her head. She stared up at him, at the five-point star on his chest, splattered with her blood, before he brought the sword swinging down—only for it to stop in midair. Deya turned and nearly cried in relief.

Caelum, arm outstretched, violet eyes almost glowing with his power, strode through the clearing towards them. At that moment, the other soldiers crashed into view. Caelum's purple eyes fixed on them; his sword drawn. With a grunt, he thrust his fist upward, sending the brute who had been about to slaughter her spinning into the air with a yell. And then he lunged for the remaining soldiers.

Gone was any of the previous weakness and fatigue he had exhibited after their escape from Ironbalt. His power seemed to have come back to him in full over the last few days. Deya watched in awe as, with a practiced stroke, Caelum spun his sword over his head, catching the Praiton soldiers' blades one by one.

Deya struggled to her feet, reaching for her own sword, even though she had no idea how she would help. But the Nodarian did not seem like he needed it. He moved in a choreographed dance, each blow, strike, and parry strong and resolute.

He struck one soldier, before spinning to throw another in the air with his Celestial Magic, striking them down on the descent. And then, the captain sprang into the fight.

Deya shouted to warn Caelum, who caught the blow at the last second with a crash of his brass sword, his purple eyes glowing and furious. The two battled across the clearing until Caelum's hand snapped forward like a viper, blocking the captain's blade, suspending it with Celestial Magic, and striking him down with a yell of fury.

The captain's body hit the ground with a dull thump, and for a second, Deya thought it was over. Until, with a huff of irritation, Caelum clenched his fist and brought his hand crashing down. With a rush of air, Deya looked up just in time to see the body of the brute who had initially attacked her, hurtle to the ground, hitting the Earth so hard that he exploded in a surge gore. Bone fragments and bits of brain and blood rained down on them both. And then everything was quiet.

For a moment, Deya sat there, feeling the soldiers' blood drip down her face. Bile bubbled in her throat, and as her eyes roved over the grisly pile of dismembered bodies, she felt her gut heave. Doubling over, she emptied her stomach into the grass beside her.

Caelum stood in the clearing, his purple eyes glowing, splattered from head to toe with dark red blood. Those menacing eyes alighted on her, and he seemed to be radiating murderous fury.

But then, something moved out of the corner of her eye. Without thinking, still lightheaded, bleeding, and aching all over, Deya ran straight towards the Nodarian male, hurling herself between Caelum and the lone soldier who had advanced from the trees, and threw all her strength into blocking the blade of the last surviving soldier.

The soldier's eyes were wide as they met hers over the warring blades. Caelum turned, just in time to see Deya shove the soldier to the ground with every bit of strength she could muster. The male hit the dirt, trembling and fearful as Deya's sword hovered above him.

"P-please," the male whispered. Deya froze. The soldier was young— even younger than her. She had seen faces like his in the infirmary, laughing with his friends, still innocent and unmarred by battle and blood. And now, she held a sword to his face . . . and she was expected to use it.

"What are you fucking doing?" Caelum yelled. "*Kill him!*"

But Deya couldn't. She had been taught to save these men, to *help* them. Even as she stood, bleeding copiously, and soaked in the blood of his fellow soldiers, she couldn't do it. Couldn't kill him.

In her second of hesitation, the soldier scrambled to his feet and took off running into the forest. Caelum swore and pushed past her, attempting to give chase, but it was too late. The soldier had already disappeared between the trees.

Caelum spat blood out of his mouth and turned to look at her where she stood, bleeding and quivering, the faerivaine shackles still draped across her wrist.

"What the *fuck* is wrong with you?" Caelum panted, storming towards her. He flicked blood from his face with his sleeve, but it was rather pointless. Their clothes—once clean and smelling of lavender—were now covered with blood and gore. "You let him go! Why did you not kill him?"

Deya could only stutter. Nothing she could say to him could answer that question in a way he would approve of. Her silence seemed to infuriate him more. Swearing at the top of his lungs, he whirled away from her, stepping over the dismembered bodies of the Praiton soldiers. Soldiers he hadn't so much as hesitated to kill.

"I'm sorry," Deya said, her voice barely a whisper. "I just . . . I just couldn't—"

"*Couldn't?*" Caelum echoed. He stalked towards her, violet eyes still glowing with that unusually strong Celestial Magic. Deya stared up at him, a little awestruck. Val had said he was powerful, but she hadn't seen it yet. But watching him throw soldiers into the air as if they weighed nothing . . . not to mention having the strength to send them crashing so hard into the Earth that they exploded on sheer impact . . .

"You hesitated to kill Praitonians because *you are one*," he hissed at her. "You are still loyal to them. After everything they have done to you—to your friend! And yet you still hesitate to fight back." He shook his head, disgusted, but Deya felt a surge of anger flare up in her again.

"I am *not* loyal to them!" she insisted defiantly, but her voice shook and even she did not believe herself. "I was taught to *heal* these people, not to kill them." She wrapped her arms around herself defensively. "You think I do not know they have no loyalty to me? You think I do not realize what horrors they have committed? *I do.* But I can't . . ."

She dribbled off. Caelum was staring at her intensely, a mixture of distrust and something else on his face. It felt naïve hoping it was sympathy.

"How did they find you?" he asked, a hint of an edge still in his tone.

Deya's shoulders lifted but she couldn't feel them. A numbness of shock and exhaustion had set in like frost. "A creature chased me into their camp . . . A horrible thing with long claws—looked like a nightmarish dog."

"A nyraxi, probably," Caelum said. His eyes swept the clearing. The body of the creature lay a few feet away, headless and smoldering, black haze still undulating from the limp mass. Caelum kicked it, rolling it over with the toe of his boot. "They're shadow creatures. Demons of the underearth. You're lucky the soldiers got you instead."

A shiver crawled up Deya's spine as she remembered the way those bloodred eyes had locked onto her . . . the sound of its claws striking dirt as it chased her.

Caelum crossed the clearing towards one of the fallen corpses. Leaning down, he began to root through their clothing.

"What are you doing?" Deya asked, cringing as Caelum's fingers picked through the soldier's pockets and armor. He didn't answer her. He rose, clutching a worn piece of parchment stained with blood. Unfolding it, he gave it one look and scoffed with disgust.

"What is it?" Deya asked, and Caelum tossed her the blood-stained paper. She recognized it instantly. An official Praiton memo. The Praiton crest was printed at the top, and below it, an emergency order gathering all soldiers in the Aunecia area to look for . . .

Deya's eyes flew down the words on the paper, reading the description of the person they were looking for. A person who sounded an awful lot like her. The words *Armed with dark, dangerous magic* swam in her vision. Pushing the paper aside, suddenly feeling sick to her stomach, Deya looked back at Caelum.

"What did the soldiers want?" Caelum asked, his voice a bit softer now. "Why were they trying to capture only you?"

Deya shook her head. Her throat burned and her eyes stung, as if tears were waiting behind her eyelids. "They called me a demon," she told him. "Said that Lord Decius wants me back. He finds my new power . . . concerning."

Caelum's face darkened. He contemplated this, his hands clenching and unclenching on his sword hilt. Deya shifted uneasily but stopped, doubling over when the gashes on her arms and back flared in pain, a sound that seemed to shake Caelum from his reverie.

"Come on." He seized her arm and marched her away from the pool of blood where the soldiers still lay, back towards the creek.

Shoving her down on top of a rock on the edge of the water, he ripped off a long strip from the bottom of his tunic. Tearing free another sliver from his sleeve, he dunked the cloth into the river and turned towards her.

"I have to take off your tunic," he said gruffly. Deya didn't have it in her to give him a hard time. Numbly, she reached for the bottom of her tunic and pulled it off, allowing him access to her wounds. She had wrappings around her breasts—something Ironbalt had given their female prisoners for modesty, she supposed. Now, she was extremely grateful for it. She didn't need the added shame of Caelum having to save her, then tend to her wounds while she sat naked and shivering before him.

His hands moved from the minor gash on her arm, to the much deeper one on her back. It spread from the center of her spine towards the side of her ribs. She felt him pause as he took in her back, his hand stilled.

"It's fine," she said to him. She knew he was staring at the deep, jagged scars on her skin, hiding under all the blood. "We all have them, right?"

He cleared his throat and didn't answer, merely proceeding to clean her wounds. His hands were gentle against her skin, the water making her hiss in pain as it trickled down the deep ruptures. And yet Caelum was quiet, almost pensive as he dabbed at them.

She felt him hesitate above her bare skin. He was riled and hot from the fight, and yet the space between his fingers and her naked skin felt cold. It prickled every nerve ending in her body, made her instinctively arch her back in anticipation of his touch. And when he touched her, Deya had to hold her breath to keep from reacting.

"It's concerning to me," he said. "How fast they found us. And that Praiton is now hunting you for your power."

The words sent an unpleasant tremor of panic through her. "It concerns me, too."

Caelum continued his work, his brow furrowed. "I had hoped that word of what had happened at the whipping posts would not reach Praiton so quickly."

"Praiton has soldiers everywhere," Deya replied, her fingers clenched tightly to the bloody tunic in her hands. "They are expected to be the eyes and ears of Lord Decius. I was naïve to think it *wouldn't* get back to Stonehall."

Caelum did not answer. He dipped the thin rag he was using to clean her wounds into the water and methodically reached back for her bare skin.

"It would help if you could still heal yourself," he grunted, cupping water in his hands and trickling it down her back, clearing off the blood.

"There should be some myrrh," she said. "In the thicket back that way. It's the tree with the jagged leaves. And some chamomile flowers. Mashed together they make a useful healing ointment."

Caelum looked down at her for a second. His purple eyes no longer glowed, but rather simmered. Then, quietly, he stood up and walked towards the forest.

While he was gone, Deya took advantage of his absence by pulling off the undergarment she was wearing and plunging into the creek to wash the rest of the blood off. The feel of still being coated in the soldier's blood was making her queasy. She scrubbed herself until her skin turned raw, all the while holding back the panicked tears at the memory of those broken corpses they had left in the clearing.

By the time Caelum returned with a fistful of plants, Deya was dressed

117

again and now washing the remaining blood off her discarded tunic.

"Give them here," Deya said, reaching for the plants. He handed them over, and she proceeded to grind them up on the rock using the hilt of her sword. Mixing it with a little bit of water, a thick paste began to form. "That should do it," she murmured. She began to rub some on her arm, then attempted to slather it on her side and back but winced when the wounds protested the movement.

Caelum watched her struggle for a minute, before letting out an aggravated sigh and picking up a handful of salve. "I'll do it," he grumbled. "You look ridiculous trying."

When he touched her, Deya was surprised to feel it was gentle, almost tender. It was not what she expected from the snarling, biting male, but then again, Caelum had been full of nothing but contradictions since they had met.

"Can I ask you something?" Deya said quietly.

His purple eyes flashed. "No," he grunted, still running his fingers full of salve down her spine. His touch was making her skin prickle with goosebumps.

Ignoring his grunt, Deya said, "You have an extremely strong amount of Celestial Magic, yet you don't look like a Nodarian. Why is that?"

She felt his hands still upon her back, the heat from his hand warming her in the cool, biting breeze of the Aunecian forest. She had asked this question, expecting him not to answer it, to bark a nasty retort at her about how it's none of her business and stomp away.

But, to her surprise, Caelum answered.

"My mother was from Bridah," he said, and then spoke no more. And while it didn't answer her question, Deya took his mere reply as a small victory.

Caelum finished wrapping her wounds tightly with the strip of fabric he had torn from his shirt. Deya pulled her tunic back over her head and the two of them began to head back towards camp using the creek as a guide, but this time on high alert.

The appearance of Praiton soldiers had increased the anxiety that

Deya had already felt since leaving Ironbalt, but the taste of danger was still so fresh in her mouth. They were after her now. The knowledge that she was being actively hunted caused her to continuously move her head in a swivel, her ears pricked in order to pick up the slightest movement.

Caelum remained silent for most of the walk. His tunic was still stained with blood and was now torn and misshapen in places. She was too afraid to say any more to him—to even thank him, though she wanted to.

"Those scars," he said. "On your back."

Deya looked over at him, surprised. "What about them?"

It looked like every word pained him. Gritting his teeth, he said, "Those weren't from Ironbalt. They didn't get to whip you at the whipping post. So . . ." He trailed off. Deya knew he wanted to ask the question but his pride and stubbornness—his absolute refusal to deviate from being the coldhearted bastard he had committed himself to being—stopped him.

"I was imprisoned because someone in power at Stonehall Castle accused me of treason," Deya said. He had shared something with her, no matter how small. And besides, after coming to her rescue, she figured she owed him something.

Caelum looked at her out of the corner of his eye. She didn't know what he was thinking. His face gave away no emotion, and he didn't press her any further. Quietly, they both returned to camp.

CHAPTER
11

"What in the *Mother* happened to you two?" Val cried. They had awoken the next morning—early as usual, per Caelum's request—to pack the carriage. Although both Deya and Caelum had washed in the creek after the fight with the Praiton soldiers, the blood proved harder to wash out than the soot of the mines from Ironbalt. Red splatters stained their shirts—though Deya had been sure to rub herself down with lavender again to ensure that none of the smell of death lingered on her.

She had to admit, Caelum looked the worst. His shirt was torn and fluttered in the cold breeze; the bottom now much shorter than it used to be. Deya found herself looking a little too long at the patch of exposed, scarred skin that appeared when he raised his arms to lift himself into the carriage.

"Praiton soldiers," Caelum said bitterly. "We need to move. Quickly."

Val turned to stare at him, mouth agape. "Praiton soldiers? *Here?*"

Even Rayner whipped his head around to look at them, fear apparent in his bright blue eyes.

"They are hunting *her*," Caelum said, jerking his head at Deya roughly, still not meeting her gaze. "News of her power has reached Praiton."

Val looked towards Deya this time, her amber eyes taking in the bandages peeping out from underneath her bloodied tunic. "Do you even know how to fight?" she asked Deya as they climbed back into the carriage and set off again into the woods.

Deya shook her head, pulling at the bandage around her bicep. "Fighting is not really my thing," she muttered. "I was lucky Caelum found me, honestly." She wouldn't have admitted that if the male was in earshot. Thankfully, he and Rayner were arguing in the front seat over which direction they should take to get them to Latchside faster.

Val hummed thoughtfully, looking out the window at Caelum and then back to Deya. "And here I was thinking you finally got him to take you on the forest floor or something."

Deya almost choked on her own tongue, causing Val to laugh and thump her on the back as she began to cough and splutter, her face a bright, lurid red. Was it her imagination, or did Caelum stiffen and cough a little up at the front, too?

This was supposed to be the last stretch of their journey to Latchside Landing, according to Rayner, but the journey this time was laced with tension and fear. Knowledge that Praiton was actively hunting her set the whole party on edge, though Deya was especially nervous. The panicked fluttering in her chest made it difficult to breathe as the carriage trundled its way through uneven forest, bumping and rocking over rocks and roots littering wild country.

Rayner explained he could sense water and had been tracking the coast, taking them southeast towards Latchside and its otherwise small harbor town. This explained why he had opted to stay up front with Caelum, who was in an even more unpleasant mood today, most likely due to his and Deya's encounter last night.

Caelum had hardly looked at her twice that morning. She wondered if it was because he was angry about her failure to kill the soldier, the fact that Praiton was actively seeking them, or about the information they had shared with each other afterwards. It could be that Caelum considered it a weakness, a loss in his battle to not let any of them know him at all. Maybe he was mad at himself that Deya now knew even a little detail about him that the others did not. Either way, she vowed not to let his hostility affect her. She was already on edge enough.

It turned out that Rayner's navigational skills were impressively accurate. The forest and subsequent wild country began to thin, until they could see the beginnings of a small town in the distance. Out of the forest, Aunecia was a rocky, bleak region. The glacial fjords of Bridah could be seen from a distance, and the strong gusts of icy wind blown off them was bone chilling for the four escaped prisoners in nothing but their thin rags.

Val was bouncing up and down beside Deya, eager to get into town and maybe buy a meal, but before they could even exit the forest, Caelum stopped the cart.

"Why are we stopping?" Val cried, thrusting her head through the window and right between the two males to glare up at them accusingly.

"We have to sell the mares," Caelum said. "We can't just roll into town with a damn prison cart. We need to ditch the cart, sell the mares, and get on a boat as quickly as possible. Things are more complicated now that we know Praiton is seeking us. Ironbalt will no doubt have alerted all the towns nearby that there are escaped prisoners on the loose."

Even Val didn't have a pithy retort for that.

"Who's going into town then?" Deya asked cautiously, looking between the three of them. Every single one of them stuck out like a sore thumb. There was Val, her long mane of red hair had been tamed in the creek, but her features were still starkly Manielian. Then there was Rayner with his blue gray skin and webbed ears. Worse of all of them was Caelum. His purple eyes, an obvious tell that he was Nodarian, coupled with his silver white hair and they may as well slap the faerivaine shackles

122

back on themselves now.

"I'll go," Caelum proclaimed immediately. Val snorted.

"Oh, right, and you won't stick out at all with that hair, princess."

Caelum's hand leapt instinctively towards the dagger on his hip, but Rayner grabbed his wrist almost like it was second nature to him.

"Bridah is a bordering kingdom," Caelum said through gritted teeth. "I won't stand out *that* much."

"And no Bridanians are crazy enough to leave their own region for fear of capture by Praiton," Val challenged.

They glared at each other, lightning virtually crackling between them as they stared each other down, as though willing the other to back down first.

Rayner then cleared his throat awkwardly. "Honestly, Deya is the least conspicuous out of all of us," he said hesitantly. Deya's eyes widened, and Caelum let out a harsh bark of laughter.

"Yes, let's send the girl who has a fat bounty on her head for incinerating half of Ironbalt's guard into town on her own."

"I did *not*," Deya grit out, "incinerate *half the guard*."

Caelum snorted humorlessly. "Praiton released her description specifically. And besides, she will never be able to broker a deal for the mares," he snapped. "One of us will have to go with her."

"Then I will," Val proclaimed. She smoothed her red hair down, her lustrous locks shining an array of ruby red hues in the morning light. "Manielians happily joined Praiton. No one will question a free roaming Manielian."

Caelum sneered at her. "If they're walking around in prison clothes, they will."

"Val comes with me," Deya said, cutting off the no doubt scathing retort the female had at the ready. "We'll be sure to stay out of the main town until we can purchase cloaks to hide our features. Val will help me bargain a price for the mares and we'll use the coin to buy us new clothes. Then we can all make it to the docks. Okay?"

She directed this question mostly to Caelum, who looked like he wanted to argue with her, no matter what she said. But it was Rayner who broke the stalemate.

"That sounds like a fine idea, right?" he proclaimed, elbowing Caelum sharply in the side. The male grunted but didn't disagree.

"Excellent," Val said, and she grabbed Deya by the hand. "Come on. Let's go show the boys how it's done."

Caelum muttered something under his breath which was no doubt nasty, but Val ignored him. She and Deya set off on foot, through the forest and onto the path leading towards the town, each pulling along a mare.

"The Bayard mares should fetch a pretty penny," Val said, reaching up to stroke hers, who whinnied gently. Since they had detached the mares from the cart, they had shrunk down in size, each adjusting to their respective heights. Bayard mares had a special magic that allowed them to change in size based on who was riding them. Deya was a tad smaller than Val, so her mare was a bit shorter as a result. "What do you think? Should we take some coin and grab a hot meal, too? Just for us?"

"What about Rayner?" Deya asked. "Don't you think he'd appreciate a hot meal, as well?"

Val huffed. "I know, but if we bring things back for Rayner, then we'd have to bring some back for that white-haired bastard, too." Deya chuckled, and they continued towards the town with Val ripping Caelum apart while Deya smiled quietly.

The harbor town of Latchside was small and bleak. Rain and sleet battered the wooden huts that were set up along the pathway. Once painted bright colors, the houses were chipped and fading, giving all the buildings a washed out, sad hue.

The people who walked by barely looked at them, all their eyes cast downwards. Funnily enough, Deya thought she and Val blended in nicely in the town. Everyone looked emaciated, pale, and downtrodden. A perfect place for two escaped prisoners to hide.

"Food shortages must have gotten worse," Val whispered to Deya, her eyes following a female and two children, both of whom looked skeletal and wan. Val's eyes were filled with pity. "Since Praiton took Ganiea, food has become sparse everywhere else in Krigor."

Deya watched the family shuffle down the street, their clothing nothing more than rags as thin and dirty as their own. She knew Ganiea was responsible for most of the food production of the realm. She had heard rumblings of hard times and food shortages throughout Krigor, but it had never personally affected her. Food in Praiton's capital was always abundant, almost wasteful. The all-too-familiar feeling of shame welled up in the pit of her stomach again as she and Val made their way further through the town. It was getting harder to swallow.

They managed to find a suitable buyer for the mares. Deya insisted they find a farm to take them in, and not merely some owners interested in selling them off or leading them to die in battle. Val thought she was being ridiculous, but Deya didn't care. She would not have any more innocent things die by her hands.

With a small bag of coin in hand, Deya and Val made for a merchant and bought up four cloaks, several tunics, and breeches, as well as new boots for all of them. By the time they were done shopping for clothes, their moneybag was significantly lighter. This, however, did not stop Val from going to a tavern and ordering three large meat pies. And after a great deal amount of ribbing from Deya, she reluctantly bought a fourth.

They returned to the two males, sitting in the abandoned cart, waiting for them. It seemed like Caelum was not in a very chatty mood, because when Val and Deya emerged from over the hill, Rayner leapt up to greet them, as though overjoyed at having someone other than the brooding Nodarian to speak to.

"We come bearing clothes and . . . food!" Val announced, holding the brown sack with the meat pies in the air as if it were Lord Decius's head. "Warm meat pies! No more Ironbalt gruel, or slop after today!" Rayner and Deya both seized theirs eagerly, but when Val—rather reluctantly— held out Caelum's to him, it was met with a rather sour look.

"Don't you think we should possibly save any rations for the several day boat journey we're to be embarking on soon?" he asked snidely.

Val looked like she was about to explode. Steam almost escaped from her ears, and Deya could've sworn that her hand twitched towards the sword on her hip. Hastily stepping between them, Deya swiped the meat pie from her hand and pushed the female back towards the carriage.

"Go get changed. I'll deal with him," she added to her in an undertone.

Val hesitated, before snarling at Caelum and slinking away.

Deya rounded on him. He was back to looking unconcernedly at anything other than her. She realized, rather belatedly, that this was the first minute alone that she had had with the male since last night's misadventure.

"Can you just take the damn pie, Caelum?" she asked, exasperatedly, waving it back in his face. "Or does every little thing really need to be a fight?"

"Did you and the Manielian really not bring back any spare coin after that transaction?" he asked, ignoring her completely. "What, did you just *give* the mares away to any good home?"

She flushed. "No, of course not," she spluttered, but the look Caelum gave her was enough to confirm that he knew that she was lying through her teeth.

"I figured as much," he snarled, and snatched the meat pie from her.

"Don't forget your clothes, too, you absolute *ass*," Deya snapped, and hurled a black tunic, a pair of breeches, and his boots at his silver head. She did not know what it was about this male that brought out the usually nonexistent fight in her, but she couldn't seem to stop the fury boiling in her blood.

Caelum ducked, and the boots soared over his head, hitting the tree behind him. Deya whirled away from him, but, with extraordinary swiftness, he seized her wrist. Gasping in pain, Deya was hauled back against him, her arm bent painfully behind her.

"Throw something like that at me again," Caelum breathed in her ear from behind. "And I will throw this knife back. And I promise you, I do not miss." Deya stiffened against him, his breath hot in her ear.

"Are you threatening me?" she hissed, though her voice was strained as she struggled to free her arm from his grip. This resulted in her being pressed even harder against him.

"Yes," he snarled, and then he shoved her off him.

Stumbling, arm aching, cheeks blazing, Deya threw him one last filthy look, before hurrying back towards the others. Val looked up from where she was tying up her new rust-colored corset.

"Did he take it?" Val asked. Deya grunted in response, her cheeks still flaming, the feel of Caelum's fingers still making her wrist ache. Val let out a knowing bark of laughter and shook her head.

Deya dressed, marveling in the feel of the new cream tunic accented with a soft, mossy green corset, brown breeches, and leather boots. She even allowed Val to help her plait her hair into a thick braid down her back. Several minutes later, Caelum emerged from the forest, tugging down the sleeve of the all black outfit they had picked out for him.

"Black suits you," Val said venomously from where she was braiding part of her hair into a coronet on top of her head. "Matches your soul."

Caelum's jaw tightened and Deya saw a vein throb in his forehead before he jerked his head towards town. "We need to get going."

Val gestured towards a small pile of their prison clothes now lying on the forest floor. "Throw yours in there first," she commanded. "We need to destroy them."

Wordlessly, Caelum chucked his prison uniform on the top of the pile. They were the sorriest looking rags Deya had ever seen. Val approached the heap, and with a flick of her hand, a fire erupted on them.

All of them gathered around and watched their clothing go up in flames, and with it, the last of their lives in Ironbalt.

Deya and the others all pulled on the thick, warm cloaks that she and Val had spent the majority of the money on. Rayner and Caelum pulled the hoods over their heads, to hide their more conspicuous features. Deya felt like sighing as the heavy cloak rested around her, like a warm blanket, keeping out the brisk Aunecian wind.

Dressed in the new clothes, Deya felt more alive than she had in months. She couldn't remember the last time she had worn something other than that horrible healer's dress, even before she was imprisoned.

When they set off towards town, leaving the prison carriage behind, they all no longer felt like escaped prisoners.

Caelum was on edge. His hand remained clenched on the hilt of his sword underneath his cloak the whole way through town, his violet eyes darting around constantly, studying every individual who passed. Deya knew he was looking for guards, for Praiton soldiers, for someone who had been alerted to the possibility that four escaped prisoners would try to reach a port.

The walk to Latchside Landing was short. Latchside itself was an exceptionally small town, with not much coming and going. This made Deya a little concerned about the conspicuous nature of the sudden appearance of four cloaked strangers lurking about it. Caelum seemed to have a similar fear because he stopped the group at the harbor.

"We need to split up," he said. Some of those passing them were beginning to stare, their eyes lingering a bit too long. "Rayner, Val, you two need to find a boat. Any will do," he said. "Rayner, find one that you think you can control to get us off this continent."

"Oh, I see," Rayner said, crossing his arms grumpily. "Since I'm the Laenimorian, I *must* be a sailor."

Caelum's eyes narrowed into violet daggers. "No, but you and your Water Magic are our only hope to get us *out of here*."

"And what will you do?" Val cut in.

"Deya and I will see if we can gather supplies," he replied tersely.

Deya's head shot up in alarm. "*We* are gathering supplies?" she spluttered.

It was her turn to receive his vicious glare. From underneath his hood, the effect was even more menacing. "We will meet up at the docks. The farthest harbor at the southernmost dock," he instructed them.

Deya stuttered some more. The panic of having to go *anywhere* alone with Caelum was starting to take over.

"But . . ." she blustered, looking at Val, as though asking her for help. Val opened her mouth, probably to do just that, when Caelum snarled and seized Deya's wrist.

"The farthest port," he repeated to Val and Rayner. "One hour." And then he dragged Deya away, muttering curses under his breath. "For fuck's sake," he hissed to her, her wrist still in his viselike grip. "What in the Mother do you think I'm going to do to you?"

"Well, you *did* just threaten to kill me not even an hour ago!" Deya hissed back. "So, who knows what you may do to me? For all I know, all that bleach you put in your hair may have addled your brains."

Caelum stopped dead in his tracks, but his fingers tightened so hard around her wrist that Deya bit down on a little cry of pain.

"*I. Do. Not,*" he growled, his face so livid Deya didn't know whether to laugh or cry. "*Bleach. My. Hair.*" His grip tightened on her until she really did moan in pain. With a snarl, he released her, leaving her face flushed. "You've been spending too much time with that obnoxious Manielian," he snapped. They began walking into town at a brisk pace, still bickering under their breath.

"You just don't like Val because she doesn't put up with your nasty, moody bullshit," Deya shot back at him. She didn't know where this newfound courage to go head-to-head with Caelum had come from. It could be the memory of him bending her arm backwards, of being crushed into his chest that still sent her face flaring with color. But, if she were being honest with herself, she wasn't sure if it was out of fury or something else.

Caelum glared at her from under his hood, a look she returned with equal force. They were both snapping at one another with such ferocity that they were beginning to draw attention. As they stepped foot into the market bazaar, heads swiveled to look at them. Deya and her long brown plait hanging innocently under the hood of her dark green cloak was not exactly anything to be alarmed about. The great, hulking, hooded figure who radiated irritation and fury, however, was another story.

"How exactly do you expect us to gather supplies when we have no money?" Deya hissed at him.

They edged along small, modest looking booths. Some sold food—dried fruits and salted fish—some sold wares like swords and armor, tunics, and breeches. But what each stall had in common was the look of downtrodden despair upon each of the vendor's faces. The sight of them tugged a bit at Deya's heartstrings—even if all those faces were giving them suspicious, wary looks as they passed.

"How do you think?" Caelum retorted. His eyes latched onto a shabby booth which sold tins of salted fish. The owner—a rather weather-beaten female—was busy talking to another shopkeeper across the way, leaving her booth empty.

"We are *not* stealing from these people!" Deya hissed, seizing Caelum's arm as he made towards the female's unattended booth.

He pulled his arm free and grabbed her by the wrist *again*, pulling her so close she was practically underneath his hood. The same power that had caused his purple eyes to glow that night with the soldiers was coursing through the violet irises again. "We will *die* out at sea," he hissed, shaking her slightly. "Without food and water, we will *not* make the journey. And since you and Val decided to just give away those mares, we have no money, thus, no choice."

Caelum's hands were still on her, and Deya couldn't understand how this kept happening. His pincer-like grip bit into her skin and she felt a surge of anger, a flare of heated fury so strong that the destructive power in her core bubbled up. It flashed within her, filling her veins, looking for an out, a way to explode out of her. It met the faerivaine necklace, slammed against it with such force that she wondered if it would hold. Thankfully it did, or Deya was sure she would have reduced Caelum to no more than a ball of soot on the ground.

Whether Caelum noticed the power flashing through her eyes or how truly pissed off she was, he released her as though she were made of hot coals.

"Stay behind if you must," he snarled. "But at least attempt to distract some of them." He then disappeared with a whirl of his cloak, like some oversized albino bat. Deya glowered after him. Gods, Val was right. He was definitely a hard potion to swallow.

Caelum swooped around the booths, the occasional tin of dried fruit or salted fish disappearing under his cloak. Deya attempted to look natural, perusing the wares in front of her.

"You lookin' for something particular?" an older female asked gruffly. She scowled up at Deya, the expression exacerbating the lines on her worn face. Deya jumped, her hand going to her faerivaine necklace when that instinctual surge of power started to rise from her core.

"N-no," she stuttered. From the corner of her eye, Caelum swished by, a bushel of apples disappearing under the tail of his black cloak. Deya didn't know where in Mother's name he was stashing all these stolen goods, but none of them slowed him down. "I'm just looking for a present . . . for my mother."

It was a flimsy lie. The female only had wooden trinkets for sale and the occasional fruit or loaf of bread. The wooden carvings in front of her featured an array of small, female figurines. She recognized the set of scales the female was holding. It was simple and a little crude, but the likeness of the Mother Goddess Mav was undeniable.

"These are lovely," Deya mumbled to the female, meaning it. The female's face did not soften, but she did incline her head slightly to her.

"My mother carves these. Silly trinkets. I tell her no one will want them, but she keeps making them. She even makes the other goddesses . . ." The female stopped, wavering as if she realized what she had admitted. Fear flashed through her features as she looked up at Deya properly for the first time.

Deya's heart panged when she realized this was what Praiton had wrought. Banning the other goddesses, persecuting those who still believed, still worshipped. They had ruined these people without even trying.

"May I see them?" she whispered. The female hesitated. She knew that the mere acknowledgment of any of the five other goddesses was punishable by imprisonment, and yet Deya wanted to see them. She wanted to look upon these magical beings that were still responsible for all the realm's magic, no matter how much Praiton did not want to admit it.

The female sank behind the counter and pulled out a bundle of figurines. Deya reached for them, standing them upright.

She could vaguely distinguish one from the other purely by the element each was holding. The Celestial Goddess, Astrea, a star in her palm, was slim and beautiful, a slinky barely-there gown covering her; Eula, the Sea Goddess, holding a lantern, waves beneath her feet; the Ember Goddess, Calida with her baby dragon curled around her shoulders, the details in the wood surprisingly clean and impressive; the Frost Goddess, Flykra, snowflakes in her hair and cradled in her arms. And then, the Harvest Goddess, Arista.

She was as Deya remembered. Long hair falling over a plain flowing tunic, and in her arms, she held a basket of fruits and vegetables. Although the carving was unrefined and a little rudimentary, Deya found herself lingering on the goddess's face, her finger carefully tracing the lines, the tips of her delicately carved ears.

Reaching up, she began to unfasten the silver broach from her cloak, before holding it out to the female.

"For Arista," she said quietly.

The female looked surprised, but then a small smile appeared on her face. "From Ganiea, are you?"

"Distantly," Deya said. "I have never been. But I had a figure like this. As a child. I always thought she was pretty."

The female nodded. "Very pretty." She took the broach and handed Arista to her. "Mother will be pleased," she remarked.

Deya smiled. "Please tell her that her work is beautiful."

The female nodded and bowed her head to her. Clutching Arista to her chest, Deya moved on from the female's booth, only to catch sight of Caelum swiping a loaf of bread from a small stall. Right in the line of view of a guard.

Deya's heart sank as the guard cried out, and Caelum, caught unawares, began to sprint from the market. The guards took off after him, tearing into the small town. Deya, panicking, decided to follow suit. With one last look at the female—who had turned her attention elsewhere—she took off after Caelum.

CHAPTER
12

Caelum ran like hell. How had he been so stupid? How had he missed that guard? Most likely, it was because the guard didn't look anything remotely like a real soldier. In shabby, worn leather armor, he had looked more like a poor farmer than anything. But, either way, as Caelum sprinted out of the market and plunged into the town itself, he blamed Deya. The stupid girl was off buying silly trinkets while he was attempting to steal to ensure their survival.

He gritted his teeth and cut sharply between huts, causing the guard to lose track of him. They began calling out to the others, asking for help. Caelum, cursing under his breath, took off back towards the harbor. Maybe Rayner and the obnoxious Manielian had found a boat already. Maybe they could—

He turned down an alley and collided with something small and light. With a cry, the female went flying backwards, bringing him down with her in a shower of feathers. Wild geese and ducks from the farm beside them squawked and honked in protest.

"What the—" Caelum cried.

Deya spat out a feather, but there were still about a dozen of them stuck in her hair.

"What happened—" she began, but Caelum didn't let her finish.

He seized Deya around the waist. Pulling her against him, she let out a surprised squeak of terror, which Caelum ignored as he took a deep breath. His magic had barely had a chance to return in strength after last night. But he had no other choice. He drew the shards of his Celestial Magic from deep within him, then, with a grunt, he propelled them into the air.

They crashed onto the roof of a building. Deya let out a small cry of pain, but Caelum wrapped a hand around her mouth. Dragging her into him, he threw their bodies behind the chimney of the thatched roof.

"They will not look up if you don't give them a reason to," he hissed in her ear. Her terrified gray eyes looked up at him from around his hand. Caelum didn't know what it was about this female that kept causing him to have to carry her, hold her, or otherwise be very, very close to her. It wasn't like it was *entirely* unpleasant. Her thick, chestnut hair tickled his face, smelling strongly of lavender and pine. The only worry Caelum had was that she would bite his hand, which was still pressed into her warm, soft mouth.

Deya growled behind his palm, and he shushed her and held her mouth tighter.

Caelum watched from the roof as the guards met, looking around confusedly. They conversed for a second, all of them looking around, perturbed, before they headed off.

He released Deya, who spat out a mouthful of hair and glared at him spitefully.

"Was that really necessary?" she snapped.

Caelum glared at her. "I'm sorry, did you want to go back to Ironbalt over a few tins of fruit and fish?" He released her waist—which, he realized belatedly, he was still holding onto—and shoved her away from him. Deya looked affronted at the shove but didn't seem too upset to no longer be touching him.

"Can we get down?" Deya asked hesitantly, peering over the edge of the thatched roof into the alley below.

Caelum looked down with her. The guards had cleared out, but he wasn't sure how far they'd gone.

"Scared of heights, are we?" he sneered at her.

"No," Deya retorted, but it didn't sound too convincing. Caelum snorted and she flushed. "I'm . . . not used to it, is all."

Caelum leaned back against the chimney, his heart still pounding from the adrenaline, making it difficult for him to steady his breathing. "Just give it a minute," he told her. "Let them get a head start somewhere else first."

Deya nodded, but he didn't miss how her fingers dug into the thatched roof as she stared down. They couldn't be more than a few feet above the ground—the huts in this area were low and dilapidated—but still, Deya's petrified face didn't turn away from the edge.

Caelum shifted awkwardly, his hip brushing against hers. He hadn't been around people, hadn't so much as held a simple, pleasant conversation, in over fifty years. Since he had been in Ironbalt, he had kept to himself—besides the occasional fights that landed him on that middle column at the whipping posts, that is. All who interacted with him simply thought he was a captured Bridanian, imprisoned for refusing to help Praiton infiltrate the heavily insulated region.

Already, his Celestial Magic had begun to elicit questions from his traveling companions. And after last night, he felt like the Praitonian girl now knew too much. The encounter with Praiton had shaken him, had rattled all his common sense. Now that the girl was being hunted, her magic something that they coveted, it filled him with no short amount of dread.

What was more, he was angry at himself for taking pity on her afterward. The tears in her eyes when she had to denounce Praiton to him, the betrayal on her face . . . He wondered briefly how much all of this must be crushing her inside. And then he wondered why on earth he even cared.

Telling her the tiniest, innocuous detail about his mother—something that still caused a dull ache in his chest—made him want to kick himself. But after seeing her last night . . . covered in blood, wounded, holding the sword like an absolute child, but still throwing herself thoughtlessly between him and that soldier he had failed to notice . . .

Saving him.

As angry as he had been with the stupid girl for running into the forest at night, he couldn't help but respect her effort, how she had held her own. She had faced death purely to get away from him. A fact he had not missed.

"Well, I guess we can say our cover was blown," Caelum said bitterly, mostly trying to distract her from the way she had started trembling while looking down from the roof.

"Did you at least get enough supplies?" she asked shakily.

Caelum nodded. "Enough to get by, at least. It depends on how powerful the Sea Fae is. If he can push us on a strong enough tide, we can get to Elbania much quicker."

Deya nodded. If she was confused or even found it odd that she and Caelum were having what could almost be construed as a pleasant conversation, she didn't let on. He was thankful.

"How long do you think the trip will be?" she asked softly.

"Not sure. I'm assuming several days."

Deya nodded again but said nothing more. Caelum watched her out of the corner of his eye, taking in how her long, delicate fingers twisted the end of her braid, how her small frame shook imperceptibly against him, and he wondered how it was so easy to be angry at something so helpless.

He had felt a switch flip inside him as he watched Deya toss and turn last night. Between that, and her flippant mention of how Praiton had brought back a Nodarian spice after they had finished burning his kingdom to the ground had made him see bright, violent red.

This anger had only grown when she had woken up screaming from a nightmare, one that felt eerily familiar to him. Knowing that he had been exceptionally cruel to her for no other reason beyond seeing himself in her. How his own nightmares had sent him jolting awake, screaming the same way. How he was angry that someone from Praiton had any right to suffer the same way he had.

Eventually, Caelum felt sorry enough for her that he decided they had waited long enough. He stood, still hunched over to stay out of sight and offered his hand.

"We don't have much time until the hour is up, and we need to meet the others."

Deya looked surprised at his hand. He couldn't help but feel a little ashamed of how much of an ass he must have been lately for her to look this taken aback at his help. His father had always taught him to look out for females—especially his younger sisters. He knew he would be furious at him for how he had been acting. Even if the Manielian female pissed him off to no end.

Hesitantly, Deya took his hand. With an almost apologetic nod to her, he wrapped his arm securely around her waist again. And then they jumped off the roof.

The walk back to the harbor was terrifying. Deya walked so close to Caelum that their sides kept brushing together. She figured with how much time she'd already spent pressed up against the Nodarian that this shouldn't matter anymore. However, Caelum bristled like a cat held over water every time she came in contact with him. He had handled her as roughly as the guards had at Ironbalt, and yet, it was . . . different.

Every time they touched, it was like being shocked by a bolt of lightning. She briefly wondered if it was his sheer hostility that caused these unpleasant little jolts. In fact, this wasn't the only curious side effect about being around Caelum.

Deya tended to be mild-mannered and slow to anger. She often suspected others found her to be a bit of a pushover. And yet, Caelum seemed to bring out all the rancor and fire inside her. She couldn't help going head-to-head with him, challenging him every snap for bite. No matter how much the male riled her, she hated to admit that being around him was exhilarating.

They walked at a brisk pace through Latchside towards the harbor. Each time a person passed, Caelum would stiffen, his hand clenched tightly on the hilt of his sword beneath his cloak. Deya was inclined to grasp the dagger hanging from her hip, not confident enough in swords to reach for hers.

The harbor came into view, the grayish wood of the docks the most welcoming sight she had seen all day. From a distance, she could see the glint of bright red hair at the end of the piers. Val stood out in stark contrast from the rest of the gray and gloom around her. She and the cloaked figure that Deya knew to be Rayner were loitering around a small dinghy, barely bigger than a rowboat. This stood out to Caelum, too, because he cursed under his breath and quickened his pace. His legs were much longer than Deya's, who was already struggling to keep pace with his long strides.

"Could you slow down—" Deya began, but her voice died in her throat when she caught sight of a group of guards moving towards them out of the corner of her eye. These were not the same guards that had chased Caelum out of the market bazaar, but different ones—*familiar* ones.

Reaching out, she seized Caelum's arm, pulling him back sharply.

"*What?*" Caelum spat, but Deya held out a shaky finger, pointing in the direction of the group of soldiers coming from the market, a familiar green and white crest on their breastplates.

Caelum's face went as white as his hair. "Praiton," he breathed. He grabbed Deya's hand and began pulling her along, her legs barely keeping up.

They began to walk briskly, keeping their heads down, hoping against hope that the soldiers wouldn't notice them. Deya could see them scanning the crowds, craning their necks, attempting to locate something—anything suspicious. But Caelum and Deya were the only hooded figures in the harbor, making them easy to spot.

No sooner did they break out of the crowd and reach the long stretch of wooden dock that would take them to the southernmost port of the harbor, than the soldiers noticed them. There was a scuffle, a shout rang out, and soldiers, pointing and shouting, made right for them.

"Go!" Caelum cried, and then they were running through the harbor towards Val and Rayner, Deya's hand clenched tight in Caelum's.

The bronze armored guards began to run, too, weaving in and out of the fisherman's carts and barrels, shoving innocent meandering fae out of their way. Deya and Caelum were more fortunate. It was a straight shot down the harbor's wooden dock towards Val and Rayner, who both appeared to catch on to what was going on. They began to unwind the small boat from the dock, Rayner jumping into the hull and helping Val in.

Caelum began to pick up the pace. Soldiers shouted behind them, commanding them to stop. And then the arrows came. They flew through the air, narrowly missing Deya by an inch—whizzing past her ear, taking some strands of hair with it. Deya yelped, but Caelum tightened his grip on her hand, hauling her down the docks toward the tiny dinghy. Another arrow sailed by, nearly hitting Caelum this time. He cursed loudly, losing his footing as he dodged it, causing Deya to stumble in turn.

"Come on! Come *on*!" Val was yelling, waving frantically from the boat, which Rayner had already started pushing out to sea.

From behind them, Deya could hear a half dozen arrows being loosed at once. It happened so fast that she could barely process it. One second, her hand was securely in Caelum's, the next, he was shoving her in the back and a strange, tingling sensation spread from where his palm connected with her spine. And then, Deya was airborne, flying through the sky with the force of Caelum's push and his Celestial Magic, and landing, hard, right in Val's waiting arms.

It took a second for the shock of being catapulted through the air to wear off before she was scrambling to the edge of the boat. Deya watched in horror as Caelum sprinted for the edge of the dock, arrows flying all around him.

"Caelum!" Deya yelled. Caelum had his sword drawn, but he didn't seem capable of using it as he ducked arrows left and right. "*Jump!*" Deya screamed at him. "*Jump, Caelum!*"

With a roar, Caelum threw his arms down, just like he had to the soldiers the night before. He flew into the air, his legs flying underneath him. It dawned on Deya a second after he had launched himself that Caelum could only *suspend* gravity. He could not physically *move* things.

He managed to leap into the air, making it off the dock and over the water, before coming to a stop, suspended between the pier and the boat. The look of panic on his face was evident, his hesitation one moment too long. An arrow whizzed through the air, and this time, its aim was true. The arrow collided with Caelum's shoulder, throwing him right from the sky and straight into the ocean below.

Val and Rayner yelled, scrambling to the edge of the boat with Deya to see where he had disappeared to, but Deya didn't stop to think. Stripping off her cloak, she plunged headfirst into the icy sea.

The freezing water was an immediate shock to her system. Sound cut off as she descended, the chaos from above distant, almost belonging to another world. Her eyes adjusted to the darkness, her faerivaine necklace floating up around her neck. Several feet in front of her, she could see dark red tendrils of blood swirling through the murky waters.

Deya kicked towards them, swimming as fast as her legs could carry her, the water turning darker and darker with the color of blood. There, floating in the depths, white hair swirling all around him, was Caelum, unconscious, an arrow protruding from his shoulder and dark swirls of blood unwinding from the wound like spiraling ribbons.

She struck out towards him, fear gripping her stomach. The injury looked superficial. The healer in her knew that it had not struck anything major, that it was a flesh wound. But the amount of blood undulating from him filled her with no small amount of panic.

Seizing Caelum around the middle, Deya kicked and fought with all her might towards the surface. As she ascended, Caelum's weight slowing her down, the water began to clear. Weak sunlight shone down, its dim rays refracting against the water, making her feel like she was trapped in a mirrored box of light.

She could hear shouting and yelling, could see the bottom of the small boat Val and Rayner were in, could almost reach it . . . before it started moving rapidly away from her.

Frantic, Deya kicked after it as fast as she could, dragging Caelum along with her. But he was too heavy, and she was too slow. She couldn't understand why her companions were leaving them there. Had they decided to abandon them? To sacrifice them to save themselves?

Arrows struck the water, raining down upon the sea like falling stars. They sluiced through the surface before floating harmlessly, but, rather belatedly, Deya realized what was happening. And how dire the situation was.

Grunting in pain, she readjusted her hold on Caelum's limp form. Already, her lungs were beginning to tighten, the effort of holding her breath and keeping them afloat was weighing on her almost as much as his body. She had to surface soon, she knew this, but feared the minute she did an arrow would slice through her skull.

Deya swam at an angle, ascending as fast as she could while still staying beneath the surface. The boat was getting further away from her, a jet of bubbles propelling it out of her reach. She knew it had to be Rayner's magic, pushing the boat away from the Praiton soldiers.

Her head began to spin, her lungs screaming out in agony. She couldn't put it off any longer. Kicking furiously, Deya closed her eyes, and then her head broke the surface.

Immediately, an arrow flew by, landing several inches away from her.

"*Deya!*" Val screamed. The boat was getting further away from them, attempting to outrun the arrows while not leaving them behind. Val was standing at the bow of the ship, flaming sword in hand, fielding any arrows that came their way. Already, Deya could see arrows protruding from the wooden helm of the small dinghy.

Deya heaved Caelum's head above water so he could breathe. They were only above water for a few seconds before, with a yelp, Deya was forced to plunge back down to avoid another projectile.

"*Deya! Swim!*" Val's voice was drifting towards her. Breaking the surface of the water again, gasping and spluttering, Deya looked at the red-haired Manielian, whose eyes were wide and frightened, illuminated by the flaming sword in her hand. And then, towards the Sea Fae beside her. His one hand was raised, pointed toward the water. Their eyes met.

"*RAYNER!*" Deya yelled. She wasn't sure what she was expecting, whether she was asking for help or knew exactly what needed to be done, but either way, the Sea Fae acted.

Reaching towards Deya, he let out a roar, and the water around her began to bubble and churn. Arrows were still cascading around them, one even nicking her in the shoulder as it fell. Then, Deya and Caelum jetted through the water. Deya shrieked in surprise, barely able to cling to Caelum's still unconscious form as they skipped like a stone towards the dinghy. Then with a grunt, Rayner pulled his fist back, and Deya and Caelum shot into the air, thrust upward by a jet of water.

They landed with a crash in the small wooden boat. It bucked with the force of their weight, nearly ejecting Val and Rayner from it. Deya smashed into the wooden seat, her forehead banging against it. Swearing, head spinning, blood dripping into her eyes, she yelled, "Rayner, *go!*"

Rayner threw both hands out in front of him, directing them both at the rear of the boat. The water began to churn and bubble viciously, the same way it had under Deya and Caelum, and, with the force of a cannon firing, the small dinghy shot forward, and then they were off in a shower of arrows.

CHAPTER
13

"Are you okay?" Val cried. She scrambled from the bow of the boat, the flame that had encased her sword extinguishing as she knelt in front of Deya and Caelum. The force of their landing into the boat had roused Caelum into consciousness. He was coughing and sputtering, gagging out large quantities of water.

Spitting out her own mouthful of seawater, Deya gasped, "F-fine. I'm fine." But then she turned to Caelum. He was panting, trying to steady his breathing. Making to sit up, he winced, his hand going up to feel the arrow still protruding from his shoulder.

"Let me," Deya said. Caelum looked up at her. His eyes registered her soaking wet clothes and hair, how she had wet blood on her brand-new tunic and breeches.

"You went in after me," he rasped. He sounded stunned.

Deya reached for the arrow's tail and snapped it, causing him to flinch again in pain. "Consider us even now," Deya said. His eyes flashed, his scowl coming back in full force, but it froze in place as Deya handed him the wooden end of the arrow.

"You may want to bite down on this," she said. Caelum looked at her hand wrapped around the middle of the arrow. It had not been a clean entry and exit. The arrowhead was still deeply embedded in his shoulder. Thankfully, it had seemed to stop the bleeding . . . for now.

"Fuck," Caelum muttered, and he obediently put the wooden stick in his mouth and bit down. With a swift, well-practiced hand, Deya pulled with all her might. Caelum let out a roar of pain and the arrow came free, the tip covered in blood. Deya tossed the tip aside and let out a long-held breath.

Val collapsed down onto the wooden bench, her sword clattering to the floor. "Well," she said, her breathing still unsteady. "That could've gone smoother."

With a groan, Caelum reached for something beneath his now soaked and dripping cloak. Removing a heavy satchel that he definitely did not have before; he threw it on the bench next to Val.

"I stole a healing pack," he said to Deya, jerking his head towards the bag. His eyes were closed in pain, his hand now soaked with blood as he pressed down on the open wound.

Surprised, Deya reached for the satchel and began to root through it. Salted fish, dried fruit, several loaves of bread, a few apples—all surprisingly unharmed thanks to the sheepskin bag Caelum had shoved them in—before she extracted a small burlap sack. From within it, she could smell herbs like chamomile, eucalyptus, and myrrh. Inside, she was relieved to see bandages, as well as a variety of premade ointments and salves.

Caelum let out another hiss of pain as Deya laid him down against the hull of the boat.

"Is he okay?" Rayner asked from the head of the ship. He was breathing heavily too, no doubt exerting a significant amount of energy keeping the boat moving at this fast of a pace.

"He'll be fine," Deya said, reaching towards the bottom of Caelum's tunic, pulling it loose from where it was tucked into his breeches.

Caelum jerked away from her, his violet eyes snapping open to stare at her as if she'd lost her mind.

"I have to get to the wound to apply bandages, don't get too excited," Deya snapped.

She was impressed that he was able to imbue that much hatred into his glare even when he was, no doubt, in an excruciating amount of pain.

Not even bothering to ask his permission, Deya pulled the damp, black tunic over his head and zeroed in on the open hole in his shoulder. She had to focus or else she knew she would be too easily distracted by the thin black lines of the tattoos on his body.

On closer inspection, it was hard not to marvel at the letters that looked to be nothing more than sharp lines spread from his chest and shoulders, up his neck. As she bound his injury with bandages, what she found herself most distracted by were the scars. They were closer to her than the night Caelum had shouted at her, and this time, she was able to see them. Some were thin, nothing more than hairline blemishes, others raised and brutal looking, as though he must have bled for hours before his fae body healed itself.

This was the problem with fae. They healed fast, often clotting within minutes. A healer was often unnecessary for smaller injuries. However, if a fae had been so injured that their body couldn't heal itself, that was when they called upon a healer.

In Caelum's case, his wound was still bleeding as she applied a poultice to it, then wrapped it firmly with the bandages. However, a blossom of blood bloomed through the dressings, causing Deya to swear under her breath.

"I don't know why you're not clotting yet," she whispered to herself. Val, who was watching all of this with some manner of fascination, looked around the boat, her amber eyes coming to rest on the arrowhead that Deya had discarded. Picking it up between calloused fingers, she wiped off some of Caelum's blood, then sniffed. She instantly recoiled.

"Iron infused with faerivaine," she said, chucking the bloody arrow at Caelum, who caught it with a grimace and a dirty look towards Val. "It explains why he plummeted out of the sky like a fat, flightless hen when he got hit." Caelum made to lunge at Val but was stopped partially by Deya and partially by the obvious pain from the still bleeding wound in his shoulder.

"Knock it off, both of you," Deya admonished. Her hand was still pressed over the wound in her attempt to help it clot. She felt a surge of anger and despair when she unconsciously looked for her Healing Magic and came up empty.

For a brief, horrible moment, Deya wanted to cry and scream over such a large part of her being stripped away. Her fingers curled on Caelum's skin. She felt his violet irises shift towards her, searching her.

Their gazes met. Was it her imagination, or did Caelum show a glimmer of recognition of what she was feeling?

Clearing her throat, she looked away. "You won't begin to heal fully until the faerivaine is out of your system," she said.

She released him as if he had burned her, and sat back against the side of the boat, staring out at the large, fathomless expanse of water around them.

For a second, all four of them sat in silence—even Rayner's magic had quieted down, allowing the boat to drift along at a gentler, yet still brisk pace.

"I haven't seen the ocean in so long," Val breathed. She was still sitting on the bench, elbows on her knees, her face cradled in her palms. She stared out into the sea, towards the setting sun—which was brilliant and vivid now that they were far from the continent, as though paddling towards the molten red center of it. "I had three friends in my unit in the Legion . . . Sisters to me. We used to sit on the coast of Elbania on nights like these and watch the ocean."

She smiled, her gaze distant. "I feel like I was in that place for centuries," she whispered. "Only seeing mines and stone, never knowing when my body would give up or my life would be taken on a whim. Never knowing when I would see something like this again. Not knowing when I'd see *them* again."

Their eyes followed the setting sun. Even Caelum was silent, contemplative.

"When I was captured," Rayner piped up from his place at the head of the boat, "they ripped me right out of the water. It was not long after they overthrew Laenimore, when they decided to exterminate the nymph race. My mother was a nymph who lived below Pentworth Harbor in their underwater city of Lyledell. Praiton came and set fire to the water. I was the only Sea Fae there capable of going to land to fight, to push them back. They tried to kill me. They almost did . . . but then they saw I was a halfling. And instead of killing me, they captured me."

Rayner's blue gray hands tightened on the wooden edge of the ship, his eyes lost in the water beneath them, reflecting the reds and oranges now shining down on them from the sun. It was then that Deya spotted the discoloration on his hands, something she had not noticed until then. They spread from the tips of his fingers all the way into the sleeves of his dark blue tunic, which were now rolled up. His blue-gray skin was mottled with dark gray scars, as if they had come from intense burns.

"I have not seen the water since," he murmured.

After that, none of them spoke anymore, instead choosing to drift along on the surface of the water and watch the sun set over them.

The brightness of the full moon was keeping Caelum awake. He tried to block it out, but every time he closed his eyes, he could still see the way the moon looked on his last night in Nodaria. How the smell of fire trickled down the hallway of Atlas Keep like a shadow monster.

The image of his eldest brother, Aelius, rushing him and his brothers and sisters into the servants' quarters while the sounds of Praiton soldiers thundered through the Keep . . . It all still echoed in his mind. A recurring nightmare that never ended.

Caelum rolled over, attempting to shift in the tiny rowboat, which was rocking gently over the waves of the ocean below. Planks of wood dug into his side as he tried to shield his eyes from the bright glow of the blasted orb above him. But with each flicker of light, he could see his brother, sword in hand, his head of wavy, midnight-black hair illuminated in the light from the glowing stars built into the Keep's immense ceiling. They twinkled like genuine starlight, but they almost flashed that night, as if they were attempting to warn them of impending danger.

"I need you to protect them," Aelius had whispered to Caelum. *"You and Aten are the eldest. Look out for the others. I know you can do it."*

How many times had he relived this moment? How many times did he recount the look on his brother's face as he pushed him and his siblings to safety? How many times had he hated himself for letting him, even all these years later?

He could still feel every bone in his body screaming to not leave his brother behind, to stand and fight with him, yet he had ignored it. Instead, he'd obeyed and left his brother in that throne room. Leaving Aelius to face the army alone.

Caelum's eyes opened and moonlight flooded his vision again. He was staring up at the inky black sky, stars twinkling overhead. For a second, he thought he was back at Atlas Keep. The throne room had been designed to resemble a planetarium—large gold replicas of all the planets and moons had hung suspended in the air, and real, blazing stars shone from the ceiling.

It took him a second to remember where he was, to take in the small wooden boat that was drifting upon a natural wave. To see the Manielian, Rayner, and Deya all asleep in the boat around him. Deya had insisted Rayner take a break from pushing the ship along, trying to stop him from burning out and stranding them at sea.

Caelum looked back up at the sky, the fear he had felt in that memory still coursing through him, the pain in his chest having nothing to do with the wound in his shoulder. He had been so scared then. And because of his fear and his weakness . . .

He blinked and looked away from the sky only to find a set of gray eyes beside him, staring back. He started, unable to hide his surprise at finding her looking back at him.

"You don't sleep," Deya said softly, her voice barely a whisper to avoid waking the others.

Caelum looked away, back towards the sky. "My shoulder is throbbing," he lied.

Deya didn't look away from him, though. "You didn't sleep even before you got shot."

For once, Caelum could not think of anything biting or scathing to say in return. He didn't understand this girl at all. Had she been watching him? Had she noticed how he took all nighttime watches? Did she notice he had dismissed her, Rayner, and Val from their shifts multiple times over the last couple of days?

"I sleep just fine."

Deya nodded and looked away, following his gaze up towards the sky. The stars here were so bright, so clear. He couldn't remember the last time he had stared up at them like this. He must have been very young still.

"Were you born and raised in Nodaria?" Deya asked, her eyes still on the sky.

Caelum hesitated, but then nodded. He did not trust this girl, yet something in him always felt inclined to answer her.

"Does that mean you know how to read the stars?" she asked.

"Not as well as some," he replied. "I was never much of a seer. But we do learn the basics as children."

Deya lifted a hand and pointed towards a cluster of stars, her delicate fingers illuminated in silver by the glowing orb overhead. "Do you know what those are?"

"Centaurus," Caelum responded automatically. It was amazing to him how much the lessons of the old star seers had stuck with him. He had *hated* stargazing. Was absolutely abysmal at it. Yet, he and his siblings had sat in the lessons at the observatory in the Keep, had constellations and planets and their various brightnesses and cycles hammered into them until Caelum could draw a star chart with his eyes closed.

"Those three are planets," he said, using his good arm to point towards several of the brightest specks in the sky. "Their colors and brightness can predict good fortune for those born under it."

"Is it true Nodarians can garner full prophecies from the stars?" she asked.

Caelum shifted, the movement causing a dull throb to flare in his left arm again. But his discomfort wasn't from the arrow wound. It was from the debilitating, burning pain that he could still feel when he had received the tattoos that now partially covered his body.

"Yes," he answered. "Prophecies are made frequently all over Nodaria by the star seers, always given in our ancient tongue that few speak. And when they are made, they appear on the subject's skin." He peeled back the cloak he had covering his bare torso. He hadn't bothered to put his tunic back on, knowing it would hurt like all hells to put it on now. Deya's eyes moved from the stars to his skin, the blue-gray orbs sweeping up him, lingering. It made his hair stand on end.

"That's a prophecy," she whispered, eyes wide.

"Yes."

"Do you know—"

"No," he said quickly. "I do not know what it says."

Already he was regretting telling her this, but it was not a secret. The Nodarian Prophecies were a well-known fact. Many Nodarians were covered in them, making it a common sight for most.

"I've never seen them before," Deya said softly, her eyes still locked on his skin. "Nobody back home in Praiton has—" She fell silent, darting a nervous glance up at Caelum, as if she just realized what she had said.

The familiar flicker of anger burned his insides again at the mention of her homeland. Gritting his teeth, he rolled onto his side, ending the conversation. "I'm tired," he snapped, and then feigned sleep until he was sure she had let it go.

But there was now anger and panic bubbling within him. The girl did not know of Nodarian Prophecies because she had never left Praiton. He had sat and listened to Val and Rayner share their pasts, the stories of their captures, their eyes haunted and pained. They had lost everything to Praiton, just as he had. The girl, however, had never known . . . could not understand. She did not know of their cultures or their people, had lived in ignorant bliss of the war that their people had waged in order to stay free from her lecherous kingdom.

She did not know of the pain. She did not know of the ultimate cost. And that filled Caelum with such an inexplicable rage and hatred that he couldn't sleep for the rest of the night.

Deya managed to fall asleep for a few hours and woke only when the faintest rays of dawn were beginning to appear, as though it had crawled from under the surface of the water on which their boat floated.

Rayner was already up, climbing back to the bow of the ship, a loaf of bread from Caelum's pack in hand.

"Morning," he said, smiling down at her.

Deya's neck ached, and her muscles felt stiff and tender. She supposed sleeping upright with four others in a boat not meant to fit more than two had its consequences.

"How are you feeling?" Deya asked him, struggling to rise.

"Surprisingly rested," he replied.

Deya realized that she had fallen asleep side by side with Caelum, her head resting on his arm. He was still asleep and had not noticed it or she feared he would throw the boat across the water out of pure spite.

After their conversation last night, his eyes had filled with such an intense anger that it had taken her aback. She thought they were having a cordial—maybe even pleasant—conversation. For once, he spoke to her as though she were a living thing, and not something that disgusted him. She had liked hearing about Nodaria, had wanted to know more about Oswallt's favorite place. And then the iron shutters had come back down around him, and he shut her out again.

"How far do you think we have left until we get to Elbania?" she asked Rayner. Val gave a tiny snore across from her, her wild red hair covering her face, making both Rayner and Deya share a secret smirk with each other.

Rayner looked contemplatively across the horizon, craning his neck in every direction before shrugging. "I'd say about maybe half a day. It's surprisingly a short journey across the Gray Gap."

"The Gray Gap?"

"The channel separating the main continent of Krigor and the Exile Continents, as they're so lovingly called," Rayner said.

Deya reached for Caelum's pack, laying open underneath one of the wooden benches. She sorted through it and removed an apple.

"Have you been to Elbania before?" she asked Rayner. She took a chunk of the apple but found she couldn't really taste it. Chewing slowly, she assessed the texture of the fruit in her mouth, the feel of the juice sweeping over her tongue, but tasted nothing of the sweetness she knew it should have.

Rayner shrugged, his hands twirling above the water, causing a gentle jet-stream of bubbles to erupt, pushing the boat along again at a much brisker pace.

"Once or twice. I joined the rebellion when we caught wind that Praiton had turned its sights on Laenimore after it had felled Ganiea and absorbed Maniel. There were a lot of us who joined at that time, who went out to fight in small battles across Krigor. But in the end, we weren't enough to stop them from taking Laenimore," he said, his voice heavy with sadness.

Deya felt the same grief mixed with a bit of shame. The shame of ever being part of the staff that healed the soldiers who had destroyed these kingdoms for their own gain. But still, the apprehension she felt for going to the Pillar Legion, of *joining* them . . .

Promise me you will warn them. Praiton cannot get what they seek. Promise me that you'll tell them.

The memory of Os's final request made her shift and squirm, triggering a familiar nervous flutter in her chest. Rayner was watching her carefully, his electric blue eyes taking her in. Deya had wondered what the Sea Fae had thought of her, if he mistrusted her like Caelum or had forgiven and accepted her like Val seemed to. He had always stayed neutral and kind and totally inscrutable.

"You're nervous," Rayner said softly.

Deya looked up at him in surprise. "What?"

"You're nervous. About going to the Legion. About joining us." He gave her a small, comforting smile, as though he could sense all of this churning inside of her. "It's alright. It's understandable. You can't unlearn all you have been taught in a few days."

Deya felt herself flush and looked down at her feet.

"I . . ." she began, but nothing felt genuine enough. Nothing seemed right to say. "I don't know how I feel," she admitted. "It's been . . . overwhelming. Learning what my kingdom . . . what *Praiton* has done." Her chin wobbled, but she forced herself to remain calm. She *needed* Rayner to know, needed someone to understand. He was listening to her, his face calm.

"If I had known the extent . . . the truth," she whispered. "I think I would have fought back a long time ago."

"But now?" Rayner asked.

Deya shook her head. "Now I am torn," she admitted. "Torn about wanting to fight back. Fight for you and Val, and—" She stopped short of saying Caelum's name, before biting her tongue.

"I am not a fighter," she said, smiling at him grimly. "But I would have stood against it. I *know* I would've. But the obedience that has been drilled into me stops me every time. I feel sick at the thought of betraying them, even though I *know* they have betrayed *me*. So why do I still feel any shred of loyalty?"

Rayner did not react. She worried whether she had said too much. But then, he spoke. "You were brainwashed your whole life," he said. "Forced to believe their dogma and their lies, punished when you questioned or disagreed. It is not loyalty you feel, Deya. It is fear."

She didn't speak for a moment, but as she and Rayner looked at each other, something profound seemed to pass between them. A moment of understanding. A moment of forgiveness.

A heavy lump formed in her throat, and after a long pause, she took a breath.

"Are you very old, Rayner?" she asked, eager to change topics.

Rayner burst out laughing, the tension breaking like cheap glass. "Old enough," he said, chuckling. "But not as old as Val, I assure you. I'm taking that you're very young?"

Deya nodded. "I was born into this regime," she said. "I didn't know the world before Praiton began to take over."

Rayner sighed; sadness evident in the sound. "That's a shame," he said. "The world was beautiful then. Rich with all the kingdom's different cultures and magic. We were able to move freely between kingdoms, welcome as guests anywhere. Now, everyone is suspicious. We have all been conquered now, besides Bridah, and what used to make each kingdom special and unique is much . . . less," he finished, his voice heavy.

Val stirred across from Deya, and she rose, looking groggy and bad tempered, a faint wood-textured imprint on her golden cheek.

"What are you two talking about?" she mumbled, rubbing her eyes.

"Krigor before Praiton," Rayner said, leaning back against the bow of the ship, magic still being concentrated towards the water. "Deya is too young to know."

Val grumbled something, clearly not much for morning conversation. Deya looked towards the sunrise, trying to see if she could still see the continent they had just left, when she noticed Caelum's eyes were open. He wasn't looking at any of them, had not so much as made a noise. How long had he been listening? Did he hear the whole conversation between her and Rayner?

"Only half a day left, I reckon." Rayner, who also realized Caelum was awake, nodded towards him. "How's the shoulder?"

Caelum sat up, pulling his cloak back to check on the bandages underneath. Deya's handiwork was tight, professional, and neat. Only the smallest blossom of dried blood blemished the white bandages. He looked at Deya.

"Have I healed, then?"

Deya reached towards him, feeling more nervous than usual. Was it her, or was the coldness radiating from him in waves today? She supposed that was better than full out hostility, but she didn't like the frostiness in those purple eyes, how they appraised her as she peeled back the bandages to look at the wound underneath.

It had healed a good deal, but was still open, pus oozing in places as his body secreted the faerivaine. Still, it looked several days older now.

"Getting there," she informed him, wrapping it back around him tightly. She tried to do this while touching him as little as possible. Childishly, she felt that the chilliness coming from him would give her frostbite. "You probably have to give it one more day for the faerivaine to fully leave your system."

Caelum didn't respond. He reached around her and seized the food satchel and his discarded tunic. He threw the tunic over his head with only a slight wince, rooted through the satchel, grabbed an apple, and began to eat it without so much as a glance at any of them.

Deya, Val, and Rayner all exchanged bemused looks. Val cleared her throat and turned to Rayner, as if determined to break the tension.

"So only half a day?" Val asked, ignoring the glowering male next to Deya.

Rayner nodded. "Give or take. Less if I push it."

"Please do," Val moaned. "I haven't been back to Elbania since I was captured, and I think the suspense is nearly killing me."

"Did you spend much time in Elbania before this?" Deya asked.

"I lived there," Val said, sighing. "The minute I abandoned Maniel, I left for the Exile Continents. They house more than just rebels. Most who are displeased or displaced by the war all try to flee to Elbania or Havia across the Gray Gap."

"I'm amazed Praiton hasn't tried to stop them," Deya admitted. "Why haven't they put guards to patrol the Gray Gap? Stop potential rebel allies from joining?"

"Don't go giving them ideas," Caelum sneered. His words were still cold at best, acidic at worse.

Val shrugged, like she couldn't help but agree with Caelum—a rare thing. "I'm not sure why they haven't," she said. "We've often wondered that, but it's not like they don't do enough policing of the main borders. Places like Zulon and Dritus—the other Free Countries that border the Gray Gap—have all taken Praiton's position. They allow Praitonian guards to police their borders and harbors, to stop any who tries to flee. Aunecia is one of the few places that aren't heavily guarded, since the prison is what's being watched."

"They may change that now." Rayner smirked. "Having *four* flee Ironbalt will surely change policy. Especially since we actually made it to the Gray Gap."

Val nodded in earnest. Deya chewed quietly on her apple. It tasted like sand in her mouth. Ever since they had escaped, since she had lost Os, she hadn't been hungry. She ate when she could no longer ignore the hunger inside of her, but it was a feeling that was faint and went away quickly. Chewing slowly, she lowered the apple.

They continued in relative silence, Val yawning, Caelum glowering, and Rayner singing a small tune under his breath in what sounded like Laevish, Laenimore's ancient tongue. It was a beautiful song, its melody twisting and curling around Deya's ears, its foreign words sounding like a magic spell.

When Rayner fell silent, she would ask him to sing more, something which appeared to please him to no end. She expected Caelum to object, to argue and snap a little more, but he didn't. He remained silent and cold, steadfastly staring across the water, not looking at them and not saying a damned word.

They ate together in the center of the small boat—the only time Rayner allowed himself to take a break. Sharing a tin of dried fruit and salted fish, Val and Rayner chatted, wondering aloud who would still be at the rebel base that they knew, telling stories of their various battles, and those they had met. And all the while, Caelum and Deya sat together, still shoulder-to-shoulder, listening.

Deya smiled and laughed with the others, but Caelum sat, arms crossed, his face a mask of indifference. It made Deya squirm, sitting so close to him. She wondered several times if he was responsible for the icy breeze that swept around them, pushing them faster across the Gray Gap while Rayner was busy eating and laughing.

In the end, Rayner was right again. Within a few hours after nightfall, Val let out a cry of surprise, jumping to her feet—causing the small boat to rock fiercely, and for Caelum to hiss in protest—and pointed at something Deya had to squint to see.

"Land!" Val cried. Rayner was laughing too, his Water Magic intensifying with his joy. It propelled them forward, the boat skipping merrily across the dark water. Shortening the distance, they had left of the Gray Gap, the boat cleared it within minutes and crashed onto the sandy banks of the shore.

Val jumped out of the boat, splashing into the sea, and throwing herself down onto the sand, laughing.

Deya couldn't help but smile at her—this female that she now tentatively considered a friend. Rayner leapt out of the boat as well, leaving Caelum and Deya to round up the supplies.

Deya clambered out of the boat, the soles of her boots soaking up the water as the dark shores of the Gray Gap slithered up to lick at her heels. Deya spotted Caelum struggling to pull himself out of the boat without losing balance, his injured arm still proving to be cumbersome. With a brief pause, Deya held out her hand to him—an offer, an olive branch.

Caelum looked at her offered hand for a whole second. Then, he sneered at her, and although it was obvious it caused him a great deal of pain, he planted his hands on the edge of the boat and heaved himself over it, splashing water into her face.

Rage flared deep inside her. It was like a monster in her gut, hammering at the faerivaine shackles she had encased it in. In that second, Deya wanted nothing more than to shove the white-haired bastard right into the ocean, stab him in the heart, and wait for the Sea Beast to come eat him. She would've done it, too, except she had a feeling even stabbing him in the heart wouldn't kill him.

"Do you have to be such a fucking—" Deya burst out, anger clouding her vision. Caelum turned to face her, his expression darkening, causing her to cut off midsentence. Water lapped at their ankles, soaking their boots. Val and Rayner even paused to look around, laughter dying out.

"Be such a fucking *what*, exactly?" Caelum hissed, his purple eyes flashing.

At that second, Deya couldn't think of something strong enough to describe what Caelum was being. An *ass* didn't seem to do it justice anymore.

"A *prick*," she breathed, fury trembling on the word. She heard Val draw in a sharp breath.

Caelum advanced towards her, water splashing around him, causing Deya to take an instinctual step backwards, hitting the hull of the boat as he neared her. That same menacing purple glow was igniting his irises, causing no small amount of fear to course through her.

"Let me make one thing *very clear*," he breathed. He had cornered her against the boat, so close to her again that she was surprised he couldn't hear her heart hammering out of her chest. "You may have saved my life, and I may have saved yours, but we are *not friends*. I do not have to be friendly to a girl who has to question her loyalty to an *evil* fucking *empire*. And if that makes me a 'prick'," he growled, leaning into her face, pressing her even further back against the boat. "*So be it.*"

And then, he stormed away, splashing out of the surf, and up the bank, past Rayner and Val, their expressions astonished and even a little angry.

"I'm taking the first watch," Caelum shouted, not even looking back at them before disappearing into the trees.

CHAPTER
14

Deya, Val, and Rayner awoke on the sandy beaches of the coast of Elbania, the fire they had lit the night before still smoldering between them, and Caelum nowhere to be seen. He hadn't awakened any of them to take over the watch. Deya wondered if he was, once again, not sleeping, but then chastised herself. Why did she even care?

Val sat up, sand clinging to her dark auburn hair, peering around, as though she expected a rabid animal to be lurking around their camp. Deya knew, however, that she was only looking for Caelum.

"Do you think he was eaten by a monster?" Rayner asked, his brow furrowed, also scanning the surrounding area for the white-haired Nodarian.

Val snorted. "What monster could choke down all that bitterness?"

It was then that a gust of icy cold wind blew through the trees, causing all three of them to draw their cloaks tighter around them. Caelum strode out of the forest, looking as intense and indifferent as he always did.

"The rebel base is a few miles from here," he said, disregarding pleasantries altogether. "Pack up and let's get moving while it's daylight." He didn't wait for them to respond as he picked up the satchel of supplies and turned back towards the trees.

Val scoffed. "Just when we thought he couldn't get any cuddlier," she muttered. Then she looked over at Deya, as if remembering what the cause of Caelum's bad mood was. "Are you okay?"

Deya shrugged but said nothing. She couldn't deny that she was still incensed about how Caelum had treated her last night, but she had decided to ignore it. Fighting with Caelum was as useless and futile as fighting a mountain troll.

"I wouldn't take it personally," Val reassured her. "It's how he treats all of us. He's tried to draw his sword on me several times already."

Deya glowered. Maybe she should have let Caelum be. It wasn't like he was only exclusively awful to her. Val was right: he was consistently awful to all of them. Still, as they trooped after Caelum's distantly retreating figure, she couldn't shake the way it felt whenever he advanced on her. How his fingers were like molten ice, clenched around her wrist when he had grabbed her. How different it had felt when he had smoothed salve down her bare back. How *he* had been different.

Elbania was undeveloped. Wild country spread out around them, the forest here similar to what they had left in Aunecia, the only difference being that the weather here was much warmer. This was something she hadn't realized with that strange icy wind that had seemingly followed them from the continent, as if it were swept right off the top of Bridah's fjords.

Rayner hurried to catch up with Caelum while Deya and Val hung back, watching the Sea Fae jog after the hulking, brooding figure.

"I don't know whether he's brave or stupid," Val said, watching after Rayner.

Deya shrugged, her feet slipping over mossy stones, sword clanging against her hip. "Rayner's just a kind soul, I suppose. Maybe he sees something we don't."

Val gave a disbelieving snort. "I don't think that's the case," she said. "If anything, the only person that white-haired bastard has seemed to show a different side to has been you. Perhaps it's why he hates you so much." The grin Val gave her made a flush creep up her neck from her collar.

"What do you mean?" she stuttered. "He has never shown me any other side besides pure hostility—" But she paused, realizing that was a lie. Because Caelum *had* shown her a different side. She had even been contemplating it earlier while they had been packing up the camp.

Val smirked, interpreting her silence for exactly what it was. "See," she pointed out smugly. "He has saved you multiple times now. And gave you that necklace. I'd wager he probably hates you because he *doesn't* hate you."

Deya didn't reply, the flush now engulfing her from head to toe. It didn't matter, she decided. It didn't matter the small kindnesses he had previously shown her. They had been a fluke, a small break in the hostile wall Caelum had around him. And to excuse how he had treated her, to turn a blind eye to the threats and hostility he had already heaped on her specifically . . . No, she would not even entertain that thought.

"Either way, it doesn't matter," Deya muttered. "I stand by what I said yesterday. He's a complete prick."

Val laughed and threw an arm around Deya's shoulder. She jumped, the casual, affectionate contact causing something innate and primal in her to startle. With a pang, she realized her body was not used to receiving contact that wasn't dangerous or violent.

"You're right," Val said, tightening her grip on Deya's shoulder, her warm touch seeming to dissolve the panic that had begun to set into her body. "He *is* a prick."

They continued through the forest, Deya allowing Val's arm to remain across her shoulders. It would take some practice, she decided, to get used to feeling . . . safe.

The forest felt never-ending as they marched on for hours, only stopping now and then for water in a clear crystal creek, or some dry fruit and salted fish. The supplies had been dwindling rapidly over the last two days. Rayner had to eat a lot to replenish the amount of magic it took him to push them across the Gray Gap.

Deya, however, had barely touched any food since the apple the morning before, only eating a small, dried sardine during their break. Caelum had deigned to slow down long enough to join them, shoving half a tin of dried fruit into his mouth before moving on, hardly even looking at the rest of them. Rayner sighed at this and hurried after him.

The further along they plunged through the forest, the colder it got. Soon, the surroundings began to grow mountainous and rocky, rapidly changing the farther inland they went. When Deya mentioned this to Val, she only nodded.

"Elbania ranges in terrains," she panted as the incline turned steep, the mountain path they were ascending unforgiving in its climb. "The Legion set up in a mountainous region, in the base of a cliff. They built the fortress there. We figured it was the best option to defend."

"Do you know where we are?"

Val nodded, sweat gleaming on her brow. "We're close. We used to train on these footpaths. Used to use them to build stamina."

"I can see why," Deya gasped, and they both fell silent, concentrating solely on putting one foot after another.

After close to an hour, when Deya's legs were about to give out, and her tired, malnourished body begged for a break, she opened her mouth to ask Val how much further—then she saw it. The footpath they had been ascending for a straight two hours broke off, opening to a cliff's edge that looked down upon a massive valley. At the apex of this valley was a large mountain with two enormous stone doors carved into the face.

Beside her, Val let out a soft cry, and fell to her knees on the cliff's edge, tears of joy running down her face. Rayner, too, looked like he couldn't believe where he was. He came to stand next to Val and put his arm around her, like Val had to Deya earlier that day, and they both sat on the edge of the cliff and stared down at the valley, at the home they had been taken from for decades.

Once again, Deya found herself to be an outsider to a moment she felt she had no right to see. And, once again, she was facing this moment with Caelum right beside her.

Looking at him out of the corner of her eye, she watched him observe Val and Rayner, his face surprisingly passive. She had expected impatience and derision, some nasty comment about how they were wasting time, perhaps. But instead, he stood a fair distance back, allowing them their moment, just as she was.

It was then she noticed the dark circles underneath those violet eyes. With a pang, she realized that he must not have slept the whole night, must have stood guard or else simply brooded.

Deya wanted to say something to him—even opened her mouth to do so—but stopped. She didn't know what there was left to say. The words "I'm sorry" rang flat, insincere. Because she *had* meant what she had said to him. Meant every uncharacteristically nasty, rage-filled word. But what she wanted to say was something she wasn't quite sure she was ready to admit to herself: how she wished it could be different.

Caelum must have felt her gaze on him because he turned to look at her, his face, for once, neutral. She opened her mouth again but stopped, the memory of what happened last time she attempted to speak to him normally flashing through her mind. The words died on her tongue.

After a minute, Deya said, "I think we should probably go now, don't you?"

He cleared his throat and nodded. "I can take us down the rest of the way," he said. "It'll be quicker." It was stiff, polite, but at least he wasn't snarling at her and even that frostiness seemed to have abated. Either that, or he was too tired to keep it up.

Caelum took Val and Rayner first. Both looked terrified at the prospect of being suspended in midair—with Caelum controlling it, no less. But both capitulated in the end. Deya supposed the desire to get down to the mountain base overrode the fear Caelum would drop them like a boulder to their death out of pure spite.

Deya watched as Val and Rayner wrapped their arms around each other securely and gave Caelum a nod. With a deep breath, he raised his hand. Wind whipped past Deya, rustling her hair as Rayner and Val ascended into the sky. Val's eyes were wide, and she was muttering a string of colorful curse words as she stared down at the rocky ground below her. Rayner, however, opted to keep his eyes shut tight and asked Val to tell him when it was over.

With a grunt, Caelum began to lower them to the ground, eyes glowing. Deya couldn't help but wonder if he maybe let them go a bit *too* early, since they thudded to the ground in a heap on the rocky floor below.

Val's shouted curses up at Caelum rang up from below the cliffs, and Deya couldn't help but let out a little snort. Chuckling, she turned to look at Caelum. She could've sworn that—just for a split second—she saw his lip twitch an infinitesimal amount. It was gone in an instant.

"Let's go," he said and held out his arm. Deya hesitated. She had been in this position before, been pressed against this male so many times at this point it was a wonder how he had tolerated it thus far, given how much he apparently loathed her.

His face twitched with annoyance. "Come *on*."

Scowling, Deya stepped into his arms, his hand coming to wrap around her waist. And then their feet left the ground.

She didn't think she'd ever get used to the feeling of weightlessness that came with Gravity Magic, much less the swooping sensation in her gut when Caelum had leapt off the cliff while holding her. She remembered he couldn't physically move objects, only lift, and lower them down. She wanted to ask him more questions about his magic, having never met a Celestial Magic user of his caliber before, but knew he would probably bite her head off if she tried. Especially after last night.

Caelum's grip on her was surprisingly warm, and his body heat against hers proved to be an effective, even comforting barrier from the cold wind on the mountain top. And as they descended—as slowly as Caelum could, which, no doubt, exerted a lot of his energy—Deya didn't know what to do with herself as she clung to him. Every nerve ending was on fire where they touched, where she pressed into him.

Caelum's violet eyes flashed to her in that moment, as if he also felt the absurd amount of heat pooling in her belly at the way his hard chest felt pressed against her breasts. Or how his fingers were splayed across the small of her back, digging into the bit of skin between her breeches and her shirt.

It was the longest minute of her life. Everything from his body heat, the feeling of the hard muscle of his chest, even his scent—like a forest on a crisp, cold day—sent a nervous bolt of energy through her. Gods, she better not *blush* . . .

Their feet hit the ground, and Caelum released her as if she were on fire. He swept past her, Rayner, and Val without so much as looking at any of them, making his way towards the stone doors in the mountain. Rayner hurried after him, yelling at him that he wouldn't even get to the doors without them. Val, however, turned her amber eyes towards Deya, a small, smug smile on her face.

"Not one word," Deya snapped, and Val snorted, and gestured for them to follow the males.

The stone mountain loomed before them, bigger and more imposing now that they were on the ground in front of it, looking up. For a rebel fortress, it certainly had an impressive presence. The stone doors were intricate, heavy, ornate, as though they had been there for generations, carved by ancient fae as part of an old temple. This would not have been an obscure thought—all the Pillar Kingdoms had several temples devoted to their goddesses, with all being disbanded when Praiton took over.

As they neared, Deya got a better look at the carvings adorning it. A beautiful engraving of a forest crawled up the large twenty-foot door. Laced in gold leaf, it followed the grassy slopes, the large trees, the shrubs, and flowers, before leading to waves, water, surf. This transitioned easily to stars, sky, planets, the moon, before moving to fire, flames, and then frost, and ice. The carvings were so detailed and elaborate it took Deya's breath away.

In the center of the stone doors was a knocker in the shape of a set of scales. *Mav*, Deya thought. These scales were everywhere in Praiton, on buildings, carved into city streets, emblazoned onto books and signs. It only then struck Deya what Mav was supposed to be: balance.

Val held out a hand, stopping them all from getting any closer.

"Let me go first," she murmured to them. She cast a look sideways at Rayner, and they both exchanged a knowing nod. Deya glanced at Caelum, trying to see if he understood what that look was, but he was dutifully not looking her way. *Jerk.*

Holding her head high, Val stepped forward. All at once, the unmistakable sounds of dozens of bowstrings being drawn at once filled the clearing. Deya gasped, and she felt a sharp tug on her sleeve as a hand pulled her back. Whipping around, Deya saw Caelum's hand gripping the edge of her tunic and dragging her backwards behind him. His purple eyes were sweeping the top of the mountain, taking in the glints of silver arrowheads that caught Deya's attention. Dozens of soldiers had their aim trained on them. And all were ready to strike.

Val's hands went up, but she did not waver.

"Declare yourself!" a voice yelled out. Deya's eyes shot up, trying to identify who was speaking, but couldn't discern between the many faces above them. Caelum's hand tightened on her sleeve.

"I am Valeria Augusta, captain of the twenty-second regiment of the Pillar Legion, leader of the Fireflies," Val called back, her voice loud and strong. Her chin raised imperiously, and her amber eyes shone in the sunlight. "I am home."

There was a tense silence, a moment when it felt like all the bowstrings collectively quivered with Val's words. And then they lowered.

"Approach!" The voice echoed throughout the mountains again. Only then did Deya feel Caelum's hold slacken.

Looking back over her shoulder, Val jerked her head, an indication for them to follow her.

Advancing across the clearing with the rest of them hot on her heels,

Val knocked hard on the door, not even bothering to look up at the gold-embossed etchings. She had the air of someone who had been there many times before.

Both she and Rayner were trembling with excitement at being back here. Caelum, however, was standing beside Deya, his head tilted back, his violet eyes sweeping up the expanse of the stone door. She noticed his eyes lingered on the section of the stars and planets, how tiny the stars looked, how detailed the planets were as they arced over each other in a perfect ellipsis.

The large stone doors began to open, yawning apart with the sound of a giant waking. The four of them had to take several steps back as it opened outwards, the beautiful, carving disappearing to be replaced by a stone hallway lit with torches . . . and about a dozen armed soldiers, all with their swords pointing towards them.

CHAPTER
15

"Who are you?"

The demand was given by an impressively tall, imposing male in gold armor, who stood at the forefront of the pack. His large, equally gold sword was aimed right at Caelum's face, who was the only one who had refused to take a step back when the doors opened.

"What kind of welcome home party is this?" Val demanded. She stepped out from behind Caelum, her face bright, the torchlight enhancing her foxlike Manielian features, making her even more striking.

The male froze when he saw her, his heavy gold sword dropping to his side in surprise.

"V-Valeria?" he whispered. It was as if he had seen a ghost. A million expressions passed across his face before his sword clattered to the ground.

All around them, the soldiers lowered their swords, a few surging forward to greet Val—Rayner, too, once they realized he stood with her. They swarmed around them, clapping them on the back, embracing, smiling, and laughing uproariously.

Shunted to the side, Caelum and Deya stood back, once again outsiders.

"I suppose we should get used to this at some point," Deya muttered absently to Caelum, but she was smiling as she said it. To see her friends reunited with their adoptive families, the tears, and the joy on their faces warmed Deya's heart and broke it all at once.

She thought of her mother—alone in that small village in Wexbridge. Was she still oblivious to what her only daughter had gone through in the last several months? Then there were the so-called 'friends' she had left behind at Stonehall. They would never be happy to see her like this again—probably never had been if she were being honest.

Caelum shifted next to her, his hand still clenching and unclenching around the hilt of his sword. "I suppose," he mumbled back.

She was shocked he had answered her. And so normally, as well. Before she could reply, the throng around Val and Rayner began to break apart.

"Wait, meet our friend!" Val was saying, pulling away, her face flushed and filled with joyful tears. She staggered free of those still attempting to hug and greet her, and grabbed Deya by the arm, leaving Caelum behind as if he were just some fungi on the cave wall.

"This is Deya," Val proclaimed, presenting her with a sweep of her arm. "She's the reason we were able to escape." Deya didn't know whether to curtsy or bow after an introduction like that. Instead, she lifted an awkward hand, as if she were waving to the crowd before them.

"Hi," she said.

The male who had been leading the group emerged from the throng, his hand outstretched.

"Hi, Deya." He shot her a devastating grin as he approached her.

Now that he wasn't on the offensive, Deya was struck with how *handsome* the male was. His jaw was chiseled, cheekbones high, his head of dark hair was neat and perfectly styled—as was the rest of him—but it enhanced the startling beauty of his features. He held out a severely calloused hand for her to shake, which she did after the shock of staring at such a perfect specimen had worn off. "I'm Aris, General of the Guard here at Light's Tower."

She could've sworn she heard Caelum snort derisively in the corner.

Deya ignored him, turning back to Aris. "Light's Tower?"

Aris nodded, gesturing behind him towards the cavernous hallway they were standing in. "That's the name of this fortress. It used to be an old temple here in Elbania, set up to worship all the goddesses. It was left abandoned over a century ago, and we have since repurposed it," he explained. "But, come, let's not stand here and receive *Lady Valeria Augusta* in the doorway." He shot Val a wink, which did not faze her one bit.

Rolling her eyes, Val scoffed. "Still as arrogant and pigheaded as ever, I see, General," she said, breezing past the male, but she was smirking.

"Well, of course," Aris replied, falling into stride beside her. "Someone had to take up the mantle once the Princess of Pigheadedness got herself captured."

"I'm sure it was an extremely tiring transition," Val simpered. "Did the big strong general find it difficult to fill my boots?"

The two carried on like this, teasing and taunting each other mercilessly, leaving Deya in slight disbelief at how there could be a male who could keep up with her new friend.

The group was ushered through the torchlit hallway. The stone walls were old and worn, but clean and adorned with shields and tapestries from across Krigor.

Up ahead, Aris and Val conversed in hushed voices, their heads together. The handsome general's face was serious as Val spoke rapidly to him, the bustle of people making it difficult to discern what they were saying.

Aris led them through an antechamber towards a large room located in the center of the mountain. Several of the guards who had tagged along to chat with Rayner bid them farewell and resumed their patrol.

The great hall of Light's Tower certainly lived up to its name. Standing sentry around the large, circular stone room were enormous pillars carved with the likeness of each of the five goddesses. Towering over them at almost twenty feet—the same height as the doors at the entrance, she noted—they stared down at the large wooden table in the middle of the room, circled with highbacked chairs.

They all took seats, Deya perching on the edge of her chair.

"So," Aris said, throwing himself down into the chair at the head of the table and looking at them with an arched eyebrow. "Tell me all about this escape from Ironbalt." He was mainly looking at Val and Rayner when he said this, but then did a doubletake when he noticed Caelum lurking in the background, the only one to not have taken a seat.

"I don't think we've met," Aris said, rising from his chair again. As he approached Caelum, the other male bristled, his violet eyes appraising Aris with a look of leery contempt. Aris held out his hand to Caelum, just as he had Deya. "I'm Aris. And you are . . .?"

"None of your business," Caelum snarled.

Rayner, Val, and Deya all seemed to collectively groan at once. Leave it to Caelum to be an arrogant jackass to the general of the rebel forces.

"Don't mind Caelum," Val cut in. "He's a *prick* to everyone."

That word made Caelum's nostrils flare, a small movement that wasn't lost on the general.

His patrician eyebrows raised even higher, and his self-assured smile grew even more catlike. "Caelum, eh?" he said. He circled him, his hazel eyes sweeping over the other male, as though he were analyzing, assessing. "Forgive me for assuming, but do you happen to be from Bridah?"

Caelum let out a scathing snort. "Funny," he leered. "I pegged you for someone a little more astute, General."

Aris finished his revolution around Caelum, returning to his seat, his eyes still narrowed on the white-haired male. "Caelum," he repeated. "You're right . . . that name is not a Bridanian one."

Caelum's eyes flashed as he moved out of the shadows, coincidentally framed between the Goddesses Flykra and Astrea.

"You don't say," he growled.

Val let out a little moan and buried her face in her hands.

Caelum threw himself into the chair three down from Deya—an island to himself. Despite Val's dread, Aris did not seem to be angry by Caelum's insolence. In fact, he merely looked amused, and almost frighteningly intrigued by his standoffishness.

"You definitely have the gift for gab," Aris drawled, leaning back in his chair, boots thumping onto the table in front of him. "What's wrong, Caelum? I promise, we don't bite here at Light's Tower. Not unless you're a Praitonian soldier, that is."

Deya's body twitched involuntarily, but no one noticed. Caelum sat in his chair, arms crossed, face dark, purple eyes shining bright as he snarled at Aris.

"Has anyone ever told you that you are just as annoying as the Manielian female?" Caelum said through gritted teeth.

Aris let out a bark of laughter that was devoid of any warmth at all. "Now that," he said, "is the most insulting thing you could ever think to say to me."

Val threw her dagger at Aris in retaliation. It landed with a thud, embedded right into the oak table in front of him. It only caused him to laugh harder.

"Lecherous pig," Val mumbled. Aris chuckled and reached for the hilt of the dagger and pulled it out of the wood, shooting a lewd grin at Val. His fingers traced over the blade of Val's knife, his eyes never leaving hers. Deya almost shivered at the intensity of his stare and how his fingers touched the steel in an almost sensual way. If Val noticed, she ignored it.

"Are you two done slinging your cocks around yet?" Val snapped, glaring at him and Caelum. Deya's eyes widened to the size of saucers while Rayner choked on a laugh. "We get it. Two alpha assholes in the room. Now do us all a favor, General, and get down to business." She planted her slender hands on the table, twin flames burning in her amber eyes as she looked towards the general, who matched her heated stare. "The Fireflies," she insisted. "Where are they? Where have you moved them to?"

Aris's face fell, and he didn't speak for a long moment. "Valeria, you and Rayner have been locked away for more than three decades," Aris said finally, his cocky smile fading.

"I know this."

A pall fell over the room as Aris hesitated, looking down at the table, as if he couldn't look Val in the face. After a moment, he said, "Valeria . . . I don't know how to tell you this."

The golden hue of Val's skin paled, and her fingers clenched the tabletop.

"After the skirmish in Maniel where you were captured, your unit snuck away from camp to go after you. They tracked the band of soldiers who were said to be transporting prisoners. However, they had been misinformed."

Val's eyes widened, tears beginning to well in them. "No . . ." she whispered.

Aris bowed his head. "Lucia, Atria, and Katia were all captured and then killed," he said. "We retrieved their bodies from a ditch by the camp they had infiltrated. There was . . . enough left of them to give them a proper burial. They now rest in Bellston Gardens atop this mountain."

A horrible, pitiful sob burst from Val's mouth. She fell back against her chair, the tears that were of joy mere minutes ago now full of sorrow and pain.

Rayner bowed his head, a hand clasped over his mouth, and Deya felt her own heart splinter for Val. Aris watched Val attempt to steady herself. Her shoulders shook violently, the tears falling swift and fast until, with a deep, trembling breath, she stilled.

"I am sorry, Valeria," he said quietly.

She shook her head, still not able to look at him. Aris sighed, and his gaze shifted towards Caelum and then, to Deya. Her spine stiffened. The general's piercing stare lanced through her and, what was more, his expression was no longer easy-going and arrogant. It was now serious, business-like. The general of Light's Tower was now sitting before her.

"I do not know where you two hail from," he told her and Caelum. "But obviously Rayner and Valeria have trusted you enough to bring you here. However, if you choose to stay, then you choose to join us. Our ways, our mission, our secrets, they are to be kept and adhered to. Am I clear?"

There was a long pause. Both Deya and Caelum stayed still. Val sniffed through her tears and rounded on Caelum furiously.

"You have lost everything to Praiton," she snapped, her voice still thick with emotion. "Have lost most of your grown life in Ironbalt and suffered who knows what other horrors in the Battle for Atlas. Who has more reason to fight than you?"

Caelum remained silent, but Aris sat up a little straighter. "The Battle for Atlas?" he said. "So, you are a Nodarian?"

Caelum's eyes shifted to Aris, and Deya saw the moment when the general noticed the characteristic purple Nodarian irises.

"Do you hear me denying my intentions?" Caelum murmured, a menacing lilt to his voice. He paused, looking around the table, as though weighing his options . . . his consequences. His gaze landed on Deya, but swiftly looked away. "I want Praiton to burn," he proclaimed. "I want them to pay. I want to kill Praiton soldiers and watch them suffer." The intensity and fury to which he said this made a chill creep up Deya's spine.

"However, I do not have reason to fully trust the rebellion," he continued. His eyes flashed to Aris. "Where were you and your useless forces when my kingdom fell? Nodaria and its army were left to face Praiton alone. No one came. No reinforcements. How am I to sit here and pledge my allegiance to you, *General*, when you allowed my kingdom to fall?"

The echoing silence after this pronouncement seemed to ring throughout the stone walls. Rayner, Val, and Deya all stared, dumbstruck at Caelum. None of them had heard him speak this candidly about what had been brewing behind those angry purple eyes. He sat before Aris, teeth bared, breathing short. Aris, however, appraised him seriously. The cocky grin did not return.

"You know that no one was able to make it in time," Aris said. "The only being in all the realm with the known ability to teleport was King Castor himself. His Celestial Magic gave him the ability to open portals through space, which was the only reason he was able to come to Bridah's defense when Praiton attempted to attack it several decades before the Battle for Atlas. None of our forces have that power. When King Castor fell, our legion was attempting to fight through the army of Praitonian soldiers surrounding the capital city, Arctos. Praiton knew Castor would call for reinforcements after the sneak attack caught them off guard, and they had prepared accordingly. We did everything we could to reach Arctos in time."

He stared Caelum down, unblinking as he said, "I am truly sorry from the bottom of my heart for the loss of Nodaria. It was a blow to many of us here. King Castor was a good king, a strong one. Losing him was not easy. Watching it happen was worse."

The expression that flickered through Caelum's eyes sent a jolt through Deya's chest. For, in that tiny moment, a look of such intense pain and grief flitted across his face that it hurt her to her very core. Particularly in the place in her heart where all her own pain, sorrow, and grief was kept. She knew that look all too well. And then, it was gone.

"Why has the Legion been so ineffective at stopping anything Praiton has done?" Caelum glared at Aris, the pained look on his face replaced with disgust. "It has been fifty years since Nodaria fell, yet your pathetic Legion has hardly done anything to stop Praiton's conquests."

Aris inclined his head, his expression still cool as glass. "I will not deny that we have taken a step back with more active resistance. Since Castor fell, King Makis of Ganiea perished, and Queen Arnora of Laenimore has disappeared, we have lost any advantage against Praiton we may have had in the past." The general's fingers tightened on the dagger he held, just enough for Deya to recognize the frustration he was tamping down. "However, our numbers grow daily. Thousands strong across the realm. Dozens of units and outposts. We do what we can to stop Praiton. Destroying camps, sabotaging supplies, and military maneuvers, killing their officials. But I promise you, our day to strike will come. And the question is will you be the next one in line to slaughter a Praiton commander?"

There was a long pause, before, "Fine." Caelum spat the word out, the cold indifference back. "Fine. I shall join your forces, then."

Aris nodded, almost as if in appreciation of this. But then his eyes fell back on Deya, who was still silent.

"Deya," Val breathed, almost as if she were pleading with her to speak. But Deya was staring at the general of the Pillar Legion. And he was staring right back.

"Valeria told me you were born and raised in Praiton. That you worked within Stonehall for a few years," Aris said coolly. Deya felt herself nod.

Aris appraised her over tented fingers. "I know from my spies within Stonehall that Praiton does quite a number on its citizens. They shield you and lie about what their greed and prejudice has done to this world."

Deya's heart gave an unpleasant leap at the word "spies," but she held her head high and willed her voice to remain steady.

"That's right."

"And yet you are here," Aris continued. "But where do you stand?"

Her heart pounded in her ears as she felt everyone's eyes on her—particularly, a heated purple gaze. But then she caught Rayner's gaze. There was something calming about the way he looked at her, as if he was simply reminding her of something she already knew.

"I spent my whole life in Praiton," Deya began, her voice quiet and scared. "I served them with honor and distinction. And they repaid me by imprisoning me and torturing me. No jury, no trial, no chance to explain. They betrayed me. I had been lied to my whole life, and I blindly believed in them. The one time I ever spoke contrary to the kingdom was my last." She paused and looked back at Rayner again. He gave her the smallest of encouraging nods.

"They shouldn't be allowed to treat people like this," Deya said. "What they did to me . . . what they did to all of you . . . They need to be stopped." She stared at the handsome general, whose hazel gaze was sharp and analyzing. "I stand with you, General," she said. "And all who have been wronged by Praiton. As I have."

There was a moment of silence. She was holding her breath, waiting in trepidation to see if they believed her, if it was enough, when Aris smiled.

"Any enemy of Praiton," he said, "is a friend of ours."

Deya gave him a small smile, which he returned, and she breathed again.

"Now that's settled." Aris sat up straighter in his chair and leaned towards her. "Valeria says you were the reason for their escape. How, may I ask, did you manage to break out yourself and three prisoners from the most highly guarded prison camp in all of Krigor?"

Deya swallowed hard and looked around the table. Rayner was watching her apprehensively while Val was still staring, numb and shaken, at the table in front of her. Caelum's purple eyes were on Deya, his gaze cold and steady.

"When you mentioned *spies*," Deya said hesitantly. "Did there happen to be one that was . . . a bard?"

Aris's eyes narrowed. "Why do you ask?"

Drawing in a shaky breath, and with a feeling akin to diving headfirst into freezing cold water, she told Aris everything. She started at the beginning, unsure of what he wanted to know, what she should withhold. She told them of what she had overheard from Clarita Killoran and Lord Decius, what she suspected, what they had done to her. She told him about Oswallt, of his friendship and kindness. Of his death. Of the awful, terrible power that had ripped out of her. And then of the ashes.

Aris took this all in, the dagger he had taken from Val lying limply in his fingers. He looked, for once, at a loss for words. Even her companions were staring at her in total incredulity. The one that surprised her the most, though, was Caelum's expression. For once, a look of pure shock stole his cold indifference.

"You mean to tell me," Aris breathed. "That the King of Praiton,

King Rodric, has been being *poisoned* by his steward for a near *century* now?"

"I cannot be certain," Deya whispered, her voice trembling. The last time she had spoken this terrible theory out loud it had cost her everything. Each time she had spoken this to someone, it had ended in nothing but despair. "It would explain his symptoms. King Rodric was always of strong health and mind. His decline was sudden, and dare I say suspicious. None of the healers in the castle were ever called upon to look after him. I always found this odd. The High Mother was the only one asked to see him, and she possesses average, even weak, levels of Healing Magic."

It had been the reason Clarita hated Deya so passionately. Deya had upstaged her several times when they were asked to heal important officials after battles. They had always called upon Clarita first, assuming her to be the strongest of her healers. While it had irritated her to fail, it had enraged her to watch Deya do what she could not.

Aris sat back dully in his chair, his hazel eyes seeming to process this, comprehend it. "We did have a spy in Praiton named Oswallt," he said. "I did not know he had been imprisoned. It would explain why we hadn't heard from him lately."

So Oswallt *had* been a spy for the rebellion. The totality of this realization crashed upon her, and Deya's heart sagged in her chest. Her mind was racing as she felt everything from the last few months come tumbling down around her. Oswallt's friendship . . . their time together . . . his story of his imprisonment, the things he had confided in her. Were any of them true? What else had he not told her? What else had died along with her friend?

A lump welled in her throat and her eyes burned.

"It would explain a lot," Aris muttered to himself, not noticing how Deya was fighting tears. He still appeared to be processing her information. "Rodric was always against war and conquest. He was a proud Ganiean who loved the kingdom he had hailed from. Yet he felled our kingdom first . . . or so we thought."

"You're from Ganiea?" Deya asked, momentarily forgetting the sharp ache behind her ribs.

Aris gave her a small, sad smile. "I was part of the king's guard. Obviously, I failed my king, too," he added, looking over at Caelum, whose mouth tightened.

Deya felt that pang in her heart again. She had known of the High King of Ganiea's death. King Makis faced the first Praiton invasion completely unawares. No one had anticipated Praiton turning rogue and attacking a Pillar Kingdom. It had been mayhem. No Pillar Legion existed, no allied kingdoms on guard. It had just been King Makis and his small Ganiean army . . . and the king's guard.

Deya looked at Aris, and she knew he could see the sadness in her eyes.

"His son lives," Aris said. "The crown technically goes to him, Prince Minos . . . my best friend. Minos is still in Ganiea. His mother begged him to bow to Praiton after Makis died fighting. So, Minos was given a place of *honor* on the council as a *diplomat*." He spat these words like venom onto the oak table, his face darkening behind his cool mask.

"They killed everyone within the Green Fortress," he continued, his fingers tightening on the dagger in his hand. "I fought my way to Minos, but when he bent the knee, he banished me to *save* me. His final act as what should have been High King of the Harvest Throne." Aris's words were cold, calm, but there was something scary and deadly behind those hazel eyes. "I was exiled but spared on Minos's request. And now I fight to free my kingdom from the *bastards* who destroyed it."

Silence rang within the halls, his words echoing and rebounding off the five goddesses who stood sentry over them.

Deya hesitated. She knew it was now or never. The heaviness of Oswallt's final words had been weighing her down, as if she had dragged them with her across the Gray Gap. The truth of Oswallt's identity was still burning a hole in her chest, but there was no denying it now. She knew who he must have meant—knew what she had to do. She had pledged her allegiance to the Pillar Rebellion. And now it was time to avenge Os.

"There is more," she said, and every head in the room whipped around to look at her again. "Before Oswallt died, he told me something. Told me that Praiton was searching for something dark and dangerous. He told me to warn someone, begged me to promise him that I would. I didn't know who he meant . . . until now."

Val glanced at Aris and back at Deya, but the general's gaze did not leave her face.

"Something dark and dangerous," he repeated. His finger began tracing the silver knife again, over and over in small circles. "Oswallt was stationed close to the King. Close to Decius. He would've been privy to much information." He looked at Val and Rayner. "You mentioned that she was being hunted by Praiton. That she has a price on her head because of her magic." Glancing back at Deya, he asked, "Could it be *you* they are seeking?"

"That's impossible." Deya jumped at the sound of Caelum's growl. To this point, he had not so much as breathed a word, only taking in everything she had told Aris. "She had not even unlocked that power yet. How could she be the one they were already looking for?"

Aris hummed in agreement. "Fair point." He sat silently for a second, lost in thought, before he looked up at all of them and gave them a small smile. "Well, we will not solve this mystery in a night. Thank you for telling me this, Deya. Oswallt was a good male. I am glad he had someone like you in his final moments."

Deya knew he had meant it as a comforting thing, as a token of appreciation, but his words hit her like a slap in the face. Because if it wasn't for someone like her, Oswallt would still be alive.

Reaching into her pocket, Deya pulled out the small, wood carving that she had bought from the vendor in Latchside. Arista, the Harvest Goddess, the Goddess of Ganiea. Slamming it down on the table in front of her, she looked at Aris.

"I may be from Praiton," she said, her voice stronger than she felt. "But I do not condone what is being done. And if I am right, there may be a way to end this."

Aris paused, but then smiled at her. A strange, icy breeze drifted down to them from the ceiling. Looking up, Deya saw a stained-glass window up above them, staring right up into the heavens. It was of the Mother Goddess, Mav, scales in hand, staring down at them from her place above.

CHAPTER
16

After their meeting, Aris's guards escorted them to small chambers in the upper levels of Light's Tower. The tower itself was constructed of spires and narrow turrets that climbed upwards through the mountain. Deya and Caelum followed the guard up, and up, and up, until Deya began to get dizzy and lose her footing.

While Val and Rayner had chosen to stay downstairs with Aris and the others, Deya found herself worried about her female friend. The look on her face when she had heard of her friends' deaths . . . She hoped that Aris and Rayner were looking out for her. When they had left, Val still had the stunned, crushed look of someone whose entire world had just fallen out from underneath her.

The sleeping quarters were located at the topmost tower in the east wing. When the spiraling staircase ended, it led to a narrow hall with thick wooden doors lining its walls. The guard pointed to two rooms across from each other, gave them both a nod, and headed back down the endless staircase.

Deya and Caelum paused before their respective doors.

"So, I suppose I'll see you tomorrow?" Deya said.

Caelum paused, his hand on the handle. "Why didn't you say before?" he asked. The words seemed to explode out of him, yet he was talking to the doorknob, not looking at her.

Surprised, Deya tilted her head. "Say what before?"

"What you were imprisoned for. What your friend said to you . . . Everything."

She looked at him curiously. This moment reminded her vividly of their walk back to camp after their encounter with the soldiers. Caelum had been just as hesitant, just as reluctant to ask her something not filled with resentment or anger. For a second, he looked . . . concerned.

"Because I hadn't decided . . . about where I stood in the war," she admitted, her voice soft . . . ashamed.

She expected him to lose his temper. After all, she was admitting to the thing he had always suspected her of. Had always *hated* her for.

Caelum paused for a long moment, and then, "And you've made up your mind now?"

Deya nodded. "Yes."

He did not look at her, instead he stared at the doorknob so hard, he looked as if he were trying to set it ablaze. Then he jerked his head in a small nod. "Good night," he said and then disappeared into his room.

Shocked that she had even gotten a "good night" from him, she did the same.

Her new bedroom was small, but clean, and cozy. A fire crackled in the worn fireplace by the door underneath a foggy mirror. There was a rough set of dresser drawers and a vanity desk with a stool. But what made Deya let out a moan of longing was the small double bed beneath the window. The mattress looked like a mix of goose feather and hay, and when Deya shed her dirty clothes and collapsed onto it, she couldn't stop the groan of absolute bliss that escaped her.

It had been months since she had had a bed. Months since she had even had a blanket. And this one was heavy and soft, made of some animal hide. The bed was underneath the small porthole of a window, and when Deya propped herself onto the bed and gazed out of it she nearly gasped. There was nothing but miles and miles of rocky slope plunging down from her ledge. The number of stairs they had climbed had not been in her imagination. They were miles above in the sky.

Flopping back down onto the bed, Deya let out a long, heavy sigh. She was safe, she realized. Safe from Praiton, safe from Ironbalt, safe from the monsters in wild country, safe from that horrible and inexplicable power that was now locked inside her.

And with that thought, she fell into the deepest sleep she had had in months.

Deya slept and slept. Every time she would open her eyes, she would look out the window, see the sun and the clouds, and drift back to sleep.

She found herself thinking about everything and nothing. About Oswallt and the Pillar Legion. Of the infirmary in Stonehall . . . of Clarita Killoran . . . of the whipping posts . . . of the soldier she had spared. Of her mother, alone in Wexbridge, unaware and unprotected while she sat there with an enormous bounty on her head. And every time the wood in the fireplace snapped or crackled, Deya would flinch, the sound of whips still fresh in her ears.

All of this swirled around her, faces of the ghosts of all her failures beating tiny fists down upon her. But she could not do anything about it, so she sat, and she slept, and occasionally the nightmares would find her, and she would jolt awake and stare at her ceiling for hours.

She counted two sunsets before there was a gentle tap on her door. Deya raised her head from where she had been resting against her pillow, surprised at the intrusion.

"Come in."

A familiar scent of burnt poppies filled her nose and Val poked her head in.

"So, you *are* alive," she said, grinning. "We were worried about you."

"I'm alright," Deya said, attempting to match her smile, but knew it looked as weak as it felt. Val, however, looked better than she had the other night in the great hall. There was color back in her golden cheeks, and her amber eyes were brighter—though still red around the edges. Deya wondered if she had been crying. Instantly, she felt ashamed of herself. Val had just found out three of her friends had died. She should've been there to comfort her, to look out for her.

But instead, she had been lying in bed, sleeping through her own sorrow.

"How are you?" Deya asked, sitting up in bed, sheepishly attempting to smooth down her sleep ridden hair.

"I'm okay." Val perched on the edge of her mattress and gave her what could only be described as a brave smile. "It's hard being back here without . . ." She trailed off and her face fell.

Without thinking, Deya reached out for her hand. "I'm so sorry about your friends, Val," Deya whispered.

Val's lips trembled as she shrugged, the smile unsteady on her face. For a moment, she stared off into the corner of Deya's room, her leg jiggling.

"I never had sisters," she said. "Only brothers. Brothers that were cruel and heartless, supported Praiton, and joined their army quite willingly." She shot Deya another sad grimace. "You can imagine they did not take well to having a traitor for a sister."

Deya's heart clenched. "That's awful."

Val shrugged again. "I thought so, too. Until I came here. And then I had three sisters." She gave a long, shaky sigh. Deya knew she was trying to be brave, but she didn't miss the quiver of her bottom lip, the shimmering of her eyes.

"They died for me," she whispered, more to herself than to anyone. "They gave their *lives* for *me*."

Deya did not know what to do. Ever since she had gotten out of Ironbalt she had flinched at the slightest movement, jumped at the smallest touch. Yet Deya tightened her grip fervently on Val's warm hands. She tried to convey in that one small squeeze all the pain she felt for her friend, the grief she recognized as clearly as her own.

"They loved you."

Val's head dropped and she nodded. For a moment, it looked as if she was going to let the tears loose, before she breathed in, her golden fingers tightening on Deya's, letting out a controlled breath.

"You remind me of one of them," Val added. "My third in command, Katia. She was gentle and kind. Loved animals. Maybe that's why I wanted to be your friend."

"I appreciate you wanting to be my friend," Deya said, her cheeks flushing as she gazed down at their hands, piled on top of each other. Pale skin over golden brown. "Considering where I came from."

"Where you came from is irrelevant to me," Val said firmly. "Look where *I* come from. My kingdom has done just as many wicked things as Praiton. You are not your kingdom, Deya. And I have no doubt Katia would've liked you, too." She trailed off, her gaze shifting out of focus again as she stared across the room at the empty fire grate that Deya had long since given up lighting. With a sigh, she turned to look back at Deya.

"Are you really okay?"

"Of course," she replied automatically, but Val gave her a knowing look.

"Katia was a lot like you. She was a strong, fierce warrior, but she was sensitive." Val peered at her before saying gently, "She struggled to bounce back from hard times."

Deya blushed and looked away, shame filling her insides again. She knew Val was not trying to be judgmental. After all, she *had* locked herself in this room for the last two days, hadn't even left to eat or speak to anyone. Val had every right to be concerned about her.

"I'm just tired," Deya said. It was her turn to give Val a weak smile. "It's been a long few months."

Val nodded. "I understand, trust me I do. But it can't be healthy staying in here. Wasting away . . ." Her amber eyes swept over her. She had no other clothes besides the ones they had bought in Latchside, so she was currently only wearing her undertunic. It hung on her body, the neck constantly sliding off her thin shoulders.

"I think you need to keep yourself busy, Deya."

She blinked at her. "Busy how?"

"Everyone in the rebellion pitches in somehow. We have cooks, priestesses, healers . . ." She gave her a pointed look. "You can help in the infirmary."

Deya's heart sank, and she tried to ignore the instant prickle of sadness she felt at the back of her throat.

"My Healing Magic is gone. I would be no help in an infirmary now." The words hurt to say out loud, but she knew it was true. Poultices and ointments were of no use to anyone if there were normal healers around.

"Then train with us," Val implored. She still held Deya's hand, and this time she was the one whose fingers tightened earnestly. "Learn to fight. Become one of us."

Deya did not understand why she balked at this, but she could feel herself shut down at the suggestion. Pulling her hands free of Val's, she tucked her bare knees to her chest, looking away from the Manielian female, whose hands were scarred and calloused—a trademark symbol of a seasoned warrior.

Deya's hands were slender and soft, her long fingers designed for gentility and mending. She was not a fighter. The fact that she had crawled into this hole of a room and refused to come out for days only made this more evident.

"I don't fight," Deya said, speaking to her hands. "It's not who I am."

Val's expression fell slightly, but her resolve only seemed to intensify. "I don't believe that's true," she said. "You *do* fight back."

Deya let out a snort of disbelief. "Really? When?"

She did not expect Val to have a real answer, but the Manielian replied instantly. "You don't let Caelum push you around. I've noticed that you fight back with him. It's how I know that you have a fighter's spirit within you, Deya."

Deya resisted the urge to scoff again. She did not want to be mean to Val, but she had never felt less like a fighter than she did now. Her body had gone into hibernation, her mind an empty vessel of shimmering fog that—if she looked too closely—would reduce her to tears. She jumped at every sound and movement, even flinched at the sound of fucking firewood crackling, and Val expected *her* to be a soldier?

"I'll help in the kitchens," Deya said, still not able to look Val in the face. "I'll start tomorrow. I promise."

Val looked like she wanted to object, even opened her mouth to do so, but she closed it a second later.

"Okay," she said, giving her a tight smile. "If that's what you think is best."

"It is," Deya said, but she knew she was lying. Now that she had finally found safety and warmth, she didn't think she'd ever have the courage to leave it again. Not even for her friends.

The following morning, Deya washed in the modest bathing room—taking advantage of the soaps that were available to her—before dressing and descending the many, many stairs back towards the main level of Light's Tower. She hadn't seen much when she arrived besides the antechamber and the great hall. But as she wandered, she saw there were more rooms, some open, some closed and locked.

Every wall was decorated with artifacts from around Krigor. Intricate tapestries depicting Ganiean grasslands, battle-worn shields with the Nodarian crest, oil paintings of old High Kings, and even one of High King Makis. Deya paused in front of him, taking in his warm brown eyes, frozen in time forever.

As she strolled further, she passed an open door and hesitated. There, standing behind a desk with his arms folded and brows furrowed, was Aris. And standing in front of him, eyes blazing, almost nose to nose with him, was Val. They appeared to be in a heated discussion, one that Deya did not feel safe to interrupt. It was too late, though. Aris tore his gaze from Val and started when he saw Deya lurking in the doorway.

"Good morning," Aris said, giving her a tight smile. He still looked exceptionally bothered, as though he and Val had been going at this for a long time.

Val whirled around, her red hair flying in a wave of fire. "Deya!" she cried. She hurried out from around Aris's desk and walked towards her, smoothing her hair down. "It's good to see you out."

Deya eyed them both. Val looked flushed and winded. She couldn't tell whether it was because they were having a heated argument, or something else.

"Thanks . . ." She looked between the two of them sheepishly. "I didn't mean to interrupt."

"There is nothing to interrupt," Val snapped. She shot a warning look at Aris, who blinked up at her innocently, that same, smug smile sliding up his face.

"Yes," he murmured. "Absolutely nothing to interrupt, Deya."

There was a long, tense pause, to which Deya looked from the handsome general and back to her friend, getting the distinct impression that there was more to this situation than she knew, before Aris cleared his throat and smiled at her.

"Valeria mentioned you wanted to help in the kitchens," he said.

Deya glanced at Val, whose arms were folded stiff over her body. She was determinedly not looking at him.

"That's right," she said.

"Well, we are fully staffed in the kitchens at the moment," the general said, sitting back down in his highbacked chair behind the desk. "You would merely be a hindrance in there. For the time being, why don't you join Valeria in the training ring with the others?"

Deya's mouth sagged open, a protest bubbling up her throat. But her well-practiced restraint stopped her. She was never one to disobey an order, especially if it was a reasonable one.

"Alright," she mumbled. She caught Val's eye and noticed that even she looked surprised at Deya's acquiescence.

Val shook the shock from her face and grabbed Deya's arm, looping it through her own. "Come on," she said. "Let's go."

Deya wanted to question the Manielian about the sudden change of plans about her duties for the day. But, judging by the tic jumping in her friend's slender jaw, she could tell Val had nothing to do with Aris's decision. Not to mention the fact she was obviously still worked up over whatever she had walked in on.

"What was that?" Deya asked leadingly, smirking at her friend as she ushered her out of Aris's office.

Val's face was as red as her hair. "Nothing. Aris is insufferable, he always has been."

A little pleased that she now had the upper hand with teasing Val for once, Deya raised an eyebrow at her. "He didn't seem insufferable to you the night we arrived."

The glare that Val shot her made her snort with laughter. Val's face turned even redder. "He has been insufferable since I met him decades ago," she snapped.

Deya knew it was mean to keep prodding her like this, especially when the usually unflappable Val looked *very* ruffled now, but she couldn't resist. "What could he have possibly said to you to upset you so much?"

"It was nothing," she said stiffly. They were walking so fast through the hall that doors blurred past as Val dragged her by the arm as far away from the general as she could. "Aris is an unbearable lout."

Deya hummed in a knowing way, and it made Val huff.

"Have you and he . . ." Deya began, but Val had already let out a snort of derisive laughter.

"Absolutely not," she scoffed, but she had turned a lurid pink. "No, Aris is my general. He's a good leader, an excellent fighter, but an absolute *ass*."

Deya chuckled some more but decided to let it go. It was sort of entertaining to see Val this incensed. Even Caelum had failed to get her going like this.

"I think the boys are in the training ring," Val told her, and they headed through the main floor, across the antechamber and through a set of heavy double doors. Sunlight poured in, causing Deya to shield her eyes, the first taste of the outdoors that she had had in days filling her lungs. She breathed it in, taking in the scent of trees and a warm, mountain breeze.

The training ring was a large expanse of rocky ground, cleared, leveled, and surrounded by tall, jagged cliffs. It was the perfect defense, Deya thought, reminding her vaguely of the fjords that surrounded Bridah. From a distance, she could see guards pacing the span of the mountain tops, walking on what appeared to be wooden pathways that had been constructed within the sharp rock.

In the center of the open space were weapons racks and individual platforms and arenas. Already, a half dozen males sparred with swords and other weapons. Across the way, Deya spotted a head of white hair and a familiar Sea Fae.

Caelum and Rayner had swords out, circling each other. Both males had discarded their normal leather armor, opting for the lighter fabric of their undertunics. Sweat gleamed on both their brows and where Rayner looked tired yet good-natured, Caelum looked menacing.

"You keep dropping your elbow," Caelum said. "It leaves your left side vulnerable."

Rayner lunged clumsily towards Caelum, their swords clanging. Caelum whipped around Rayner's blade, parrying expertly.

"Better," he said in between blows, his teeth grit, his face a mask of furious concentration. Caelum struck and lunged at Rayner, who struggled to match him move for move, until, with a whirl of his blade, Caelum spun away from Rayner's sword and stopped short of swinging the sword against Rayner's neck.

Rayner's face split into a grin. "You're not half bad, Nodarian," he said, panting. "Then again, I'm much more of an archer than I am a swordsman."

Caelum didn't so much as crack a smile. He was breathing hard, his white hair damp with sweat. He had threaded a small braid on the side of his head, hanging beside his ear. It accentuated his Bridanian features even more.

"You're going easy on him, Rayner," Val crowed as they approached. Caelum's head jerked to look at her, his eyes doing their usual ominous glow, before freezing when they noticed Deya. Deya knew better than to expect any sort of greeting from Caelum, no matter how many days had passed. She could've been dead in her bedroom for all he cared, she knew that. Still, the way his eyes froze on her, as if they were taken aback at seeing her standing there, did not escape her notice.

"Pick up a sword and say that again, Manielian." Caelum sneered, jerking his eyes away from hers.

Val gave Caelum a catlike grin as she swaggered into the ring. "Fine," she said. Any of the previous bluster she had shown in front of Aris was gone, replaced with her usual cool, confidence that bordered on arrogance. She strutted towards the weapons rack and brought out two blades. "How about two swords?" she asked, grinning.

Caelum glared at her, twirling his weapon around him.

"If you don't think you can win with one," he snarled, "then who am I to deny a handicap?"

She let out a harsh laugh and spun the swords around her, so fast that they looked like a hummingbird's wings.

"No magic," Caelum growled.

"Don't worry," she purred. "I won't need it."

The two moved so fast that Deya blinked and almost missed it.

Val's swords moved so quickly that Deya had no idea how Caelum was managing to parry them all at once. She expected Caelum to give up or falter, but instead he seemed to push harder, his sword moving with an equally impressive amount of speed. They fought back and forth, pushing each other from one end of the ring to another.

Val's confident smile faded when she realized Caelum could keep up with her. Her teeth bared, and her face furrowed with intense focus.

Rayner came to stand by Deya, smirking as he watched Val and Caelum battle it out. He was shouldering a new longbow onto his back; the wood intricately carved with Laenimorian symbols and stained a dark cerulean on both ends. It was only when he got closer did Deya discern the carvings: it was the Sea Beast, etched into the dark wood, attempting to eat its own tail.

"It's good to see you," Rayner said, shooting her a furtive smile, which she returned.

"It's good to see you, too, Rayner."

"What happened to you?"

Deya hesitated. She felt pathetic to admit that she had slipped into a black hole for a few days. Now, back in the world and around people again, it all felt so silly now. "I just had to catch up on some rest," she said.

The crash and clang of swords intensified as the Manielian and white-haired Nodarian battled each other across the ring, kicking dirt up into the air in a cloud of fury.

"How much you want to bet Caelum would die rather than lose to her?" Rayner asked her, smirking.

Deya laughed. "I'd bet the treasury of every kingdom that you're probably right."

At that moment, Caelum ducked one of Val's flying blades. He dropped to the ground in one fluid motion and kicked Val's feet right out from under her.

Val hit the ground with a thud, a gasp of breath exploding out of her. For a moment, she lay there like a turtle on her shell, staring up at the sky with the look of the utmost incredulity on her face. Even Rayner looked dumbfounded, his mouth sagging open as he watched Caelum point his sword at Val's golden throat.

"You were saying?" he panted. His eyes glowed with fury and something a bit like triumph.

Val blinked and seemed to come to her senses long enough to shoot a loathsome glare at Caelum. "Lucky try," she snapped, furiously getting to her feet. Caelum burst out laughing—a sound that was so foreign and so *strange,* coming from him, it was almost unsettling.

Val stormed off, brushing past Rayner and Deya, her face bright red.

"That," Rayner proclaimed, his mouth still hanging open in astonishment, "was both incredibly lucky and incredibly dangerous all at once."

Caelum huffed and leaned against his sword. Sweat soaked his shirt, his tattoos standing out starkly underneath the damp, white material.

"I'm not afraid of her," Caelum sneered, lifting the hem of his tunic to wipe at his brow. Deya had to look away.

"Val was one of the best swordfighters in the whole Legion," Rayner told them. "You *should* be afraid of her. Because she will most likely attempt to kill you until she regains that title. You *beat her.*"

Caelum shrugged. "She can try."

Rayner let out a disbelieving laugh, shaking his head as he looked at Caelum with something grudgingly like respect. "I should go check on her," he said. "She does not take losing easily." He hurried out of the training grounds, breaking into a jog to follow the red-haired female who had blazed an angry, fiery path back towards Light's Tower.

Caelum still had a faint smile on his face as he twirled his sword a few more times, as though stretching his muscles.

"Where did you learn how to do that?" Deya asked him. He glanced over at her, as if he had forgotten she was even there.

"You're back," he grunted, ignoring her question. Turning away from her, he slashed his sword in midair. Deya stood and watched him from a distance, hugging herself.

"I didn't go anywhere."

"Well, you weren't here." He darted one bright purple eye back at her. "What happened to you?"

While his tone was still coldly indifferent, even the tiniest bit of lukewarm concern from Caelum took her aback.

"I . . . I was just catching up on some sleep," she replied, her canned answer much more readily available now that she had given it several times to other people.

Caelum gave a derisive snort. "You slept for two days," he said. "How much sleep did you really need?"

Deya glared at him. The memory of Val pointing out that she did not let Caelum push her around echoed in her mind. A spark of irritation flared within her as though in compliance with this. No matter how strong, deadly, and *nasty* the Nodarian male was to her, she could never suppress the urge to lash back at him. And that fact exhilarated her.

"Where did you learn how to fight like that?" she asked again, ignoring his question this time.

"Training."

Deya scoffed. "Thank you for that very helpful answer."

Caelum shot her a look that, for once, was not hostile. She wondered for a second if it was even *amused,* before he turned his back on her and began walking to the weapons rack.

"Why do you even care?" he said, thrusting his sword with the others. "I thought you don't fight."

"I don't," Deya said. "And I *care* because I'm curious. It's not like I *want* to learn to fight—"

"I think that's a great idea." From the edge of the ring, a glint of gold shimmered in her peripheral. Striding towards them with all the swagger and confidence of a celestial being, Aris stepped into the ring. He grinned at them both, his golden green eyes twinkling as he took in Deya's bemused expression and Caelum's furious one. "Deya should train. She should learn to fight."

"I—" Deya began, but the protest died on her tongue with one look at the vein that was beginning to throb in Caelum's temple.

"Great idea, *General*," he sneered. The word dripped with all manners of impertinent sarcasm. "*You* teach her, then."

Aris's eyebrow arched, and that look of unfettered entertainment only grew as he appraised Caelum. "If I just heard correctly," he began coolly, "you won in a sparring match against Valeria."

Caelum no longer looked pleased about this fact, but he did not deny it.

When he did not reply, Aris smirked. "I thought so." Then, from in between his impressive gold breastplate, he withdrew a folded piece of parchment. "I received this in a raven from one of our spies on the mainland." He unfolded it and handed it, not to Caelum, but to Deya. Hesitantly, Deya reached out and took it.

Her own face stared back at her. A crude drawing that made her look gaunt and sickly. The picture shimmered with the magical ink that had been used to create it.

Deyanira Krey, the flyer read. *Wanted for treason and threats against Praiton. Highly dangerous.*

It was as if a flame had been lit in her stomach. She felt a melting sensation, the same quickening of fiery wings in her rib cage. She knew she should not care. This flyer should come as no surprise to her—she *knew* Praiton hunted her. But to see it like this, to see her own face on an official Praiton flyer—the five-pointed star with Mav's scales emblazoned in the corner—made an infuriating heat prick her eyes. Attempting to swallow past a lump rising in her throat, she shoved the paper at Caelum, who had leaned in to look over her shoulder. She hoped he did not see the tears that were welling traitorously.

"As you can see," Aris's calm voice said, "you are no longer safe anywhere you may go, Deya."

Deya blinked rapidly, attempting to clear the tears from her eyes, hoping they would not betray her and fall. From beside her, Caelum scoffed, and tossed the flyer back at Aris, who caught it with one hand.

"We knew this already," he snapped at the general, who only smiled.

"Yes, we did. But I don't think Deya fully understands." He looked at her, and in the way that those hazel irises appraised her, she knew he did not miss the way her eyes had misted. "You are in danger, Deya," he said. "To learn to fight is to survive."

Deya wanted to scream at him that she was tired of fighting—maybe not with swords and shields and magic, but with her whole mind and body. With her entire soul. She was tired and beaten and sick of having to struggle to survive. She was safe *here*, wasn't she? Why did she have to learn to fight? She would simply never leave.

Then she felt herself deflating. Realizing almost as fast as she had thought it, that never leaving Light's Tower would be as sad of an existence as the life she was supposed to have in Ironbalt.

But she said nothing. She couldn't bring herself to agree, to relinquish this last bit of control over her life that had slipped so far from her grasp.

Aris seemed to take her silence as capitulation, because he nodded and looked at Caelum, that sly grin quirking the corners of his perfect mouth. "You will train her," he said to him.

Caelum's face darkened, those purple eyes beginning to glow. "No."

"As your general," Aris said. "*You will train her.*"

"Ask the Manielian to train her," Caelum snarled, advancing towards the general, who did not so much as flinch at this.

"You beat her," Aris said, smirking. "*You* will train her."

Breathing hard, Caelum stared Aris down, the fury emanating from him thickening the air. But he did not object, and Aris grinned.

"Excellent," he said. "You will start tomorrow. Good day." And he turned with a last glint of gold and strode out of the training ring.

There was a long, tense silence. Deya felt like she was trapped in a ring with a carnivorous animal. Caelum was staring after Aris, the anger still rolling off him like a cold wind. He took a step towards her, a menacing movement that made Deya instinctively take a half step back. They came almost chest to chest, a familiar dance they kept finding themselves in again and again. He leaned down towards her, their foreheads nearly touching.

"I will break you," he whispered. "You train with me, and it will be the hardest thing you have ever done. That is the Nodarian way. We break our bodies to build them back stronger. I will *break you.*"

It was a threat, a promise. Maybe even a warning. Yet, Deya wouldn't let him intimidate her, no matter how close he was to her, no matter how much he still smelled like a cold forest breeze, even though he was sweaty and filthy. She stood tall and stared right up into those malevolent purple eyes. Her answer surprised even her.

"Good." Because she wanted to break. In that moment, she wanted to feel the collapse of her useless body, one that matched what she felt in her heart and in her soul. She wanted to crumble like the ash her life had been reduced to. And she didn't care how it was done.

If he was surprised at her answer, he didn't show it. Instead, his jaw tightened, and his face darkened. "Meet here at six tomorrow morning. Not a second later." He turned to leave, to walk away from her, but before she could help herself, she was calling out to him again.

"Who trained you?" she asked. The question had burst from her before she could shove it back in. She didn't know what made her ask again, only that Caelum was beginning to feel more and more like a book she hadn't read, a book she *needed* to read. She was more curious about the male than she ever wanted to admit to herself.

His back stiffened. He froze in his retreat, hesitating just a moment, his head almost turning back to face her. The familiar battle appeared to be raging in his head. It always seemed to cost him a tremendous effort . . . the decision to talk, to answer her questions. To not fight back.

"My brother," he said. "He trained me growing up."

"Oh," Deya said, surprised. "I didn't know you had siblings."

He paused, and that same look she had seen cross his face in the great hall their first night here appeared again like a passing shadow. "I don't anymore," he said, before turning and walking away, leaving a cold, blistering wind in his wake.

Caelum had slept well for the first time in nearly six months. Having a bed was a luxury he had almost forgotten. In fact, he almost couldn't fall asleep the first night due to how soft the mattress was. And, for the first time in he didn't know how long, he did not have a nightmare.

He felt lighter, rested . . . Alive. For the last week of travel, he had been unable to get comfortable due to an unnatural cold and was constantly overtaken with chills. But after a night in a bed, under heavy blankets, and in front of a fire, the chills had subsided significantly. He wondered if he possibly had a fever.

Beating the Manielian female had also been incredibly satisfying. He hadn't remembered the last time he had laughed that hard—had actually, genuinely *smiled*.

And then the Praitonian girl happened. And it had all gone to shit.

He was so angry he had agreed to train her, so angry she had successfully pried, once again, into his business. And he had let her. Again.

His fury was so intense he instantly began to feel the chills again the minute he had stormed away from her. Was this girl the reason for his fever? Was *she* causing these chills?

That night at dinner, Caelum sat next to Rayner in a corner—far away from Deya and the Manielian, who appeared to have recovered since he had thrown her to the ground. That thought did make him smile a little again.

"What are you smirking about?" Rayner asked. The food at Light's Tower was exceptional. It appeared that Aris the Heiress had offered sanctuary to not only displaced members of the fallen kingdoms, but to their priestesses and lost castle staff as well. It was truly something to behold; the rebel fortress was bustling with people from every kingdom.

As someone who had grown up in Nodaria, the white sheep in a sea of dark-haired fae, he found that he was fairly inconspicuous here. Except, he noted, that he was still the only white-haired fae that he could see.

"I'm just remembering the look on the Manieliean's face when I dropped her on her smug behind," Caelum said, smirking as he took a bite of chicken.

Rayner sniggered a little. "Don't be getting too cocky, my friend," he advised. "Valeria may be a bit rusty. She will surely re-challenge you again."

"I hope she does," Caelum said, shrugging.

Rayner cut into his potatoes, peering at Caelum with a look of interest. It made him shift a little.

"Do you like Light's Tower so far?"

He shrugged again. "It's fine."

"You seem much better these days," Rayner commented, watching him closely. "Happier."

Caelum lowered his fork, glaring at the Sea Fae. "Don't be stupid," he mumbled. "I am the same as I ever was."

"You *smiled*," Rayner said. "Actually *smiled* today. With teeth and everything."

Spitefully, Caelum shot Rayner the biggest, widest smile that could fit his face. It felt unnatural in every muscle.

"See, nothing unusual."

"You just looked like you wanted to eat me," Rayner said. "The other smile was a *real* one."

"Forgive me for indulging in taking that female down a peg," Caelum grunted, shoveling another potato in his mouth. Gods, it was good. Warm. He hadn't been full in ages.

Rayner chuckled, shaking his head in mock disapproval. "Val is confident in herself and her abilities," he said.

Caelum snorted. "That's a nice way of saying arrogant as the day is long."

Rayner burst out laughing. As if alerted to the sound, Deya looked over at them. Their eyes locked, and Caelum felt that same surge of chilly coldness in his blood. He jerked his eyes away from her.

The Sea Fae noticed this, his eagle eye darting between Caelum and Deya, before taking another forkful of chicken from his plate.

"Did you two have another fight?" he asked. His tone was cautious, but leading. Caelum chewed his food but didn't reply. Rayner guessed exactly what his silence meant. "What was it about this time?"

"Aris demanded that I train her."

Rayner stared at him for a second, before he roared with laughter. "*You*? Train *her*? No offense, friend, but I don't think either of you should be around each other armed."

"He wants her to be trained," Caelum said coldly. "I'll train her."

Rayner gave him a derisive look. "No, you'll *torture* her."

He shrugged dismissively, remembering his threat to her. That he would break her. And he would. His training throughout his life had been brutal and unforgiving with the master of arms at Atlas Keep. Caelum and his brothers were trained to be warriors, no matter the cost. At the time, Caelum had been too young to understand the rigorous nature of the exercises and he'd often struggled to keep up with his older brother. But Aelius had tutored Caelum on the side, always trying to help him when he had fallen behind.

He couldn't deny the pride he felt at how far he had come. Beating the Manielian was no small feat. He had nearly lost several times during that match, would have fallen if he had faltered even a little. After fifty years of imprisonment, Caelum had still practiced in his cell at night. Had kept up with the exercises, the stances, everything that Aelius had helped him master. It had kept his form sharp, his instincts honed, his muscles in shape.

But today was the first day he had been able to use a sword, to attempt the actions as they had been intended. He was pleased that the Master of Arms, Master Orion, had not led him astray. He and Aelius had taught him well.

"I once had to mentor someone as well. During my time in Laenimore's capital," Rayner said. His long blue fingers toyed with his fork; his eyes downcast. "I felt the same way you did. She was still practically a child, inexperienced, and frankly a bit spoiled." He shook his head, and his electric blue eyes looked troubled . . . almost haunted. "But over time, teaching her how to use a bow, how to protect herself . . . it is still something I am proud of. We both learned from each other."

Caelum did not reply. He was grinding his teeth together, irritation swirling in him. The thought of learning something from Deya should be laughable, but seeing her standing in the training ring yesterday, the look of satisfaction in her eye at the thought of being broken, of being shattered and repaired . . . It was a feeling he was all too familiar with.

"Caelum." Rayner put his fork down to look at him. Caelum growled at the intrusion, but reluctantly looked back at the Sea Fae. "Deya has gone through a lot," he implored. "She was tortured by Praiton. By those she thought were her friends. Her people. Her whole world has been turned upside down. Do not add to that girl's pain. Please, Caelum." Rayner's eyes were pleading. It rankled Caelum, his teeth grinding in aggravation.

"Why should I care about a Praitonian girl's suffering?"

"Because," Rayner said, "she is not just a Praitonian anymore. She is one of us."

Caelum had heard enough. He finished his meal, eager to get away from the Sea Fae and stormed from the dining hall, furious at the prying, overly empathetic male.

Why should he dump his sympathy for the girl onto him? He did not care about her pain or her trauma. Did not care how it gave her nightmares, had corrupted her Healing Magic, had reduced her to the trembling skeleton of a girl that stood in front of him. She never ate, he realized. He had watched her put a particle of food in her mouth here and there and chew it slowly, as if she were masticating rocks.

He remembered how scared she had looked the night he had given her the faerivaine necklace. How she had trembled, tears on her face as she took in the devastation that her once pure magic had wrought. She had looked so thankful when he slipped that iron chain around her neck, had looked up at him with tear-filled eyes . . . how he could count every knob in her spine that protruded from under her skin.

Caelum strode through Light's Tower. Some people were milling about and moved out of his way as he blew like an angry cloud through the hall. He stormed out the double doors leading towards the training ring, which was deserted and dark. The sun had long since set, and the only light came from the torches high above in the watchtowers. He headed around the weapons racks, past the arenas and fences surrounding them, his mind racing.

Deya had told him that night in the forest that she had been imprisoned for treason, but never what that treason entailed. For some reason, hearing her tell Aris what she'd overheard, what had been the piece of information that had cost her everything, had set him extremely on edge.

He had been determined to hate her. Determined to not allow a member of Praiton's castle to get close to him, to even *know* him, no matter how hard she tried. He gritted his teeth, his fists clenching as he pushed out a side gate and kept going, plunging into the wooded area surrounding Light's Tower.

Overhearing the girl tell Rayner about her confusion over her loyalty to Praiton during the boat ride to Elbania had made his blood sizzle. But she had sat there before the general of the Pillar Legion and told him everything she knew. *Valuable* information against Praiton. She had pledged her allegiance to the rebellion and that was good enough for Aris, Val, and Rayner. So, shouldn't it be good enough for him too?

The gate leading out of the arena took him to a small forest clearing. To his right, stone steps descended upwards, back into the shelf of the mountain. Hesitating only slightly, Caelum headed towards them. The stone steps were crude, flat stepstones that took him on a steep climb up the rocky expanse of Light's Tower.

He kept climbing, his breath coming out in clouds of mist. Like the stairs up to their chambers, these seemed to go on forever. He climbed higher and higher into the starry sky, his breathing growing heavy and labored, sweat beginning to bead on his brow.

After twenty minutes of climbing, the terrain began to level out, and the steps opened up to a grass-covered plateau. Panting, Caelum looked around. The plain before him was flat and peaceful. Flowers blossomed from the dark green grass, which was manicured and surprisingly healthy for how high up the hill was. The only blemishes on the plateau were a series of white marble markers. As Caelum approached them, he realized what they were: tombs.

Dozens and dozens of headstones littered the meadow, all the same height, all the same pale, bone marble that stood in stark contrast to the dark grass. Caelum traced his finger over the top of the nearest one, its surface cool and smooth. The name on it looked Laenimorian.

Caelum wandered from grave to grave. He remembered Aris telling Val how her friends had died and were laid to rest atop the mountain. That must be what this place was . . . Bellston Gardens. In other words, a mass grave for the fallen soldiers of the Pillar Legion.

Caelum didn't know how long he wandered amongst the headstones, his fingers tracing names from all five Pillar Kingdoms. He was amazed to see some Bridanian names—their reclusiveness usually meant he was always the only white-haired fae for hundreds of miles. It was truly remarkable how many of them had come out of hiding, only to die fighting to protect the other kingdoms.

After about a half hour of walking among the dead, the tombstones began to lessen. They grew fewer and farther between, until the ground became unblemished again, clear of any markers. It seemed Light's Tower had left a decent space to bury their future dead. The grassy plane went on for at least another few miles in either direction—an impressive find for a mountaintop this high.

He kept walking, grass crunching under his feet, that blasted winter chill still sweeping around him as he went. He thought about Deya, about the look on her face when she had asked him about his siblings. The look on her face when he answered her.

It still hurt him. All of it still hurt him. To talk about Aelius . . . to think of him. To think of Aten, Astrid, Seren, and Sirius. The worst part of it all wasn't the grief, though—it was the guilt. The bone-aching, soul-wrenching guilt that he carried in that now black heart of his, that he still dragged along behind him like a heavy weight.

He had seen that same look in Deya's face. Had seen it when she woke screaming that night in Aunecia, how she had muttered in her sleep about needing to save her friend. How she had obviously failed again. How many times had he had the same dream? How many times had he woken screaming his siblings' names?

The cliff opened up, the edge looming into view. The night sky spread out before him, a familiar face welcoming him with open arms. It had been a long time since he had seen the stars this high up. He and his youngest sister Seren often used to go to the top of Atlas Keep where the astronomers and star seers liked to dwell, to stare at the moon and stars.

Shakily, Caelum sank to the ground, his eyes never leaving the heavens. Seren had been so small, he remembered, had barely made it to Caelum's hip. She had a mess of jet-black hair that stood out starkly against her pale skin and purple eyes. She had been the perfect Nodarian female. Smart as a whip, energetic, and a gifted star seer, even at such a young age.

Seren had revealed three prophecies in her short life. Two of those they knew not who they were for. Star seers went into trances when the prophecies were formed, reciting them in the ancient Nodarian language of Nadarak. But Seren had taken her studies of the heavens seriously, had even been attempting to learn Nadarak on her own, a dead language few spoke outside of trances.

Out of all his siblings, Caelum had been the most mediocre, the most run of the mill. His powers had taken a long time to develop, and then they had sat, dormant and encaged for fifty years.

"What are you doing up here?"

Caelum started, springing to his feet, his hand flying towards his sword, but stopped when he saw who was approaching him. Red hair purple in the moonlight, Val stepped towards him, a bundle of flowers in her hands.

"Gods, don't sneak up on me like that," Caelum spat, re-sheathing his sword, and sitting back down.

Val sneered at him. "Jumpy, are we?"

"I have every right to be," Caelum muttered. "You could be back here for a rematch for all I know."

Val let out a derisive laugh, but she still walked towards him, flowers cradled in her arms, and joined him on the cliff's edge. "I will, don't worry. Just not right now."

They sat together, shoulder to shoulder, in a tense silence. Caelum had never spent so much as a second alone in the Manielian's presence, would never have wanted to, either. But tonight, there was something different about her. She wasn't bursting with fire, crackling with energy and passion. She was subdued, like a flame that was smoldering quietly, burning out.

A minute passed without either of them speaking, and with each second, the tension diffused. Both of them deflated; the need to fight petering out.

Val was staring at the flowers in her arms, a collection of night blooms and lilies. Caelum found himself looking at them, too.

"My unit would have hated these," she said, smiling to herself sadly. "They were some of the few females from Maniel who defected and joined the Legion. They would have wanted fire poppies, but they do not grow in Elbania."

Caelum stayed silent, but not out of irritation for once. He let the female talk, the sadness radiating off her like ripples of heat.

"I couldn't bring myself to come up here to see them . . . until now." Val's chin dropped, her red hair falling like curtains in front of her face. "They died coming to save me," she whispered. "I should've been able to at least bring them fire poppies." Her lips trembled. "Just another thing I have failed at, I suppose."

Caelum didn't say anything—what could he? They had never had a normal conversation, let alone one that was like this. Vulnerable.

"I came out here," Caelum said, "to look at the stars. They remind me of my family."

Val nodded, her amber eyes looking upwards, too. "You lost them in the Battle for Atlas, didn't you?"

He didn't know why it was easier to admit this to Val than to Deya. Maybe it was the armful of night blooms for her dead friends, or maybe it was the fact he knew exactly where Val stood in the war. Whatever the reason, he nodded.

"I thought so." She looked over at him, a shadow of sorrow in her eyes. "I'm sorry."

Caelum found himself looking back at her, taking in the golden skin streaked with freckles and moonlight, her ruby hair the color of blood under the night sky. "I'm sorry about your friends, too."

"It's never easy," she said, looking down at the flowers in her lap. "To lose someone . . . To blame yourself. I spent decades in that prison and all that time, I never knew of their fate. I always wondered . . . hoped. I carried that hope for three decades, just for it to shatter at my feet the other night." Her fingers rubbed a dark blue petal of the night bloom and plucked it free, holding it for the wind to take. A breeze blew it from her grip, taking it over the edge, drifting towards the stars above them.

"No," Caelum whispered back. "It definitely is not easy."

Val gave him a grim smile. She clambered to her feet, shifting the flowers in her arms so she could hold out a hand to him. Caelum just stared at it.

"Come on, don't start being an asshole now," Val said. But she said it with a small smile. Caelum grunted and took it. She pulled him up, and together, they walked through the cemetery, looking through the headstones. Several minutes later, Caelum stopped in front of a marker and called Val's name.

Val hurried over to his side, and together, they stood in front of three headstones. They had been buried together in a row. Lucia, Atria, and Katia. Val's lip trembled as she approached.

Falling to her knees, her hand still clenched onto the marble that bore Lucia's name, a sob broke loose, and her shoulders shook as her grief poured out. It was the most gut-wrenching moment Caelum had ever witnessed.

He didn't know what to do for her, whether to leave her be, or perhaps comfort her. The thought of putting his arm around her didn't feel right, so Caelum stood next to her, quiet and patient as she sobbed for her friends. Her tears splattered the grass; her golden hands clenched the marker so hard that her fingers sank into the stone, leaving molten holes beneath her fingertips.

Caelum bent down and scooped up the night blooms from her lap, his hand tentatively touching Val's shoulder. Her body was hot through her clothing.

"Let's put their flowers down," he whispered to her. Val nodded, but she was still crying so hard that he was unsure if she heard him. Caelum placed a bouquet down in front of each of the headstones. Lucia, Atria, and Katia in that order. Then he lowered himself down next to Val and together, they sat in front of the headstones, Val's tears echoing off the marble around them.

For a second, Caelum imagined these headstones were his siblings. Were Aelius, Aten, Astrid, Seren, and Sirius. His breath caught, and he felt even colder than he had before.

CHAPTER
17

When Deya staggered into the training ring the next morning, the sky was still dark. She had stayed up late last night, sitting with Rayner and Aris, listening to their stories, and soaking in the laughter and conversation. She hadn't partaken herself, opting to sit comfortably in a corner by the fire, a quiet observer.

Now that she was out of her room, she grappled with feeling like an outsider in Light's Tower, detached from all those around her that were bonded in blood and tragedy. Instead of sharing the burden, her suffering was her own to bear. It felt like something she carried around with her, secretly cupped in the palm of her hand, like an injured baby bird. She was afraid to move too much, to breathe too hard in case she jostled it, hurt it. She was afraid to do much of anything for fear of awakening that pain again.

Yet, here she was, staggering bleary-eyed into the training arena, just to see Caelum bright-eyed and bushy tailed, holding his sword and working his way through various poses and lunges. He looked a little funny, as though performing some elaborate dance, and she stifled a giggle as she approached him.

His eyes narrowed when he saw her face. *"What?"*

But she smiled and shrugged. "Nothing, just a lovely morning, isn't it?"

If steam could come out of his nose like a bull's, she had no doubt that it would. He jerked his head towards the weapons rack.

"Pick up your sword."

Deya approached the rack and reached for a simple brass sword when something seized her wrist.

"A *wooden* sword," Caelum growled, his hand squeezing her tightly.

"*Wooden?*" Deya wrenched her hand out of his grip. "Why am I using a wooden sword? I've used a real one before!"

"I've seen you use a sword before," Caelum snapped, pulling the blade from her, and shoving it back into the rack. "You held it like a child. We're using wooden swords. End of story."

Scowling, Deya reached for the hilts of about a half dozen wooden swords pushed towards the back of the weapons rack. They looked old and barely used.

Fighting back the anger she felt, she pulled one free and was stunned by how heavy it was. Her shoulder dropped from the weight of it, and, embarrassed, she glanced back at Caelum, hoping he hadn't noticed. By the nasty smirk he wore, she knew he had.

Caelum had put his own sword away and replaced it with a wooden one as well. They headed back into the middle of the ring, and he stood before her, an evil glint in his eye.

"Right," he said. "Let's begin."

It started with a two-mile run around the ring. Caelum ran beside her, his wooden sword still clenched in his hand. He, however, was not panting like she was. Deya's legs trembled with each step, her sword heavy in her hand, weighing her down. Her breath was coming out in short gasps, and her body was begging her to stop.

"Faster!" Caelum would bark from ten paces ahead, and she would surge forward, her movements sluggish and labored. She made it three times around the ring—two short of the last mile—before she collapsed hard in the dirt, her wooden sword thumping to the ground beside her.

Caelum stopped from up ahead, turning to look back at her, his lip curled. Deya could hear his footsteps coming closer as she struggled to raise herself from the dirt. Her palms smarted from where they had broken her fall, bits of rock and gravel clinging to them. Coughing from the cloud of dirt that had risen when her body hit the ground, she slowly got to her feet again.

Caelum stopped in front of her. His eyes roved over her body, and she knew he could see her knees shaking, her arms quivering as they held the wooden sword aloft, weak, but determined to keep going.

"What did you eat this morning?" Caelum demanded.

Deya opened her mouth to answer, but stopped, sputtering slightly. The answer to his question was nothing. She had half an apple in the dining hall, which was all she had managed to choke down before coming out to meet him. Food still tasted like sand and ash, her body seeming to reject it. Anything she ate hit her stomach with the weight of a cannon ball, sitting heavy in her gut for hours. She didn't think anything of it, just that she must not be used to comfortable amounts of food anymore.

But with the way Caelum was looking at her, she was beginning to worry that maybe something *was* amiss.

"I had an apple," Deya said defensively.

Caelum's eyes flashed. "*Just* an apple?" he said, moving closer to her. She was still trembling, her arms giving out and she had no choice but to lower her wooden sword and lean on it like a crutch.

"I wasn't hungry."

A cold finger lifted her chin. The touch shocked her. His fingers were cold—as if he were outside in a blizzard rather than exercising hard on a warm autumn day—but also gentle. His fingertips were as light as they had been the night he had put salve on her.

"You think I don't notice?" he said, his voice as cold as his fingers, not matching the feel of his touch on her chin at all. "You claim I do not sleep, but *you* do not eat."

Deya's heart quickened, the flutter of wings beat in her chest. She tried to duck her head, to look away from him, but his fingers kept steady on her chin, so she could only avert her eyes.

"I try to eat," she whispered, trying to ignore the treacherous pace of her heart—the fluttering of those tiny wings. "But it all tastes like ash to me. I can't . . ."

Caelum dropped her chin and seized her wrist. "Come," he said, and pulled her up. He dragged her along, back towards Light's Tower, her wobbly legs struggling to keep up with him.

"But what about my training—" Deya began.

"You cannot train if you can barely stand," Caelum snapped. She immediately missed the gentle touch of his fingers on her chin because his grip on her wrist was an icy shackle.

Caelum marched her through Light's Tower like an errant child, striding her past several groups of patrols, and a few important looking males who were speaking to Aris in the doorway of the great hall. Aris paused, mid-conversation, to look at them curiously as Caelum frog-marched her through the dining hall, towards a small wooden door at the far end of the room.

Deya had never been in this room—hadn't even noticed it during the times she had been in the dining hall. The minute the door opened, Deya was overwhelmed with the hustle and bustle of the busy kitchen. The ovens were at full blast, and the heat hit her in the face. All around the large stone room, various kitchen workers hurried around, stirring pots, preparing loaves of bread, chopping vegetables. A few looked up as they entered, and went back to their work, not perturbed at all by their sudden appearance. Caelum paraded her through the kitchen, his hand the only cool thing on her skin. He led her to a small wooden table in the back that was empty and pushed her down onto a stool.

"Stay," he commanded, then walked into the middle of the kitchen, only to return a moment later with a heaping plate of food.

He slammed it down on the table, and then sat himself across from her.

"Eat," he ordered, pointing to the plate. Deya looked down at it. It was filled with the roasted chicken from last night, a large side of garlic potatoes, and a few root vegetables beside it. Deya would have killed for this meal a month ago. She had daydreamed with Oswallt about a chicken like this—its skin crisp and speckled with seasoning. But now, when she looked at it, her stomach only gave an uncomfortable squirm of disgust.

Picking up the fork, she glanced up at Caelum, who was watching her intently. When their eyes met, he jerked his chin towards her plate again, egging her on. Tentatively, Deya speared a potato, then placed it in her mouth.

She chewed and chewed and chewed, the potato like gravel sloshing around her mouth. She still couldn't taste anything, couldn't taste the rosemary and other herbs that were clinging to the sprouts, but still she forced herself to keep chewing until it was small enough for her to choke down.

Caelum's purple eyes watched the potato travel down her throat, and he nodded in approval. "Keep going," he demanded.

Deya stifled a small groan but continued. She dived for a bit of chicken this time, Caelum's eagle-eyed stare watching each piece of food cross her lips.

"Where did you disappear to last night?" she asked him, desperate to distract herself from the tasteless mush she was attempting to swallow.

Caelum looked like he was about to snap at her but paused. She wondered if he saw the pain in her eyes and decided to humor her.

"I went on a walk. I climbed the mountain to Bellston Gardens."

"Bellston Gardens?" Deya echoed. She paused in her battle with the chicken, trying to remember where she had heard that name before.

"Light's Tower's cemetery," Caelum said.

This jogged her memory. Aris had told Val that her friends were buried there. She then remembered Val leaving dinner last night, telling her she was going out on a walk to look for flowers.

"Did you see Val there?"

He hesitated but nodded again. "She came to pay her respects to her friends."

"You weren't mean to her, were you?" Deya asked, cringing a little.

Caelum glared at her. "You may be surprised to learn that I'm not always *a prick*," he said pointedly.

Her face flushed, and she hung her head. "I know you're not," she admitted. He grunted noncommittally at this, but the guilt made Deya put her fork down and say, "I'm sorry I called you a prick, Caelum."

He stared at her for a moment, his purple eyes, for once, not piercing, or angry. For the first time, he looked at her as if he were seeing someone else.

"Don't worry about it. I deserved it." He nodded towards her plate, that glint back in his eye. "Now, eat your chicken."

Deya obeyed, but mostly because she was hopeful that this little moment was proof that the ice was thawing between them. Even as she sat there and gagged down bite after bite, Caelum stayed with her, his eyes neither judging nor impatient. Instead, he sat with her as if he were there for support.

"Can I ask you something?" she said, pausing from the chicken leg which was now a quarter eaten. It had only taken her a half hour to get to that point.

Caelum rolled his eyes. "This again?"

"Well?" she implored. "Can I?"

"Eat another potato and you'll get a question."

Obediently, Deya popped a potato in her mouth. It took her almost five minutes to get it down.

"Is what keeps you up at night the same thing that keeps me from eating?" she asked quietly.

Surprise washed over his face. His mouth went slack with shock before he looked away. Then his hand shot forward and swiped a potato from her plate.

"Hey!" she cried, but he waved her off and took a piece of chicken next. "I thought this was supposed to be for me," she mumbled.

Caelum shrugged; his mouth still full. "If I waited for you to finish this, we'd be here all night."

"You may not be a prick, but you are rude," she said, swatting his hand away from the food. "At least get a fork, your fingers are filthy!"

She could have sworn he almost smiled. Maybe more of a smirk, but it was still something not filled with antagonism.

He got up to get a fork and another plate of food, and they ate together. Caelum wolfed it down like a starved animal while Deya still attempted to swallow the most miniscule of bites.

"You never answered my question."

One dark eyebrow rose as he watched her cut a small potato into halves and then quarters.

"I have never seen a person cut a potato into sixteenths," he said flatly.

Deya ignored him. "Why do you not sleep?"

"You are extremely nosy." His voice was cool, positively frosty. "I didn't pry into why you don't eat."

She paused and fiddled with her fork. "I didn't realize I wasn't eating," she admitted. "I thought my stomach had just shrunk from starvation. That I wasn't used to having enough food anymore."

"That could be part of it," he said, not looking up at her, concentrating on his plate.

"But that's not what it is, is it?" Deya asked him. She wasn't sure why she was asking Caelum this. This was a conversation she should save for Val, someone who cared about her and worried about her well-being. Caelum had always made it abundantly clear that he did not give even the smallest of shits about her or her well-being. However, he was being so . . . normal, right now. He wasn't snarling and snapping. He was sitting before her, calmly cutting his chicken, listening to her, replying—albeit tersely.

"You would know the answer to that question better than I would," he replied.

"You knew about my magic inversing," she insisted, willing him to look at her again, for him to understand. "How were you the only one who had any kind of theory about what happened to me? Val and Rayner are both decades older than either of us, yet they had never seen anything like it. How did you come to that conclusion? Have you seen something like it before?"

He put his fork down and the look he offered crashed into her. It shot goosebumps down her arms, raising the hair on the back of her neck.

"The star seers have mentioned things like this," he said, those eerie purple irises seeming to flash between blue and purple in the dim lighting of the kitchens. "They studied ancient magic and history in order to learn of old prophecies and forgotten planets. They once said something to us about how certain magic is tied to our emotions. To our very core. When that is compromised, it affects our magic. This is why you may have felt your magic fluctuate in power based on how you were feeling in the past."

Deya nodded, her attention wholly on the Nodarian.

"When I heard you were a healer, it was the first thing I thought of," he said, shrugging.

She shook her head, a little shocked that he had even remembered something so distant. "I didn't think that it had affected me like that . . ." she murmured.

Caelum studied her. His plate was almost empty at this point, nothing but stray chicken bones and a few potatoes. "Pain like that manifests in strange ways," he said. "That is something I've learned in Ironbalt."

"How old were you when you were imprisoned?" she asked quietly.

He shifted, that uncertainty of whether he should answer her flashing in his eyes again. "Barely a teenager," he said. "When I was captured, my magic wasn't even at its full capacity yet. I was something of a late bloomer."

This was his attempt at levity, she supposed, and she gave him a small, grim smile for his efforts. "It must not have been easy," she said. "To lose your childhood to tragedy and adulthood to prison."

Caelum's eyes narrowed on his plate. Rage, sadness, and fear danced behind them. She had never seen an ounce of fear on the male's face before. He had always faced everything they had encountered thus far with stoicism and a large helping of hostility and rage. To see him like this . . . it did something to that broken bit of her heart that wanted to reach out towards likened things. The broken bird in her chest seemed to cry for him.

"I have endured worse," he said, and his tone was final. The conversation ended, and Deya turned her attention back to her plate.

Caelum decided to start his training with Deya in the dining hall instead of the training ring from then on. Every morning, they met for breakfast where he would inhale his own food and then proceed to watch Deya with sharp-eyed intensity as she put one tiny bite of toast at a time into her mouth.

He wanted to scream and shove it down her throat after the twentieth nibble, but he stopped himself. Their conversation yesterday in the kitchens had made him look at her a little differently.

It pissed him off to realize everyone commenting on his change in mood was not exactly unfounded. He *did* seem to have more patience. The effort it took to keep up the wall of impenetrable hostility had cost him a great amount of energy. And now that he was there, an official part of the Pillar Legion, he felt like he had a direction, an outlet, a path. He would seek vengeance on Praiton, one way or another. And that thought gave him more solace than anything.

Even the Manielian—Val, he supposed, he should call her—had stopped trying to get a rise out of him every chance she got after the night in Bellston Gardens.

But Caelum found himself worrying that he was revealing too much of himself. Especially to the Praitonian girl . . . to Deya. The way she looked at him—as if she understood, as if she *saw* through him to what he kept so tightly locked inside. It riled him to his core. So, to distract from this, he threw all his efforts into their training.

They ran laps around the ring first thing in the morning. Deya was able to keep up with him a bit better after he had force-fed her an egg and a whole piece of toast. It had taken her nearly an hour for her to choke it down—with much gagging and sips of water—but she had managed.

Then, he would put her through the exercises. First, the basic strength building: sit-ups, push-ups, curling weights. He found it funny that she tried so hard when she had not even wanted to learn to fight. But she was so small, so frail, that she could barely lift the smallest weight the training ring had available. Instead, Caelum had to supplement her with the wooden sword that he had decided she was also not yet ready to use. This decision had been met with a lot of irate foot stomping that made him think unconsciously of his younger sister when she had been denied access to the astronomy room past her bedtime. The thought made his heart clench.

Deya wasn't ready for the swordplay exercises yet, he decided. She could barely stay standing after he made her lunge across the entire training ring, even though he was right behind her, and doing it while carrying a heavy weighted plate in his hands, no less.

Within a few weeks of being at Light's Tower, Caelum was starting to notice a marked difference in his own physique. He had been eating heavily, training hard, and the difference had been staggering. No longer was he thin, pale, and emaciated, but he was beginning to bulk up, his muscles coming in. The tunics that used to hang loose on his arms and shoulders like a sheet on a hat rack now were much tighter across his chest and arms.

Deya, however, did not improve much over the next few weeks. Her eating did not get easier, and as a result, her strength was still minimal. She was beginning to get frustrated and angry every time her body betrayed her, and she'd fall to the ground again and again.

And what was more, *Caelum* was starting to get frustrated as well.

When Deya hit the ground again for the second time that day, Caelum had to draw in a slow, controlled breath. He wanted to scream at her, snap at her like he had been snapped at in his youth, but he held back. His patience for her may have grown, but it was beginning to wear thin.

"Are you going to get up any time soon," Caelum said, the tremor of irritation just barely audible in his low hiss.

Deya spat out a sweaty tendril of hair and glared up at him with such intense fury, it almost made him laugh. "I'm *trying*."

She was dirty, sweating, and swearing. Her chestnut hair was plastered to her forehead and spilling out of the braid she always wore. The third lap and the last fifty push-ups were what felled her this time.

Caelum walked around her, assessing her trembling arms and legs as she attempted to pull herself out of the dirt.

It had been days of this. Days of him watching her starve herself, even while she ate. Days of patience and compassion that were both foreign and uncomfortable to him. And yet, his frustration at watching this girl try so hard while simultaneously giving up made him want to scream with fury.

But as Deya raised her head and he saw the rage burning in her eyes, he took a deep breath. He knew what he had to do. It was the Nodarian way—the *only* way. He had been much too easy on her the last few days.

Well, he thought, *no more.*

"Try harder," he snapped, the sudden change in his tone making her flinch. "You are *weak*. You will never be ready for a sword at this rate."

The stunned pain that washed over her face made him hesitate just slightly before he shoved it back.

Deya seethed as she staggered to her feet. He had to give her credit: she always got up. But he'd never tell her that.

"You haven't even given me a *chance* with a sword!" she cried furiously. "How can you tell me I am not ready—"

"You cannot even hold a sword above your head," Caelum snarled.

221

"Cannot even run with one for an extended amount of time. These exercises are not for my amusement, no matter how much you may think I enjoy tormenting you."

Deya sneered at him. "Don't you?"

He felt his lip curl. "Oh, I do. But your suffering is just a fringe benefit."

As his shadow fell over the crumpled heap of a girl, a memory flashed through his mind: a menacing, Praiton general kicking a small, white-haired boy to the ground as he struggled to rise, to grasp a sword that was too big for him . . . the boy crying out. Pain in his ribs. Anger.

Deya shot him a loathsome look and limped back to the water jug that they kept for them on the edge of the training arena. "I have only been doing this for a week. I didn't even *want* to learn in the first place. I have never done something like this before—"

"And you will never get better unless you *eat*," he snarled. "Your meager nibbles and bites at breakfast are not enough. I do not have the time nor the patience to babysit every Gods forsaken morsel you put into your pathetic body."

Deya flinched, but he felt nothing but vindicated. All he could see was that same pathetic little boy. The boy who would not stand. The boy who did not fight back. The anger, the pain, the defeat. The memory of it rang through him with the force of a mallet on metal as he stalked towards her. And when she looked up at him, all he could feel was Deya's rage. But this time, he did not hesitate. This time, he was determined to wipe the weakness from that memory. To replace it with nothing but the fury that burned in Deya's eyes.

He *wanted* Deya to fight. Wanted her to improve. Wanted this broken girl to push back . . . Wanted to know something broken *could* be mended. That something weak could become stronger.

"*I do eat,*" she growled, the wounded look still in her gray eyes.

"Not enough. But if you don't believe me . . ." He reached into the weapons rack, pulled out a simple bronze sword, and shoved it into her arms. Pulling out a wooden sword, he held it out, tip facing her. "Then come find out."

Deya froze, looking down at the sword in her hands. "But you haven't even taught me how to properly use one!" she sputtered.

Caelum shrugged, backing up into the center of the ring again. "I thought you had used one before," he taunted her.

He spun his sword, the wooden hilt twirling in his hand—a trick Aelius had loved to do, to show off. Hours spent practicing it with the pickaxe in Ironbalt—which was much heavier and more cumbersome than a sword—left him surprised to find he was better at it now than even Aelius had been.

Deya looked as if she wanted to argue with him, but instead, she squared her shoulders, her eyes still burning with anger. Caelum smiled to himself. *There it was.*

He would never admit it, but he admired her determination. It had been surprising to him that she tried as hard as she did, seeing as how she hadn't wanted to be here in the first place. And yet, there she was, standing in front of him with her sword fisted in her small hands, looking murderously determined.

Deya lunged forward, thrusting her sword towards him. He easily parried it, spun around her blade, and thwacked her, hard, on the shoulder with the wooden sword.

She cried out, her hand flying to clutch her arm in outrage.

"Wrong," he said. "Again."

She let out an incensed roar and leapt again, but he dodged it easily. She kept swinging, and Caelum kept evading every attempt, her movements slow and heavy.

"Pathetic," he spat at her, dancing around her blade as she swung it at him senselessly. "You're barely trying."

But Deya grew even angrier, her face red and splotchy as she, in fact, tried harder than ever before to hit him, just *once.*

Finally, Caelum grew bored of her useless attempts to wield the sword. With a slow, practiced breath, he began to increase his speed. He twirled the wooden blade faster and faster, and his blows came down on hers harder than before.

He could see the panic on her face as he made contact with her blade with increasing force each time. He did not understand this girl. She fought so hard against learning to fight, and yet she was here, fighting him as hard as she could.

She had as much to be angry about with Praiton as the rest of them. He knew that she had suffered, too. And yet, Caelum could not fathom how this girl had resigned to give up for the last few days.

No, he thought. She wasn't just trying to give up. She had been trying to die.

"How are you not angry?" he snarled at her. His sword came down on hers, knocking her back a few steps. "They imprisoned you. *Tortured* you. Killed your fucking friend, and yet you aren't angry?"

Deya's breathing was labored, her eyes shimmering with tears. "I never said I wasn't!" she panted.

"Then prove it!" he snapped. "Fight back!"

And with an almighty strike, Deya's sword went flying from her hand and she hit the ground with a cry of pain and despair.

Caelum looked down at her, a sweaty mess on the floor. But when he leaned down over her, casting a shadow over her small, frail form, he only saw the small white-haired boy crying and bleeding on the ground.

"*Weak*," he hissed. "You are *weak*, and not ready."

It was only then that he noticed the tears on her face, the anger and disappointment in those gray eyes. And then, she let loose.

With a scream of anguish, Deya launched herself at him and her fist struck him, hard, across the face. Caelum felt it knock his chin sideways, yet he did not react.

Her hits kept coming. Pummeling her small fists as hard as she could, Deya screamed in fury, raining down blow after blow on his face, his chest, his arms . . . any part of him that she could reach, she hit with as much strength as she could muster.

"*Deya!*" A streak of red raced towards them. Val made to pull Deya off him, but Caelum held out a hand.

"No, leave her."

Sobbing and panting, Deya continued to thrash against him. And Caelum continued to let her, until, spent and broken, her fists began to slow, and then stopped.

Caelum reached up and grasped her wrists, which were trembling and so frail he felt he could snap them like a twig in his hands. Blood trickled down his face, bruises beginning to blossom where knuckle had struck bone. But still, he held her while she sobbed.

"*That* is how you fight back."

Deya yanked her arms from his grasp, shoved Caelum aside, and fled the training ring. She blew past all the others around them, not even noticing Val who was standing there, her hands outstretched, as though she were still about to pry Deya off Caelum. She was staring at him with such fury that her hair seemed to crackle like flames.

"I cannot believe you!" she cried, storming up to him. "What the *hell* was that?"

He threw his wooden sword back into the weapons rack, attempting to stay cool and calm while he wiped the fresh blood from his split lip. "Mind your own business," he snapped at her as she stomped towards him.

"Every time I think that you may have even *one* redeemable quality," she hissed, "you prove me wrong in such a spectacular fashion that I can hardly believe it."

Caelum snorted. "Glad to hear it."

"You are unbelievable, do you know that?" Val cried, refusing to let him off easily, and instead chasing him across the ring where he was attempting to go to get away from her. "That poor girl is in pain. She is frail and ailing, and you *know* that what plagues her is *not* physical."

"I do not care what plagues her," he spat, whirling around to face her. "They asked me to train her. I am training her. Her mental battles are her own to deal with." He knew that this was a lie, especially after he had let the girl beat him like a sack of sand. If she had been any stronger, she

225

could have caused serious damage to him, he knew that. But the second after the first punch, Caelum knew that her frustration was not for him. She had to let it out. Even at his expense.

Val glared at him with such ferocity that he could feel the warmth of her Ember Magic radiating off her in waves. "You know something, Caelum," she said, pointing a finger at him, "you and Deya are not as different as you like to make yourself believe. Your mental battles are not unlike hers. And instead of being an absolute *ass* to her, maybe you should try some compassion? You may find it gets you farther."

And then she stormed off in the direction of Light's Tower, leaving Caelum feeling like a rabid animal everyone was too afraid to be near.

CHAPTER
18

Deya took the stone steps towards the residential wing two at a time, tears blurring her vision as she went.

Weak. Pathetic. Caelum's voice echoed in her head as she ran—so desperate to get away, to go to her room where no one could see her fall to pieces.

She couldn't believe what she had done. Losing control like that. Punching and flailing against Caelum like a child throwing a tantrum. Her cheeks burned at the thought, the tears flowing nonstop. And yet, he had sat there and *let* her pummel him, not even a flicker of anger or threat of retaliation in those purple eyes.

Since she had left her room where she had initially barricaded herself in to marinate in her despair, she had done her best to throw herself into the present, to enjoy Light's Tower and her new friends. To dedicate her mind and body to training, to getting stronger. She was furious, frustrated to her wit's end that no matter how hard she tried, her body fought against her. No matter how much she tried, she could still hardly keep food down.

After the first night Caelum had sat patiently with her in the kitchens, she had returned to her room and thrown it all up. It hadn't been on purpose. She wept all night after she deposited all her hard work—the two hours of cutting, chewing, and swallowing that had been just as torturous as Caelum's physical exercises—into the bottom of the bog in her bathing room.

And while she didn't throw up again after that, it became harder and harder for her to eat more than a little bit here and there. She knew that Caelum was right—that if she did not eat, her strength would never return—but she couldn't think of anything else she could do.

All around her, were nothing but obstacles—things holding her back. She was angry and frustrated at her body, furious that it was one more betrayal. Every time she thought she was capable of making progress, healing somehow, her body would show her a new and fresh way that it had chosen to keep score.

Her boot caught on one of the winding stone steps and she went down with a crash, her head whacking against one of the steps as she collapsed. And there she wept, like the weak, pathetic urchin that Caelum had reminded her that she was.

She sobbed and sobbed, thinking that there was no end to it, no end to the pain. The broken bird in her heart was screaming with her, its wings rustling and flapping. She wanted to curl into herself, to bunch her body in as tightly as she could, as if she could somehow stamp out that fluttering movement with her knees—as if she could smother it.

That horrible power rose from her core and hammered at the iron doors she had placed on it, and she almost wished she could tear the faerivaine necklace off. For a horrible, selfish moment, she wished she could unleash all the pain and anguish she felt on the world. It was a power so big, so horrible, that she couldn't keep it inside. She wanted it out of her . . . she wanted to be free of it, even for a second.

Then a hand touched her shoulder. "Come on," a voice whispered in her ear. She flinched away from the touch, her body recoiling at the feeling, trying to run from the gentle hand that lifted her elbow and pried her off the floor.

She caught the scent of a wintry forest and groaned as Caelum scooped her up as if she weighed nothing. Because she did. She had seen it in the mirror—the first reflective glass she had encountered since she had been imprisoned by Clarita Killoran. Her cheeks were gaunt, the color of parchment, and seemed to cling to every bone and tendon in her body like wet fabric. Her body was nothing but sharp angles and points, no softness left in any part of her. She was skeleton and skin, a reflection of horror and pain.

That was all that was left of her.

Caelum carried her the rest of the way up the stairs to the residential wing, letting her cry silently into his tunic. He didn't growl or snap once, even though she expected it as her tears soaked his shirt.

When he reached her bedroom door, he pushed it open. Setting her gently down on the bed, she lay in a heap, sniffling numbly. Though she didn't look up, she could still feel him there, sitting beside her on the stool from her vanity table.

It was just like how it was in the kitchens. Caelum sat, neither impatiently nor judgingly, but almost as if he were there for support. When she snuck a peek at him, the sight of the bruises and dried blood on his face sent a pang through her. Already, the wounds were healing, but the guilt she felt for beating him like that was overwhelming.

Deya's tears eventually petered out, but they still trickled down her face, the sudden cold air drifting through the room cooling them onto her cheeks. She lay, pressed against the soft mattress of her bed, her back to the Nodarian male. His presence made the hair on the back of her neck stand on end.

After a few minutes of silence, Caelum cleared his throat.

"Val informed me that I was an insensitive asshole to you."

Deya sniffed. "You needed Val to tell you that?"

"No, I suppose not."

229

Silence fell again. Deya wasn't sure if what Caelum had said was supposed to be offered as some kind of apology. She wasn't entirely sure what to make of this situation.

Caelum let out another frustrated sigh. "I should not have called you pathetic and weak."

"You weren't wrong, though," she whispered into her pillow. "I am pathetic and weak. Look at me."

She was glad she couldn't see Caelum's face, dreading the look he would have on it. Whether it be pity or agreement, she didn't know which would be worse.

"Do you not remember what I said to you the other day," he said, and while his voice was still gentle and kind, his trademark hint of annoyance strained through just a little. "About how pain can manifest in odd ways."

Deya turned to look at him, forgetting for a second how she did not want him to see her like this. No doubt, her face was blotchy, red, and tearstained. There might have even been a little snot hanging in unattractive places. But Caelum looked upon her coolly, no hint of a sneer or repulsion curling his lips.

"You once asked me if the reason why I cannot sleep is the same reason you cannot eat," he said. He looked down at his hands which were clasped in front of him, his leg bouncing nervously as he steeled himself for whatever he was preparing to tell her. "I cannot sleep because I have nightmares of watching my siblings die."

Deya's breath caught in her throat. Caelum said it so matter-of-factly, so calmly, but she could see it—that pain, an almost mirror image of her own, reflected in his purple eyes.

"They were slaughtered in front of me," he said. "All of them. And I could not do anything to stop it. I was weak and pathetic, too. Helpless. And that will haunt me for the rest of my life."

He looked up at her, and their eyes locked. She didn't know what to say. Her mouth opened stupidly, but no sound came out.

"Pain manifests in strange ways, Deya," he said. "We may be out of

Ironbalt, but you and I are both far from being free of what imprisons us."

She felt the feeble beat of wings inside of her again, and she closed her eyes, trying to shut out the fluttering, anxious feeling in her chest.

"I keep thinking it's all a dream," she whispered. "That I'll wake up, and I'll be back on the floor in my cell in Stonehall Castle, waiting to be whipped by Clarita again. The days keep passing here and it's like I'm passing with them. Like they're not real."

Caelum did not say anything, once again just letting her talk, letting her speak what she had tried to deny in the last month since they had escaped from the prison.

"Even though I didn't want to learn to fight, I tried my hardest because I didn't want to feel like that again," she said. "But instead, I feel even more helpless. Hopeless. I cannot eat. It won't stay down," she admitted to him, shooting him an ashamed look. "Every time I try to eat something more than a nibble or morsel, as you say, my body rejects it. I throw it up within the hour."

Caelum grunted, as though this was surprising to him, but still, he did not interrupt.

"I don't know what to do," she whispered. "I just want it to stop . . . I want it all to stop."

Caelum stared at her in such a peculiar way that it took her by surprise. It was almost like . . . recognition.

"You need to find what it is inside you that makes you want to fight, to keep going," he told her. His fists clenched and his eyes flashed as he said, "I will make Praiton pay. I will avenge what has been taken from me. *That* is why I keep going. If you let them break you, they win, Deya. The only way they don't win is if you *fight back*."

"But . . ." the small, cowardly part of her whispered—the part that *didn't* want to keep fighting— "I feel like everything I had—everything worth living for—is ashes. What if that is all that is left of me?"

When Caelum looked at her, it was with intense scrutiny, his gaze spearing through her, as though he could see what was left inside.

"It does not matter if that is all that is left," he said finally. "If you fight, you will become stronger. From your ashes, you will become steel."

Deya rubbed her eyes, feeling tears welling in them again. She hadn't had a reason to keep going. For so long, she had only held onto the goal of surviving. Over the months she had been imprisoned, survival had become her only motivation in life. But for now, she was not in any direct danger. She was safe. But her body did not seem to realize this. It was still constantly at the ready, over-functioning to the point of crippling her.

She nodded to Caelum, though, still mulling over what he had said.

"I'm sorry, by the way," she added, pointing to her own face as a reference to the cuts and bruising that were fading from his skin. "For hitting you like that."

Caelum shrugged and averted his eyes from hers. "It's fine. You needed to get it out." And, as if it was just a natural, instinctual reaction, he reached out and brushed a tendril of her hair free from the sticky tear tracks that clung to her face.

Deya's mouth opened but no sound came out as she studied the white-haired Nodarian, his curious response making her head tilt. He was *such* an utter mystery sometimes.

"We'll resume training tomorrow. At the dining hall," he said to her, his hand snapping back to his side, as if just realizing what he had done. He stood and made to leave, but hesitated, his eyes on her mantle. He had noticed the carving of Arista, the Harvest Goddess, the lone decoration that she had put on display in her room. He picked it up, running his fingers over her crude details.

"Why Arista?" he asked her.

Taken aback, Deya shrugged. "My mother is Ganiean. Arista was the goddess I grew up with."

Caelum nodded and put Arista back down. "I will see you tomorrow," he said, before leaving the room.

Deya attempted to sleep after Caelum left. Her tears had left her drained, and her whole body ached from the day's training. So Deya succumbed to her exhaustion and fell into a hard, dreamless sleep. She awoke to complete darkness outside and only a sliver of moonlight falling onto her bed from her small window.

Sitting up, dazed, and groggy, she gazed out at the sky for a few minutes. She had not gotten over the view of the stars and moon from Light's Tower. From this high up in the mountain, it was like being right underneath them, as though she were placed in a bowl filled with stars.

From below, movement caught her eye. Flashes of purple light were glinting beneath the Tower, illuminating the tall, pointed trees. Alarmed, Deya stuck her head as far out the window as it could go. She was so thin now that her shoulders fit out the narrow gap without any squeezing needed.

On a lower level of the mountain, in the small gap where the trees parted, was a familiar silver-haired head. The flashes of light appeared to be pops of his magic, as if he were trying and failing to do something.

Without thinking, Deya got up from bed and grabbed her boots. Hastily lighting a candle, she shoved it onto the ledge of her window, hoping its light would be enough to guide her back, but she still wasn't sure where he was or how he had gotten there.

She tiptoed out of Light's Tower, which was dark save for a few patrols in the hallways. They all gave her a curt nod, but otherwise paid her no mind. She darted out the back, through the training arenas and towards the gate leading to wild country.

Glancing between the Tower and the stars, she was able to locate her bedroom window, the candle flickering faintly from its perch miles above in the sky. Picking her way through the forest, she listened hard for the sounds of Caelum's Celestial Magic.

A cold breeze whistled by, rustling her hair, raising goosebumps on her arms and neck. She followed it.

It led her to a small clearing, devoid of trees. The only thing in the middle of the flat ground was Caelum, his white hair gleaming in the moonlight, and his brow screwed up in concentration. He was breathing hard, and Deya watched, fascinated, as his hands pulled at the air between them. A flash of purple light flickered, and then died almost instantly. Caelum swore.

"What are you doing?"

No sooner had the words left her mouth than an invisible hand gripped Deya by the throat. She let out a strangled yell as it wrenched her into the air, her feet leaving the leaf-strewn Earth.

"Caelum—" she gasped, but recognition dawned on the male's face, and his concentration broke.

"What the *hell* are you doing out here?" he shouted at her. He dropped her to the ground, not even bothering to lower her down gently. She crashed to Earth and glared up at him from her crumpled heap in the dirt.

"I saw you from my window!" she cried, pointing backwards to where Light's Tower glinted above the treetops, a massive black spike on the horizon. "I thought you may be . . . in trouble or something." This was a lie. She had seen he was practicing magic; known he had come out here where nobody could see him. And she wanted to know why.

"Well, I'm just fine, thanks," he snapped, waving her off. "Now get back to the Tower before you get us killed."

"What are *you* doing out here, if you could be killed?" she asked waspishly, rising to her feet, and brushing off the dirt from her breeches.

Caelum drew a deep breath through his nose, his purple eyes almost rolling into the back of his head from sheer impatience.

"None of your fucking business."

Deya folded her arms. "Oh, so we're back to this again, are we?"

He turned his back on her, and she suspected that he was trying everything in his power not to lash out at her. She had hoped the last few interactions they had were proof things were improving between them. That while Caelum was always destined to be grumpy and cranky, the hostile part may abate as they found more common ground. The fact he turned away from her instead of lunging for her throat boded well.

"Deya, for the love of the Mother," he moaned. "Just *leave me alone* so I can get back to work."

But Deya ignored him and moved closer. Her eyebrow raised as she circled, eyeing him.

"Are you merely practicing to get better or are you trying something different?"

"Does it *matter?*" he snarled, his purple eyes doing their usual murderous dance. The more she and Caelum got to know each other, the more she was beginning to find his general crankiness amusing rather than frightening.

"What are you trying to do?" Deya asked again.

Caelum whirled to face her, anger boiling over in every feature of his face, but then he froze. Deya heard it, too. Large, echoing crashes. They reminded her of Clarita's footsteps, except massive . . . dangerous. Slowly, she turned to see what had Caelum looking so horrified.

A shadow fell over them, and what looked like two enormous tree trunks the size and width of a large boulder thudded down in front of her. Deya's eyes roved upwards.

A large mountain troll towered above them, its skin gray and scaly. She had only ever seen pictures in tomes in the library, crude drawings of creatures that lived in mountain passes, who carried clubs and feasted on animals or stray travelers. It was obvious now that those pictures did the terror of this monster no justice.

Large mossy rocks grew out of its shoulders, arms, and back, as if it had fallen asleep one day in the woods and had become part of the Earth. Its face was blank, too stupid to think, its black, expressionless eyes roaming across the ground. The beady orbs landed on them, and its gash of a mouth opened to reveal teeth like jagged rocks. It let out a roar so loud that the trees were blasted back by the force of the sound. The reverberations sent Deya flying backwards into Caelum, who caught her, his eyes wide with terror.

"*Run!*" he cried, and snatching her hand in his, they took off flying into the forest. The troll let out another mighty roar, and its crashing footfalls began to thunder throughout the woods, trees quaking, stones bouncing from the sheer weight of its steps.

Deya and Caelum ran, weaving through trees, dodging branches. The troll, however, pushed trees out of its way as if they were mere brambles, the entirety of the trunks being ripped from the ground with barely a flick of its large arm.

"Where are we going?" Deya shouted at Caelum. Now thankful for all the running he had made her do in the past few days, her feet seemed to fly underneath her as she struggled to keep up with Caelum's long strides.

"We need to find someplace to hide." Caelum's head jerked backwards to see where the troll was. The look on his face told her that it wasn't far. The footfalls were getting closer and closer, each reverberation more severe, causing the ground to buck underneath her, making it difficult to keep her footing. "Someplace small . . . where it can't reach us—"

"Can't you just hold it with your Gravity Magic?" Deya cried. A branch whacked her in the face, tearing into her skin, making her yelp.

"I depleted too much energy training . . . It's too big . . . there's no way I could hold it for more than a few seconds at most—"

Another roar rent the forest, so loud this time that the force of it knocked them both to the ground. The troll crashed into view, its feet smashing everything beneath it. It stormed towards them, barely giving them a second to scramble to their feet and dive out of the way.

Swinging a club-like hand at them, it missed Deya by an inch. She screamed and threw herself behind a tree. The troll's fist blasted the tree to smithereens, sending branches and leaves flying. Caelum rolled the opposite way to avoid one of its enormous feet, but now he was separated from Deya by the troll itself.

"Deya!" he yelled, but the troll had already turned its sight on her. Beady black eyes glinted at her hungrily, its large mouth gaping. A bead of drool hung from one of its incisors and Deya could see herself reflected in the glistening goop.

It let out another tremendous growl and lunged for her with the grace of a bull elephant, its hand swinging towards her when its feet lifted from the ground. Suddenly, it was floating, stunned, in midair. Its massive head swiveled, its expression confused and disoriented as its giant form rose higher and higher.

Bewildered, Deya looked around to see Caelum, standing across the clearing, arms outstretched, his face screwed up with the effort of keeping the colossal beast airborne.

"What are you fucking waiting for?!" Caelum yelled. "*RUN!*"

Deya ran. She sprinted for Caelum who, with an almighty yell, brought his arms up over his head, just to bring them crashing down. The whole Earth shook with the force of the troll, its girth slamming into the ground—but not hard enough.

Unlike the soldiers from Aunecia, the troll was massive. It was evident it had taken most of Caelum's magic to lift the troll as high as he did. The force of its descent was nowhere near as devastating as what he was able to achieve with the soldiers. In the end, Caelum's effort did nothing more than buy them a bit of time . . . and, of course, enrage the troll even more.

"Fuck," Caelum breathed as the troll screamed in anger, but Deya was already reaching for his hand and pulling him along, both pelting pell-mell back through the forest.

"This way!" Deya cried, pulling Caelum, who kept looking backwards over their shoulder. The troll was raging now, running at an even faster pace, slamming its fists into the trees and ground around it. They ran towards the outskirts of the forest, making a hard turn back towards the mountains.

If only they could find a crevice, Deya thought. If they could find some small bit of rock to squeeze into . . .

The mountainside came into view and Caelum seemed to know exactly what Deya was onto. From behind them, the troll blundered and roared through the trees, the impact of its footfalls being the only way they could tell where it was.

Caelum began to pull Deya straight towards the mountain wall that was piled high with rocks and boulders. She opened her mouth to scream to Caelum that they were about to crash, headfirst into the wall, when Caelum reached out an arm. With a strangled shout, he lifted his hand. An enormous rock that she had thought to be one with the mountain rose, revealing a small crevice behind it. He threw Deya in before barreling in after her and, with another grunt, the slab of stone crashed back to the ground, barricading them in.

She could hear the troll roaring, its arms flailing, attempting to smash anything it could find. The ground underneath them trembled, but they kept quiet, nothing but their heavy breathing filling the cramped space.

The troll's yells became more frustrated, the banging becoming frantic, as if it were searching for them on the ground. But its senses were lacking, unable to detect them panting and sweating, hidden behind the rock—surely, they would reek to any other predator nearby. But the troll did not pick up on this. It roared once more, before they heard it lumber away.

Caelum's breath was tickling the hair on her forehead. His hands were splayed on either side of her, their bodies pressed tight together. Now the danger had ultimately passed, she felt her breath catch at his proximity. Caelum seemed to notice this at the same time as she did.

A sliver of moonlight fell through the gap in the rock, letting her see the look on his face as he realized how close she was. In fact, there were a lot of things she hadn't noticed about him before now. Like how his eyes were violet with an almost blue starburst around the pupil, how he had a small scar on his eyebrow, or how his lips . . .

She felt her head tilt, just slightly, and for a second, Caelum's purple eyes—still glowing with his power—glimmered as they homed in on her mouth, too.

"This is your fault," he breathed. "I told you to go back to the bloody Tower."

"Are you kidding?" she laughed. "This is the best training you've given me all week."

Caelum snorted, but she could've sworn she saw it—an actual smile. He cleared his throat, shifting against her, every inch of his body touching every inch of hers, and it sent a molten flush through her.

"We should probably go before it comes back," he said gruffly.

Deya nodded, clearing her throat. He shifted around her, attempting to get an arm loose to lift the rock. When he managed to raise it clear of their crevice, they fell out of the hole, the cool air rushing to meet them.

"Now, try to keep your damn voice down," he said, but it lacked his usual bite. Deya smirked.

Together, they headed quietly back up to Light's Tower, neither of them speaking. But this time, the silence was pleasant, comfortable . . . almost friendly. It made her think about how it felt with Oswallt as they sat beside each other in their separate cells in Ironbalt, too tired to speak but grateful for each other's presence. And in that moment, his final words came back to her.

"I figured it out," she told him. "What it is that makes me want to keep going, I mean."

Caelum gave her a look that could've been anywhere from curious to skeptical.

"Oh?"

"I didn't even realize it, but Oswallt actually gave it to me," she said softly, her eyes watching her boots take one step at a time. "He made me promise . . . made me swear that moment at the whipping post. He made me swear that I'd fight this. For the both of us." She gave him a small smile. "So, you were right. I have to fight, don't I?"

Caelum's purple eyes did not leave her face. They scrutinized her, but she did not look away. She could still picture how his head had tilted in that tight cave, like he, too, had considered the impossible.

"Revenge is always a heavy motivator," he said, and nodded to her. "We will make Praiton pay."

She nodded back, and together, they headed back towards the mountain in silence, but the feel of his body against hers did not fade as they made their way towards the black tower.

CHAPTER
19

Saying aloud to Caelum what Oswallt had made her promise gave Deya a new zeal for life. It was almost as if she had forgotten that last moment she had shared with her friend until she had confessed it to the brooding male. But he had been right: it had set her free, in a way.

The next morning, she was in the dining hall before Caelum, and had loaded her plate with eggs and toast, even going so far as to add an apple and a glass of milk. She sat in the far corner of the still empty hall, attempting to tackle her food when Caelum entered. He did a doubletake when he saw her there already—and with a full plate—before he made his way towards her, his own plate in hand.

"Ambitious," he remarked, looking at her heaping dish. For the last few weeks, she had only been attempting to choke down one egg and a piece of toast. She would've settled only for the toast, had Caelum not insisted she needed the protein.

"Can't very well make Praiton pay if I can't hold a sword," she said. Picking up the toast, she took a brave bite. Food still felt like sand, but she persevered, chewing as fast as she could and choking it down before tearing off another piece.

"Careful," Caelum warned her, reaching out to pull the toast back from her mouth. "You need to slow down, or you *will* throw it up again."

But Deya was determined. She had awoken that morning with a driving electricity in her blood, as if she were being pumped full of life. The broken bird she felt in her chest was shaking the bars she had encaged it in, wanting out, wanting blood. She didn't know how she hadn't considered it before . . . revenge . . . anger. She had been holding on so tightly to the sadness, to the sorrow and grief she had felt. Not only for Oswallt, but for her home, what she had thought to be her friends.

Praiton was where she had grown up, what she used to consider the biggest and best kingdom in all of Krigor. She was proud to be a part of it, proud to be part of such a vast and important region which boasted life from all corners of the realm. When she had been hired on as a healer for Stonehall Castle, serving the king himself, she had been bursting with pride. It was where she belonged, her calling. And while she had struggled and fought for her place in Stonehall's ranks, she felt she had earned it.

But it had all been ripped away from her. When Clarita had imprisoned her, the loss and betrayal of what she had thought was her home was so rife, it had often kept her awake and in agony on the floor of her cell in Stonehall. Ever since her imprisonment in Ironbalt—especially now that she was here at the headquarters for the Pillar Legion's rebellion—she had felt exiled, outcast. Her kingdom no longer wanted her in it.

She had spent weeks unconsciously mourning this, grappling with the loss of her home and her friends all at once. But it had taken the conversation with Caelum yesterday for her to realize something. That while Praiton had thrown her away, she finally realized that she no longer *wanted* to be a part of it. This realization had emboldened her.

And as she feverishly chewed her food, she found it tasted a little less like ash.

It took her only thirty minutes to finish the toast and half the apple—a large improvement from the days before. Even Caelum had given her the tiniest hint of an encouraging smile. Well, his attempt at one, anyway.

Caelum didn't seem able to look her in the eye that morning. She wondered if it was because of their awkward, charged moment in that crevice. If she were being honest with herself, she found it hard to look him in the eye after that as well. She could still see the way his purple eyes had lowered to her mouth, how his head had turned the slightest degree to mirror hers in that moment.

It all made a shiver run down her spine. And not necessarily in a bad way.

"Well, isn't this quaint." Rayner and Val appeared at their table, grinning down on them like two cats who had got fed a large, fat rat. Val looked positively gleeful at the sight of them eating breakfast civilly in front of each other. "Deya, have you finally taught him table manners?"

Caelum's lip twitched into its familiar cold sneer as he took a bite of his eggs. "If only she could teach you how to use a sword, Manielian."

Val stuck her tongue out at him. They plonked down beside Caelum and Deya, their plates clattering on the table.

"Are we still attempting to train Deya?" Val asked, tucking into her eggs and kippers.

Deya shot her an offended look. "What do you mean *attempting?*"

"Sorry, love, but I've been watching your last few training sessions, and they haven't been pretty," she said, wincing. "Though I don't think it's your fault, rather your very *ineffective* teacher."

"If I'm so ineffective," Caelum spat, "why don't *you* take over for today?"

Val's heart-shaped mouth stretched into a delighted smile. "You know, I think that's a perfect idea," she announced, clapping her hands together, causing Caelum to hiss like a wet cat. "Have you just been teaching her the Nodarian style of swordplay?"

His eyes narrowed. "Naturally."

"There are different kinds of swordplay?" Deya asked.

"Each kingdom has their own unique style," Rayner supplied, taking a bite of his eggs. "Laenimore specializes in a style called Rain Dance, which is a much lighter, fluid form of swordplay. I'm not much for swords, but I can try to teach you what I know."

"And Nodarian style is mostly all about discipline and strength," Val said, looking pointedly at Caelum. "Which is probably why she is struggling to master your exercises. Swordplay doesn't always need to be about who is the fittest and fastest."

"If you want to be good it does," Caelum grumbled, glaring at the Manielian who tittered at his death stare.

"Not true. The Manielian style of swordplay is mostly double bladed. It is all about a sense of self-awareness, seeing the blades as an extension of yourself and being sure of that."

"If it is so good," Caelum snarled, "then how did it lose to the Nodarian style?"

"How's this," Rayner cut in—always the diplomat. "Deya can take turns learning from each of us. She can adopt what works for her and discard what doesn't. That way she can have the best of all three styles."

Deya looked between the three of them hopefully. "Is that possible? Do you think I can benefit from learning from all of them?"

Val nodded enthusiastically, but Caelum barked out a harsh "No."

"Why not?" Val cried, rounding on him.

"These disciplines are separate for a reason," Caelum snapped. "They each have their own strengths and weaknesses. And, in case you two have forgotten, they were created to compliment the magic of each region."

Val and Rayner both fell silent, telling Deya that they did, in fact, forget this. And what was more, they were both remembering that Deya's particular brand of magic was sealed away, too dangerous to let loose. Deya felt a surge of frustration and her fingers twirled the faerivaine necklace around her too bony neck.

She looked between the three of them—these three unusual companions that she was beginning to consider more and more as friends. Even Caelum, despite their ups and downs, had seemed to come around to her—and her to him. It was only because of this that she was able to take a deep breath and ask for the thing that scared her most.

"Do any of you think you can teach me how to control my magic?"

All three of them stopped dead at that question. Deya knew it was a lot to ask—knew it meant asking them to put their lives in danger as she attempted to master this horrific power. But she didn't know who else to ask, who else to *trust*.

"I . . . I would not even know where to begin," Val murmured. She glanced between Rayner and Caelum, both of whom were still staring, dumbly at Deya. "I have never seen anything like her magic, have you two?"

Rayner shook his head, but Caelum did not respond. He sat and peered at Deya, his purple eyes taking her in for the first time all morning. Val noticed his silence and turned towards him.

"Caelum?"

A second passed without the Nodarian moving or answering before he murmured, "No. Her situation is definitely rare. Possibly unique. However, I do believe it is still a part of her Healing Magic . . . almost a mutation."

Val's brow furrowed, and Rayner crossed his arms, looking pensive.

"You mean like her magic has . . . gone bad?"

"Not bad, just changed," Caelum said. His eyes never left her face as he said this, as though he was attempting to stare through her to see the very essence of the magic inside. It made her shift uncomfortably, her traitorous mind replaying that tiny tilt of his head last night over and over again.

"So . . ." Rayner began. "If it is a mutation of her Healing Magic, do you think it can be tamed?"

"Possibly," Caelum murmured.

All three of them lapsed into silence, lost in thought, all staring at Deya now as if she were a particularly interesting specimen. She could feel her face turning pink under their scrutiny.

"I suppose we can all try," Val hedged. "I'll even ask Aris if he'd be willing to help. He is also from Ganiea. He may not be from a noble family, but his Earth Magic is still fairly strong. Maybe he can help?"

"Oh, if *Aris* can help . . ." Rayner muttered, smirking. This caused Val to turn from pink to red in rapid succession. She smacked Rayner on the arm so hard that the Sea Fae nearly fell out of his seat.

Caelum sipped at his mug of orange juice, quiet as Val and Rayner squabbled. His eyes locked with Deya's, and she could have sworn that a hint of a smile played on his lips again.

That day, Val took over her training from Caelum. She still insisted that Deya do her warm-up exercises with him—a grueling and exhausting task that even the large breakfast she had managed to put down did little to alleviate. However, she managed to make it through the seemingly endless run alongside Caelum, and the push-ups and sit-ups he commanded her to do.

Eventually, Val allowed her to pick up a sword. She reached for a second one, but Val stopped her, smiling at her.

"You are not ready for two yet, love," she said. She twirled her own plain silver sword around her lithe body—which had filled out since she had left Ironbalt. Her hips and curves had come back with such a vengeance that the corset vest she had on pushed her breasts almost to the heavens. It made Deya a little envious. Her own body looked like a skeleton in clothing. She had always been more on the petite side, but now she looked like she was barely clinging to life.

"I used to have beautiful gold swords," Val said wistfully, watching the dull silver blade flash in the sunlight. "Manielian-made and gorgeous. They were engraved with our family crest and lineage." Her eyes paused on the rusty brass hilt of the sword in her hand, and she sighed. "Sadly, I lost them when I got captured."

Deya gave her a small, sad smile, which she returned, but it didn't quite meet her eyes.

Deya proceeded to train with Val for the rest of the day—under Caelum's steely-eyed supervision. Working with Val was much less unforgiving than working with Caelum. She led Deya through the motions and exercises with a practiced patience and gentility that Caelum had severely lacked. Val taught her how to view the sword as an extension of her arm, making her perform motions over and over again until they began to become second nature.

Even with her bigger than usual breakfast, Deya's arms and legs still trembled like leaves in the wind, her shoulders aching from performing the dancelike maneuvers Val performed with an athletic grace. She, however, felt like a newborn, unable to master or control the smallest movements Val had instructed her to do.

When Val announced that she had had enough for the day, Deya almost collapsed in the dirt in exhaustion.

"You'll get the hang of it," Val said, patting Deya on the shoulder with an encouraging smile. "It's all about practice."

Caelum had been sitting on the outer edge of the training arena next to Rayner, arms crossed and eyes glinting as he observed Val and Deya.

"You'll have Rayner tomorrow," Val said, reaching out a hand to help her up. "You'll get better if you keep at it, I promise."

Deya was greatly looking forward to staggering into her bathing pool and sinking like the Sea Beast beneath the water. Her muscles ached and she felt sweaty and grimy. But Caelum rose from where he was sitting and prowled towards them.

"You're not done yet. We need to work on your magic now."

Val opened her mouth to protest, but Caelum sent her a look that could kill, and she only sputtered in response.

"Caelum, she's had a long day," Rayner interjected, hastening over.

"Exactly," Caelum said. "It's better to test this when she's tired, or she may disintegrate the whole lot of us."

Deya felt her heart sink. It only then dawned on her the enormity of what she had agreed to undertake. She had not taken off the faerivaine necklace since Caelum had slipped it around her neck over a month ago. But she could still remember that awful, terrifying power that had exploded out of her that day at the whipping post. The memory still filled her with an unbearable amount of dread.

Caelum led Deya into the same clearing she had found him in the night before. Bits of tree and bark still littered the clearing—a mess left behind courtesy of their run in with the troll last night. Val and Rayner trailed after them, Val's eyes flicking around the destruction, opening her mouth as if to ask, but seeming to think better of it when she caught sight of Caelum's face. Caelum never appeared to look anything other than angry . . . except when his head had tilted the other night, that is.

Caelum directed Val and Rayner to stand twenty feet back from Deya. He had positioned her in front of a large, thorny bush in the clearing before stepping back to join Val and Rayner, out of her range.

"Take it off," he commanded. Deya's heart skipped for a second at the way he said that. It took her a moment to realize he meant her faerivaine necklace. Blushing, Deya reached up with trembling hands and removed the chain from around her neck. The high-pitched, tinny ringing in her ears from the iron subsided. For now, the power she knew to be in her core lay dormant, quiet.

"Aim at the bush," Caelum demanded. "Do what you tried to do to the flower that night." She caught sight of the questioning look Val shot at Caelum. She had never told Val about that night.

Deya took a deep breath and took aim at the plant. She tried to reach for her magic the way she used to, by digging into her core. But she found nothing. She adjusted her stance, breathing in harder, narrowing her vision. Still, there was nothing to pull from.

They were far enough away from her, but Caelum could still see Deya getting frustrated as her power failed to come forth. Val shifted beside him, also unnerved. She had never seen Deya's power in person, the devastation she could bring.

"Why is it not working?" Rayner whispered to him.

Caelum did not answer. He was studying Deya, her frustration and impatience growing the longer she stood in front of the bush. He had thought it obvious that her pain and fear activated this power, but he couldn't be entirely certain. They had experienced plenty of both since leaving Ironbalt.

The few times her powers had sprung forth, all of them were on edge, scared, shell-shocked. He couldn't have been sure then if that was the reason. But now that she was safe, relaxed and at ease, this would be the real test.

Deya stomped her foot and turned towards them. "It's not working!" she moaned.

Caelum wanted to shake her whenever she moaned like that. It was a sound he hadn't been able to get out of his head since the night before with the troll. He hadn't been able to look her in the eye the entire morning, either. He was still kicking himself for how he had looked at her in that damned crevice.

Her mouth had been so near to him . . . her lips pink and full, and for some damn reason, he had found himself momentarily entranced by them. He could have sworn that she had looked at him like that, too. The thought made him flush with a mix of anger and embarrassment.

Caelum broke away from Val and Rayner and stalked towards Deya. He heard Val gasp and she almost reached out, as if to pull him back, but he ignored her. Deya saw him marching towards her and the shock and fear on her face was evident.

"Caelum, wait—" She reached for the faerivaine necklace, but he held up a hand, not slowing his pace as he advanced towards her.

"Leave it off," he snapped.

Deya looked horrified. "But, Caelum, I could hurt you . . ."

"Good." He moved around her to stand behind her. She made to face him, but he seized her by the hips and rotated her back to the bush in front of them. "Your fear triggers your powers," he breathed into her ear. His hands guided her into place in front of the plant. "Your pain and agony were what caused it."

She turned to look at him in horror, the terror vivid in her eyes. "I . . . I have to channel *that*?" He knew what she was thinking—could only imagine having to dig into the trauma and hurt that she had most likely buried within herself to keep her going.

"Channel it and control it." His fingers dug into her hips, almost as if he were trying to drag her closer to him. A quick flare of anger at himself for even considering it stopped him, though. "Your despair was out of control at Ironbalt and when you first escaped. Now it is time to master it."

She looked at him, naked terror in her eyes, but she still nodded, determined. It was the thing that he admired most about her. How many times had he watched her fall only to get back up again? And now she was readying herself to plunge back into everything that terrorized her, traumatized her, haunted her . . . and she was doing it willingly.

Deya turned to look back at him. "Okay. I'll try. Just go back to Val and Rayner."

"No."

"*No?*" Deya cried, but then against his better judgment, Caelum pulled her backwards. Pulled her straight back into his chest, so close he could smell the sweet scent of roses in her hair.

He breathed into her ear, "You're going to *only* destroy the shrub in front of you. If you lose control and blast apart everything, you kill me, too."

Deya tried to whirl around to face him, to yell at him, her eyes alight with fury and panic, but he refused to let go of her waist, holding her in place as she fought him, tooth and nail.

"*I am not doing this with you here,*" she said through gritted teeth, her face panicked, but he was bigger than her, stronger. He held her right in place.

"Do it now," he growled. "Do it. I thought you were not weak and pathetic. I thought you were going to master your weaknesses."

Deya was now breathing hard, her breaths ragged as she stared at the bush in front of her. He knew what he was doing, egging her on, pushing her.

"Do it," he hissed in her ear. "You weren't too scared to destroy those guards. You weren't *weak* then. You even obliterated what was left of your friend—"

Caelum may have told himself that this was all cold and calculated, all done with a purpose, but the minute he said it, he sensed the ground tremor, as if something in the girl he was holding between his hands had broken. At his words, she whirled to face him—fighting against his grip— her face wild, furious . . . hurt.

Tears shone in her eyes as she turned and screamed, "*Shut up!*"

The ground underneath them seemed to tremble. Something was happening to Caelum's fingers. They felt as if they were vibrating.

"*Destroy the plant!*" Caelum shouted at her.

Deya let out a scream, a howl of pain and rage, tears running down her face. She was fighting herself; he knew it. She didn't have the ability to control this magic that was now so thick in the air he could almost taste it. His fingers tingled, now totally numb resting on her waist, until Deya threw herself out of his grasp.

She collapsed on the ground in front of the bush, and an agonizing, gut-wrenching scream exploded out of her. Caelum stumbled back, just in time. It was like watching a sped-up image. The bush and the grass surrounding Deya began to wilt—to turn gray, as if someone pulled away all the color. It happened so quickly that Caelum blinked and one minute it was green and whole, the next . . . ash. His eyes roamed down towards his feet. The ring of dead grass stopped right at his toes.

Panting, he flexed his fingers. They still felt numb and tingly, but otherwise, workable. Deya, however, lay in the circle of devastation and sobbed, just like she had when he had found her, collapsed on the steps in Light's Tower.

Footsteps thundered past him, and a flash of red appeared in his peripheral. And then a hand with a fistful of fire slapped him, hard across the face.

Stunned, cheek smarting from a light burn, Caelum stood there, too shocked to react as Val rushed past him towards Deya. She slipped the necklace back over the head of the trembling girl in the dead grass, her hands smoothing her hair, gathering her up.

"You're fucking psychotic," she spat at him. Then she picked Deya up, slinging her arm over her shoulder, and began to carry her back to Light's Tower.

Caelum put a hand on his cheek, the skin tender, blistering as if he had brushed his face against a hot stove.

Rayner approached, his eyes on the small circle of destruction that Deya had wrought. Caelum could see his eyes trace the circle, could see him note where it had stopped—right where Caelum stood. Then, the Sea Fae glanced at him. Shaking his head, he turned away, as if he couldn't bear to look at him, and headed after the two females.

CHAPTER
20

The Mother wanted to ensure we took extra special care of you. The sound of the warden's final words echoed in her head as Val half-dragged, half-carried Deya back towards Light's Tower.

She mentioned how much you agonized over watching others suffer. So, how will it feel to watch your friend suffer for you?

Caelum couldn't have known. To use himself to test her, force her. She felt so drained that her head spun. She was only faintly aware of the toes of her boots dragging over the threshold of Light's Tower, the warmth of Val pressed into her side.

"What happened?" She recognized the voice but was too weak to lift her head. Aris hastened to her and Val's other side, grabbing Deya by the arm and lifting her up, helping to support her as they walked through Light's Tower.

"Caelum is a dick," Val said through gritted teeth. "He pushed Deya to use her powers in a way that she wasn't ready for."

"Take her to the infirmary."

Before she knew it, Deya was being placed gently onto a small bed. She was swimming in and out of consciousness, but she could still hear Val and Aris whisper about her a few feet away.

"Did she lose control of her powers?"

"Caelum forced her to unleash it while he stood in range. He forced her to control it, but it cost her. She has no control over the radius. She nearly killed him."

Deya closed her eyes, squeezing them shut.

I nearly killed him.

Somehow, she fell asleep, even with Aris and Val still whispering around her. The warden's sadistic smile as he prepared to make Oswallt pay for her mistake flickered in and out of her dreams. Clarita knew her weakness, and apparently, Caelum did too.

When she awoke again, she didn't know what time it was or even what day. A small female in a gray dress was bending over her, a washcloth in hand. A healer. When she saw that her eyes were open, the healer smiled down at her.

"How are you feeling?"

Deya did a quick body scan and was surprised to find that she felt rested. Even the aching in her muscles from the training and using her magic had abated.

"Fine," she said. In fact, she felt like she was even rested enough to make training—with Val, that is. She didn't much fancy seeing Caelum right now.

She sat up and attempted to stand, stunned to find her legs were quite steady.

"I'll get Captain Valeria," the healer said, and she hurried from the room.

Deya walked to the basin and wet the washcloth the healer had left behind, wiping it down the side of her neck and face. The faerivaine necklace was back in place between her collarbones, a relief to see. Her fingers brushed it, and she remembered Caelum slipping it around her neck. Then the thought of him pulling her against him in that clearing, of holding her hips so tightly, of refusing to let her go, of growling in her ear, egging her on . . .

The infirmary door opened. Aris stepped over the threshold; his handsome face clean-shaven this morning. The hilt of his gold sword glinted in the sunlight shining through the mullioned windows of the infirmary.

He smiled when he saw her standing. "Valeria is temporarily indisposed," he told her, that cocky smile oozing his patent charm. "So, I came to see you instead."

Deya put the washcloth down, and Aris gestured to the bed she had just vacated. "Why does that sound oddly suggestive?" She was teasing, but Aris's face stiffened imperceptibly, before relaxing back into that cocky smile again.

"If only it were that," he said lightly. "No, I'm pretty sure she's hunting for your friend Caelum." Deya's heart gave an uncomfortable squeeze. "I believe she's trying to keep him from coming to see you. Most likely by force, knowing Valeria."

"Well, I appreciate that," Deya mumbled. "I'm not really in the mood to see him, to be honest."

Aris studied her. "Valeria told me about what happened and a bit about you and your power. She said you used to be a healer."

Deya nodded. The thought of her power—both old and new—made a numbness settle over her like frost.

"Valeria has asked me to facilitate your magic training going forth," he said. "She seemed adamant that Caelum not help with that anymore."

"I don't want to do it again." The response flew from her mouth before she could stop it, but she found she meant every word. The possibility of feeling that power again, of having to dig into that well of pain inside of her . . . Her palms began to sweat, and her heartbeat quickened.

Aris paused. His hazel gaze was piercing and contemplative. The general was never ruffled or riled, but always thoughtful and deliberate. This was no exception.

"Are you sure?"

Deya nodded. "Please," she whispered. "Don't make me do it again. I . . . can't. Not right now."

For a moment, she thought he would deny her. He held her gaze for a second too long, before nodding. "If that is what you choose," he said. "But I insist on the continuance of your sword training. It is still important that you learn to defend yourself."

And just like that, Deya began her training with the general of Light's Tower. Aris was a much more calculated tutor than Caelum, or even Val. She spent days under the general's careful observation, testing her swordplay, experimenting. She began to learn the strong, solid stances of the Ganiean sword form, something that came easier to her than the rest. Some days were harder than others, but she found herself slowly gaining footing with a sword, a feat she never thought would happen. And all this time, she did not see hide nor hair of Caelum.

All the while, the Pillar Legion was busy executing their schemes against Praiton. From what Val had told her, the Legion worked diligently across Krigor, sabotaging supply chain deliveries to Praiton, destroying Praiton posts and camps, protecting nearby cities from Praiton's bloodthirsty lot.

In the weeks that followed, Deya began to see more soldiers coming and going, smelling of blood and battle. Aris and the captains of Light's Tower met often in secret—Val included—and Deya sometimes went days without seeing the handsome general while he and his small unit completed clandestine missions no one else knew the details about.

Amidst all the movement, she still practiced her sword work with Val and Rayner, finding a cozy medium of both individual styles. She found she was lighter on her feet, quicker than she had known she could be. And while she didn't eat like she used to, her food intake improved to the point where she was eating small quantities again with little to no issue.

For a while, things seemed calm. She trained, ate, slept, and talked with Val, Rayner, and Aris, but all the while, she couldn't help but wonder where Caelum was. She worried that Val had actually succeeded in crippling him, as Aris had alluded to. But nobody mentioned him to her, and she was still too angry to ask.

It was all too quiet. Until one day, weeks after the incident with the bush, Aris stormed into the dining hall, his expression grave, causing all of those assembled to instinctively jump to their feet.

"Everyone report to the great hall," Aris roared to the room at large. Val rose from her bench beside Deya, concern lining her foxlike features.

"General," she began, but the general did not slow. He looked at Val and gave her a stern nod.

"We need you to lead your old unit, Valeria," he said.

"But . . . what . . . why—" Val began but she didn't get to finish.

"Praiton is attempting to breach Bridah again. We move out in one hour. Prepare quickly."

The next ten minutes were a blur of activity and near panic. Deya did not know which way to look as, all around her, soldiers of the Pillar Legion rushed back and forth, gathering weapons and armor while the main captains met with Aris in the great hall.

Val was one of those captains. Rayner, though, was only a lieutenant for one of the Laenimorian squadrons, so he took off with the rest of his unit, giving Deya a gentle squeeze on the elbow as he went.

"Deya, go to your room," Val said as she rose from her chair.

"What?" Deya cried, leaping to her feet as well. Soldiers rushed past her, buffeting her slightly with the crowd. "You're really sending me to my *room*?"

"This is Legion business, let us handle this," Val said as she followed the other captains towards the great hall. "*Go!*"

But Deya was seething. She wasn't going to be dismissed like an errant child. How could they expect her to stay back and let all of them fight and *die* while she stayed in her room, in the dark?

Hands balling into fists, Deya gave one look back at the stairs leading to the residential wing, before turning in the opposite direction and jogging after Val.

The five captains were in the great hall, most of which she hadn't met yet. They all looked deathly serious, and Deya couldn't help but feel intimidated as she slipped into that room behind the last one.

She didn't know how on Earth she would be of any use to this room of intense looking males, but she sure as hells knew she would be better off here and in the know than helpless upstairs in her room.

Val was the only female in the room. She stood out starkly amongst the large, imposing figures gathered around the wooden table with Aris at the head.

Deya found herself huddled in the corner of the room by the fireplace, a fly on the wall, as the captains took their seats around Aris. They were too preoccupied and harried to even realize she was there.

"What's going on?" a male Sea Fae with much harder features than Rayner's demanded of Aris.

"Patience, Elric," Aris purred. His presence was certainly commanding. He was dressed now in full golden armor, the hilt of his sword clutched in his hands, resting on top of the pommel. "We will wait until we are all settled for the briefing."

"Patience?" Elric barked. "If you are telling us they are once again attempting to breach Bridah—"

With a crash, the large oak doors leading from the antechamber into the great hall burst open. Caelum strode into the room, purple eyes glowing in a menacing fashion. Deya watched as all the captains turned to stare at the white-haired male striding into the room. Caelum looked as if he were about to face the demons of the hells all on his own.

"Ah," Aris drawled. "Nice of you to join us, Caelum."

"What is this about Praiton attacking Bridah?" Caelum demanded, not even looking at anyone else in the room, zeroing in wholly on the Pillar Legion's general. "Why are you sitting on your pompous ass instead of going to their defense?"

Deya could see the captain closest to her—a dark haired male with familiar tattoos crawling out from the collar and sleeves of his armor peering at Caelum. His purple eyes—a deeper and richer shade than Caelum's—appeared to study the male standing before them, panting with fury, as if he had just run there.

"Why don't you join us for this briefing, Caelum, and you shall find out," Aris said.

Caelum prowled into the room but froze when his eyes landed on Deya. Their gazes locked and all the air left her lungs, a spark of electricity crackling through his purple irises. It had been weeks since she had seen him, and her own eyes greedily devoured him, drinking in every detail. He looked thinner than he had before the training incident, the dark circles under his eyes more pronounced. He also seemed angrier than ever before.

"What is *she* doing in here?" he exploded at Aris. The eyes of the Legion's command staff simultaneously snapped towards Deya, and she wilted against the mantlepiece.

"*Deya*," Val breathed, the groan she didn't release was evident.

But, to Deya's surprise, Aris did not dismiss her. Instead, his perfect mouth rose into a small, cunning smile.

"Ah, Deya. Both of you, please, join us." The captains around the table looked at Aris with barely concealed confusion, which was nothing compared to the fury threatening to burst from Caelum.

Heart thumping, cheeks burning, Deya walked forward on unsteady legs as all the captains stared at her before perching herself in a chair next to Val. Caelum, on the other hand, threw himself down into the farthest chair away from the group of captains, glowering at Aris, who merely smiled.

"Anyway," the general said, returning to business. "We have just received a raven from our insiders within Praiton's army. They are preparing to lead an assault on Bridah via an entry point in Maniel." His hazel eyes turned to Val, whose golden skin had paled at this news.

"An old tactic. I'm not surprised," the dark-haired male sitting closest to Deya remarked. His purple eyes parted from Caelum, the sparkle of intrigue still in them, as he turned to look back at Aris. "As the bordering nation, it is not as if High King Titus does not have one of the largest advantages when it comes to war."

The generals all murmured in agreement. Val still looked stricken.

"I'm sorry . . ." Deya began, her voice coming out in a tiny squeak. All heads turned to look at her, but she could feel Caelum's gaze on her the heaviest. "But what advantage does the High King of Maniel have? I know they are Ember Magic wielders and can maybe survive Bridah's conditions but . . ."

Aris smiled at her, almost indulgently. The other captains appeared impatient with her ignorance, shifting in their seats, rearranging their swords. Still, Caelum sat and stared at her, unmoving.

"Don't you know, Deya?" Aris said. "Titus is one of the only members in the entirety of the Manielian royal line to do the impossible." He looked at Val, as if pausing to ask her permission first before saying, "He has tamed a dragon."

Deya's heart slid down into her chest. "A *dragon*?" she echoed, dumbstruck. "I didn't even know they existed."

"Oh, they exist," the Manielian male closest to Caelum spoke. He was scruffier than Val, his hair an almost orange instead of her deep, flaming red. He gave Val a reproachful look as he said, "But *Lady Valeria Augusta's* own dear cousin Titus was the only one crazy and bloodthirsty enough to go to Mount Cinis to claim one, much less make it back alive."

Deya turned to look at Val, aghast. King Titus was her *cousin*? Val's face was set, stonelike, but the color was still drained from her cheeks.

"We do not have time for these ridiculous history lessons," Elric roared, slamming his large, blue-gray fist on the table. "What do we plan on doing about it, General?"

"I have already sent a raven to Bridah, warning them of the plot," Aris said, his hazel eyes flashing in anger at Elric, a look that made the Sea Fae recoil and lower his fist sheepishly. "And if you would be so kind, *Captain,* to prepare your fleet. We need to cross the Gray Gap to our post in Zulon. We will head them off."

"When do we expect them to invade?" Caelum demanded from his lone island seat across the table.

"In three days' time," Aris said. "We are to leave immediately. Elric, you and the other Laenimorians are needed to power the ships. We will need all hands on deck to get us there as soon as possible. Valeria, Lycus"—He turned to address Val and the other Manielian male— "your guidance through Maniel and the ways of their army will be of the utmost importance. I will look to you, Valeria," he said, nodding to her. Val gave him a stiff nod in return.

"As for the rest of you," Aris continued, "Gather your troops. Prepare them for battle." The captains all rose as one and headed for the door. Deya, Caelum, and Aris remained.

"Now," Aris said, getting to his feet and looking between them. "Deya, with that bounty on your head, I think it wise that you stay here at Light's Tower where you are safe—"

"You're telling me to stay behind?" Deya demanded, incensed. She strode towards Aris, who watched her calmly. "I am going, Aris. I will not stay behind while you all fight."

She didn't even want to look at Caelum, though she could feel his eyes burning purple holes into her back.

Aris stared at her for a long moment, as if he were considering something from all angles. Those hazel eyes swept her from head to toe, then came to rest on her faerivaine necklace. "Fine," he said. "You can join Valeria's unit. She will look after you. Caelum, I want you to join Saros's unit—"

Caelum turned to glare at the general so fast that his eyes flashed like daggers.

"I go with her."

Deya looked at him, alarmed. Aris had the grace to stay composed.

"Saros has a team of Nodarian fighters that you will be invaluable to," Aris said, his voice like silk, as if finessing the angry Nodarian.

"I don't give a shit. I'm not going with Saros," Caelum spat. "I go with her or not at all."

Aris stared him down, and Caelum stared right back. The crackle of electricity between them was almost audible: the angry hostility from Caelum; the cool, calculated appraisal from Aris.

"Fine," Aris consented again. "Deya, you are assigned to Saros's unit. Caelum is to go with you."

Caelum stilled and for a second, Deya had an insane impulse to laugh. Caelum looked so angry that she could practically see the gears turning in his head, attempting to undo Aris's command.

"Fine," she said, and Aris stood.

"Dismissed." He gave them both a wide smile before he swept out of the room.

For a moment, Caelum and Deya stood in the great hall, alone. Their eyes locked. Deya shook her head and strode out the door, right behind Aris.

Caelum watched as the ships were loaded, each unit filling into one of the Pillar Legion's ships. The dark blue and orange banners of the Legion waved from the mast of each vessel, standing out starkly against the gray sky of Elbania. And somehow, Caelum found himself packed into the helm of the Nodarian unit led by Captain Saros. Deya wouldn't even look at him.

They sat together in the steerage cabin below the ship, surrounded by other soldiers, all dressed in full armor. Deya sat next to him stiffly, arms crossed, their shoulders touching with each shift of the waves under the boat. And still, she would not look at him.

Caelum did not know how to apologize for the last time they saw each other, nearly two weeks ago now. Every time he attempted to speak, the words wouldn't come. Perhaps he never learned how to properly apologize.

The boat rocked violently, and Deya clutched at the wooden bench, eyes shut tight.

"You should have stayed back," Caelum hissed at her.

Her eyes snapped open, and she shot him such a furious glare that it almost made him recoil. "Why do you care? Where have you even been the last few weeks?"

"Staying away from you, as the Manielian harpy demanded I do," he snarled. He had been shut up in his room for days. He had even gone as far as to strike out away from Light's Tower, exploring the many refugee camps that were built several miles in the heart of Elbania. At least there he had remained anonymous.

Deya didn't respond. The ship bucked, and she took a deep breath, her eyes squeezing shut again.

"You should have stayed at the Tower," he said again. She looked healthier, a little stronger and less fragile since he had last seen her. It angered him to think that she had fared better under the tutelage of the Manielian and her arrogant dick of a general. "You're not ready for battle."

"I'll be fine," she snapped. "I would've been safe if you had allowed me to go to Val's unit. She would've looked out for me."

"Yes," he growled. "What a shame you just have me now."

Deya turned to face him incredulously. "*You?*" she asked, disbelievingly. "Just like you looked after me that day during training?"

Caelum sighed, dreading this part. He had spent the last few weeks second-guessing his tactic when he had trained her, had felt the guilt for days at how he had pushed her. Still, he wouldn't admit that.

"You needed to be pushed. I knew you would not have hurt me."

"And how were you to know that?" Deya cried, turning to face him, her gray eyes wide and pained. The hurt that she felt at what she must believe to be a severe betrayal was raw in her eyes. "Even *I* did not know if I would hurt you, Caelum. And I nearly did."

"But you *didn't*," he insisted. "And I knew you would not, and it was important for you to know it, too."

Deya's nostrils flared, and tears glimmered in her eyes. "Do you know why the warden at Ironbalt decided to beat Oswallt instead of me?" she asked him softly. Caelum hesitated but shook his head. "Because Clarita Killoran had told him that my weakness was other people. And that the best way to punish me was to punish someone I cared about. I had always wondered why the guards let me remain close to Oswallt, but I realize it now. They wanted to have someone to use against me. And it worked." A tear slipped down her face, which she wiped away furiously. "Threatening harm to someone I care about is what they considered my weakness. And you exploited it the same way they did."

And, with that, she turned away from him, putting an end to their conversation, and leaving Caelum to process the fact that she may have just implied that she actually cared about him.

After an hour, Caelum grew tired of being ignored and rose from the bench, pushing past Deya and the other soldiers and climbing to the top deck of the ship.

The winds whistled around him, the sky gray with an impending storm. Some soldiers milled around, but for the most part the decks were free of prying eyes.

He walked to the bow of the ship and stared out onto the Gray Gap. Their first journey across these same waters felt like another lifetime ago. So much had happened, so much had changed. His fingers tightened against the wooden railing, and he closed his eyes, the hurt in Deya's face flashing through his mind. He never would've imagined caring about her pain the first time he had set across this ocean . . . never would have believed it was even possible.

Across the gray waters, the main continent was already in view, the free country of Zulon looking to be only another half hour away. The Sea Fae below decks were funneling mass amounts of strength into propelling them to the continent as soon as possible.

It was then that he felt someone come up to stand at his side. Turning, he saw the dark-haired captain, his similarly tattooed arms folded over his black leather armor.

He and Saros stood at the helm of the ship in silence, watching the Gray Gap disappear underneath them, until the captain spoke.

"I know who you are."

Caelum stiffened, but he did not speak as the captain chuckled a little to himself. "Honestly, I am surprised no one has recognized you yet. The White Sheep of Nodaria is not typically easy to forget."

Caelum bristled at the name and slowly, he turned to look at the captain, whose dark purple eyes gleamed a familiar color that shook him to his core.

"Who have you told?" Caelum growled. Saros smiled wider.

"I may have mentioned it to one or two of my colleagues, but do not worry. I will keep my silence."

Caelum snarled. "Telling one or two of your colleagues is not keeping your silence."

"My *colleagues* deserve to know who is in the Legion," Saros said, flicking a piece of dust from his arm. "Especially since your . . . particular presence is very important."

Caelum could barely feel the wooden edge of the ship underneath his fingers. His whole body had gone numb, replaced only with a white-hot feeling of dread and panic that was beginning to spread through him.

"Why have you not revealed yourself, yet?" Saros continued curiously. "You could turn the tide of this war. Could avenge all you have lost. So why have you remained hidden all this time?"

The captain's words washed over him, but he could barely register them through the roaring in his ears. A wintry wind buffeted around them, his traitorous white hair whipping into his face, but still, he did not respond.

Saros studied him, his purple eyes sweeping the side of Caelum's face, taking in the tattoos, the prophecy on his skin. "I was the First Lieutenant of the Nodarian army under High King Castor," Saros said. Caelum knew this. Had experienced a horrific jolt of recognition upon seeing the male sitting at the table with the rest of the captains, had known it may come to this.

"You should be dead," Caelum snarled, glaring at the captain.

Saros smirked. "I should say the same for you, my friend."

Caelum turned back to look at the looming shore of Zulon, his fingers digging into the skin of his palms.

"Anyway," Saros said, his tone casual, as if they had merely been discussing the weather. "We have plenty of time to discuss these matters after we reduce these Praiton scum to blood and bone. War approaches." And then the ship crashed onto shore.

Deya and the rebel forces streamed out onto the coast of Zulon. She knew that it would be a day's journey to head off the Praiton forces in Maniel, and she did not know how she would do it. It was as this fear washed over her, she caught sight of a head of white hair.

Caelum blew off the ship like a tornado, his face dark and strained, a hint of panic in his features. She felt her mouth open, her hand reaching out instinctively towards him, when she caught herself and pulled back. She would not give him the satisfaction.

They marched through Zulon—a barren, desert-like region surrounded by red clay. Deya trooped alongside the Nodarian rebels, her eyes reluctantly scanning for Caelum. He had promised to look out for her, but she couldn't see him at all in the sea of soldiers. So, she kept her head down and marched.

Aris was at the head of the pack, leading them on. He insisted they walk through the night to reach the base the Legion had constructed on the border of Zulon and Maniel. So Deya walked alongside the Nodarian captain, Saros, not breaking ranks except for the occasional meal as they descended towards the base.

After hours of marching, a large dome-shaped building appeared on the horizon. Surrounded by gates and guards, the armored troops waved to open the doors when the blue and orange banners of the Light's Tower legion approached. Deya almost cried from relief upon seeing it. Her feet and legs ached tremendously, and she was thankful she had trained so hard recently, or she may very well not have made this journey.

Aris led their forces through the gates of the base. The Burningtide Sanctum opened up before them, more blue and orange banners waving in the breeze of the impending storm. At the apex of the gates stood a large Ganiean male, clad in bronze armor, his dark brown hair long and pulled back. As the Light's Tower forces surged into the courtyard of Burningtide, the male looked at Aris and nodded, his face grim.

"Aris," he said, holding out a large tan hand.

Aris seized it. "Good to see you, Petrus. Have you made the preparations?" The captain of Burningtide nodded again, and the general and captain disappeared into the main sanctum, leaving the troops and their generals to be directed to various positions.

Deya was buffeted in the crowd, being pushed and jostled by the mob of rebels as they dispersed. And then, through the throng, a white-haired head flashed in her peripheral before a strong, firm hand wrapped around her wrist.

"Where are we going?" Deya asked Caelum. She couldn't deny that no matter how angry she was at him, she was secretly relieved to see him.

"Out of the way," he responded, and she let him pull her along, almost indifferent to where they would go next.

Burningtide Sanctum resembled a large eye, pushed into the ground, and surrounded entirely by high fences. It was not as large as Light's Tower, a mere outpost in comparison to the size of the Elbanian fortress. The small sanctum heaved with bodies as she and Caelum pushed their way through the crowds, attempting to find one little corner that was not filled with large, armor-clad soldiers.

After a great deal of pushing and shoving, they found themselves in a small turret leading up to the battlements. This particular turret was far enough away from the rest of the watchtowers, giving them a bit of space and privacy.

The minute they reached the top of the battlement, Caelum let out an enormous breath. He slumped against the stone wall and . . . breathed. It was such a rare moment of vulnerability for him that Deya couldn't help but stare as he tried to gather himself.

"What's wrong?" she asked. It hadn't been her imagination, then. There had been something on his face when he had gotten off the boat, an expression mixed between rage and panic.

Caelum was still breathing hard when he shook his head. "Nothing."

Deya rolled her eyes. "It is *not* nothing. I have never seen you like this before."

Caelum sank to the floor against the stone wall, his eyes closed as he breathed, as if he were attempting to take in as much air as he could. Deya moved forward, pausing only slightly before sinking down beside him.

He did not even open his eyes to look at her as he took short, rapid breaths. Deya didn't know what to do for him. She almost wanted to reach out and hold his hand but didn't know how he would react to that.

"What is it?" she asked again, softly. A cold, icy wind whistled by them swirling around Caelum whose nostrils flared as he breathed it in. His eyes opened to rest on the moon in the sky. It was blood red tonight.

"I'm sorry I tried to use the people you care about against you."

Deya's breath caught. "I . . . it's okay."

He looked at her sideways. "Is it?"

"Well . . . no, but you're upset, so I forgive you," she said, and that's when it happened. He laughed. Actually laughed. And Deya couldn't help it. She laughed with him.

"It was like this the night before the Battle for Atlas, too," he said, his eyes still lingering on the blood moon. "The moon was red that night, too. It was what alerted the star seers that war was on our doorstep."

Deya leaned back to look up at the sky with him, their shoulders touching and the scent of a forest on a winter night filling her brain like a heady perfume.

"Do you think a new war is upon us?"

Caelum shrugged. "I have always been a rotten seer, but if I had to judge the planets now, I would say that it is coming sooner than we think."

The wind picked up, whipping Deya's hair into her face, the chestnut tendrils sweeping against the side of Caelum's cheek. She made to push it away, but then his hand reached out and brushed it away for her, just like he had that day in her bedroom.

Their eyes met. His fingers lingered on her face as they tucked the errant lock of hair behind her ear, those purple eyes a lurid magenta in the light of the blood moon. Like the moment in that cave, Deya found her eyes falling to his mouth, watching as his own did the same to hers. Their heads tilted.

"When you said they used people you care about against you . . . Does that mean I am someone you care about?" he murmured.

She opened her mouth, so stunned by the question that she didn't know how to respond.

But then, a large ball of fire came careening into view. For a second, it illuminated all of Burningtide, throwing everything into sharp relief against the darkness, before it crashed into the battlements and engulfed the entire wall.

Burningtide Sanctum was under attack.

CHAPTER
21

The fire ball hit the watchtower directly in front of Caelum and Deya, sending all the guards patrolling it up in a wall of flames. The blast knocked her and Caelum halfway down the stairs of the turret which they had climbed, Deya's braid smoking slightly and the sleeve of Caelum's black leathers smoldering. There was screaming, guards below shouting, and then a shadow passed over the blood moon.

A large dragon sailed over them, red and scaly, straight out of the books in the library, and more terrifying than even her nightmares could imagine. It emitted a large roar that drowned out the screaming of the rebels below it. Deya could see the next fire-ball brewing, fresh in its throat, preparing itself for another blast.

She scrambled to her feet and made to scream at Caelum, to prepare him for what was coming, when the next explosion ripped the world apart. The fireball blasted right into the turret they were in, sending Deya flying out the small open window in the tower. She tumbled down, the swooping in her stomach reminding her of the baby bird of fear that was now shrieking its head off inside of her and then she hit the ground in a cascade of burning rubble.

Coughing, spluttering, black with ash and soot, she looked up. The turret was nothing more than blackened debris, still smoking and flaming in places. Panic began to set in, molten and hot in her chest.

"Caelum!" she screamed, but her voice was drowned out amongst the yelling of the rebels attempting to rally their forces as the large shadow of the dragon flew overhead.

She hadn't seen where Caelum had gone, hadn't seen if he had managed to move before the fireball had blasted apart the tower.... Didn't know if he was dead or alive.

A hand gripped her underneath her arm and dragged her into a standing position.

"Move, Deya!" It was Rayner, his longbow out and an arrow clutched in his hand, blue and black armor glistening in the flame from the burning turret. He shoved a sword into her grasp—the spare one that he had kept on his back—and began dragging her away from the fire.

"Rayner!" Deya gasped, trying to breathe through the smoke and the sheer panic choking her. "Caelum was in that tower!"

Rayner's eyes darted back towards the smoldering rubble. "We can't do anything now!" he cried. "We've got to move, Deya!"

"What's happening?"

Rayner's eyes darted back and forth; his hand still clasped protectively on Deya's wrist. "It was a trap! A trick to lure us here! Praiton is marching on us, intending to wipe us out in one fell swoop!"

At that moment, a large crash echoed throughout the Sanctum. The steel doors that had encased the dome gave a shudder, as if something had been thrown against it. Almost as one, the Pillar Legion, Deya and Rayner all froze, their attention on that door. It gave another enormous jolt, a dent forming in the middle. Then, with an explosion of dragon fire, the doors burst inwards, and a stream of soldiers surged in. All clad in armor and steel, Deya caught sight of a flicker of the green and white banner of Praiton flying high.

And then they attacked.

Deya was wrenched away from Rayner as soldiers and rebels clashed around her. Swords went flying, magic of all kinds erupting around her head, and she was thrust to the ground, nearly trampled by the boots of the fighters surrounding her.

She covered her head, cowering, attempting to roll and avoid the fire and blood that had begun to rain down around her. Then, a hand grasped her by the hair and wrenched her up. She screamed in pain, coming face to face with a Praitonian soldier. He leered down at her, missing teeth, and blood in his mouth.

"Thought you could hide down there, did you, pretty thing?" he rasped. His hands moved towards her body, as if to touch her, and Deya felt the flare of fury explode in her chest. She was not going to hide, not going to cower, helpless among soldiers who were aiming to kill her friends. She had vowed to never be helpless again.

Reaching for the sword Rayner had given her, Deya slashed it before her body, taking the soldier unawares. Blood showered around her, splattering her face and clothes as his disembodied hand went spinning into the battle around them. His howl of fury and rage echoed like the dragon's roar above them.

His sword flashed, and she parried it easily, the muscle memory of her weeks of training with Caelum, Val, Rayner, and Aris seeming to spring to life. She battled the soldier backwards, joining the fray at last.

The Rain Dance of Laenimore and the Fire Stance of Maniel surged through her as she spun, ducked, and parried around the brute's blows, before, with a great roar, she swung for the throat. Her aim was true. The soldier's head spun clean off his shoulders, blood spraying from his neck, and then his body dropped like a stone.

Deya only had a moment to take it in. Her first death by steel. It made her a little sick, her stomach heaved at the sight of the headless soldier, his neck still gushing blood, before she was forced to rally as another soldier took his place.

She had not been ready for this, she knew that. Aris may have been right to beg her to stay behind at Light's Tower. But still, she fought alongside them all, battling her way through the courtyard of what was left of Burningtide, smoldering bodies and blood all around her. She was able to hold her own until, before she could blink, she was surrounded by Praiton soldiers, not a rebel amongst them. Panting, covered in blood and soot, sporting several cuts and injuries to her arms and legs, Deya held her sword firm.

If only she could use her magic, she lamented. This fight would be over before it even began. But instead, it was useless to her. Locked inside, too dangerous to touch. Even when staring death in the face.

The Praiton soldiers moved into position.

"What's a pretty little thing like you doing here?" The soldier closest to her snarled, his face splitting into a malicious grin. "Why not come over here and join the fun?"

Deya was panting, the blood pumping so hard in her temples from her bounding nerves that her vision danced with light. Even after all her training, she was beginning to tire. She couldn't keep up much longer.

She hoped, rather naïvely, that they would deal with her one at a time instead of all together, but that hope proved to be just that: naïve. They all moved at once, and Deya immediately sprang into the third form of the Rain Dance. Rayner had taught her to move in a wave, fending blows from all sides. She had struggled with this for weeks, and even now her form faltered. She caught all their blades, twisting, turning, and spinning her lithe body in a single movement, fending off any additional injuries, but without time to strike back.

They began to laugh, their blows relentless, and her stamina waning.

"You can't dance forever, girl!" one of the soldiers jeered.

It had been a long day, Deya thought. She had walked miles and miles from Zulon to Burningtide, had barely eaten since she had woken up that morning in Light's Tower . . . Gods, had it only been that morning? Light's

Tower felt so far away now, so long ago . . .

And as she thought about Light's Tower, her form slipped just slightly. She didn't turn in time to block her back left, and a sword caught her on the back of the shoulder, causing her to fall, just to receive another blow to the back of her leg. She screamed in pain, her left side dropping, blood splattering, but still, she did not stop. Staggering, body screaming, she continued the Rain Dance, but now her entire left side was compromised. The pain blinded her, white spots appearing in her vision.

A flash of gold appeared on her side, and then a blade slashed around her. It was an expert movement, a single twirl like a golden tornado, and all the soldiers around her fell. Aris stood before her, his handsome face covered in blood and soot, but otherwise unharmed.

"Get to the battlements!" he commanded her. "Hide! You are too injured to keep fighting!"

Deya nodded, but she couldn't speak. The pain was so intense it was all she could do to limp from Aris's side and obey his command.

The battlements seemed unprotected. All the soldiers had flocked to the center of Burningtide's courtyard, like one large training ring. Deya dragged her bleeding leg towards another turret, untouched by the dragon fire, and heaved herself up the steps towards the battlements, leaving a grisly trail of blood in her wake.

She did not know where the dragon was, had not seen its large form fly above them since the battle had started. Had it gone? Perhaps it had only been used to catch them unawares? Where was High King Titus? It had to have been his dragon that had blown half the Sanctum apart.

She climbed and climbed, the pain in her leg and shoulder nearly causing her to black out as she ascended the turret to what turned out to be the highest lookout of Burningtide. And there, bathed in the orange light of the blood moon, was the Praiton commander.

Deya recognized him from her time in barrack's duties. He hadn't been there often, but she knew the heavy steel armor embossed with the green and white crest of Praiton, the shield she had proudly polished in the infirmary for many years, now stained with blood.

He turned to look at her as she froze in the doorway of the outpost, blood dripping from multiple parts of her body.

"Ah," the commander murmured, his eyes alighting on her. He must have been of Ganiean descent, she thought, like King Rodric. He had hair that was once brown, now flecked with gray and white, and eyes that flickered with the flame around them. She had always thought Ganieans to be soft, gentle creatures. So how, she wondered, did this male standing before her seem to exude nothing but evil?

"Deyanira, the Traitor of Praiton," he said, moving towards her, his heavy silver longsword glinting in the flames. "It must be my lucky day. I did not expect to find you here."

"Why are you looking for me?" Deya panted, her hand digging into the wound on her leg, trying to staunch the bleeding.

The commander's smile only widened. "Why, you're famous back home, my girl. Wanted and hunted in all parts of the realm. You being here with these rebel scum explains why we have not found you yet. Your treason knows no bounds, apparently."

Deya's heart pumped hard between her ribs. Butterflies in her chest fluttered so furiously she felt her feet might leave Earth. The longsword the commander held was the length and weight of her entire body. She knew it could cleave her in half with one blow.

"The High Lord has put a large price on your head," the commander continued, a large finger running across his blade. He smiled cruelly. "And while he asked for you alive, I'm sure he wouldn't complain if I brought back just your head."

She couldn't fight this male. Even uninjured, she had barely held her own against a few low rank brutes. This male was the highest level of the Manielian extension of the Praiton army. Deya knew what the Praitonian commanders were capable of, had watched them in training during barrack's duty, had tended to the wounds of those who had gotten on their bad sides. She would not survive this.

"So, Deyanira," the commander said, drawing his blade back. "You have two choices. Come with me to be turned back over to Praiton or die here resisting."

His name came back to her in that instant, the long-forgotten shards of her past life in Stonehall Castle—a willing disciple of a corrupt empire—flashing before her eyes. Commander Maelor, three-star commander, reporting to Lord Decius. She had seen him flittering about the lord at the few feasts she had been allowed to attend. Decius had entrusted him to lead the most bloodthirsty sect of their militia.

Deya raised her sword. "I will die before I return to Praiton," she said with every bit of conviction she had left in her aching, bleeding body.

The commander's eyes flashed with glee, as if he had been hoping she would say that. "Very well, then," he purred, and then the longsword came down on her.

Deya leapt aside and chunks of battlement shattered underneath the heavy silver sword. She rolled across the stone floor, swearing as her shoulder and leg screamed in protest. With shaking hands, she raised her blade, which looked pathetic in comparison to the commander's immense weapon.

The commander's eyes danced with joy, a fox cornering its prey, delighted that he had found a meal willing to fight back. As if he enjoyed the challenge.

He twirled his longsword with surprising agility and Deya parried, the force of it knocking her sideways, lowering her defense, leaving herself open to a swift kick in the chest from the commander's enormous foot. His heel cracked her rib cage, and she was sent flying back into the wall of the battlements, wheezing and gasping for breath, feeling as if he may have broken her sternum.

"Out of respect for your service to my troops," the commander said, that feral grin exacerbated by the flickering flames as he neared her again, readying himself for another blow. "I will give you another chance. Surrender, or die."

Deya looked up at him, her whole chest feeling caved in. Finally, she had the wounds to match how she had felt since Praiton had betrayed her. Finally, the hurt and pain she had kept safe had manifested itself into real blood and broken bones. And as she looked up at the commander in front of her, she felt herself sneer, filled almost with as much contempt as a certain white-haired male. The thought of Caelum made her heart ache behind her broken ribs.

"You will have to kill me," she rasped.

The commander chuckled. "As you wish."

And then the sword came down again and Deya, too weak, too short of breath, was unable to defend it. But something was wrong. As the commander swung the sword with the force that should have ended her, it halted in midair. Maelor's expression changed from satisfaction to confusion as he fought against the longsword, which almost appeared to be resisting him. And then, it flew up and hit the commander squarely in the face, bloodying his nose, causing the male to howl with fury.

Deya knew who it was before he even appeared. White hair turned black with soot, several gashes on his arms and face, Caelum emerged, sword in hand, and purple eyes gleaming with Celestial Power.

The commander whirled around to see who had dared interfere with his execution, clutching his bloody nose, the excitement of an easy kill replaced with that of pure, unadulterated rage.

"What the—"

But Caelum, sword drawn, merely sneered at him. "Fuck you," he snarled. And then his sword slashed the air so fast that Deya almost missed it. Reacting fast, Maelor countered him, growling with anger, and then the two males were locked in battle.

Deya didn't dare blink as both males brought their swords down upon each other in rapid succession. Although Maelor's sword was heavier and larger than Caelum's, he still moved it with alarming speed and dexterity, a sign of a skilled warrior. Caelum's own sword was small, nowhere near strong enough to fend off a heavy blow, but he kept Maelor on his toes with pure speed. Caelum danced around the longsword, dodging and weaving around its heavy downfalls. Maelor began to get angrier and angrier with each miss.

Then the commander moved in a different way. His sword went down instead of up, sweeping Caelum's legs, and taking them right out from under him. The sword sliced across Caelum's shins, causing him to cry out and fall to the ground. Blood poured from deep gashes across his legs and his yell mingled with that of Deya's, her aching lungs straining with the effort to scream his name.

But Maelor did not stop. His sword fell again, not giving Caelum even a moment to pause in his pain. He deflected from the ground, eyes glowing purple with fury. But he didn't have an opening to use his Celestial Magic. Maelor's blows came too fast, too hard. And then, with a flash, Caelum's sword was knocked from his hand, the white-haired male being tossed aside like a rag doll.

Maelor was panting, grinning wildly as he gazed down at Caelum. He raised the end of his sword and pounded the pommel into Caelum's skull.

It came back to her in flashes . . . broken, agonizing, suppressed memories. Oswallt tied to the post, helpless as the warden smashed his head in again and again while Deya stood and did nothing but scream and cry, as she was doing now.

Before the commander could raise his sword to hit him again, she moved. Shoulder smarting, legs bleeding, ribs aching, she lunged at the hulking commander, jumping onto his back, her sword plunging into his arm—the one piece of unprotected flesh she could find.

The commander let out a snarl of fury and threw Deya off him like a flea from a dog. He whirled to face her, blood pouring from his arm. Caelum was motionless on the floor, his head bleeding. It was not caved in, but she couldn't tell if he was still breathing.

"I grow tired of this, little healer," he snarled, kicking Deya hard in the already broken ribs. She let out a cry of pain which quickly turned into a wheeze when her lungs pressed against fractured bone. "I will enjoy watching your head roll," he sneered. The tip of the longsword touched her face, its sharp point pressing into her soft cheek, as if he were teasing her. As he pressed down, Deya shrieked as he ripped a cut down her face.

"Goodbye, Traitor of Praiton," the commander said, and then raised his sword.

A deadly, blistering cold wind cut through the harsh heat and smoke that surrounded the top of the battlement. It was so cold that even Maelor paused, looking around, perplexed. Deya couldn't see where it was coming from as it grew colder and colder until both her and Maelor's breaths came out in puffs of mist.

And then, Deya saw it. From underneath the crumpled form of the white-haired Nodarian, frost grew. His hand reached out and slammed against the stone underneath him, pushing himself upwards, ice and frost exploding from underneath his palm. His other hand came down the same way, more ice appearing as he went. Then, he was standing in front of Maelor, but the look on his face was one Deya would never forget in all her life.

"Get the *fuck* away from her," he growled, and then cold wind and frost erupted from the white-haired male, sweeping past Deya to engulf Maelor where he stood. Caelum, his face screwed up in concentration, advanced towards the commander, fist outstretched, concentrating all the Frost Magic towards the enormous male, whose face was stunned.

Caelum's eyes glowed blue as he lifted a second hand and pushed the magic straight at Maelor, whose body began to freeze, growing rigid and cold. In what seemed like a second, the commander was frozen where he stood, the longsword clattering to the ground.

Bending, Caelum grabbed the longsword, and, with a roar of fury, slashed at the frozen Praiton commander. Maelor shattered like glass, exploding in a torrent of cold wind and ice so strong that Deya had to shield her face to keep the shards from piercing her.

Then, the wind died, and Caelum dropped the longsword with a clatter. He swayed, barely able to stand on his injured legs. Tremulously, he looked over at Deya.

"Are you okay?" he rasped.

But Deya did not answer. She stared at the male before her, too shocked for words. His once purple eyes were glowing a bright, effervescent blue that she had never seen before, and it rattled her to her core. Slowly, her voice found her.

"Okay," she breathed. "What in the *hells* was that?"

CHAPTER
22

Caelum's whole body shuddered with cold and exhaustion as he collapsed onto the floor beside Deya. His fingertips were frostbitten, his teeth chattered, and every strand of magic inside of him felt different . . . rearranged. Deya had been watching him with an expression of the utmost incredulity, as if she did not know who or even *what* he was anymore.

The cold in Caelum seemed to freeze the blood in his veins as, below the ramparts where they stood, the Pillar Legion pushed back against the Praitonian forces. With the fall of their commander, the rebels were able to send Praiton into retreat not too long after. But Deya and Caelum stayed on the battlements, surrounded by slush and rapidly melting ice as the fires from the burning parapets warmed the air around them.

His body was spent, and he was still bleeding from his legs and head, but he could already feel his fae body beginning to repair the more minor abrasions. He was still shocked by what had exploded out of him, could still feel the cold and ice in his blood as it gradually melted back into his veins. Slowly, he turned to look at Deya. She was staring at him, eyes wide.

"How . . ." she breathed.

Caelum looked away from her. Cinders fell from the sky, clouding the air and his vision as he struggled to breathe . . . struggled to explain. He pulled himself into a sitting position, wincing as he felt every wound in his body.

"I don't know," he said finally.

She nodded, still looking shell-shocked. Bits of ash and snow clung to her chestnut hair, turning it gray. "But . . . to have *two* types of magic. Two *strong* types of magic . . ." She paused, and he could see her gray eyes seeming to calculate the situation. He could almost see the moment it dawned on her. Slowly, she turned to look back at him. "Caelum . . . who are you?"

He drew in a slow, deep breath. "I am the son of Castor Hesperos, High King of Nodaria."

Deya looked as if she had stopped breathing. She stared at him, gray eyes wide, blood still trickling down her face.

"His *son*?" she breathed.

Caelum looked away. "His *bastard*." He wiped away his own blood that was leaking into his eyes and gazed down at the remainder of the frost on the ground. "Castor was a good male. A good father. But he fathered six children, only three of those being from his wife, Nova." He bowed his head, the shame that he had been taught to feel hammering into him. "I am not a Hesperos by birth. A bastard does not get a surname in Nodaria. And I never knew my mother. Don't even know her name. Castor never told me."

Deya watched him, her eyes wide as the blood moon that was now a faint outline in the sky. "Caelum," she whispered. "She had to have been from a very powerful bloodline. *No* offspring of two different magic wielders *ever* inherit *both* powers. It's unheard of."

Caelum didn't speak. He knew this. Had been just as surprised as she was when that Frost Magic had exploded out of him. It had come from a different place than his Celestial Magic, as if he were speaking a different language. When he told her this, she looked even more aghast.

"You didn't know you had this power?"

Quietly, he shook his head. "I've been feeling . . . strange since we left Ironbalt," he admitted to her. "Cold all the time. Like I was catching a fever. It was probably this power lying dormant inside of me. I have been in faerivaine shackles all my adult life. It took me until nearly adolescence to develop just the Celestial Magic." He looked down at his hands. They looked foreign to him now. "I don't know where to even begin with this magic. It feels . . . different."

Deya didn't say anything for a moment. All around them, sounds of the battle ending washed around them. The moon was fading, and a golden glow was beginning to emanate from the horizon. Daybreak.

"Caelum," Deya said. He looked over at her. She looked scared. "How . . . how did you survive the Battle for Atlas?"

He had been dreading this question. Been dreading it his whole life, really. He took in a breath, closing his eyes for a moment, as if to shut out the pain remembering that day would bring.

Finally, he spoke. "My eldest brother Aelius was always the better warrior. He was destined to take over after Castor. He was the strongest magic wielder, the strongest fighter. My younger brother, Aten, and I always looked up to him. Which is why, when the battle began, Aelius sent us all to hide."

He could still see it so vividly. Aelius was the spitting image of Castor—handsome, dark-haired, with deep violet eyes that were always glowing with power, no matter what he did. Aelius had rushed them into the lower level of Atlas Keep, telling Caelum and Aten to protect his three youngest siblings—Nova and Castor's trueborn daughter, Astrid, and the two other bastard children from the same common Nodarian female: Seren and Sirius.

Caelum had listened to the Praiton guards fight Aelius from the other room they had been locked in. He and Aten had stood, swords raised, surrounding their younger siblings, fearing the soldiers pushing through that door because it would mean that Aelius was dead.

The sounds were awful. They had heard clanging swords, screaming, the sounds of Aelius's powerful Celestial Magic ripping apart soldiers. Until a heavy thud sounded, so loud that it shook the door of the room they had been hiding in. And then the face that haunted his nightmares for years kicked down the door: General Morlais, holding a large, black longsword, just like the one the commander he had killed had used. From behind Morlais, Caelum would always remember the sight of Aelius's severed head on the black marble floor, his purple eyes dim and lifeless for the first time in his whole life.

After this, it was all a blur. Caelum and Aten fought Morlais for their lives, but both had been young and weak, flicked aside so easily that Caelum had realized Morlais was playing with them. He had knocked Caelum to the ground, and began to attack Aten, and that was when it happened.

From the corner of his eye, he remembered Seren's face going blank. She and Sirius had been cowering in the corner, merely children, unable to defend themselves. Seren's eyes had rolled back into her head, and then a strange noise had begun to come from her mouth. He had only seen this happen one other time before—from another star seer. A prophecy.

Only this time, as the foreign words came from Seren's mouth, Caelum had felt his skin prickle. And then it had begun to burn with an intensity of a thousand flames, as though he was being roasted alive. He remembered screaming in agony, collapsing on the ground as his skin felt like it was being peeled from his body.

Aten had paused to yell his name, allowing Morlais to cut the young boy in half. His screams of pain then became screams of grief and horror as he was forced to watch, prostrate in pain on the floor as the prophecy finished branding his skin, as Morlais hacked Sirius down next. The young boy had rushed out to help when Aten had fallen, but he was too small . . . too weak.

Astrid had screamed herself hoarse, but had never been a fighter, had always been like her mother, Nova, content to sit and do needlework and paint. Although she had not particularly cared for her illegitimate siblings, she died screaming for Sirius.

Seren had barely finished the prophecy, barely spoken the last word in Nadarak before she fell silent and closed her eyes, peaceful, as if she knew what was coming next. Morlais cut her down as easily as if she were a blade of grass.

Caelum had lain, panting on the floor, skin still smarting as if he had been burned, tattoos now glistening blackly on his arms, neck, and chest. Tears were in his eyes as he lay, surrounded by his siblings' bodies, as Morlais had turned towards him.

"Now the last of Castor's children dies," he said, grinning down at him. Caelum had almost been unconscious at this point, waiting for death, praying for it.

The next memory was hazy. To that day, he was unsure whether he had imagined the frosty wind that had whistled by, had wondered if the Bridanian forces that his father had begged to come had actually made it in time. He could have sworn that a lithe, white-haired female had charged Morlais, engaged him in battle. That they had fought until the Keep collapsed, signaling the end of Castor's life and magic. Morlais had fled, but the Bridanian female lingered.

He could vaguely remember her blue eyes looking at him on the floor under the rubble, before a look crossed her face that he couldn't describe. Had it been horror?

He remembered being scooped into her cold embrace, rushed from the collapsed room of Atlas Keep towards what was left of the servants' quarters, where he was laid down with the other children. And after that, it had all gone black and the next thing he knew, he was waking up on a ship to Ironbalt.

He finished recounting this entire story to Deya, barely stopping even to register what he was telling her. He told her every detail, even the ones that he had denied himself from revisiting. Afterwards, the pain was so intense in his chest that he felt like crying for the first time since that horrible, horrible day. But, at the same time, he felt . . . lighter. Because when Deya looked at him, her eyes grief-stricken and filled with horror and pain for him, she was looking at *him*. For the first time in fifty years, someone knew who he was.

She took his hand, her fingers warm against the still-cold flesh of his own.

"I'm so sorry," she whispered to him. He nodded, having to look away from her because the way she was looking at him was causing a lump to rise in his throat.

Gently, her fingers touched his neck, tracing down to his chest, pushing aside the leather armor he wore to study the tattoos that were now etched on his skin. Her touch made him shiver.

"This prophecy," she said. "You really have no idea what it says?"

He shook his head. "Nadarak is only spoken by very old star seers," he told her. "Most of them only spoke it when in a trance and could not tell you what it said afterwards. Even Atlas Keep had only one or two that could read and speak it. I'm not sure if any of them survived the battle."

Deya lapsed into deep thought. Caelum realized her hand was still in his.

"We need to figure out what it says," she said. She was staring so intensely at him, those gray eyes blazing. He opened his mouth to protest, but she cut him off. "That prophecy came to you at a time when your entire family died, a pivotal moment in this war," she insisted. "It could be significant, something important that could lead to the end of all this."

Caelum's mouth hung open slightly, at a loss for words. He hadn't thought about this possibility, hadn't even considered it. Loads of Nodarians had unknown prophecies on their skin, many of them dying without ever knowing what it said. How could his be so important?

As if she could tell what he was thinking, Deya tightened her grip on his hand. "Your sister *died* giving that prophecy," she implored. "Don't you want to know why?"

Until she said it, he had never even thought about it. He remembered what Saros had said earlier. *You could turn the tide of this war. Could avenge all you have lost. So why have you remained hidden all this time?*

"Saros knows," he told her. "He recognized me."

Deya nodded. "So that's why you were so panicked getting off the boat," she mused, and he grunted in response. Pursing her lips, she looked at him inquiringly. "Why did you not tell us?"

He shook his head. "Because," he spat. "I am the *bastard* of Castor. If I am his only surviving heir, people will expect me to pursue his crown, his legacy. I do not deserve it. It was Aelius's to take. His *true* son. I am nothing more than the White Sheep of Nodaria." He spat the final title out like venom. It was given to him as a child, teased mercilessly by those in the Keep—those like Aten and Astrid, even some of the other servants finding it funny. Never Aelius, though. Aelius was always above that.

"Caelum," she whispered. It was like she could tell what he was remembering. He had been mocked and teased, stood out like a sore thumb with his white hair in a sea of dark-haired fae. All his life had been a fight, a struggle to fit in. Seeking an acceptance that he never would earn. "Forget being the White Sheep," she said, clutching his hand tightly, shaking it in hers. "When the Nodarians learn that you have survived, it may be different. You may very well be the White *Hope* of Nodaria."

And with that, he looked into her eyes, how they gazed at him imploringly, how she clutched his hand in hers, and he felt that same, inexplicable tug towards her that he had felt from the start. The tug that used to anger him, infuriate him, but now, it seemed natural . . . expected.

Slowly, he nodded.

Deya and Caelum returned to the courtyard that was now reduced almost to cinders. There were bodies everywhere and, as she picked her way through, her hand remained clasped with Caelum's, as if they were afraid to lose each other again.

Everywhere, rebel soldiers gathered the dead, throwing them onto a pyre that was already constructed in the center of the courtyard. Deya's eyes scanned the crowd, looking desperately for a glimpse of red hair or a blonde Sea Fae amongst the living.

A streak of red flashed in her peripheral, and without warning Val threw herself on both her and Caelum, nearly knocking them over.

"You're alright!" she sobbed, clutching them both so hard that she thought Caelum's head might pop off his shoulders. "I saw Deya being attacked by that group of soldiers and couldn't get to you . . . I was so . . . so worried!"

"We're alright!" Deya cried, laughing, and holding onto her friend tightly, Caelum still grunting uncomfortably in the middle of them. "Just a little banged up, but fine!"

Val released them and stopped to look down, noticing their clasped hands. Her eyes narrowed. "When you say *banged up . . .*"

Caelum and Deya immediately released each other, both turning a bright red.

"You're as crude as ever," Caelum snapped, and he marched ahead of them, towards the Sanctum, which remained scorched but intact. "Move it!" he yelled at them. "I need to talk to you and Aris. *Now.*"

Val rolled her eyes, and she took Deya's hand.

"Are you sure you're okay?" Val said to her. "Honestly, I don't know *what* Aris was thinking allowing you to come with us—"

"I demanded to come," Deya told her. "It wasn't Aris's fault."

"Oh please," Val scoffed. "The general does not let anything happen that he does not want. Aris always has a reason . . . even if it is completely psychotic."

Deya fell silent, contemplating this, Val's hand hot in hers. Together, they jogged after Caelum.

The inside of Burningtide Sanctum was cool and dark. Injured soldiers were being tended to everywhere there was free space. Healers bustled from one side of the room to the other, and Deya felt a slight pang in her broken chest at the sight of them.

Aris was standing with the captain of Burningtide, in a small room with one large table surrounded by maps. Both were covered in soot and bleeding from various places, but otherwise uninjured. They both looked up as Caelum, Deya, and Val appeared. Deya recognized the hint of relief in Aris's eyes upon seeing them—especially when he looked at Val.

"You're all alright," he said.

"What in Mother's name *was* that?" Val cried.

Aris's gold armor was scorched, his face bloodied, but Deya could see the darkening of his features.

"It was a declaration of war."

"What were they after?" Val demanded. "Was it—"

Deya felt Aris's gaze shift to her for a split second, before looking back to Val. "It was several things. Our recent attacks on Praiton have caused significant damage to their supply chain and military. Tonight, I assume they meant to handle us. I suppose we are lucky we weren't all burned alive by Titus's dragon."

Val didn't reply. Both she and Petrus exchanged serious looks— captain to captain—and Deya knew there was more than what they were saying.

"Where is Rayner?" Deya asked hesitantly, breaking the tension in the room.

It was Petrus that answered her. "He is being tended to with the others. He is fine, just a little burnt."

Deya's heart clenched at the memory of the burns on Rayner's hands, pitying her friend for having to collect more of them.

"I need to talk to you," Caelum demanded. "And . . . Saros, if he is near."

Deya expected the general to look curious, even worried, but instead, a small smirk tugged at his lips. "Valeria, go fetch Saros for me," he said with a casual nod, and he gestured for all of them to sit.

Val disappeared only to return a second later with the Nodarian male by her side, his black hair singed in places, but also unscathed. He noticed Caelum and smiled haughtily.

"Good to see you have survived," he said to Caelum, nodding at him, before sitting down in front of them. Aris sank into the seat at the head of the table and appraised Caelum.

"Well?"

Deya expected Caelum to launch into the story of what they had discussed, the plan they had formed, but instead, his eyes narrowed first to Aris, then at Saros.

"You told him," he demanded of the captain.

Saros shrugged. "My colleagues deserved to know."

Aris smiled dolefully at Caelum. "It is very nice to meet you, Caelum Hesperos."

"I am *not* a Hesperos," he snapped. "A bastard does not have a last name."

Saros did not argue. Instead, his dark purple eyes studied Caelum. "You are the last direct survivor of the greatest High King Nodaria ever had," Saros said firmly. "Regardless of who your mother was, I don't think it much matters now."

Caelum blinked. Val, too, looked shocked at this revelation, but did not interrupt.

Aris cut in. "Saros and I believe," he said steadily, "that you are the only way to reclaim Nodaria, and thus finally gain an upper hand in this war."

"I do not want his crown."

"You do not have a choice," Saros snapped. "If you want to save our kingdom, you have an obligation to recognize your birthright, Caelum." Caelum averted his eyes from the captain, arms crossed, eyes blazing. "Castor was my cousin," Saros said, and Caelum looked back up at him in surprise. "And he never loved any of you less for being bastards. He would have wanted it this way."

Like he did to Deya on the battlement, slowly, Caelum nodded. He then proceeded to tell the two captains, the general, and Val an abridged version of what he had told Deya, about the Battle for Atlas, the prophecy, and their plan to go to Nodaria to see if anyone could translate it.

Saros nodded. "I agree," he said. "The prophecy is indeed important. For it to appear at that instant, it *must* mean something."

Aris mulled this over, appraising them over peaked fingers. "And you two are willing to undertake this venture? Alone?"

Both Caelum and Deya nodded simultaneously.

"I will come, too," Val announced, springing to her feet, but Aris held up a hand to stop her.

"I need you, Valeria, to stay with your troops." And when Val tilted her head at him, he looked back at Caelum. "We will begin moving out on foot towards Arctos today. We will attack Nodaria at your signal, Caelum," he said, and all the air seemed to dissipate from the room. "We will reclaim the Celestial Kingdom, and a Hesperos *will* sit on the throne again."

Deya was mended by a healer who bustled between her and Caelum, before they both set out to depart, each carrying a bag full of supplies against their hips. They were to leave at once for Nodaria, not even able to rest or eat before Aris shooed them on their way.

Saros accompanied them out the gates of Burningtide, the male quiet and pensive as he walked beside them.

A half mile out of the gates, they stopped, and Saros nodded to Caelum. "Can you?" he asked.

Deya did not know what they meant, but Caelum nodded. "I've been working on it."

Saros stood back and Caelum took a deep breath and closed his eyes. When they opened again, they glowed a bright, vivid purple. Deya watched as he performed the same movement she had observed him practicing the night with the mountain troll—his hands pulling apart the air between them. Except, this time, a bright, spiraling portal appeared before him.

Deya gasped and Saros let out a deep chuckle. "If there was ever any question you were his son," he said to Caelum, "there isn't now." He clapped him on the shoulder, gave Deya a nod, then stepped back.

Caelum looked at her and held out his hand. Without hesitation, she walked into his embrace. And then they both stepped through the portal.

It was like being sucked into a vacuum. For a second, Deya could not breathe, and it felt like every molecule in her body was being compressed and condensed, until both she and Caelum were spat out and collapsed onto the hard Earth, coughing, and panting for air.

"Well, that was pleasant," Deya gasped.

Caelum sat on his back, eyes wide, taking in a rasping breath. "That was my first time doing that," he confessed, sitting up and rubbing at the back of his neck. "No wonder my father didn't do it often."

They both sat up and looked around. Caelum had teleported them to what appeared to be a wide rocky clearing. The ground underneath them had craters and bits of fossil embedded in its gray soil. It looked like what Deya had always assumed the surface of the moon to look like.

"I overshot it a bit," Caelum said, getting to his feet, squinting at the morning sun around them. "We're a few miles out of Arctos."

Deya rose, taken aback by how empty Nodaria seemed. Caelum, too, looked sad.

"Castor kept it permanently at twilight," he said, gazing at the sunny sky. "It was better for star-seeing. I guess it's just another thing that died with him."

Deya gave him a small, consoling smile, which caused him to clear his throat and move out.

Things were different between them—charged, tense, yet at the same time more relaxed than they ever had been. Deya felt antsy around him for some inexplicable reason. She almost wished he would snap and snarl at her again, like she was used to.

They began the walk towards the Nodarian capital city of Arctos, but Deya's legs were beginning to shake and tremble. She was tired . . . so tired. She realized she hadn't slept for over a full day, and now that the adrenaline of the battle at Burningtide had worn off, she was beginning to feel it. Caelum, too, looked exceptionally weary as they trooped their way farther and farther across the rocky terrain.

It was as the city of Arctos came into view that Deya's legs gave out. Caelum caught her before she hit the ground.

"I'm sorry," she stuttered, panting slightly. "It's just . . . the day is starting to wear on me."

Caelum nodded grimly. "It's starting to get to me, too," he said. "But Arctos is only another mile ahead."

Deya shook her head. "I just . . . need to rest for a second."

"We can't afford to rest," he said through gritted teeth. "We need to get out of the open before nightfall. In case you forgot, you seem to be a special type of bait for monsters in wild country, and I don't fancy being eaten because of you."

This bit of venom made her narrow her eyes at him as glimmers of the old, crotchety Caelum shone through like the morning sun. Or the fireball from a dragon.

"You will not be eaten because of me, you condescending *ass*," Deya growled, shoving him off her, adrenaline suddenly roaring in her veins as she drew her sword defiantly. "In case *you* forgot, I can defend myself just fine, no thanks to you."

"Really," Caelum sneered, drawing his own sword, too. "You want to have a rematch? Do you remember what happened the last time you faced me?"

"Fine," she snapped, squaring him up. "If I win, we rest. If you win, we keep going."

Caelum's eyes glinted, his lip curling up into a characteristic snarl. They glared at each other, now back to familiar territory. He had such an uncanny ability to get under her skin—an almost maddening pull towards each other, only to be met by a hard shove away. And in that moment, he looked so smug, like he knew he could beat her, that she lunged for him.

Caelum caught the wrist holding her blade with his free hand and with one fluid motion, he shoved her against a tree, pinning her to its trunk so hard that she gasped for breath as her still-sore lungs were pounded against the bark, Caelum's sword glinting at her throat.

"*I win*," he breathed in her ear. Deya snapped at him, pushing hard against him, trying to break free, to shove him off her, but only succeeded in pushing herself closer, molding herself even more against him.

The contact made molten warmth spread from her face to her chest, all the way down, warming her in all the places he touched. And she felt that same annoying pull she always felt around him, the same magnetic force that dragged her eyes downwards from his hooded purple eyes to his lips, which were parted as he regarded her the same way.

An angry, deep growl rumbled from the back of his throat. "Fuck it," he muttered, and then his lips were slamming into hers.

She moaned into his mouth, the sword she held dropping right into the dirt with a dull thump. Caelum threw his own sword away and gathered her tighter, their mouths opening, moving deeper, plunging further into each other.

Her hands in his hair, his hands on her hips, Deya felt herself melt into him. Even though he was cold to the touch and a blistering, wintry wind whistled by them, their kisses grew faster and hungrier. Suddenly, Caelum slammed his fist against the tree and pulled back, breathing hard, eyes unfocused.

"We keep moving," he panted, and he broke away from her, picking up his sword and walking quickly away, leaving her pinned to the tree by a thin layer of frost and ice.

She stood there for a full second, blinking as if she could not believe what had just happened. And, honestly, she couldn't. Did Caelum just *kiss* her? And, more importantly, did *she* kiss him back?

The only sign that it had even happened was the frost coating her body except for her lips which were the only warm things left, the feel of his mouth still lingering.

By the time she managed to peel herself from the tree and bent to retrieve her sword, Caelum was already almost a half mile ahead of her.

The rest of the walk to Arctos was spent in an agonizing silence. The weight of their frenzied kiss back at the tree seemed to rest only on Deya as they trooped on, Caelum dutifully not looking at her.

The sight of Arctos made the breath catch in her throat, driving out all thoughts of Caelum and his confusing mixed signals.

They froze at the edge of the city.

Arctos had been reduced to nothing but rubble and ruin. The small spire-like houses and dome-shaped huts surrounding the enormous Keep were empty, abandoned, many of them sporting caved in roofs or missing walls. There was no sound in the city. Not a footstep, a whisper, or even a bird chirping.

Arctos was a tomb, its buildings like skeletons encased inside it. A memorial for the Battle for Atlas.

Caelum stood on the bridge leading to the city, his feet rooted to the spot. His purple eyes were wide as he took in the wasteland of the place where he had grown up, where he was born and raised . . . where a part of him had died.

Deya reached out and took his hand. He jumped, as if he had just remembered she was there. His fingers tightened within hers, but he didn't look away. The bridge was decaying and dilapidated, the lanterns set on the posts leading across it were empty and covered in cobwebs. Caelum reached out a hand and brushed his fingers through the dust.

"These used to be filled with starlight," he whispered, his voice hoarse. "It was always nighttime here, so the city needed to be filled with other sources of light. These were always lit . . . always."

They walked over the bridge, the wooden planks bowing under their weight, creaking as they stepped across it. Deya could see it—how Arctos was once a beautiful, vibrant city, one that Oswallt had crowed about to her during those nights in their cells when nothing felt like it could ever be beautiful or vibrant again. The hollow lanterns on every available corner, empty of the starlight Caelum said they were supposed to have, were reflective of the city as a whole. Devoid of light.

They reached the edge of the town and Caelum stopped again. His eyes widened and Deya felt his fingers flex in hers, as if they were the only things holding him upright. Deya opened her mouth to ask him what was wrong, but then she saw it.

Atlas Keep must have once been an impressive, beautiful structure. It resembled a long, tall cylinder of black stone, stretching up towards the sky. At the top, half of the building had been rebuilt and sealed up, but the way that Caelum stared at it, Deya knew something was missing.

"The astronomy tower," he breathed. "It collapsed when Castor died. It's just . . . part of the building now."

Deya made to walk towards the Keep, to head towards the entrance that was located almost a mile over another long, wooden bridge, but Caelum stopped her.

"We can't go to the Keep," he said, shaking his head.

"Why not?"

"It's the only place in all of Arctos that is guarded. Look."

Deya looked. Soldiers. Hundreds and hundreds of soldiers, all wearing the Praiton crest, were milling about the grounds of the Keep. Deya was shocked to see that the only numbers in all of Arctos were Praitonian soldiers.

"Besides, that is where General Morlais resides now," Caelum snarled. Deya looked back at the Keep. She could not imagine the evil Praitonian general sitting on the Celestial Throne, perhaps still in the ruins of the destroyed astronomy tower. The thought made Deya sick. "They can't know we're here," Caelum said. "He'd remember me, I have no doubt."

"But what about the star seers?" she asked, looking around the deserted road. Not even a breeze swept through the abandoned buildings. "If we can't go to the Keep, where do you expect to find them? There's no one here."

"There's one last place," he said. "One place where there may be people left."

He led her through the winding streets, up and down the steps of the elevated city. The cobblestones underneath their feet were cracked and scattered, making for rocky terrain as the two of them plunged into the center of Arctos.

It was hard to see the city like this. She couldn't imagine what Caelum must be feeling. This was where he had grown up, now in ruins.

There were many crumbling statues devoted to the planets and stars located on street corners, making the ruinous city somehow even more tragic. But Caelum took her right past them, walking quickly, as if he was attempting to block it all out.

They came to a big, round building, alone at the top of a hill. From its roof, a large glass lens reflected in the sunlight, almost like a cyclops' eye. It was an observatory. Like all the rest of the structures in Nodaria, it was dome-shaped and tall. She assumed that they were built this way in order to ensure a better view of the heavens. This building looked old and important. A crumbling orrery was erected at its entrance, large brass stars lying broken on the floor underneath a dilapidated moon.

"What is this?" she asked him softly, for his eyes looked haunted, his face troubled.

"This was our observatory. The library that our priestesses studied at," he said. Every word seemed to be costing him immense effort. She tightened her grip on his hand and led him up the stairs, away from the sad sight of the broken-down planetarium.

Hesitating, Deya pushed open the heavy stone doors. Inside, there was nothing but dust. Books were pulled off the shelves, several bookcases and desks smashed, and the large bronze telescope in the center of the library, held high above their heads, looked shattered and broken. Caelum drooped beside Deya, and she knew that this was destroying him. This whole walk through this once bustling, lively city was destroying that one bit of him that had persevered after all this time. The love for his kingdom. The grief hitting him as he beheld what became of it.

Footsteps, muffled by dust and debris, shuffled from behind one of the bookcases, and both Deya and Caelum jumped, hands flying to their swords instinctively. But, edging out from behind the bookcase, was a small, trembling priestess. Her dark purple robes swished against the floor, swirling dust up around her as she clung to the edge of the heavy wooden bookcase.

"Who . . . who are you?" the quivering thing asked. She was shaking so hard that the heavy books in her hand seemed liable to hit the floor at any moment.

"We're looking for the star seers," Caelum said in a surprisingly gentle tone. "Did any of them . . . survive the battle? Are any of them here?"

The priestess's eyes darted nervously between them as she toddled to one of the few spindly tables left standing. "No," she whispered breathlessly. "They have all fled. As has everyone else."

The relief washed over Caelum's face. "So, they fled? They didn't die in the battle?"

The priestess shook her head, now anxiously staring at Caelum.

Deya cut in, "Why are you still here? Are you alone?" She tried to ask it gently, but still the girl flinched as if Deya had advanced towards her, weapon drawn.

"I . . . I was tasked to maintain the building by the new g-government," she stuttered.

Caelum's expression darkened. A familiar icy wind swept through the library, causing the priestess to shiver slightly.

"Where did the seers go?" he demanded of her, forgetting the kind, patient Caelum and reverting right back to the old one in a quick flash. Deya groaned inwardly. "It is important. *Where did they go?*"

The priestess shook like a leaf, her words stumbling and stuttering as she cowered from them. Deya could tell she was afraid to tell them, afraid to betray the last of her peoples' whereabouts to strangers.

Reaching out a firm hand, she seized Caelum by the wrist and dragged him forward. "I know he may not look it," she said to the priestess as kindly as she could. "But he is one of you." She pulled the sleeve of his tunic up, revealing his tattoos. The priestess's eyes widened, and she looked at Caelum closer. Her gaze roved from the white hair to the prophecy, and then to his violet eyes.

"Please," Deya begged, inching towards the priestess, as if she were attempting to reach a scared animal. "Tell us where they went. We *need* to know."

The priestess hesitated. And then, she sighed. "Mount Mors," she whispered. "The remaining seers and priestesses have taken refuge at Mount Mors."

Caelum looked at Deya. He nodded.

They burst out of the library, running down the empty streets, Caelum shaking his head. "I should have known," he said angrily. "They would not have stayed here. Mount Mors is the safest place for them in all Nodaria."

"What *is* Mount Mors?" Deya cried, struggling to keep up with him as he cut through side streets and alleyways, muscle memory of the familiar city, no doubt, kicking in.

"It's our temple," he said. "It's located high in the cliffs of the mountain range, which is as far north as you can get to the Nodarian border. Praiton would not have been able to attack it. It was always too well defended by nature alone."

"Then how are we to get there?" Deya panted.

"How do you think?" he said and made the motion of pulling the air apart. A portal sprang open. He seized her around the waist, and threw them both, headfirst, into the black hole again.

CHAPTER
23

The portal was not in any way more comfortable than the last, and when it expelled them out again, it was for Deya to fall headfirst into a pile of bushes, Caelum rolling to rest beside her. They were both gasping for breath.

For a second, she could only lay in the uncomfortable thorny bushes as her lungs tried to remember how to expand again.

"*Warn me* next time, will you?" she gasped angrily, attempting to swat him on the shoulder in retaliation.

Caelum coughed, but ignored her, brushing her flailing fist away as he rose from the bushes on unsteady feet.

"Fuck," he breathed.

"What is it?" Deya didn't know how much more bad news she could take. It had been the longest day of her life. Already she was beginning to grow irritable from sheer exhaustion.

"I think my magic reserves are running low," he said angrily, pacing back and forth from where they had landed. It was a field of rocky terrain—much like what they had landed in outside of Arctos. A few trees, bushes, and general greenery were around, but for the most part,

Nodaria looked like the surface of a faraway planet. "The portal only brought us halfway."

"*Halfway?*" Deya echoed. She struggled to rise to her feet, but the bushes tried to pull her back in. What was more, her legs felt like noodles, causing her to wobble like a baby deer. "Caelum, you are out of your mind if you think we can make it there today. *We have to rest.* Your magic reserves are depleted, and you're exhausted, too."

Caelum's jaw clenched in irritation. She knew it killed him to agree with her, regardless of their newfound common ground, or whatever in Mother's name happened back at that Godsforsaken tree.

"It's already late afternoon," Deya reminded him. "Wild country, remember? We should find some place now before it gets too late."

Caelum let out a growl. "Fine," he snarled. He looked back at her, and those purple eyes were still glowing with the power it had taken to get them this far. "Keep up. I won't slow down for you."

Deya mumbled an angry epithet under her breath, which Caelum ignored as they began to walk due north.

It took almost an hour to find a cave—a small gap in the rock that yielded just enough room for them to squeeze into—with enough space for them to lay down comfortably around a fire.

Caelum left to bring back flint, kindling, and wood, and Deya got busy attempting to start the fire as he made up camp.

"I miss Val already," Deya muttered five minutes later as she continued to rub the stick against the rock at a rapid speed to no avail. Smoke was billowing from around the flint, and the occasional spark, but otherwise not much else.

"That makes one of us," Caelum said. "Move over, you're doing it wrong." He leaned over and plucked the sticks from her hand, shoving her aside, causing her to hiss at him.

Deya sat back, rummaging through her satchel of food as Caelum got the fire going. She picked out a tin of salted meat from Burningtide's supplies and began to eat.

Fire burst from underneath the flint rock, and Caelum sat back with a groan of exhaustion that she knew was not intentional. He reached for his own supplies, and silently, they sat on the floor, the crackling of the fire filling the small cave, embers dancing on the walls of the rock and stone around them.

"So," Deya said, chewing slowly on a piece of dried meat, which had begun to taste less like ash as the weeks had gone by. She peered at Caelum sideways, who was not looking at her, instead focusing dutifully on his can of fruit. "Are we not going to talk about it?"

Caelum grunted. "Talk about what?"

"About what happened back in Arctos. At that tree."

A tic began to work its way in Caelum's jaw as he ground it together, stabbing at a piece of fruit with his tin fork.

"We don't need to talk about anything."

She had expected this. Had debated even bringing it up to him. It was obvious he would ignore the fact that it ever happened if she let him. But she was not going to let him.

Deya scoffed and leaned back against the wall of the cave, picking at another piece of jerky, even though she wasn't remotely hungry now.

"Fine," she said coolly. "We won't talk about it . . . even though you nearly gave me frostbite."

Caelum slammed down his tin of fruit, his eyes blazing with an irritation that almost made her laugh. She *loved* goading him like this. Had begun to learn how to take the tiniest bits of pleasure in watching that vein in his forehead almost explode every time she prodded at him.

"Is this your idea of not talking?" he grumbled.

Deya tried not to smile, but it was hard. A tell-tale flush was creeping up his collar. "No," she murmured. "But I'm just worried is all. I didn't think you were so repressed—"

Deya had barely gotten the word out of her mouth before he was seizing her roughly by the waist, pulling her towards him so abruptly that she let out a little yelp of shock as she came crashing into his lap.

"Why," he snarled with a tone of tortured frustration that made the words die in her throat, "does it *have* to be *you?"* His hands seized her by the jaw, pinching her chin in its grip, holding her steady.

"Why does *what* have to be me?" she breathed. Her lips were so close to his, that same maddening attraction already starting to pull her in again. Except this time, she knew what his lips felt like, knew how he tasted. And Gods, why did she want to do it again?

"Why does it have to be you that I'm so . . ." He tightened his hold on her jaw for the briefest moment before they both seemed to break at once.

She wasn't sure if he kissed her first or she lunged for him, but all she knew was that his lips were crashing over hers and the moan that escaped her was almost embarrassing in its desperation.

Caelum's hands moved from her chin to her waist, pulling her roughly on top of him so she straddled him, their kiss growing deeper, more frenzied.

Their hands ripped at each other's clothing, Deya's unsure where to go first. Caelum didn't seem to have that issue. He tore at her vest, his hands fumbling over the laces. She got so impatient that she let go of where she had his hair in her fist to help him out.

"Didn't think the Prince of Nodaria would be beaten by some laces," she breathed against his mouth, and to her surprise, she felt him smile against her lips.

"Trust me, those won't stop me," he murmured. And then the vest was off as he shoved her tunic off her shoulders, leaving her mouth only to kiss the gentle curve of her neck. Her head fell backwards at the touch, but she wanted more . . . needed more.

Reaching for his tunic, she pulled it up over his head, revealing all his tattoos and scars, exacerbated by the firelight. She had seen him shirtless before, had always found herself trying hard not to look too closely, but this time was different. This time she could look all she wanted . . . *touch* all she wanted. And she did. Slowing their desperate pawing of each other, she stopped to run light fingers down the tattoos—studying each delicate twist of the Nadarak letters, how they intermingled with the white scars on his body.

Caelum was still breathing hard, still had that hungry, glazed look in his eyes as he too slowed at her touch, her inspection. His own hands came up to her under-tunic and gently, he eased it off her shoulders and to the floor, exposing her to him.

His gaze went down to her breasts, small but pert, and the moan he let out was stifled as he took one peaked tip in his mouth. The sensation caused her to cry out, her head tilting back. Gods, she didn't know how much more of this she could take. She could feel him, hard, underneath her—such a strange and overwhelming feeling.

It was like an out-of-body experience. She had never imagined that she would find herself here, with *Caelum* of all people, like *this*.

And when he flipped her onto her back and began to pull off her boots and leather breeches, she had to try and steady her breathing. All this touch, all this sensation . . . She had now lost the ability to decipher the flutter of her heart and whether it was from fear or anticipation. Or were they the same thing?

Her breeches off, Caelum stared at her, naked save for the faerivaine necklace, on the cave floor, her hands attempting to cover herself instinctively. Never had she been this exposed to someone, this on display. She had had no time for lovers back home, had never been touched or looked at the way Caelum was doing right now.

And yet, she breathed in, held it . . . Caelum had seen her at her absolute worst. Had never moved or walked away, even when faced with his own possible destruction.

And that gave her strength.

He pulled her hands away from her body, shaking his head. "Don't you fucking dare. Have you not learned yet that you don't have to hide from me?" he murmured, and the breath caught in her throat. With shaking hands, she lowered her arms.

He spread her legs, his fingers tracing around her breasts, down

304

her abdomen, all the way down to the apex of her thighs, sliding down, feeling the wetness of her. The pressure of his finger made her cry out, the sensation too much and yet not . . . fucking . . . enough.

"*Caelum*," she snarled, her impatience getting the best of her.

Caelum raised one eyebrow at her, his fingers still exploring her, teasing, and pressing in all the best ways. "Impatient, are we?"

"I swear to the Gods, Caelum . . ." But her threat was swallowed by her moan when Caelum's mouth found the sensitive bud he had just been playing with. And she almost blacked out. The pressure built with each swirl of his tongue, each tug and nip had her moaning so loud she had no idea how all the monsters of wild country weren't coming to see what all the noise was about.

She was nearly delirious with need by the time he released her, his hands moving to his own trousers, and this time, she really had to tell herself to breathe.

"Are you sure about this?" he murmured.

"Isn't it a little late for that question?" she snapped, sitting up on her forearms to glare waspishly at him.

He smirked. "Never too late for that question."

Deya rolled her eyes. "Yes, I'm sure," she snapped, and she hurriedly reached for his pants, helping him unlace them, then pull them down. When he sprang free of his breeches, Deya's mouth went dry.

"Still sure?" he asked, and that smirk was so *smug* that Deya let out a furious little growl and pulled him towards her.

He fit inside her slowly, the inching bit by bit driving her to the brink of madness. She was so desperate to have him, to feel him fill her, that her legs hooked around his waist, driving him all the way into her. The moan they both let out was instantaneous.

As they moved together, a cold wind roared through the cave, nearly obliterating the fire in its wake.

And as Caelum moved inside her, each thrust harder and more furious than the last, his hands braced above her, and Deya seemed to dissolve within herself. For a moment, the broken panic in her chest was silent.

With a moan, Deya shattered first, pushed completely over the edge in what felt like a shower of sparks. And then, soon after, with a roar, Caelum grabbed at the ground to brace himself and fell apart, and an explosion of ice and frost erupted around them.

CHAPTER
24

"You made it snow." Caelum heard Deya giggle a little while later as snowflakes drifted from the cave ceiling and danced in the air, landing on her bare shoulders and in her hair.

"Fuck," Caelum groaned, rising from his partially collapsed position beside her to look around them. The entire cave was covered in a thin layer of snow. Icicles hung from the ceiling and flurries floated down upon them.

"The fire went out, too," Deya said.

Caelum groaned again, collapsing back down again, and she laughed even harder.

"I hate this damn power," he grumbled. He was lying on his stomach with his head against her chest, right in between her breasts, listening to the gentle beating of her heart. "I wish I knew how to control it."

"Well, let's hope you being turned on isn't what triggers it, because if so, I might have some questions about the Battle of Burningtide," she said, the smugness still evident in her suppressed yawn. He turned to glare at her, and she giggled again.

Deya rolled onto her stomach, dislodging his head from her chest so she could pull his thick cloak out of the nearest pack. She threw it around them, to shield them from the sudden cold that his Frost Magic had brought about.

"There," she said. "Problem solved."

Caelum's eyes lingered on the side of her face. The delicate curve of her chin, the way her dark eyelashes cast shadows across her pronounced cheeks. He soaked it all in, this moment he had denied himself since they had met—the rare opportunity to gaze as long as he wanted at this Praitonian girl and every small, beautiful feature that he'd tried to ignore. But there he was, throwing it all away just for the chance to look at her . . . to touch her.

Deya, sensing his stare, looked over at him with a small smile. "What?"

Caelum shook his head. "Nothing." His fingers reached out and touched her bare back. The scars he had noticed that day in Aunecia were now in full view. They were raised and brutal, as thick, and obvious as veins on a forearm. His touch made her spine stiffen, but as she had touched his scars, he touched hers.

"You hesitated," he said softly, his finger still following one ragged line. "At the very end . . . I felt you stiffen, just like that."

Deya fell silent, the laughter and euphoria of the last hour fading from her face. "My body doesn't know sensations anymore," she whispered. "It has a hard time . . . deciphering what to feel. It's like it was filed down . . . made into something only designed for survival. Pleasure can feel like panic. Nerves can feel like the end of the world. Sometimes, it takes me a moment to untangle them."

"Were you nervous?" he whispered to her. He didn't know what it was that made him whisper, like he didn't want anything in the world to hear him, to eavesdrop on this moment.

"A little," she whispered back. She reached out a hand and touched his face, reaching for the braid he kept twined beside his ear, the only part of his Bridanian heritage that he had ever adopted. "But only because I'm afraid of what all of this means."

Caelum didn't answer. He couldn't tell her that he was afraid of the exact same thing.

"I thought you hated me," Deya said, laughing softly, her fingers playing with his braid.

Caelum shrugged, his own fingers still walking the map of the many scars on her back. "I did. But I think it was because I always saw a bit of myself in you. It was strange. I hated how you would look at me sometimes. It was always like you . . ."

"Understood?" Deya whispered. Their eyes met, gray against purple. And he nodded.

"I never got to have friends as a child," Deya murmured, laying her chin down into her arms, speaking softly to the cave floor. "My mother didn't trust any of the families in our village. She kept me away from all of them. When I got to the infirmary in Stonehall, it felt like the first time I ever had friends." She gave a sad laugh. "Perhaps that's why I clung so tightly to Praiton. I guess all I wanted was to belong."

Caelum didn't speak. An image of himself as a child, constantly bobbing along behind his siblings, being laughed at, rejected . . . He watched her eyelashes flutter, covering those mystifying gray eyes of hers. And once again, he felt like she could see that child he once was. That she understood him.

They fell asleep shortly after that, too exhausted from their long two days to stay awake. And when they awoke again, the ice had thawed, and bright, radiant sunlight streamed into the small crack in the cave.

"*Fuck*," Caelum groaned, shielding his eyes from the sun as both he and Deya struggled to open their eyes. "How long did we sleep?"

Deya mumbled something, attempting to pull the cloak over her head. Caelum stood, still naked, and poked his head out of the cave and swore loudly.

"*What?*" Deya moaned.

"We slept clear into the afternoon!" Caelum cried, furiously grabbing his pants, and attempting to shove his legs back into them. "There's probably barely any daylight left for us to get the rest of the way to Mount Mors."

Deya shifted, stretching, catlike upon the cave floor, causing the cloak to slip off her, revealing her petite frame, still as naked as he was. She caught him looking and gave him a lazy smile.

"Or we can just take one more day in the cave," she purred.

Caelum froze, his eyes taking her in greedily. Gods, he had never been more conflicted in his life. Here they were, on the cusp of starting a war on a whole kingdom, and all he wanted was to fuck this girl silly until he couldn't think anymore.

The worst of it was that he felt like he could have kept sleeping for another couple hours. Last night with Deya had drained him in more ways than just his magic reserves. And Gods did he want to do it again.

"We *have* to get to Mount Mors," he said sternly. But it didn't come out very convincing. Deya seemed to hear that, and she smiled a bit wider as she stood up, the cloak falling off her.

"Then we'll just brave wild country," she said, walking towards him. "*Or* you just have to make sure that lovely Portal Magic of yours actually gets us there in one shot this time."

Caelum's eyes raked her naked body. He could feel himself harden again looking at her.

"Fuck it," he growled and then seized her by the back of the neck, bringing their lips crashing together again.

In the end, they didn't leave the cave for another two hours as he took her on every available surface he could find. They only decided to leave because the amount of snow and frost Caelum had accidentally sent exploding out of him had left the cave virtually uninhabitable with ice forming on the ceiling and snowflakes falling around them.

As they were getting dressed, Caelum caught Deya cringing slightly as she laced her vest back up.

"What?"

"I just thought of how Val is going to react to this," she said. "She'll probably die from laughing so hard."

Caelum grunted at the thought of the Manielian female. He could picture that gloating, foxlike face now. He still couldn't quite get the moment out of his head when she had told Deya that she thought he had "finally taken her on the forest floor" back in Aunecia. Mostly because now, he wished he had.

"Can't we just not tell her then?" he growled, shoving a foot into his boot in one furious motion.

Deya snorted. "You can try. But judging by our inability to leave this damned cave, I have a feeling it might not be an easy thing to hide."

Caelum grunted again, knowing she was right. Anyway, he intended to fully take advantage of having a bed with her back at Light's Tower, Val be damned.

They emerged from the cave a little while later, and Caelum paced around the outskirts of the cliff, looking at the sky and the horizon, trying to get his bearings. Eventually, he was able to make out a speck in the distance. Little jagged edges that must be the mountain range of Mount Mors, due north of them.

He took a deep breath.

"How are your magic levels?" Deya asked beside him.

He rolled his neck, taking a brief inventory of the magic within him. "Not at capacity, but it should get us there," he said.

The fact that he was not at full capacity worried him. One thing Castor had always stressed was the dangers of Portal Magic. Done wrong or pushed too far, he could lose whoever he was transporting within the folds of time and space.

He could not risk losing one of them just because they were impatient. He didn't add that his magic may have been completely restored if he hadn't accidentally expended most of it on Frost Magic he couldn't fully control while making furious love to her all over that fucking cave.

But, once again, he didn't need to say it. The little hint of a smile on her lips told him she could guess it.

"You know who might be able to help control your Frost Magic," she began.

He knew what she was going to say before she even finished her thought.

"*No.*"

Deya rolled her eyes. "Come *on*, Caelum. Frost Magic is the sibling of Ember Magic. They are two sides of the same coin. Val might be your best—"

"I would sooner eat my own sword," Caelum grit out, and Deya rolled her eyes.

"So dramatic," she muttered.

Glaring at her, he turned away before he did what he wanted to do, which was seize her by the throat, push her back into that cave, and teach her a lesson for constantly trying to goad him. But they didn't have time for that.

He closed his eyes and gathered his Celestial Magic. Now, when he reached into his body for it, it was like he was touching more than one strand of power. He now had to detangle which he was looking for, careful to avoid pulling from the place where the Frost Magic was always desperate to escape.

With a grunt, he pulled the air apart again. Castor's Portal Magic had been tricky to get the hang of. To his knowledge, nobody other than the late High King had been able to do this. Even Aelius had been unable to do it before he died—though Castor had tried to teach him. Ultimately, those lessons Caelum had been allowed to sit in on were what got him to this point. Still, it took an immense amount of his energy and power just to do one portal. He was still nowhere near what his father once was.

A swirling black and purple tear erupted out of the air between Caelum's palms, spinning into position in front of them. Panting slightly from the effort, Caelum turned to Deya and held out his hand. It was a different gesture this time. They both knew it. Her eyes were soft when she looked at him, and he couldn't seem to muster any of the previous ire he used to have with her. In fact, he was pretty sure he had the softest, doughiest, most pathetic expression on his face when looking at her.

It was almost easy . . . natural. In finally yielding to the pull between them, it was as if something had slid into place that had fought to be there all along.

Smiling, Deya took his hand.

They plunged into the portal, the tight vacuum compressing them to near suffocation before spitting them out, face first, into the dirt.

They both gasped and spluttered, Caelum's lungs inhaling the newfound air before he looked up. Nothing but a solid rock wall was in front of them. His eyes roved upwards, and he felt his heart lift.

There, reaching towards the sky was Mount Mors—the large mountain was jet black, something truly alarming in the late afternoon. A hulking black mass that appeared to spread out for miles and miles on either side of them, Mount Mors was a formidable sight. At the apex of the mountain, a large telescope jutted from the black rock—the brass shining in the setting sun.

"How do we get up there?" Deya panted, sounding like she was still struggling to intake the breath she had lost in the portal. "Can you portal us up there, too?"

Caelum shook his head. "Portals don't work up there," he said, and Deya stared at him dumbly, making him chuckle. "The mountain is protected by ancient magic from the seers back in Astrea's time. All magic is nullified around it. This is as far as we go."

"You mean to tell me that we have to *climb* that behemoth?" Deya cried.

Caelum laughed out loud, the feel of it still foreign to him. "This is why," he growled, reaching out to pull her towards him, his mouth grazing hers, "I told you we needed to leave that damned cave and get moving before nightfall."

"I still say we should've just stayed another night," she purred, grinning, her lips brushing his back, and Caelum growled in annoyance before taking her mouth in his for a slow, languid kiss.

Deya groaned. "Okay, *focus*," she said, pushing him away. "How in Mother's name are we going to get up there?"

"How do you think?" he asked, smirking at her. "We climb."

And he laughed again as Deya let out a moan of agony. He wrapped Deya in his arms, and then with what little power he had left, he lifted them with his Gravity Magic, taking them up the black sheet rock of Mount Mors, all the way towards the base of the mountain. It was almost a hundred feet from where they had started, but the amount of mountain still left to climb was substantial.

"That's as far up as we can go with Magic," he said, releasing her and pointing towards a narrow stone path of black, flat steps. "We start the climb there."

They began the ascent up the narrow, carved steps, the pathway too tight for them to take side by side, so Caelum led the way ahead of her. The first thousand steps were easy, if not a little arduous. But by the next thousand or so, Deya was beginning to breathe a little harder, and Caelum's legs were starting to burn something fierce.

"So why doesn't Magic work up here?" Deya huffed from behind him.

"We're not entirely sure," Caelum admitted, sweat beading on his brow as he struggled to put one foot after the other. "It has been like this for as long as anyone can remember. The priestesses believe it to be from the Goddess's protection, but I think it has something to do with the rock this mountain is made of."

Deya looked down at the black slate rock under their feet. "It does remind me of iron," she mumbled. "You mean no one has looked into it?"

Caelum shook his head. "The priestesses will not allow it. The mystery of the mountain is partially what keeps it safe. If no one knows, no one can destroy or abuse it."

Deya murmured something that sounded like a vague agreement, but Caelum was too busy focusing on climbing the next step. And the next one. And the next one.

He didn't remember much of his first and only trip to Mount Mors as a child. Surely, he would have remembered *these* many stairs. But as they climbed, as the clouds grew thicker and denser, bits of memories started coming back to him: Aelius helping him up the stairs, Castor turning back to wave his sons along, dressed in his signature brocade velvet jacket, the silver pendant he always wore glinting in the moonlight. How he had put a large hand on Caelum's shoulder, ruffled his hair when they got to the top. As if he were proud of him for making it.

When they reached the top of Mount Mors, the sky was an inky black and filled with stars. The stars in Nodaria were always crisp and clear. Always breathtaking. They claimed that Nodaria was the closest to Heaven you could get in all the realm. Tonight, it looked like it.

Mount Mors was sealed by a large brass door set into the black rock. Carved with intricate markings depicting the planets and stars, it reminded him of the carving on the door of Light's Tower. In fact, it was almost the exact same markings. It was the priestess's tale of Nodaria, written in the Heavens. He had been taught to read it as a child, to decipher which stars told of the fate of the Celestial Throne.

Caelum drew in a deep breath and looked at Deya. No doubt sensing his hesitation, she took his hand. He reached out and rapped hard on the door. The force of his fist on brass seemed to echo for miles within the mountain. And then, the door crashed open.

Standing in front of him stood six young males, all with swords drawn, all with black hair and purple eyes. Caelum instinctively shoved Deya behind him and drew his own sword, but Deya appeared to have another thought.

"Wait!" she cried, throwing her hands in the air from behind Caelum, who gave an angry growl at the silly female to tell her to *shut up*. "We come in peace! Please!"

The male at the forefront of the group—a thinner, scrawny male that certainly did not look like he came from any of the high profile Nodarian military units, paused. His eyes darted from Deya, then to Caelum. The purple eyes widened.

"No . . ." he breathed, his sword dropping as he gazed at Caelum in disbelief. "It can't be . . ."

Recognition seemed to dawn on the others around him, all of them lowering their swords, whispering amongst each other.

"Is it really you?" the male asked him softly. "Are you . . . Caelum? King Castor's bastard?"

Caelum felt a flush of anger at that—the shame still present, regardless of what Saros or Aris had said to him. But at least it wasn't the White Sheep of Nodaria.

Caelum lowered his sword but glowered at the male with such malevolence that he cowered from him. "Yes," he snarled. "And this is what they put here at Mount Mors to protect what is left of our kingdom? Some scrawny knights that are too young to even have fought in the Battle for Atlas?"

The male bowed his head, a flush filling his pale cheeks. Caelum noted the faint hint of Nadarak letters coming from the collar of his armor. Another damned prophecy.

"Begging your pardon," the male said, his voice trembling. "But we were all that was left." He looked up at Caelum, and he found that his expression had not softened one bit. "We did not know you were alive."

"No one did," he said impatiently. "Now, will you let us in, or must we continue to have this very unpleasant conversation outside?"

The soldier jumped to attention and he and the group stepped back, allowing Caelum and Deya to enter. The soldier was jumpy and nervous. He looked as if he didn't know whether to bow to Caelum or not. Even Caelum didn't know where he stood in all of this.

He was never considered a prince. Aelius, Aten, and Astrid were Castor's only trueborn children. They got the title, the respect, and the prestige. Caelum, Seren, and Sirius got the leftovers.

Mount Mors was exactly as he remembered it. The inside of the temple reached upwards as high as it could go. Spiral gold staircases lined the walls, crawling up to the top where the largest telescope in the kingdom sat, staring right up into the Heavens.

Bookcases filled with every tome on the stars and planets that one could imagine occupied every hole and crevice of the black cave walls. Everywhere he looked, carvings of the Goddess Astrea peered back at him—from the backs of chairs, the sides of bookcases, even in the center of a large wooden table by the fireplace. Banners depicting the silver and purple crest of Nodaria hung from the walls, and all around them were purple-robed priestesses and the signature black robes of the star seers.

Looking around, Caelum felt an intense ache in his chest. He was home, but nothing was the same. The people looked familiar, the colors the same, but he knew that there was something so terribly different . . . so irreparably wrong. It hurt him to his very core. His home as he knew it was definitively gone.

"Excuse me," the scrawny soldier piped up. Caelum shot him a flinty-eyed glare which caused the boy to cower again. "What *are* you doing here, Master Caelum?"

He snorted at that. Whatever that title was, it definitely was *not* his favorite.

"I am looking for the star seers, particularly—" He hesitated, looking at the black robed females, who were all peering up at him curiously. "Io or Cressida. Did they . . . are they here?"

The soldier looked to his men, then back at the star seers. "I . . . I am not sure, sir," he stuttered. "The star seers keep to themselves at the top of the tower. The ones down here merely help with the priestesses."

"Lady Io is here at Mount Mors, sir." A diminutive star seer rose to her feet from where she had been sitting by the fire, a book in hand. Her face was young and pretty, her hair hidden by the hood that all star seers wore. She looked to be about the age he imagined Seren would be now if she had survived. "I can take you to her. She's at the top of the mountain in her study."

Caelum looked at the girl and nodded stiffly to her.

"Thank you, Deimos," she said, nodding at the soldier. "I shall take it from here." Deimos looked faint from relief that they were being taken out of his hands. He gave Caelum and Deya a little bow that made Caelum snort derisively, and then they followed the young girl towards the narrow staircase that led to the twisting catwalks constructed in spirals leading up the mountain.

"Don't be too hard on Deimos," the young star seer said to Caelum as they began to climb the steps. "His father was King Castor's first General."

"*That* was General Pallas's son?" Caelum cried incredulously, twisting to look back at the weak, trembling boy that had collapsed in a chair when they left the room. "What in the Mother's name happened?" General Pallas had been a large, imposing male that had been constantly at his father's side. And while he may have looked formidable, he had always been kind to Caelum and his siblings.

The star seer gave him a dry smile. "When the army was wiped out, Deimos and a few of the other soldiers' children were the only survivors who had managed to escape the Keep. As they grew, they swore to protect us here at Mount Mors."

Caelum resisted the urge to scoff at that—mostly because Deya gave him a warning look that made him bite his tongue.

"What is your name?" Deya asked the girl as they continued the winding path upwards.

"Nysa," she replied. Her purple eyes shifted back to Caelum, and he could have sworn he saw color flush her pale cheeks. "You were Seren's brother."

The statement caught him off guard. He looked sharply at the young girl, wondering if she had somehow known that she had reminded him of his youngest sister. In the way she was looking back at him, he knew she had.

"You knew Seren?"

Nysa nodded; her face sad. "We studied together at the Keep for a time. She was my friend. I used to sit with you, Aelius, and Aten when we

318

had class with Lady Io."

Caelum could not remember this in the slightest. His childhood at the Keep felt so long ago that he couldn't place the young star seer's face to save his life. But Nysa smiled, as if she guessed he did not remember her.

"That prophecy," she said, gesturing to what she could see from underneath his collar. "That was from Seren, wasn't it?"

This time, Caelum was too shocked to answer. Thankfully, Deya saved him. "How can you tell?"

"All prophecies are slightly different," Nysa said. "Depending on the seer who gives it, they all will have a certain unique look about them. I have seen one Seren gave before, and I recognize it clearly."

"W-what gives it away?" Caelum hated to hear his voice tremble, but the idea that something of Seren was left with him made his body run cold in a way that had nothing to do with his Frost Magic.

Nysa gave him a small, knowing smile. "She always had big loops in her letters when she wrote. Her Nadarak letters are no different."

Caelum's eyes drifted to his rolled-up sleeves, where he could see the top of the black swirls that didn't look anything like letters to him. He decided that he would have to take her word for it.

They followed Nysa up in spiraling circles, the brass steps rattling underneath them with each footfall. The catwalks began to get narrower and narrower as the mountain peaked, and then they were circling around the large golden telescope. It looked well-polished and maintained, the same model as the one that used to be in the astronomy tower at the Keep. Except *much* bigger.

Nysa walked them towards a dark blue door in a circle of identical doors around the golden platform. She raised a pale, delicate fist and knocked on the wood.

"Enter," a familiar voice called from in the room.

Nysa looked at them and inclined her head, stepping back and allowing them to enter the room.

Io's office was the same dark blue color as the door they pushed open. It was a small circular chamber with bookcases up to the ceiling and little brass instruments on every available surface. The old star seer sat behind her desk, the black robes and hood accentuating the lines in her pale face, her gnarled hands delicately holding a spindly brass object to her eyes, which she lowered slowly to look up at them.

"Ah," she murmured. "The lost Prince of Nodaria. Welcome home. We've been expecting you."

Deya found herself struck by how old the female was. The elderly star seer peered up at them from over the tiny gold object she had been looking into. Age and time moved slowly for the fae. It took decades—even centuries—for their appearance to change just a little after they reached a mature age. For this female to look this old, she must be positively ancient.

"Hello, Io," Caelum said softly. Deya hadn't missed how he had bristled at the title: Prince of Nodaria. She found it funny how he hadn't minded it when *she* had called him that when they were tangled together in that cave last night. The memory alone made her flush.

Io took off her half-moon spectacles and squinted up at Caelum, her purple eyes cloudy, yet still sharp and full of wisdom. "I always knew you survived," the old female said, rising to her feet, smoothing down the folds of her long black robes. "The stars told me long ago. The Heavens glowed bright on the day you were born. I will never forget it."

Caelum shifted uncomfortably. "Funny," he mumbled. "I never felt particularly special."

Io walked around the table, her eyes scanning him from head to toe. "You came to hear what your prophecy says." It was not a question. The old female said it matter-of-factly.

"This old game again, Io?" Caelum sighed and sank down into the spindly chair in front of her. "If you already know, why even bother asking?"

Io let out a wry chuckle. "You were always a sharp-tongued little devil. Some may even say a right pain in the behind."

Deya bit back a snort.

"I did not know you received a prophecy until recently," Io continued, walking up to Caelum, and pulling down his collar with a forceful, gnarled finger without even asking. Caelum took it like a child whose grandmother was fussing over him. "It was only revealed to me through the stars about a month ago." She waved a finger at him, gesturing to him to stand. "Shirt off."

Caelum raised a dark eyebrow, but rose and, with a sardonic look at Deya, he pulled off his shirt. The old female's eyes widened imperceptibly as she took in the vast amounts of scars that intermingled with the dark lines of the prophecy. Roughly, she stretched Caelum's skin, walking around him in a circle, purple eyes roaming his whole body.

"Curious," she mused. "Very curious."

"What does it say?" Caelum asked hesitantly. Io finished her final circle around him before she returned to her desk and sank back down into her chair.

She studied him for a long moment, both Deya and Caelum tense with anticipation before she spoke. "I have known you since you were a babe, Caelum," she said. "I was there when Castor brought you to the Keep to meet his other children. With that shock of white hair and an illegitimate legacy, I knew your life would be hard. However, when the Heavens shone brighter than I had ever seen them on the night you were born, I knew something would be different about you."

Caelum didn't seem like he was breathing. He sat, motionless, staring at the old female, waiting.

"Knowing the contents of this prophecy can change the course of everything," Io told him. "Are you prepared for this?"

He glanced at Deya, as if for her help. She reached out a hand and put it on his shoulder, giving him a small, encouraging nod.

He turned back to Io. "Yes."

She inclined her head. "Very well," she said. And then, she recited, *"For what is written in snow, thus revealed in the thaw, born with a crown of ash and star, so he shall be the one to save them all."*

For a second, neither of them moved. Caelum sat as still as ice. He didn't so much as blink.

"What . . ." Deya began, causing the old female's eyes to snap to hers for the first time. "What does that mean?"

Io tutted. "I am merely a mouthpiece for the stars, girl. I do not interpret."

Deya looked away sheepishly, but the old seer's eyes narrowed on her. Her eyes moved between her and Caelum, eyebrow arching imperiously.

"You have mated," she said.

Both she and Caelum looked up sharply. Deya could feel her cheeks reddening, and Caelum spluttered unintelligently.

"M-mated?" he stuttered, but Io did not seem the least bit fazed by their embarrassment.

"Yes, your auras are different. Fused. It is a sign that you have mated, bonded by something more than just physical."

Neither of them spoke. It seemed both were at a loss for words. It was true, Deya had not been able to stop reliving their previous night in the cave—every touch, kiss, and movement felt burned into her. She could still feel all of it. And what was more, she had become more hyperaware of Caelum than ever before. Every movement and breath he took, she could almost feel it, sense it in a strange way. Was it because they were now, as Io had put it, *fused?*

"Thank you, Io," Caelum said, clearing his throat and hastily getting to his feet. He seized Deya's hand and began to pull her roughly towards the door. "We appreciate your time." But the old seer's face went blank. It was as if someone had wiped all life clean off it, leaving her eyes expressionless, empty. And then those purple irises began to roll back into her head.

Caelum's face went white. "Io?" he said. But the female had begun to shake, her thin body nearly convulsing in her dark robes, her knotted hands clenching the armrests of her chair.

"Is she okay?" Deya asked, moving towards the old seer, reaching out an earnest hand. "Caelum, is she—"

But then her spine began to prickle, as if a hot wind had blown over her. And then her skin seemed to rip apart.

Deya let out a scream and collapsed to her knees, the pain spreading from the base of her neck all the way down her back and arms.

"Deya!" Caelum yelled, but she barely heard him.

It was as if someone had taken a flame to her back, burning the already scarred skin. The pain was so intense, so surreal, that spots were beginning to appear in her vision. Soon she was face down on the rug in front of the seer's desk, screaming for all she was worth.

She felt Caelum's hands on her, rolling her over. *"Where is it Deya? Where does it hurt?"* He was yelling, but his voice sounded like she was hearing it from underwater.

"B-back," she gasped, before she let out another shriek of pain. And then Io began to speak.

A low, guttural sound, caught between a song and a chant began to issue through the room. The pain intensified as she spoke, feeling like someone with a small, flaming knife was peeling pieces of her skin off bit by bit . . .

She was vaguely aware of Caelum tearing at her clothes, holding her in his arms, searching for the source of the pain.

And then, the words stopped. The pain lessened, but still it burned, stung, and ached as if she had been flayed. Panting, still cradled in Caelum's arms, she opened her eyes.

Caelum looked horrified; his eyes wide.

The old seer gasped back into her body, her eyes flickering to the forefront.

"What does it say?" Caelum demanded angrily. He was clutching Deya so tightly that she was beginning to feel faint. "Io!" he yelled.

"Give me a second, boy," the seer snapped. "It is not easy to give these prophecies . . . especially at my age."

Deya was still panting, tears of agony falling down her face as she processed the blistering pain she still felt on her spine and backs of her arms. She heard Io rise with a grunt and her black slippered feet shuffled into view around the desk. Deya's shirt had been ripped off by Caelum, stuffed to her chest to keep her covered, leaving her back exposed as Io and Caelum leaned over her. She felt the seer's fingers touch the tender skin, and she yelped, jumping even at the gentle brush.

"Oh, dear," she whispered, running a finger down Deya's spine. Deya drew in a sharp intake of breath.

"What does it say?" Caelum snapped, and Io tutted at him again.

"Interesting," she murmured.

"*Io!*" Caelum yelled.

The old seer read carefully, her finger tracing down Deya's spine and up her arms, as if she were reading from a book.

"The balance of one, the downfall of all, only the Queen of Ash can bring about the fall."

CHAPTER
25

Caelum carried Deya to a small chamber that Nysa had led them to. He could see her falling into and out of consciousness, still crying from the pain. He knew how painful a Nodarian prophecy could be. It was like being branded, the flesh staying tender and sore weeks after the prophecy had been made. He remembered how it felt all too well.

He laid her on her stomach in the small bed, her back still exposed, the angry black marks lined in red on her scarred back. Searching for that thread inside him that triggered his Frost Magic, he gave it a gentle tug. Cold air pooled at his palm, and slowly he passed it over Deya's marks. She gave a small whimper of relief, and he let his hand glide over her skin, soothing the burns.

One hand brushed Deya's skin, the other held a pen and a piece of parchment. On it, he had jotted down both prophecies that Io had recited, staring at them, hard, trying to make sense of it. His mind kept replaying what Io had said about them mating. *Bonded*, she had said. Each time he thought the word, his heart would skip a beat, his breathing growing short.

He looked over at the female in the bed beside him. Her long chestnut hair was spread out on the pillow in her trademark twisted plait, and there were still tears on her cheeks. He knew how his body felt for her—how he couldn't keep his hands to himself, how he couldn't seem to get enough of her—but how did his heart feel? His heart, which he had always assumed was as black and hard as the rock that made up this mountain. What did it feel for her?

Io's voice echoed in his head again. *Bonded. Fused.* He had not heard much about the concept of mates. Fae mating was a rare, mysterious thing. It was a bond that was often never realized, a pull towards another that was so faint it was often easy to miss. Yet, acted on, it was said to be almost impossible to undo.

No, a small voice in the back of his mind growled. *It is not possible. There is no bond. You are bound to nothing.*

The panic was beginning to build in him as he searched within himself, as though looking for a difference in how his lungs filled, the rhythm to which his heart beat. As though this girl now had some control over it.

No, the voice insisted again—an angry, guttural hiss of fury. *No one can control that. They won't.*

For a moment, he could feel the faerivaine shackles around his neck as he was pulled into the warden's office. The way the knife would glint in the fire as the warden asked him questions about Bridah, how he would trace these questions with the blade into his skin. That no matter what he did, he could not move, could not fight back.

His eyes roved over his prophecy, the knot in his stomach tightening as he read each cryptic line.

For what is written in snow, thus revealed in the thaw . . . Was this perhaps a mention of his mixed bloodline? To his rare ability to wield two different types of magic?

Born with a crown of ash and star. Well, the star one was obvious. But ash . . .

He froze, his eyes shifting from his prophecy to Deya's, his heart rate quickening. Sitting up in bed, his hand drifted from her for a second as he read her prophecy again.

The balance of one, the downfall of all, only the Queen of Ash can bring about the fall.

The Queen of Ash.

Caelum sprang to his feet. Before he knew what he was doing, he was striding out of the room and flying up the bronze steps, taking two at a time.

He barged into Io's office without even knocking.

"For the love of the Mother, Caelum!" Io barked, clutching her heart as the door Caelum had kicked in rocked the bookcase behind it. "What is the meaning of—"

"The bond," Caelum growled. "The bond you spoke of between me and Deya. It is our prophecies that link us. That is what you meant, isn't it?"

Io peered up at him, her gnarled hand still resting on her chest. "It could be," she replied. Caelum let out a huff of irritation.

"My prophecy says I was born with a crown of star and ash. Hers mentions a Queen of Ash. It is her, isn't it? Her magic destroys things, turns it to ash. That is the bond."

Io's purple eyes did not blink as she stared up at him with an intense, scrutinizing look. Finally, she said, "I told you that knowing your prophecy may change everything, Caelum. By me reading it to you, it has set another chain of events into motion. Events that, I dare say, were waiting to be triggered. This is your fate. *Both* of your fates."

Caelum stood there, breathing hard, his mind spinning. She smiled sadly at him.

"You deserve happiness, child," she said softly. "Do not try to sabotage what is right in front of you."

Caelum left the old star seer's office but did not descend the steps back to Deya. Instead, he chose to ascend further and further to the peak of the mountain. There, several ravens roosted, all on set perches. Around them was a small table, a quill, and some parchment. Quietly, he wrote out a message to Aris. And just like that, he called the Pillar Legion to war.

When Deya awoke, Caelum was beside her, a paper in hand, chewing on a pen. Her back felt tender, but no longer as painful as it had yesterday. She sat up and saw that she was still topless. Caelum looked over. She saw his eyes take her in, before he looked away abruptly, his face stony. Gone was that softness he had in his eyes earlier. Now, it was almost as if the old Caelum sat next to her.

"How are you feeling?"

"F-fine," she murmured, sitting up and pulling the blankets with her. "I've had worse." She said it with a feeble smile, which Caelum did not return. He was still looking at the piece of paper in front of him, as though avoiding her.

"What are you looking at?"

"The prophecies," he said, his voice still brusque.

"Have you made any sense of them?"

"Some," he said. And then his eyes flicked up to meet hers. And Deya's heart sagged in her chest. The look in his eyes was cold and empty. Not a flicker of the Caelum who had kissed her softly in the morning or had traced the scars on her back. Only the hard, frigid heartlessness of the male she had first met remained in those purple eyes.

"What's wrong?" she asked, a lump in her throat.

Caelum looked away again. "There's nothing wrong."

"Bullshit." Deya sat up straighter, her hand reaching to take the paper away from him, willing him to *look* at her. "Something *is* wrong. What happened while I was asleep? Why are you looking at me like that—"

"Like *what?*" Caelum snarled and Deya flinched. Another splinter formed in her heart.

"Like you *hate me* again!" she cried, tears filling her eyes before she could stop them. "Like nothing at all has changed between us—"

"Nothing *has* changed!" Caelum roared, rising to his feet, throwing the paper and pen at the wall. Deya recoiled from him as he paced the room, breathing hard, those purple eyes glowing blue again as a cold breeze filled the room.

"You're lying," Deya whispered. "*Everything* has changed, and you know it. Even Io—"

"Io was merely referring to the prophecy," he snarled. "We are no more bonded than any two other beings. We are destined to bring down Praiton together, *that* is our fate. These asinine feelings we have for each other are just a result of the fucking prophecies. *They are not real!"*

Deya's mouth opened, and then shut again. Her chest was caving in, the cracks in her heart growing. "That . . . that's not true," she whispered.

Caelum snatched the piece of parchment from the floor and slammed it down on the bed beside her. Through tear filled eyes, she looked down at it. The two prophecies swam in her vision.

"You are the Queen of Ash," Caelum snarled. "And the crown they say I was born with is one of star and ash. *You* are what helps me reclaim the Celestial Throne. You helped me escape Ironbalt. *That* was our destiny. After this, our journey together is over."

Deya stared down at the paper, the words blurring as tears splattered down onto it, scattering the ink. Stupid, pathetic tears that made her angry with herself.

"How I feel for you," she said, her voice shaking, "has nothing to do with a prophecy, Caelum. I am sure of it."

Caelum stared at her, breathing hard. "Well, I'm not." He turned away from her, but paused, his hand on the door. "You better rest," he snapped. "Aris and the others will be here in the morning. We march on Arctos at nightfall. We will retake Atlas Keep and be done with this nonsense." And then he swept from the room.

Deya sat on the bed, still clutching the sheet to her bare chest, the tears coming so thick and fast she couldn't catch her breath. The room still felt unbearably cold, and so did she. Every inch of her body ached with the chill Caelum had left behind. Rising from the bed, she reached for her shirt he had left draped on the edge of the mattress. But then she paused.

Across the room, she caught sight of her back in the small mirror by the door. Turning, she gazed into the glass and her breath caught. Io's prophecy spiraled in thin black lines from the back of her neck, down her spine, and across the backs of her arms. The prophecy had given her wings.

Daybreak flooded Mount Mors with golden light streaming in through the mountain's peak, and Deya left her room, her heart still heavy, her back still sore. She did not see Caelum at all. In his usual fashion, he had disappeared entirely when faced with the possibility that he had broken her trust again. Except this time, she suspected he had also broken her heart.

She left Mount Mors with a nod to Deimos, and then Nysa—who gazed at her with wide-eyed concern. She almost wondered if the girl somehow knew what was happening with her and Caelum.

Deya walked the slope of the mountain, not caring where she wound up or what she might find. She reached a small area where the black rock had abated, and a small patch of grass grew. A few shrubs and a small tree grew here, a rare oasis in a field of jagged rock. Deya sank down underneath it.

She had never seen a tree like this—its bark was almost black, its leaves dark blue and translucent. White flowers blossomed from its branches, giving off a strong smell of lilacs and jasmine. It was the most beautiful tree she had ever seen, and here it grew, on this barren wasteland where even magic came to die.

From her pocket, she slowly pulled out a crumpled piece of parchment and unfolded it. Caelum's handwriting stared back at her. The words that had been running through her mind glistened in the morning sun.

The balance of one, the downfall of all . . .

Why would she be the *downfall* of all? Her fingers traced over the next line. *The Queen of Ash.*

With a sigh, she looked up at the odd leaves and the small flowers dangling from the branches over her head. She thought of Oswallt. How his face had lit up when he had told her of Nodaria, how he had described it to be the most curiously beautiful place he had ever seen.

Curiously beautiful. Much like this tree. Struck with inspiration, Deya bent to the ground, seized a jagged bit of black rock, and began to carve into the bark. It was slow work, but soon, she had managed it. Oswallt's name looked back at her, a bit sloppy, but there.

Deya placed her hand against the rough carved letters, her sad, crumpled heart aching for her friend, wishing he was here to gossip with, to cackle with. To cry with.

"I miss you, Os," she whispered to the tree. "I wish I had been able to bring your body here. But I hope this is enough." The wind whistled around her, and for a second, she almost pictured it to be her friend there with her, comforting her. "Thank you for saving my life," she whispered to the trunk, before kissing her hand and pressing it against the bark.

By the time she had risen, she looked out from the grassy slope to see a blue and orange banner waving in the distance.

The Pillar Legion had arrived.

Deya went down the mountain to meet the Legion, having to rely on Deimos to lower her to the ground with his Celestial Magic since Caelum was nowhere to be found. His absence weighed heavy on her, and it was hard to greet Val, Rayner, and Aris with a genuine smile.

Val peered at her, her smile fading when she saw her face.

"What's wrong?"

Deya shook her head. "Nothing, I'm fine," she said, and tried to give her a brave smile. It must have looked terrible because Val just looked even more concerned.

A cold wind ripped through the Pillar Legion's ranks. She felt him before she saw him. Caelum strode from the base of the mountain, right towards Aris, not looking at Val, Rayner, or Deya.

Val's sharp eyes darted from Caelum to Deya, who was also averting her gaze from him.

"For the love of the Mother . . ." she breathed. She grabbed Deya's wrist, and Deya brushed her off, but it was too late. The Manielian female seemed to be adding things up, and her eyes were bigger than the blood moon.

"You heard the prophecy?" Saros asked Caelum, approaching him.

Caelum nodded.

"Is it what we assumed?" Aris asked.

Again, another stiff nod.

Saros grinned. "So, we march on Arctos tonight. We retake the Keep from that bastard, Morlais."

Caelum was already dressed for it. In full black leather armor, he looked every bit the intimidating warrior he had the night of Burningtide. Deya couldn't help thinking he looked good, even if it made her despise herself for even acknowledging it.

"We move out now, then," Aris said. "If you are ready, that is."

It was then that Caelum's eyes shifted towards her, almost as if he couldn't help himself, just like she couldn't help herself from staring at him.

"Now," he said, and he tore his gaze away, leaving her feeling like he had ripped her heart out with it.

She was very aware of Val tracking this whole interaction. Even as the rebellion troops moved out and began the trek towards Arctos again, Val seemed to be bursting to say something. But Deya kept her head down as she walked, determined not to give her friend an opening. She didn't want to talk about it. Right now, no one knew what had changed between her and Caelum—and what had changed back so quickly—and she wanted to keep it that way.

They marched in silence—the walk feeling much like it did on their journey to Burningtide. To Deya, it was surreal, the idea of walking to war. How many of these numbers would come back at the end? Would she? She nearly didn't the last time. If it hadn't been for Caelum, she wouldn't have.

Her heart gave a tight squeeze, and she couldn't ignore the feeling of her chest caving in again. Then, a hand seized her arm, and she was dragged out of the line.

"Val!" Deya cried, squirming in her tight grip, "What are you—"

"You are going to tell me what happened *right* now, or I will go up to that white-haired bastard and make *him* tell me. Even if I have to use my swords," Val snapped. Deya sputtered as the Legion marched on, leaving them behind, some of the soldiers peering at them curiously.

"*Nothing happened,*" Deya insisted, but Val scoffed.

"Bullshit," she said, and the way she said it reminded her so heavily of how Deya had said it to Caelum yesterday. "You two were practically *friends* when you left Burningtide, and now you can't even look at each other. *Why?*"

Deya could feel the prophecy on her back itch slightly, as if it were a burn that was blistering. "It's a long story," she mumbled.

"Did you sleep with him?"

Deya looked up at her sharply, a flush spreading up her face, almost to her hairline. Opening her mouth, she gaped at Val, but her reaction was answer enough.

Val let out a bark of incredulity. "For the love of the Mother," she said again. "I cannot *believe* . . . Was it *good?*"

"Val!" Deya cried, mortified, but Val waved her off.

"It's a fair question," she mumbled.

"Can we get back in line?" Deya moaned. "We're going to get left behind."

Val capitulated, and they headed back towards the ranks.

"Let me guess," she whispered. "He panicked on you and is trying to convince himself he feels absolutely nothing." Deya did not answer. Val laughed. "Typical."

"I don't really want to talk about it," Deya muttered. Val laid a sympathetic hand on hers and together, they reformed with the ranks.

The rocky terrain of Nodaria passed under them, and Val didn't pester her for more information. Eventually, Val had to go to rejoin her unit, leaving Deya towards the back of the Nodarian squadron, alone. And that's when she felt a chill coming from her left.

"What did you tell her?" a low growl echoed in her ear. There was a cold hand on her elbow, and she snorted derisively and attempted to shrug him off.

"Why does it matter? You don't care, remember?"

Caelum's fingers tightened on her, holding on as she struggled to shake him off. "I thought we agreed not to tell that wretched harpy anything."

"Well, like we also discussed," Deya said through gritted teeth, "Val is sharper than you give her credit for. She picked up on it instantly. And besides"—With an almighty wrench, she pulled her arm free from his frosty grasp—"according to *you*, there's nothing to tell anyway."

And she stormed away from him, pushing through the ranks to stand beside Saros, her whole body shaking with rage and an excruciating sadness.

Caelum stood, fuming, beside Rayner, the city of Arctos coming into view as the sun began to disappear beneath the horizon. The Legion had stopped short of the city to wait for nightfall. Caelum was chomping at the bit, wanting to fight, wanting to hurt, wanting to stop this unbearable feeling inside of him whenever Deya looked at him. With such betrayal and hurt in her eyes that he felt it, deep in his chest. And it was getting harder and harder to ignore.

The Sea Fae beside him kept shooting him anxious looks. Rayner knew something was wrong, but he was too smart to say anything. Not like Caelum would respond, anyway.

He stood, staring at the shadow of Atlas Keep in the distance, the blood boiling in his veins.

"Breathe," Rayner advised beside him, touching his arm. Caelum snarled and jerked his arm away. "What is going on with you?" Rayner asked seriously. He didn't answer him, his eyes not leaving Atlas Keep. He could portal himself there, attack General Morlais, end all of this now.

As though Rayner suspected what he was thinking, he seized his arm, shaking him roughly. "*Caelum—*"

"*Leave it,* Rayner."

"You are thinking of storming it yourself, I can tell," the Sea Fae hissed, keeping hold of his arm. "And you are insane if you think I will let you—"

"*Let me?*" Caelum snarled. "You will not *let* me—"

"What happened between you and Deya?"

Caelum did not respond. Rayner looked exasperated. "Caelum, what did you do—"

"I did not do anything." He turned to Aris, shutting Rayner out entirely. "We march, now," he demanded.

Aris turned from where he was conversing with the other Ganiean captain from Burningtide, his obnoxiously quaffed eyebrows arching. "We move on my mark, Caelum."

But Caelum was not in the mood for the general's bullshit. Not right now. Not with Morlais so close, and Deya looking at him as if he had smashed her heart with his fist and thrown the pieces to the wind.

"If we stay here too long, someone will spot us," Caelum growled. "We attack now or risk another Burningtide."

Aris's eyes narrowed. The general never lost his cool, no matter how many times Caelum tried to challenge him. It pissed him off to no end.

"You will do best to remember who your general is, Caelum," Aris warned, his voice like cool steel. "You are not the High King yet. We move at my mark."

"And what exactly is *your mark,* General?" Caelum hissed. "What is your *ingenious* plan?"

"Lycus," Aris called, his eyes still not leaving Caelum's face. The Manielian captain whipped around from where he stood in front of his squadron, right next to Val's.

"Yes, General?"

Without looking away from Caelum, and in that same, calm tone, Aris said, "Fire."

A wave of flames exploded into the sky, arcing into the city before smashing into the nearest building.

Caelum let out a yell, but Rayner seized his arm, stopping him from leaping forward as the buildings of Arctos went up in flames right before his eyes.

"*That* was my mark," he said, and made to turn away as the first wave of soldiers breached the city. "Rejoin your unit."

It was immediately apparent what Aris's plan was. Already, Praiton soldiers were flooding the courtyard of Atlas Keep, sprinting to the source of the disturbance. Caelum's eyes darted to Saros's unit, who were already in position. The other units had also been strategically placed throughout the city. A trap lying in wait.

Aris made to turn away, but Caelum grabbed him by the elbow.

"I can portal some with me into the Keep. We can take Morlais by surprise."

Aris nodded. "Use the distraction to your advantage." Pausing, as if contemplating his next move, the general said, "Take Valeria, Rayner, and Deya with you."

A sharp spear of anxiety pierced him through the heart. "I am not taking Deya."

Aris gave him a slow, smug smile. "You will look out for her. She is an able fighter now—"

"Why are you sending her into this?" Caelum ground out, his fury making a surge of cold wind whip around him and Aris. "She will be *killed*. She should not even be participating in this fight." He was breathing hard, the thought of Deya facing Morlais filling him with an inexplicable amount of dread. She would be killed or hurt, would be in more danger than he could protect her from . . .

Aris smiled wider, as if he knew exactly what he was thinking. "Funny," he drawled. "I didn't think you cared so much for her."

The general turned, leaving him standing there, fuming. "Take Valeria, Rayner, and Deya. As your general, that is an order. We cannot spare the others. Take down what you can with the element of surprise, and we will follow to back you up. We have already sent ravens to the surrounding areas—Bridah and our Ganiean outpost—for aid. Just in case." Aris stopped and raised a hand. "At my signal," he said to the captains in front of him.

When his hand dropped, the rebels surged as one into Arctos.

The soldiers flowed around him, moving in a wave across the bridge leading to the burning city of Arctos, their blades catching the Praitonian forces that had come to meet them. Caelum drew his sword as the rest of the rebellion pushed into the city, leaving him, Val, Rayner, and Deya standing at the foot of the bridge.

Rayner nodded to him. "We go in quietly and methodically, Caelum," he said. "Our best strategy should be one of stealth."

Caelum ground his teeth. He did not want stealth. He wanted vengeance and death. He wanted to blast the entire place apart with Frost and Celestial Magic, wanted to rip Morlais's head off and throw it from the now grounded astronomy floor. But Rayner laid a hand on his arm.

"Be patient," he murmured. "I know you want blood. And we will have it. Today is our day."

From across the bridge, the sounds of battle reached them. Yelling, screaming, the bursts of different types of magic. Taking a deep breath, Caelum reached into his core and pulled the air apart.

A large, spiraling portal spun into position in front of them. Rayner gave him a nod before stepping into the gateway. Val approached it, looking back at Deya, as though she didn't want to leave her alone with him. Caelum's blood boiled at the thought that the Manielian knew anything about them.

Val made to step towards the portal, but paused, and the look she threw him was so filthy it made him inwardly cringe. "Do *anything* to her," she hissed, soft enough that only he could hear. "And I will make you wish you never touched her."

Caelum could not tell her he already wished that. Touching her seemed to have unleashed something he had not been ready for . . . something he couldn't shut out, no matter how hard he tried. He had gone back to her room after seeing Io, resolute in his decision that these feelings he had for her—these ridiculously strong, overwhelming feelings—had to only be the effect of a powerful, ancient magic. They couldn't be organic. Couldn't be real.

But then why did he feel so hollow inside? So angry and empty?

Val disappeared through the portal next, and Deya made to brush past him, when he seized her upper arm. She winced from his grip and, remembering the prophecy now branded on her, he loosened his hold.

"*What?*" she snapped, glaring at him.

That look she kept giving him pained him. And he hated that it did.

"Please," he whispered, staring imploringly into her gray eyes. "Do not go with us."

Deya stopped fighting him. She looked up, her face crumpling with confusion and frustration. The look cracked something in his cold, black heart.

"Why do you *care?*" she breathed. It was desperate, pleading, as if she truly wanted to know why he was so worried about what would happen if he released her and let her walk through that portal. How he couldn't bear the thought of exposing her to Morlais, of watching her die like he had watched all his siblings, how the very thought made him want to scream.

But he didn't say it. He could never say it.

Deya let out a humorless laugh and shook her head. "Say it, Caelum," she whispered, leaning closer to him, their lips almost touching, that damned magnetic pull causing him to tilt his head with hers again. "You *know* you were wrong. *This* is not just some prophecy, and you know it."

He closed his eyes, their foreheads resting together. The chill in his veins was beginning to overwhelm him and all he wanted was to press his lips to hers, to breathe in her warmth that always seemed to quiet this uncontrollable frost in him.

But he couldn't tell her what she wanted to hear; couldn't tell her he was wrong. And with a sad laugh, she turned from him, and stepped right into the portal.

CHAPTER
26

Deya felt a whoosh of air and she knew Caelum had teleported in behind her. Rayner and Val were already looking around curiously, Val even picking up one of the gold objects on the desk. The room that they had portaled into appeared to be a small study, which looked much like Io's office. Bookcases surrounded the circular room, and delicate gold instruments were resting on the shelves. The entire room was covered in a thin layer of dust and smelt musty. Stale.

From the outside of the heavy black door, the sound of chaos echoed through the room. There was shouting and yelling, as if the guards on the other side were assembling. The soldiers in Atlas Keep were already on high alert. They knew they were there.

"This was Castor's office?" Rayner breathed, his blue gray finger trailing through the dust.

"It was the closest I could get us to the throne room where we wouldn't make a scene," Caelum answered. Deya couldn't stop herself from looking at him a little too long. That look he had given her . . . how he had leaned his forehead against hers and breathed deeply. Deya knew what that meant, had grown used to seeing it in Caelum. He had been fighting himself.

"Stay quiet," Val whispered to them all. "They have already been alerted to the invasion and are assembling to defend the Keep."

Deya drew her sword; her chest burned with fear. Val already had both of her own swords out and was twirling them expertly—a move Deya had never been able to master.

"Stay with me," Val whispered to her. Deya nodded, but didn't miss the glare Val shot Caelum, whose jaw was clenched, as though he wanted to say something. Deya was glad he didn't.

Rayner assumed position behind the door, took one last look at them, drew in a deep breath, and nodded to Caelum. And then Val and Caelum blew the door open.

The wooden projectile sailed through the air in a burst of flame, taking a group of soldiers unawares. It rocketed into them, blowing them out of their path.

Val's swords erupted into flames, and she and Deya emerged from the room, just to catch the blades of the soldiers who came running. It was almost an unfair advantage. The minute soldiers would run into view, Caelum would hold them with his Celestial Magic, allowing the others to cut them down, one by one.

There was barely anyone in the Keep besides soldiers. As the four of them made their way through the black marbled castle, taking down any Praiton soldiers who appeared, Deya realized there were hardly any civilians inside. No priestesses or servants. Nothing but soldiers, armed to the teeth, and converging on them all at once. They pushed their way towards the throne room, Deya barely able to register the shadow of the beauty that once was Atlas Keep.

"This way!" Val yelled, pointing towards a large, arched doorway carved with gold stars. Deya and Rayner both made to move towards it, but then it was torn off its hinges. Caelum, purple eyes glowing, hand outstretched, moved past them, a murderous expression on his face. Deya paused to watch him as he advanced into the throne room, his sword bloody and a thin layer of frost crunching under his feet. Soldiers advanced on them, and they were locked in battle again.

Deya moved to the rhythm of the Rain Dance beside Rayner, who was firing arrows in rapid succession, even mirroring Val's elegant movements as best she could as she fended off blows from spears and swords. For a second, Deya thought this was going to be easy, that the mission might go in their favor as they pushed the throne room's guards back. She even had a second to take note of the large, gold orrery suspended from the throne room's ceiling—a larger, more ornate version of the one that had been located outside the temple they had visited in Arctos.

Deya paused long enough to look at the large sphere of the sun, which was rusted with misuse, when the floor beneath them trembled. And then, a roar of flames ripped through the room.

One moment, Deya was staring up into the large, gold orb above her head, and the next it was crashing down.

Deya screamed, and something collided with her, throwing her out of the way, as a large fissure in the black rock split down the middle of the marbled throne room in a blaze of heat and fire. Deya hit the ground, hard, looking up from where Caelum had thrown himself at her just to watch the enormous instrument explode onto the marble floor. Val and Rayner were both blasted off their feet, lost in the surrounding rubble as the throne room was split in two.

"What . . ." Deya coughed, dust and debris choking her. "What . . . was that—"

Caelum was breathing hard. There were cuts on his face, and he was covered with a thin layer of dust, but his eyes were wide.

"Morlais," he whispered.

And that's when she heard it. It was like a long fingernail being dragged across stone. It grew louder and louder around the destroyed throne room, until a large figure came into view.

General Morlais strode around the ruined orrery, kicking aside a fallen gold star. A large black longsword was dragged behind him, leaving a long thin scar on the marble in its wake. The sword shimmered with shadow, minute dark tendrils rippling across its smooth surface.

Deya felt Caelum stiffen, and his whole body began to cool, as if someone had opened a window in winter.

Morlais stopped in front of them. Like his brother, Decius, Morlais was pale, his hair only holding a whisper of the trademark Manielian red. Faded with age, it now was more of a light strawberry blond and, what was more, he was the size of a house. Deya could not remember ever seeing a male this large. He cast a shadow over them—lit overhead by the half-moon shining through the open, glass ceiling of Atlas Keep, unobstructed by the planetarium.

"Well," the general said, leering down at them. "If it isn't Castor's bastard. I always wondered what became of you. I had hoped that stupid planetarium had crushed you when the building collapsed." Caelum was breathing hard, glaring up at Morlais, his eyes glowing a sinister purple. "Alas," Morlais drawled, "I suppose I better not mess it up this time." Then his eyes shifted to Deya. A wicked gleam of glee crossed the red irises as he sneered down at them. "Castor's bastard and the Traitor of Praiton delivered right to my doorstep? Why, it must be my lucky day."

Caelum's hand tightened on Deya, pushing her further behind him. His body was getting colder and colder by the second, but out of fear or anger, she did not know.

From the corner of her eye, Deya saw Val and Rayner on the opposite side of the large split of the throne room, rising from the twisted gold rubble of the planetarium. Both were bleeding and covered in soot from Morlais's fire. Val made to get up, her lip bleeding, her leg dragging, and made to come to their aid. Morlais's eyes flashed in her direction, and a wall of fire erupted across the rift, sealing them off from Val and Rayner and any help they could bring.

"Now," he said, walking towards them, that awful black sword still dragging, the sound making Deya's ears ache. "How to deal with you."

The cold emanating from Caelum was beginning to make her teeth chatter. She could almost feel the thread in him break, the one thing tethering him to this world, before his anger exploded out of him.

Frost erupted all around them, blasting Deya away from him, showering her in icy shards. A thick wall of ice formed around her like a cocoon up to her neck, shielding her, as Caelum rose to his feet, eyes glowing blue, and more hatred and anger on his face than she had ever seen. The ice rose to meet Morlais's fire, but melted, no match for the immense heat emanating from the general's Ember Magic.

Morlais's eyes widened, taking in the ice on Caelum's fingertips, the wall of jagged glaciers. His surprise lasted mere seconds, before he smiled wickedly.

"Well, we're full of surprises, aren't we, bastard?" he chuckled, kicking aside a block of ice. "A hybrid of magic. How interesting."

He raised the longsword, the tip leaving the jagged line it had created on the marble floor and pointed it at Caelum. From the hilt, a burst of fire shot up it, just as Val would do. But there was something different about this fire. It was so hot, so deadly, that the red flames accelerated before her eyes and turned a blue as bright as Caelum's eyes. The wall of flames around them mirrored this, the rippling wave of heat morphing to match his sword, and the fear burned in her chest with the intensity of the flames surging up the black blade.

She had never seen an Ember Magic user have such strong flames. The heat was all around her, flushing across her face—a harsh, dry wave of warmth that was beginning to make the icebergs Caelum had trapped her in sweat profusely.

"*Caelum!*" she screamed, fighting and pushing against the cool, slick ice that surrounded her, desperate to get to him. But it wouldn't budge. Caelum was on his own.

They circled each other, the black tendrils of whatever was possessing that sword mixing and twining with Morlais's own flames. "Now, bastard,"

Morlais said, leering at Caelum. "We finish what we started."

And with a roar, Caelum lunged for Morlais. Steel clattered together, the blue flame of Morlais's sword engulfing Caelum's, causing him to be forced backwards. Morlais cackled as Caelum's blade seemed to wilt from the sheer heat. Shaking it furiously in his hand, a thick coat of frost shot up his sword, engulfing it from pommel to tip.

Caelum swung his blade and Morlais caught it easily, the blue flames attempting to overwhelm Caelum's smaller sword, but Caelum was too quick for him. Their swords clashed again, Caelum ducking underneath Morlais's heavy weapon, blue flame flying past him as he went.

He dodged one ruthless blow and hurled a knife he had pulled from his boot. With a hiss of cold air, it pierced through Morlais's armor, embedding itself in his side. Morlais swore, staggering backwards, his hand attempting to pull the knife free, but Caelum was too fast. He began to shower blows upon Morlais, attacking exactly how he had tried to teach Deya.

Aim for their weak side, he had once said. And he did just that. Blow after blow rained down on Morlais's left side, causing the general to roar with outrage and redouble his efforts.

"Your games tire me, bastard!" the general growled, blocking one of Caelum's jabs with an expert flourish, menace glowing in those red eyes.

"Then come get me," Caelum snarled, and the general spun the longsword over his head, and lunged for Caelum. His swings came faster, and, with a roar, Morlais's blue flames burst out of him. The explosion rent the air, blasting Caelum off his feet, nearly sending him headfirst into the flames. He almost went right through them, before stopping in midair, his irises now flashing purple. Dropping to the floor, an icy wind whipped around him, before he charged back at Morlais.

Deya struggled behind the wall of ice that was holding her in place. The glacier was sweating, dripping water down on her, but still it held. She wanted to scream out for Caelum with every blow the general made, the panic keeping her clawing at the block of ice.

Deya knew Caelum was struggling with the Frost Magic that was bursting out of him. He could not fully control it, as if the magic itself was reacting to his baser, primal instincts more than his conscious thought.

Deya pounded against the glacial barrier again, but knew it was useless. The wall had seemed to explode from him as if it were an answer to the only thing he could think to do . . . protect her. She knew Caelum was outmatched, even with his Celestial and Frost Magic on full display. Morlais almost appeared as if he were toying with him, relishing in Caelum's fury and hatred as he attempted to land a single blow on the general.

The knife that been embedded in the general's side had long since fallen away, and Morlais's red eyes glinted with something that made Deya's whole body tremble with fear and panic.

She saw the shift happen, could feel it when a hot, dry wind ripped past, extinguishing the chill coming from Caelum's magic. The blue flames grew, blasted from Morlais's sword, and threw Caelum backwards. He hit the ground with a gasp of breath, the wind knocked from his body. And as he struggled to breathe, to rise, Deya felt herself scream as Morlais approached and plunged the sword down.

Caelum rolled, but not quick enough. The black tip of the longsword—still shimmering with blue flames—sliced through Caelum's sword arm, burning the flesh, causing blood and ash to splatter down onto the black marble floor. Caelum yelled, clutching at his arm, barely able to hold onto his sword, when the general came down on him again. This time, a large iceberg erupted in front of him, catching the blow, causing the block of ice to explode, scattering shards everywhere. The ice was incinerated almost instantly by Morlais's fire.

"You fight like your brother," Morlais taunted, approaching Caelum, who tried to attack again with his injured arm, and was blocked with such force that his sword went flying, right into the blue flames behind him. "He thought he stood a chance against me. Thought that his pathetic Celestial Magic could best me. I had fun with him, too. But my patience is wearing thin."

Caelum was panting on the ground, bleeding profusely from his arm and his lip, his face screwed up with pain and anger. Deya could feel herself screaming his name but couldn't hear anything over the roaring of the fiery wind whipping around her, the glaciers melting bit by bit.

"I will fucking kill you," Caelum snarled, attempting to rise, but Morlais kicked him back down, edging him closer and closer to the flames. "I will make you pay . . . for Aelius and Aten . . . for my *family*—"

"Your head will roll, just like your dear brother's," Morlais snarled, that wickedly evil grin curling up his face. "I enjoyed feeding their bodies to my dogs."

Caelum let out a roar of anger and frost exploded from his body— but this was different, stronger. Jagged icebergs erupted all around, taking Morlais off his feet, as Caelum caught the general's body with his Gravity Magic and hurled spears of ice at him. Morlais smashed them to bits with his longsword, laughing from where he dangled in the air, but Caelum was useless without a sword.

Thinking fast, Deya kicked at the iceberg that was blocking her in, felt it yield slightly, and wiggled free just enough to extract her arm. And with it, her sword.

"*Caelum!*" she screamed loudly and chucked the sword with all her might. It sailed through the air and clattered on the black marble, sliding along the icy surface, and coming to rest at Caelum's feet.

Caelum seized it, and slashed at the general, who deflected, his eyes growing angry. Caelum slammed him to the ground. The general caught himself before he could hit the floor, spinning a wheel of fire to soften his fall, before whirling the longsword around his head in a perfect arc . . . and plunging it right into Caelum's chest.

Deya felt the air leave her lungs, felt her body collapse in on itself. And then her scream reverberated off the ice still clinging to her. Caelum, eyes wide, looked down at the black sword protruding from his chest. Morlais sneered down at him, pushing the blade another inch deeper.

"Go with your brother to hell," he snarled, and then, with a twist, pushed Caelum's body free.

And that's when Deya lost all control. With her free hand, she ripped the faerivaine necklace from her neck.

And she exploded from the ice.

Morlais whirled to face her, but his expression was not troubled at all as Deya staggered towards him. The power she felt in her gut was boiling, ready to erupt, but she held it back as she glared at the hulking general. Held it as she looked down at Caelum, at the blood pooling around his body, at his eyes, half open, still glowing a faint purple.

"The Traitor of Praiton," Morlais whispered, turning to face her. "I have heard about you. They say you're a demon. How curious to find you here with the Nodarian bastard, of all people."

Deya kept walking, her eyes fixed on the general, everything outside of him hazy, rippling in the heated air and in her own agonizing rage and pain. She could feel the tug towards Caelum, could feel it pulling at her rib cage, as if it were threatening to pull the heart clean out of her chest. The power rose like bile, bubbling in her throat, but still she held it, a firm grip that surprised even her.

"*Get . . . the . . . fuck . . . away . . . from . . . him,*" she breathed. Morlais opened his mouth, to continue taunting, but then she ripped open the door to her power.

That horrible, agonizing current of pain and fury rippled through her, as if she were a metal rod conducting a bolt of lightning. The pain she felt at watching Caelum be stabbed through the heart was churning in her blood, was ripping through her veins, and she let out a scream as it exploded from her body.

But this time, it was different. This time, Deya leashed the horrific shockwave that erupted from her. It was like trying to subdue a tidal wave, like trying to wrestle a troll. Deya concentrated all that anger, all that pain, all that *hurt,* right into the Praiton general, whose eyes widened.

Deya felt the floor tremble where she stood, and then cracks began to form underneath her. Fissures in the black marble, bony fingers reaching for the general as the rock splintered and cracked, becoming a wave of gray ash, that flowed right towards him.

The general scrambled backwards, releasing a wave of blue flame, aiming it at the tide of destruction Deya was trying with all her might to focus on *him*. Only *he* could feel this pain, only *he* was going to feel her fury. Dust was forming at her feet, her boots digging into the marble as her power met Morlais's blue flames, the magic battling.

Gray met blue, and the leash jerked under Deya's control, making her twist her face in concentration, pushing and pushing towards him. She was only vaguely aware of a dark wave creeping up her fingers, shooting up her arms like veins, but she did not care.

For the first time, she wasn't fighting against the magic. For the first time, she was *pushing* it forward instead of pulling it back . . . *pushing* with all her might.

"What is this?" Morlais cried, his eyes wide as Deya's gray wave of terror pushed against the flame, beating it back.

"You will release Nodaria," Deya snarled, stepping forward, throwing all her weight behind the power that had once bested her, the power that had once crippled her. "You will pay for what you have done!"

"But you are one of us!" the Praiton general cried, his eyes wide with fear, his hands shaking as he attempted to block the inevitable wave of decay radiating from her. "You are a *Praitonian!* Do you not care for your kingdom anymore, you *stupid* little girl?"

Deya gave a soft laugh. How funny it was that, only when she had Praiton on their knees in front of her, did they try to prey on her loyalty. How funny that, when she looked deep within herself, felt in her heart for the love she had once felt for Praiton, for the honor and loyalty . . . there was nothing left.

Only ashes.

"That's the thing, General," she panted, advancing towards him, the blackness creeping further up her arm. Leaning forward, her eyes taking in the fear in the male's eyes, feasting on it, she whispered, "I am *not* one of you."

The blue flames flared with light, before being swallowed by the gray wave of ash that she pushed with an almighty roar forward. It engulfed the general, and Deya was able to watch, for the first time, the true devastation of her newfound power.

Morlais froze, suspended in Deya's tidal wave of ash and death before his skin started to gray. It sunk into his skeleton, skin becoming muscle, muscle becoming bone, bone becoming ash.

The longsword fell to the floor with a quiet, finite clatter. The blue flames extinguished, and the air seemed to return to the throne room all at once.

Deya gasped and collapsed, the hold she had on her power bucking against her. She attempted to tamp down on it, to rein it back in, but she was so drained that it took everything in her to push the door closed on it. And then her eyes fell on Caelum.

She ran without knowing what she was doing. Ran to him, eyes welling with tears as she began pulling at his leather armor, attempting to expose the wound, as all her healing training had taught her to do.

"Caelum!" she panted, her hands scrabbling over the bloody wound, which was wide and gaping. It made her cry out with panic, knowing instantly that it was bad, worse than she could fix with poultices or bandages. "*Caelum*, wake up!"

His eyelids fluttered, the purple light underneath them flickering slightly as his glazed eyes focused on her. "You controlled it," he breathed, his voice a raspy gasp, barely a whisper.

She nodded, her hands coming to press against the wound, blood trickling from between her fingers at a rate even she couldn't stop. Not without her magic.

"Don't talk," she whispered to him, tears falling from her eyes before she could stop them. "The blade may have punctured a lung. You need to—"

But he shook his head. "I was wrong," he whispered, his eyelids drooping. "I was wrong."

Deya shushed him, leaning her forehead against his, tears flowing from her eyes. "Stop . . . don't speak—"

"Deya, *dammit*," he rasped, reaching up to rest a hand on top of hers. "*I was wrong.*"

She looked up at him, and his purple eyes opened long enough for him to look at her and say it again. "*I was wrong.*"

And then his eyelids drooped, and the purple light in them seemed to extinguish, just like those blue flames.

Deya shook her head. "*No*," she whispered, her hands tightening on the wound. "*No, no, no,* Caelum, stay with me! *Caelum!*" But she knew he was fading, his life was flickering like a candle, his breathing getting shallower and shallower.

"*Dammit*" she screamed, and her tears blinded her. She had never felt so useless without her magic, never clawed so desperately for that scrap of warmth that used to nestle in her chest like a comforting flame. But when she reached into her core, she felt nothing but that terrible, awful power that was being pushed down, even now.

Deya collapsed on Caelum's chest and sobbed, sobbed for that bit of her that had been taken by the pain she had endured, and was now the reason for an even more agonizing grief than she had even felt at Ironbalt.

She plunged a hand into her core, shoving a mental fist into that still bubbling magic of fury and pain and pushed through it with all that she had. Every moment that she had with Caelum, every moment of tension, and anger, every rare smile and laugh, every kiss, and touch . . .

The magnetic pull towards the male underneath her tugged, once more, at her ribcage, right by her heart. A familiar surge of warmth shot through her, taking her by surprise, causing her to sit up, to gasp as her hands began to glow over Caelum's body.

It was her magic, but it wasn't. A strange merging of pain and grief mixed with that of the love and warmth that she had always associated with her Healing Magic. It surged through her core, and she pushed all of it into Caelum's wound, pushed and pushed, until . . .

Caelum's eyes snapped open and, with a shuddering gasp, Deya collapsed.

CHAPTER
27

Caelum opened his eyes to find sunlight filling a familiar room. It was a large, circular chamber, its walls painted a calming midnight blue. Beds lined the rounded walls, and he recognized the infirmary of Atlas Keep. Sitting up, he winced, clutching his chest. Heavy bandages were twined all around him, almost stopping him from drawing anything more than a shallow gasp. Caelum grunted in aggravation as he attempted to loosen the bandages.

"You really don't want to do that," a familiar voice said.

Caelum looked up. Io shuffled into the room, alongside a small healer who he recognized from Light's Tower.

"What are you doing here?" he asked, his voice hoarse. "What happened in the battle? How—" He had so many questions, so many things that needed answers *now,* but Io held up a hand to stop him.

"All in due time, my boy. All in due time." The elderly female sank onto the bed across from him, and that's when his eye caught sight of chestnut hair in the bed opposite his. Deya was asleep, eyes closed, looking so small and frail. At least, he hoped she was asleep.

Caelum attempted to leave the bed, but Io put a firm hand on his chest and pushed him back down.

"She is fine, boy," she said. "You, however, should be dead."

"What happened to her? How long has she been like that?" he asked, frantic. He found he didn't care much about what had happened to him, only whether Deya was okay.

"Just overexerted herself," Io said simply. "She used a lot of magic that she was not used to having to defeat General Morlais. And then to save you."

Caelum looked over at her, alarmed. "*Save* me? She—"

"Healed you," the old seer replied, nodding. "Yes. She is a curious case, that girl."

Caelum looked back at Deya. She hadn't stirred. The gentle rise and fall of her chest was the only thing that kept him from rushing to her. That irritating pull towards her was now a comforting, almost reassuring sign that she was, in fact, alive.

"Her prophecy," he said. "The Queen of Ash . . . being the *downfall* of all . . . what does it mean?"

"I have told you before," Io remarked exasperatedly. "I only tell the prophecies, not interpret them."

"Have a guess, then," Caelum mumbled. The old female smiled.

"Her power is obviously two sides of the same coin. More powerful than any normal Earth Magic I have ever seen. And for that, I have no answer."

Caelum gazed at Deya, his eyes seeming to drink her in, to feast on her. *She was okay.*

He could feel Io watching him but found he didn't care.

"Our prophecies . . ." he began, but Io tutted.

"I have already told you this, boy," she snapped. "Your prophecies and the bond you have towards one another are not mutually exclusive. However, I believe you have a rather confused idea of what came first." Her deep, purple eyes flashed at him as she said, "Your love for each other and the consummation of that love made the prophecy, not the other way around. Your fear of this has absolutely nothing to do with these prophecies, and everything to do with *you*."

Caelum fell silent, his mind still spinning around the word *love* as if it were some word in Nadarak that he was attempting to make sense of.

Love.

"Io," he said, choosing to dismiss this line of thought entirely, only because it filled him with such irritation it was beginning to make his head spin. "Do you . . . do you know who my mother is?"

"Ah," Io said, smiling grimly. "I think there might be someone better than I who can answer that question." And she rose from the bed, patting him gently on the hand. "Rest, my boy. Answers will come soon."

Caelum wanted to yell at the female to come back, to answer his questions *now*, but she had already swept from the room, her black robes swishing over the marble floor.

Caelum got up from his bed and moved towards Deya's. She looked so peaceful, her thin face still beautiful, no matter how gaunt it looked at that moment. He sat down next to her, just as he had that wretched night at Mount Mors when he had thrown it all away and smoothed a hand through her hair.

And then the door opened. Aris, Saros, Rayner, and Val entered the room. Following behind them was a white-haired female Caelum did not recognize, yet who looked strangely familiar. Val and Rayner converged on him, engulfing him in a hug that made him grunt with irritation and a bit of pain as Val jostled his injured chest.

"You're awake!" Rayner cried from his right.

"We thought you had died!" Val said, and he snorted at the slight irritation he detected in her tone.

"I'll try harder next time."

Both released him, and then paused to look at Deya. Caelum, however, turned towards Aris and the white-haired female next to him, who was looking at him with wide blue eyes, as if she were seeing a ghost.

"We're glad you're alright, Caelum," Saros said, smiling at him. "We heard that it was a terrifying fight between you and Morlais."

Caelum nodded, his hand tightening on Deya's motionless fingers, as if grounding himself. He was still looking at the strange female. She was beautiful—stunning in a way—yet he could tell she was battle-hardened, and tough. A fair amount of hairline scars lined her delicate features, and the painted markings on her face made her look fierce, strong.

"You did not tell us," Aris began carefully, "of your Frost Magic."

Caelum looked over at him. "Must have slipped my mind."

Aris's eyes flashed dangerously, but he could've sworn he saw the general's mouth twitch. "Val, Rayner, Saros," he said, turning to the group. "Could you give us a moment, please?"

The three of them nodded and rose, Rayner clapping Caelum gently on the shoulder as he went, leaving him alone with Aris and the female. But Caelum had eyes only for the Pillar Legion's General. The door had barely shut behind the departing group when Caelum turned to the general.

"You sent Deya in with me on purpose."

Aris didn't so much as blink. "Yes."

Fury surged through him, and the general's unwavering expression made him want to punch the male in the face.

"Why would you do something like that?" Caelum hissed, half rising from the bed. "She was *not* equipped to fight, and you *knew* this. Yet you sent her to Burningtide *and* into the Keep to face Morlais. Why—"

"We are at war, Caelum," Aris said, silencing him instantly. "A war that we do not have the upper hand in. Like it or not, Deya's power is a weapon, one that Praiton *wants*, no less. She was our last hope if things went to hell, which I feared they would. And I was right. Deya saved you. She *won* the battle for us. It was a gamble, but it was one I was willing to make."

The anger was bubbling up inside of him, his fingers beginning to grow cold. It was a *gamble*. Deya's *life* was a *gamble* to this male . . . But he knew he was not wrong. Deya had been the only thing standing between him and certain death. In the end, they *had* won because of her.

356

With a deep breath, he willed the ice inside him to thaw. Then Caelum turned towards the white-haired female beside Aris. "Who are you?" he asked. His heart thundered in his chest. All he could think about were Io's parting words to him. *There's someone better than I who can answer that question.*

"Caelum," Aris said. "I want you to meet Kindra . . . Princess of the Frost Throne of Bridah and first-born daughter of High King Ulf."

Kindra looked at Aris for the first time, and there was something familiar in the exasperated look she shot him. "Did we really need the full title?" she said, the distinct guttural, yet melodic accent heavy in her words.

Aris shrugged lazily, sitting back in a chair by the healer's station, as if backing away. "Bridah answered our call for help," he told Caelum in that obnoxious, arrogant drawl of his. "At least, Kindra and her specialized unit of fighters did."

"We are the only ones who can travel fast enough," Kindra said.

Aris nodded in acknowledgement. "It was with Kindra's help that we were able to vanquish the Praitonian presence in Nodaria, thus taking back Arctos and the region as a whole," he continued. Pausing, he looked at Caelum. "The Celestial Throne is yours, Caelum. It was a unanimous agreement between our own Nodarians in the Legion and the citizens at Mount Mors and beyond. They recognize you as their new High King."

Caelum felt this news settle on his shoulders, heavier than any armor, and colder than steel.

"The priestesses and the star seers have also opted," he continued, "to officially bequeath you with the last name Hesperos. If you are willing to take it, that is."

Caelum didn't know what to say. His whole life he had been rejected under the Hesperos name thus he had rejected it right back. But now, he knew the Hesperos name was not just his family's name. It meant something more to the people of Nodaria than just pure lineage.

"Fine," he said brusquely, nodding at Aris. Then his eyes found their way back to Kindra. She gave him a small smile.

"It's funny," she said softly. "You look so much like your father.

Except for the hair, that is. And the eyes."

"Is it you, then?" he asked softly. "Are you the one . . ."

Kindra sat down on the bed next to him. Caelum's hand tightened on Deya's warm fingers, stiffening as the female leaned towards him.

"Do you remember that day during the Battle for Atlas?" she said. "Do you remember who stopped Morlais?"

Caelum hesitated. They were never an easy thing to revisit. But he remembered.

"You . . ." he whispered. He could recall her in fragments. Ice had flashed across the floor then, and he had seen a white-haired female fighting Morlais. Had remembered her scooping him up, taking him to the other children, to safety.

With a furious sigh, Kindra shook her head. "I wanted to come back for you that day. I *would* have, if your father hadn't fallen. I had to rush to his aid, even when it was too late, and when I came back . . . you were gone."

Caelum said nothing, his mind reeling as Kindra smiled at him sadly. "The moment I saw you," she whispered, "I knew who you were." A tear trickled down her face, and she laughed softly, wiping at it, and smudging the war paint on her angular face. "You are the only son of my youngest sister, Asti," she said. "You are the grandson of High King Ulf."

Caelum blinked at her. His eyes darted to Aris, who was watching his reaction quietly in the corner.

"How . . . how can you be sure?" he breathed.

"Your father grew up with me and my sisters," Kindra said. "I had known he and Asti had developed feelings for each other, but once your father was betrothed to Nova, I thought that was the end of it. But obviously"—she gestured to Caelum— "It was not."

"What happened to Asti?" he whispered. He almost did not want to know. Judging by the way Kindra was staring at him, he knew it could not be good.

"I do not know," Kindra whispered. "During the last attempt

by Praiton to seize Bridah, your father came to our aid. Our middle sister, Hedda, was found dead, burned alive by a Manielian soldier. And Asti . . . was never found."

Caelum's head spun dizzyingly as he attempted to make sense of this. "But . . . how do you know—"

"You have her eyes," Kindra said gently. And, with soft, cold hands riddled with callouses and scars, she laid her fingers on Caelum's face. "They may be purple, but they are there," she whispered. "There is no doubt in my mind that you are hers."

Deya awoke in an unfamiliar infirmary. She felt weak and shaken, but otherwise unscathed. And what was more, Caelum was beside her, fully dressed and looking none the worse for wear. Deya let out a cry upon seeing him, alerting him to her, and his own face melted into what could only be described as sheer relief.

"Thank the Mother," he breathed, and then he seized her by the back of the neck and pulled her to his lips. Deya wanted to cry, fighting the tears as she kissed him back with such fervor that she felt weak. He pulled back, but his forehead rested against hers. Slowly, they smiled at each other.

"You're okay," she whispered.

"Thanks to you, I hear," he said.

Deya shook her head, her hand smoothing down his face. She couldn't get the image of him dead on the floor of the throne room out of her head, had dreamed about it endlessly in the last few days of exhausted slumber.

"How long have I been asleep?"

"It's been about a week since the battle." Caelum reached out a hand to smooth the hair from her face.

"And what of the Legion? And Nodaria?"

"Everyone is fine," he said, giving her a grim smile. "In fact . . . they are crowning me High King of Nodaria tomorrow."

Deya blinked at him. "Really?"

He nodded. "They are cleaning up the Keep. Readying it for habitation again. I know that part of the Legion intends to stay for a while, in case Praiton attempts to strike back. But . . . I was wondering if . . ." He hesitated, and Deya raised an eyebrow, a smile curling her lips.

"If I would like to stay here with you?" she finished for him.

Caelum grunted, looking away from her in such petulant defiance that it made her laugh out loud.

"Yes, Caelum," she whispered, pulling his face back to her. "I would love to stay here with you."

He gave her a small smile, one that was more relieved than anything.

"Aris wants to continue the war," he told her. "He intends to strike another Pillar Kingdom, just as we did Nodaria. He thinks me being on the throne can turn the tide. That with Nodaria and Bridah, we can fight back."

Deya nodded. "We fight back," she whispered.

And with that, he leaned down and kissed her again, slowly this time, languidly. And, unsure if it was in her imagination or not, she could have sworn she felt the tattooed prophecy on her back tingle.

The next day, the remaining population of Nodaria emerged from hiding. Even those who had lived at Mount Mors before Praiton's coup had come to Arctos to watch the coronation of their new High King.

On the morning of Caelum's coronation, Deya's injuries were healed enough to allow her to get out of bed. The inhabitants of Atlas Keep had begun to fill its cavernous black-marble halls again, returning to the city after decades of Praiton occupation. Priestesses, servants, cooks, and nobility flocked back in droves, causing Caelum to be on edge. His nerves were compounded by Aris calling an urgent meeting right before the coronation.

"Just breathe," Deya told him, her hand squeezing his arm. "It'll be over soon."

Caelum was being dressed by a number of servants. They seemed to be stuffing his body into clothes that were too fancy, too *royal*. Distaste curled his lip as he assessed himself in the mirror, purple eyes glowing in a murderous way.

"These people called me the White Sheep for years," Caelum grumbled, tugging on his sleeve. "And now I'm forced to stand before them as their ruler."

Deya's hand tightened on his bicep. "It'll be alright, Caelum."

Caelum looked at her, his expression troubled . . . and almost a little sad. "This should've been Aelius," he said. His eyes darted away from her, as if he didn't want her to see the pain lingering there. "This shouldn't be me."

"Stop it." Deya pulled him to face her, and the smile she gave him was full of all the encouragement she could muster. "You know that Aelius would be happy to know that out of all the people who could've replaced him, it was you."

Caelum gave her a grim smile, before bending down and kissing her softly on the mouth.

It was a new sensation—getting used to being with Caelum like this. She never in her wildest dreams would have expected them to ever reach this point. To have those purple eyes look at her with a softness that never used to be there. Something almost like . . . love. She was afraid to think about it too hard. It felt too good to be true.

Deya and Caelum headed through the halls of Atlas Keep, the sparkles of fossilized stars twinkling at them within the black marble floors. But all the while, she couldn't swallow the apprehension of what Aris needed to speak to them so urgently about.

Caelum seemed to be of the same mind. "This better be important," he muttered, before shouldering open the doors leading to Castor's old office.

The room had been cleaned since the day Deya had portaled into it. The surfaces had been polished, books had been organized on the shelves, and all of Castor's delicate gold objects had been shined to gleam as brightly as the stars.

Seated around the large rectangular table in the center of the room were Saros and Aris.

"What is this about?" Caelum demanded the minute the door shut.

Aris smirked. "You look very nice, *my lord.*"

Saros stifled a snort by turning it into a cough, stuffing a fist to his mouth. Deya had a harder job disguising hers.

"Shut up," Caelum spat, pulling out a chair opposite the two males. To Deya's utmost surprise, he jerked his head at her to sit down before he sat next to her. "Now get to the point."

Without another word, Aris turned and reached behind him before dropping an enormous, black-bladed longsword down onto the table. Deya flinched at the sight of it. She could almost see the tendrils of shadow that had crept up it when Morlais had wielded it, could almost see the stain of Caelum's blood upon the midnight steel.

Caelum stared down at it, his eyes roving over every inch before slowly looking up at Aris.

"Is it what I think it is?" he asked softly.

Aris nodded. "A Shadow Blade."

Deya's head whipped around to look between Caelum and the general.

"A *Shadow Blade?*" she echoed. The memory of flickers of shadow twisting up the blade Morlais had plunged into Caelum's chest twined with another memory . . . one that she had a much harder time unearthing. Where had she seen those shadows before?

"A Shadow Blade is made from the bone and flesh of a species of monster," Aris said. "Shadow creatures only follow those who offer them power and blood. If Praiton is using them, it would explain a lot."

The memory hit her then. A creature of shimmering darkness chasing her, its needlelike claws pounding the dirt, Caelum kicking over the headless body, still smoking with dark shadows.

"But what makes a Shadow Blade so important?" Deya asked. She reached out her hand to touch the thing but recoiled. This blade had almost killed Caelum, had maybe even been the same sword that killed his siblings. The sight of it made her want to puke.

Caelum was the one who answered her. "For one, they're extremely rare," he said. "And for another, very powerful . . . but dangerous."

"Dangerous how?" Deya asked carefully. She couldn't take any more danger, especially where Caelum was concerned. The memory of him being stabbed had plagued her every waking thought. It was possible she would never forget the sight for the rest of her life.

Saros's fingers were tented as he leaned back in his chair. But those bright violet eyes were still locked on the shadow sword. "In order to wield the blade, you must bond with it," Saros said. "Since shadowbone takes on the power you give it, it will conform to what you feed it, thus who owns it. And it will feed in turn on its user . . . a sort of, symbiotic relationship, you could say."

Deya's head jerked up, catching on to what the males were getting at. Rounding on Caelum, she cried, "Caelum, *no.*"

Aris and Saros did not laugh. They did not even so much as crack a smile. Caelum looked up at the general, his expression stony.

"Why are you giving it to me?"

"Because you are taking up the mantle of the most powerful High King in Krigor," Aris said. "You are to hold down the only high ground we have in this war. And after what happened between you and Morlais, short of a bit of training for your powers"—Caelum growled slightly at that—"you could say we need to have a bit of an edge."

Caelum paused, his indecision clearly battling it out within his head. Then he looked up at Deya, almost as if for permission. She knew he could see the panic in her eyes, the fear of losing him, of watching him get hurt again. The thought was unbearable.

He gave her a small smile. "Come on," he murmured. "I've been through worse. It'll be okay."

Deya shook her head, but knew it was useless as Caelum reached for the sword. Shadows like black flames surged up the hilt, licking at Caelum's fingers as he grasped the handle. Then, with a deep breath, he drew the blade across his palm. Blood spilled out, splattering drops on the table, but the sword seemed to drink it up. The shadows swarmed the hilt like a cloud of locusts, devouring the droplets of Caelum's blood.

Fascinated, they watched with bated breath as the shadows sucked up every last drop of red, before dissipating. Sinking into the blade, the darkness melted into the steel, turning the sword iridescent. Caelum held it to the light where it flashed purple and black. A reflection of the male it now belonged to.

Shortly after, Caelum was shepherded away from her by Saros, who Caelum had chosen to perform the coronation ceremony. Deya watched him go, the shadow sword now on his hip.

Leaning against the wall, surrounded by the rich, dark colors of Castor's office, the morning sunlight streaming in through the window, she thought about that sword. The feeling of foreboding had only grown stronger as she watched the blade turn an iridescent purple. As if something malicious had slotted into place, like a tile waiting to fall.

Her fingers glided against the ornate gold windowpane, and as the sunlight glanced off her skin, she paused, doing a double take. Holding her hands up, she angled them towards the light, believing her eyes to be playing tricks on her.

The once white tips of her fingers were pitch black. Perplexed, Deya scrubbed at them, wondering if she had touched some ink or gotten into some dirt. But the blackness did not budge. All ten of her fingers had the same delicate streak of black, as if someone had painted them.

Deya stared at her fingers, her mind racing. How long had they been like this? She couldn't remember the last time she had properly looked at her hands.

She smudged and scraped at them. Ground them against her pants, even against the stone walls. Still, they remained as black as ever. Her heart thumping in her ears, her vision swam as a large, melodic clanging echoed through the Keep.

The sound of bells calling the citizens of Nodaria towards the throne room broke her out of her transfixed dread. Because, while she did not know what had caused this, she could not shake the fear it was something sinister. Rallying, Deya forced herself to put it out of her mind.

When it was time to return for the ceremony, the excitement in Nodaria was palpable. Hundreds of people surged into the throne room—the same room that Caelum had almost died in a week before, now mended, and clean, the large planetarium repaired and hanging from the ceiling once more.

Deya could tell that Caelum hated every second of kneeling before the Celestial Throne. Having to be anointed by Saros, who performed the ritual with the ceremonial Star Sword that had been part of the Hesperos family for generations.

And, when the coronation was finished, Caelum turned to face his new kingdom, and Deya could see it on his face. It was awe, and a little bit of fear as he looked around, as they cheered for him. Deya knew he must hate all this attention with a passion, could see it in the way his purple eyes flashed in that telltale sign of annoyance.

Val and Rayner stood next to her in the crowd as they applauded for Caelum, and as he rose from his position in front of Saros, everyone sank to their knees in front of him. Even Val, Rayner, and Aris. Even Deya.

Caelum let out a sigh. And then he closed his eyes. Deya felt the entire keep tremble. Everyone looked up, clamoring with panic as the entire roof of the palace began to shake. Dust fell upon them, some people even screamed. And then Caelum opened his eyes, and they glowed a bright, luminous purple. And then, the whole top floor of Atlas Keep separated from the lower. With a grunt, Caelum raised both his hands, and the crowd watched as the astronomy tower took to the sky once again. With one final breath, Caelum clenched his fist. The horizon darkened, and moonlight shone down on the throne room, stars twinkling as the sky became night.

There was a pause, and then the crowd erupted into cheers. Deya, clapping along with them, caught Caelum's eye. And at that moment, Caelum smiled.

AUTHOR'S NOTE

When I began writing A Crown of Star & Ash, I hadn't written for over six years. I had always been an avid writer and was always working on a novel of some kind since I was a child. But life got in the way, and eventually I stopped writing altogether. It took a life changing event to get me to start writing again.

Without going into *too* much detail, I spent almost three years in a hostile environment, constantly on edge, only to be betrayed and abandoned by people I thought were my friends. During this time, I had stopped eating, lost an unhealthy amount of weight, and was living each and every day in a state of pure panic and dread.

After two years of living in survival mode, I was told I was in the beginning stages of developing CPTSD.

Even after the dust had settled, and I had left that toxic environment, I was shocked to find that, even though I was free of the people and things that had made me sick, the symptoms still lingered, and I found my body and mind had been changed forever. I was angry and sad, resentful that the people who had terrorized me still had power over me, even though I had escaped them, and life had vastly improved.

So, one day, I sat down to do what I always did when I had to process something difficult and painful: I put it into a story.

As someone who had exclusively written YA Contemporary Romance novels her entire life, diving into the world of Adult Fantasy was both terrifying and exciting in equal measures. The story I wanted to tell and the emotions I wanted to explore did not fit into a contemporary, everyday setting like I was used to writing, so I had to pivot. Although I never spent much time reading or writing in this genre, it was like coming home in a way as I poured all of my grief, pain, and frustration into these characters and this world.

The first draft of A Crown of Star & Ash exploded out of me in one month. It was hard to believe that, just when I thought I'd never write again, this story came bursting out of me, demanding to be told.

While Deya is not a self-insert character in any way, her power was something I had thought about for many years. It was heartbreak and grief, a physical manifestation of the explosive pain a person can sometimes feel but can't release. Her power was a magical representation of anxiety, how it scars the body, leaves you transformed, and sometimes even controls you. Having Deya mourn the part of herself she lost—the person who she was before this power took hold of her—was essential to me and my own healing during this time. I still mourn the person I was before this fear had taken hold and rewired my body. I was able to grieve a lot of this feeling with Deya and I was so grateful for it.

My own frustration with my overwhelming exhaustion and mental shutdowns I felt for months and years after was frustrating, and I realized I was in a "freeze" mode of sorts. This triggered me to throw all the many dizzying, confusing, and sometimes contradictory aspects of the nervous system's responses to trauma into the other characters in this book.

All my beta readers told me Caelum was difficult to like in the beginning (and sometimes even by the end), and I was like "that's the point!" Caelum represented the "fight" mode I often found myself in. How the smallest thing would send me into a rage, how I'd get overwhelmed and snap at anyone who happened to demand too much of me at the time. It was an uncontrollable irritability that often left me feeling regretful and ashamed, which was important for me to show through Caelum.

And while Val and Rayner will also have their time to shine, I don't want to give away too much for the future installments of the series and the subsequent reveal of their stories, as well!

In the end, trauma presents differently on everyone, and I wanted to make sure, that in writing this book, anyone who reads it can feel seen in some way, and in someone within the story.

Thank you all for reading and supporting this story. I know many of you found me and this book through its trauma representation, and I am endlessly grateful to you all for taking the time to read and love these characters. I hope, from the bottom of my heart, that this book helps you believe that from your ashes, you too can become steel.

All my love,
Victoria

P.S. Keep reading for a sneak peek at the next installment THE LADY OF FIRE & LIGHT, the prequel novella all about our favorite BFF, Val!

ACKNOWLEDGMENTS

First and foremost, I want to thank my beautiful, talented, and lovely friend Veronica. If it wasn't for you forcing me into our own version of Writing Rehab, this book would never have existed. Thank you for reading it as I wrote it and being an amazing and supportive cheerleader—not just during this process, but for the entirety of our adolescence into adulthood. I'm so blessed and grateful to have you as a friend.

Second, I'd like to thank my amazing boyfriend, Cody, for—not only enduring me throughout writer's block, endless procrastination, and paralyzing perfectionism—but being there when I had questions about anything from military rankings, medieval weaponry, magic systems, or even character arcs and backstories. Thank you for always having patience, support, and *answers!* Thank you for sitting down and drawing me full battle plans and finding my characters their own theme music and being an amazing resource for all things fantasy, magic, and love. I could not have done this without you.

To my amazing group chat of talented and amazing writer friends: Carrie and Isabella—from beta readers to cheerleaders, meeting you both on this writing journey has been one of the things I am most thankful for. I have learned so much from both of you and am endlessly grateful for the long phone brainstorming sessions, the pages and pages of text message workshops, the loving pokes, and for, of course, the endless support and kindness. No matter what happens with the success of this book, meeting you both and being able to call you friends has made this journey so worth it. Having writer friends I can bounce ideas and frustrations off of has been a dream I never thought I'd have and I'm endlessly grateful to you.

To my mother and my sister, who both were invaluable sources of love, support, and criticism alike, thank you for reading, critiquing, and always being up for a brainstorming discussion. Both of you were instrumental in shaping this book (and me!) to being what it is today.

To my friend, Laura, who singlehandedly pulled me though the darkest days of my life and helped me survive my own personal Praiton, thank you. Thank you for reminding me that I can not only survive the storm, but that I *am* the storm. Your strength and kindness are forever an inspiration to me, and I'm honored every day to call you a friend.

To Sam. You are the reason I write. No matter how many years go by, or the distance between us, every time I pick up a pen or sit down at a keyboard, I think about you. Thank you for giving me the greatest gift I could ever ask for.

And finally, thank you to my editors, Noah Sky and Jennifer Murgia, and also to my group of amazing beta readers: Mary, Colleen, Lindley, Anna, Keeya, and Lucy (to name a few). This book has passed through so many hands, but you all gave me invaluable insight and *encouragement* to keep pushing and keep going. Thank you all for reading and critiquing!

SNEAK PEEK

of

— • —

THE

LADY

OF

FIRE

AND

LIGHT

— • —

A PREQUEL NOVELLA

COMING SUMMER 2024

There was blood dripping out of her hair. It stained her already red strands an even darker color than usual, matting it down. She flicked it out of her eyes as she strode through Light's Tower, her face covered in ash and soot, bleeding from various cuts and wounds, but still, she was smiling. Beaming.

"You look pleased." Aris fell into stride beside her, his handsome face a cool mask of neutrality. Only Val could see the shadow of a smile on his lips.

"You would be, too," she replied. "Especially if you had just enjoyed a lovely barbeque of Praiton soldiers. How could I not be in a good mood with the smell of burning flesh still in my nostrils?"

Aris let out a bark of laughter. "You Manielians truly are bloodthirsty wretches."

"And you Ganieans are pathetically passive," Val retorted, but she grinned at him, a sickly-sweet grin, which he returned.

The Pillar Legion's general was clad in his usual gold armor—leftover from his uniform as a King's Guard in Ganiea. It was old, tarnished, with only shadows of its former glory. She supposed some would say it was the same for its owner, but General Aris Calatos was far from being past his prime glory.

"Can you two stop flirting for once?" Katia appeared on Val's other side. The young female was also charred and bloodied, but her smile was as wide as her own.

"Trust me," Aris leaned past Val to stare into Katia's eyes, "if I were flirting, Katia, you would know it."

Val rolled her eyes and shoved the philandering general aside, causing him to chuckle and Katia to flush.

"Can you please refrain from harassing my soldiers, *General*," Val demanded, putting on her best High Lady voice that had been drilled into her since birth.

Aris just winked at her, making her stomach flutter in the most obnoxious way.

The Pillar Legion was returning from battle, and for once, they were victorious. It had been a small skirmish—an interception of supplies from the coast of Zulon—but it had still been a long, bloody battle. Val had been relieved that her unit had not had any casualties, and that all her soldiers were returning home—bleeding, bruised, and burnt, but otherwise alive.

Just then, a group of her soldiers staggered into the antechamber of Light's Tower, carrying several large crates of supplies, which they dropped proudly at Aris's feet.

"Well done," the general remarked, shooting a look at Val. "I dare say this is enough weapons and herbs for the whole legion."

"*And*," Val said, grinning broadly, "the fact that we took out a very large squadron of Praitonian soldiers. Not to mention a few Manielian stragglers." She blew a singed piece of red hair out of her face, the smoldering scent making her nose twitch slightly.

Aris gave her his patented crooked smile—one that was always imbued with charm and confidence, yet never quite met those hazel eyes of his.

"This calls for a celebration," he announced. "Marcus! Alert the kitchens! We have a feast to partake in."

The atrium of Light's Tower erupted into cheers and whistles, the smell of burnt flesh and singed clothing momentarily forgotten as the soldiers took the time to appreciate their victory. They all instantly took off towards the dining hall, laughing and talking, filling the large, cavernous room with echoes of joy and merriment.

"Go get cleaned up," Aris said to Val, giving her arm a small squeeze. "You know where to find me if you want to do a little celebrating of our own," he added in a whisper in her ear, giving her a lecherous wink that caused Val to gag and shove him off again.

"Honestly," Katia said, grabbing Val by the arm and ushering her away from the obnoxious general. "He truly has no shame."

"No," Val murmured distractedly. "He really doesn't."

This was Aris's way, though. The flirtations never amounted to anything—not with any of them within the Legion, at least. The healers and the priestesses were another story. It seemed as if Aris's conquests were always tiptoeing down the stairs right when the rest of the Legion were waking for early morning training.

The other captains, Elric, Saros, and Lycus seemed to find this endlessly amusing. Val, however, always thought it to be in poor taste.

"He is the general, though," Katia added thoughtfully. They ascended the steps of the Tower, the winding and twisting staircase towards the residential wing was an exhausting inconvenience after the day's events. "I suppose he can talk to us any way he wants."

"Are we talking about Aris?" Atria appeared out of nowhere, sprinting up the steps behind them and shoving in between them. Atria was a small, scrappy female with short, pixie length ginger hair. Strands of blonde were interwoven between the orange, and it was bound back by an array of twists and plaits to keep it out of her face. It was also burned in several places.

"Who else?" Katia huffed. "He tried to take Val to bed."

"He *always* tries to take Val to bed," another voice said, and Val flushed, opening her mouth to rebut this mortifying statement.

From behind them, Val's first in command, Lucia, stomped up the steps, cutting off all her protests. Where Atria was petite and scruffy, Lucia was tall and willowy. Her features were much more feline than the others, all accented with a shock of gorgeous, flowing tawny hair. Between the four of them, Val's hair was the darkest, the reddest, the most pronounced of them all. A ruby mixed into a pile of amber.

Lucia bumped in between Katia and Atria, pushing her way past all of them. She was the only one who wasn't covered in blood and soot, only sporting a few scratches and scuffs of dirt in places.

"He does *not* try to take me to bed," Val mumbled.

All three girls snorted at that.

"He definitely tries much harder for you than anyone else," Atria said with a snicker.

Katia hummed and Val shot her a warning look. "I mean, would it *really* be so bad?" Katia asked. "To bed him, I mean?"

Val and Atria both let out gags of disgust which caused Katia to look aghast. "*What?!* Atria, I know he's not your type" —Atria laughed at that. Her type was strictly more female than anything— "but Val, c'mon. You know he's attractive."

"Ugh, cut it out," Val moaned, giving an exaggerated shudder. "He is our general. Nothing more."

Though Lucia remained silent, Val knew she was secretly amused by it all. One of the few Manielians who also came from a noble family, Lucia's mysterious, reserved nature only melted on the battlefield.

As the staircase leveled out, Lucia seized Val's arm and flicked a wrist at the other two, shooing them off.

"Get cleaned up," she commanded them, before she steered Val towards her room.

"What, are you going to bathe with me?" Val teased.

Lucia scoffed. "Wouldn't be the first time. How many creeks have we had to bathe in together after so many years in this blasted unit?"

"Too many."

Val's room was devoid of any personal touches—no trinkets on the desk, no decorations on the wall. The only sign that this was actually her room were the many, many clothing items strewn about the small space. Armor, tunics, a few older, fancier dresses she never wore drowned all the furniture within the room.

"*Home*," she groaned and made to collapse, face-first on the bed, when Lucia's arm shot out and seized her around the middle.

"You are *filthy*," she reminded her. "I think there's still some brain matter on your shirt from the Praiton commander. Bath. *Now*."

Even though Val moaned in complaint, she knew Lucia was right. And when she dove, headfirst into her bathing pool—which had been enchanted to be much deeper than meets the eye—it felt almost as good as the bed. Almost.

When she surfaced, it was to find Lucia sitting on the small stool by the pool, picking off her gloves and examining her chipped nails.

"Aren't you going to clean up?"

"Later," she said. "I did not get nearly as disgusting as you lot."

"That's what happens when I make you the rear guard," Val said, squeezing out a large dollop of soap into her grimy hair.

Lucia did not speak for a moment, picking dirt from her nails, until "You blush every time Aris flirts with you, you know that, right?"

Val froze, her face heating.

Lucia pointed a chipped finger at her. "Yes, like that."

"I do *not!*" The mortification threatened to choke her. Did she *really* blush every time Aris joked around with her? Did he ever notice? The very thought made her want to plunge her head into the water and never resurface again.

"Oh, you definitely do," Lucia replied, smirking. "And I hope you know how much of a horrible idea it is for you to even consider—"

"I have *never* considered such a thing!" Val cried, half rising out of the pool before realizing she was naked and plunging back down. "How can you even think—"

"Because I know you hear the rumors, Valeria." Lucia's golden eyes stared down at her, silencing all her protests. "The other captains, the soldiers . . . they do not like you. They do not like *us*."

Val sank further into the tub, the heat from her face beginning to trigger her Ember Magic, causing the pool to bubble slightly.

"Well, I know *that* already." She had not missed the whispering and the rumors. No one dared to say it to her face, but they all disparaged her. As the only female captain in the whole Legion, she expected backlash. However, expected the backlash from the other captains were, it never failed to make her blood boil. To be female *and* Manielian nobility was a double sin in the Legion.

"Do not give them any reason to doubt you, Valeria," she said softly. "You are a powerful warrior. You deserve to be a captain." She rose from the stool. "And besides, Aris is a lout," she added, and left the room, leaving Val to chuckle to herself.

The feast was in full swing by the time Val descended from her room. It felt odd being clean after so many days locked in battle, living in her own filth and blood. She couldn't lie and say it wasn't amazing to have her hair feeling so soft and smelling like jasmine.

Lucia, Katia, and Atria were already seated in the dining hall, all with full plates of food and large mugs of ale. Val plopped down in front of them, her eyes scanning the hall for a familiar glint of gold, but Aris was nowhere to be seen.

She felt Lucia's eyes on her, and shifting, she cleared her throat, and tucked into her own plate of steaming beef and potatoes. Across the room, the other captains were holding court. Lycas—the only other Manielian captain—had a Priestess sitting on his lap, tittering at something he had said. Val resisted the urge to roll her eyes.

Lycas was her least favorite captain. As a commoner with little magic, he had somehow excelled as a fighter, mostly from getting into brawls. Hardened and smarmy, Lycas was the leader in her ridicule and never missed an opportunity to put Val down in front of the other captains and soldiers.

Val knew if ever given the opportunity, she would roast him alive like a pig on a spit.

Katia noticed Lycas and the Priestess as well and scoffed disapprovingly.

"She should honestly be chucked out of the Temple for that," she muttered.

Val couldn't help but agree.

As the ale flowed, the soldiers got rowdier and rowdier. Even Katia and Atria were getting a little tipsy. Lucia, however, sat calmly in her seat, nursing her mug of ale, watching the chaos with a sharp, golden eye.

Finally, Val finished her second mug of ale, feeling full and content— and a little woozy. The alcohol soothed her sore muscles and spinning mind that wouldn't stop replaying the battle over and over again. It was the curse of a seasoned warrior. Every strike, every blow, every death, her mind parsed it over and over for tactical weaknesses.

She had been trained in combat from a young age with her brothers. Her parents had hired a retired Master of Arms from the Red Citadel to train them all, and she was now a master of the Manielian sword art. All of this training and fighting, however, came at a cost.

Val stood from the long bench, and looked down at her second, third, and fourth in command.

"I'm going to bed," she announced.

"Boo," Atria moaned, throwing a piece of potato in the air at her, her eyes glazed, her body swaying. "The night's still young, Val!"

"And *you* are very drunk," Val admonished, but she smiled at the small female, who seemed to have a hard time focusing on her. "And I am very tired. It has been a long few days."

Atria began to protest again, but Lucia stopped her with a stern, motherly look.

"Goodnight, Captain," Lucia said, giving her a small, rare smile.

Val smiled back. Katia bid her another rather clumsy goodnight, and Val rose and left the dining hall. But instead of heading for the stairs towards the residential wing, she headed back to the kitchen and piled a plate full of hot food fresh from the pots over the fire.

When she hadn't seen Aris in the dining hall, she already knew where she would find him. Sure enough, as she walked down the darkened hallway of offices and studies on the lower floor, she saw the flicker of torchlight coming from the general's quarters.

She knocked, waited for his call to enter, and pushed open the door.

Aris was sitting behind his desk, maps spread across the surface, a surprisingly tired and worn look on his face. He had removed the gold armor, and was dressed in a plain, white cotton tunic that made him look more casual than she had ever seen him.

"Valeria," he said, looking up and giving her that same, vaguely friendly smile, the tiredness she had noted gone in an instant. "To what do I owe the pleasure? Did you decide to take me up on my offer to have a more *intimate* celebration?"

Val narrowed her eyes at him. "Very funny." She stepped fully into the room, and placed the plate down on the one empty bit of desk she could find. "I just wanted to bring you this."

Aris's eyebrow rose at the plate, and a small, crooked grin crossed his face.

"Thank you, Valeria," he murmured.

Val did not fancy leaving quite so soon. It was rare to see the general alone—removed from an audience for him to perform to—she found Aris to be strangely subdued. As if his true self was within reach for the first time. She moved into the room, sitting down in the high-back chair across from him.

"You did not want to join the feast that you so benevolently called for?" she teased him.

Aris let out a tired sigh, rubbing at the back of his neck. "Unfortunately, I had some work to attend to first. I thank you for the food, though. I was rather hungry."

"What work possibly takes precedent over our victory today, General?"

Aris moved a paper free of the map he had been pouring over and pointed towards a spot on it. Val leaned forward.

"Bridah," she said.

Aris nodded. "Bridah."

"And what is it about Bridah that troubles you, General?" she inquired. "Out of all the kingdoms, it is the most insulated. Surely, it is the least of our worries."

"This is true, it is very insulated by its fjords," he agreed. "However, what kingdom borders Bridah?"

She knew, but still, she felt her eyes move inadvertently to Bridah's neighboring kingdom. Maniel.

Aris saw it in her face. "Now, tell me. What is the one thing that can thwart ice?"

Looking up at him slowly, the answer they both knew remained unspoken. "They can't," she breathed. "They have tried multiple times. The fjords stop them, and if they don't, we do."

Aris did not respond. His finger traced the shape of Maniel on the map, his eyes lingering on it. "This is true," he said again. "But still . . . I worry about their ability to conquer the fjords. And if they do that, we may not stand a chance."

Val did not speak. She knew the Manielian army well—had trained with them, even fought with them in the times before the war. Titus had ensured the strongest fighters, both magically and physically, were heading his army.

"Titus is the strongest Ember Magic user in almost a millennium," Aris said. "If there was somebody who could melt the entire fjord surrounding Frostheim, it's him."

Val knew this was true, had seen Titus do awful yet incredible things in her long life. She also knew his son, Lynos, to be of the same, horrible power. The thought of Lynos made something run cold inside of her and she fought a small shiver.

"What are you thinking of doing, then?" she asked. "What precautions?"

Aris sighed, the mask of cool, confident ease slipping again, showing her just the tiniest hint of the exhaustion behind those hazel eyes. "Possibly setting up a post within Bridah to guard against any potential Manielian invasions. I have a contact within Bridah who may be willing to help us find someplace."

Val studied Aris carefully, taking in the bags under his eyes, the shadows on his defined jaw. As the founder of the Pillar Legion, Aris had every right to be considered the Knight Commander, but he had insisted on only being a general. Val had always wondered why. Aris was charming and cocksure, never one for modesty or humility, and yet he insisted on staying at a lower rank than he deserved.

"You know, we can help you with this," she told him softly. "You don't have to bear it alone." She leaned over the desk towards him and gave him a gentle, teasing smile. "That is why you have captains, General."

Aris smiled, his eyes roving her face curiously, leisurely. She never knew what it was about Aris's lingering glances, how they made her feel exposed, as if he were devouring her slowly. Even though everything told her to look away, she didn't.

"Are you offering?" he asked, his eyes still doing their slow, casual feast of her.

"I am always at your service, General," she said.

A lazy, cocky grin spread across Aris's face. "I will definitely remember that."

And just like that, the spell was broken. She rolled her eyes, and Aris laughed.

Val got to her feet and made towards the door, pausing to look back at Aris one more time.

"Eat," she reminded him. "We cannot defeat Maniel in a night, and neither can you."

Aris chuckled his eyes refocusing on her again, absorbing. "Thank you, Valeria," he murmured.

Val nodded and turned to go, feeling her heart beat fiercely in her chest, and no doubt making her turn a bright, ridiculous red.

ABOUT THE AUTHOR

Victoria mostly answers to Tori and has been writing books for most of her life. After specializing in Creative Writing throughout high school, she went on to study Communications, Journalism, and English Literature...and stopped writing completely during this time.

After a LONG break, she recently decided to delve into the world of Adult Fantasy with her debut novel A CROWN OF STAR & ASH.

She now resides in Florida and spends her day working her day job, reading, writing, playing the Sims 3 (still), and being a mother to a rotten Snowshoe Siamese cat named Sebastian.

If you want to know more about when Tori's future books come out, be sure to sign up for her newsletter and stay up to date with all ACOSAA related updates!

Visit Victoria's Website!

https://www.victoriaktaylor.com/

Connect with me on Social Media!

https://www.instagram.com/victoriaktaylorbooks

https://www.tiktok.com/@victoriaktaylorbooks

Printed in Great Britain
by Amazon

54844740R00223